The Soldier's Return

The Soldier's Return

A Novel

MELVYN BRAGG

Arcade Publishing • New York

FIRST U.S. EDITION

First published in 1999 by Hodder and Stoughton, A division of Hodder Headline PLC, A Sceptre Book

This is a work of fiction. Names, places, characters, and incidents are either the products of the author's imagination or are used fictitiously.

Library of Congress Cataloging-in-Publication Data

Bragg, Melvyn, 1939–
      The soldier's return / Melvyn Bragg. —1st U.S. ed.
          p. cm.
      ISBN 1-55970-639-2
          1. World war, 1939–1945—Veterans—Fiction. 2. Cumbria (England)—Fiction. 3. Wigton (England)—Fiction. I. Title.

PR6052.R263 S65 2002
823'.914–dc21   2002021558

Published in the United States by Arcade Publishing, Inc., New York
Distributed by AOL Time Warner Book Group

Visit our Web site at www.arcadepub.com

10 9 8 7 6 5 4 3 2 1

EB

PRINTED IN THE UNITED STATES OF AMERICA

To John Bragg in Australia

'When you go home, tell them of us and say
For your tomorrow we gave our today'

The Kohima epitaph

PROLOGUE

She got an atlas in the reference section of the library and sought out Burma. In the poky little room above the fire station in the Council yard, she stared at the name and tried to imagine what it was like to be there. She was not allowed to take it home but she returned to it more than once, willing it to yield up comfort.

Later she found a book which had a few dull pages on Burma but the photographs engrossed her: exotic-looking birds, houses built of wood, gigantic tropical forests – she could tell their size because there was a picture of elephants in a clearing – lovely smiling women in beautiful clothes, and pagodas, all sizes, some as big as the tower on Highmoor.

She mentioned the elephants and the pagodas in her letters.

He kept the letters deep in his kitbag, wrapped in a square of yellow oilskin. Every day he touched the wad of them: every morning. He knew that if he failed to do that, his luck would go.

The boy could not truthfully remember his father, not at all, but she referred to him in everyday ways and there was a presence in the child's mind which became like a memory as the years went by.

He had not thought the war would take him away for years, and so far away. Nor had she, but they were in an old island story, centuries of the men going across the sea to fight, leaving the women to weave the days, waiting at home. Yet sometimes she was glad for her new independent life. She doused her guilt by telling her son that his father would be home soon.

If he fought for any one thing it was to get back to her. And now the battles were over.

PART ONE

CHAPTER ONE

What was he frightened of, she wondered, as he burrowed his knees into her thighs and clutched at her through the cotton nightgown. She had been awake for some time, trying not to cough. In the hollow of the mattress, swaddled in too many blankets, the young woman felt a film of sweat on her brow and on her throat. The child had been uneasy all through the night; twice he had called out and prodded her with small soft fists. She, too, prickled with restlessness.

She tried to shift away from him, needing to stretch, but he held on more fiercely and even moaned a little. Perhaps they had had the same fearful and excited dreams, she thought, as the boy nuzzled his face between her shoulder blades.

Despite herself she began to cough, a barked, repressed sound which shook through her. The boy flung away and rolled over, leaving a narrow channel between them – a sword's width. The young woman turned on to her back, breathed in as deeply as she could and felt relief ripple through her body. Her hands ran down it, as if smoothing it out, making it ready.

After a while she reached across to touch her son and closed her eyes to meet the comforting slow surge of dark colour and swirl of movement, a universe of its own in her mind. She would travel there until it was time to start the big day. What time he would return she had not been told, but the day had been named. After the years, it had come so suddenly she felt breathless.

—m—

About two hours later, less than a mile outside the town, the black iron locomotive broke down again and stood inert in the bare Northern landscape. A groan ran through the carriages crammed with soldiers on the last lap of their odyssey. Still more patience demanded, even so near the end.

Sam was next to the window. He looked out and lit up. His batch would be first off. The train was headed for the west coast, calling at all the small towns and villages along the way, decanting soldiers. These men had made the longest journey back from the war.

Beside him were the rest of the solo whist school which had been in continuous session for almost six weeks, since the last sighting of the shores of India. A few miles back, in Carlisle, the regimental city, they had finally put the game to bed. Sam had vowed never again to play solo whist as long as he lived.

After the stop, the men dozed again. They were as practised in catnaps as they were in drill. Only Jackie was wide awake, rarely taking his eyes off Sam. He had not been part of Sam's section in Burma but, on the boat, he had used the fact that they had known each other back in the little town as an excuse to tag along. Sam smiled at him and said 'I'm browned off with this'. The stopping and queuing and the many unexplained halts had been just about bearable until now. With their town only a few fields away, a rush of frustration strained at his practised tolerance.

'I went mushrooming in a field over there one time,' Jackie said, nervously pointing it out. 'Never seen the like. Thousands. Whiter than white. Stripped the lot. Straight up to "King" Haney's in Water Street for him to get them off to Newcastle on the nine o'clock train. Made a fortune. Took the lot.'

Jackie's prattling had aroused a couple of the others and all of them now stared out of the motionless window looking at the dawn light stroking their native fields.

They were home. They really were. They were home. They could let the expectation loose now. Just across those fields, hidden over the hill whose rim was being more and more firmly pencilled by the steel light, was their town. They had made it back.

Sam stared hard. His mother had worked on the farm over there. He had courted Ellen in a lane which twisted down to this railway line from the Carlisle road. Abruptly he yanked the leather strap and let the window fall down. The air was so very sweet, the sounds, the farmyard, hedgerow, a light wind in the wires, just as seductive.

'Let's walk!' It was spoken like an order.

They followed him. It would be for the last time, and they knew it. Ex-corporal (once busted) Samuel Richardson, late of D Company, Ninth Battalion, The Border Regiment, 17th India Division, 14th Army. Late, too, of the war against the Japanese in Burma, and an awesome victory, sometimes fought out hand to hand, ancient warfare in sub-tropical violence against the fanaticism of a cruel warrior race. Now finally he was leading men home.

Kitbags were shouldered, presents, souvenirs and bush hats carried carefully. They set off along the railway line, soon hitting the sleepers, soon in step.

Jackie looked behind and saw others deserting the marooned train. 'All the Wigton lads are with us!' he said. He was fearful of the consequences. 'They'll have kittens up top.'

'We're out of the army now,' Sam soothed him. 'They can't touch us any more, Jackie.'

He led the men towards a long field which would take them to the very edge of the town. Cattle and a few sheep stumbled and scampered out of the way of the half-dozen men who had scaled out and now moved, from deep discipline, in martial order. In that placid Cumbrian field, in the whitening light of first morning, Sam saw lines of the same men, many thousands of miles away, in their dark jungle-green uniforms, bayonets fixed on short Lee Enfield rifles, the vicious Gurkha kukri in their belts, fifty rounds, two grenades apiece, walking steadily into fire, never breaking step. He had felt such a total love for those men, their matter-of-fact heroism and humour in a savage, disregarded war against an enemy barbaric beyond their understanding. It would be hard to beat. For a few moments he was there again and the silhouettes marching between the docile beasts were a dawn patrol swiftly sweeping up the hill to take the town.

Sam grabbed a strand of barbed wire to press it down and the points jabbed into his palm. A terrible image disrupted his mind, pumping through it, straining at his skull so that his mouth opened to cry out. Never to think of that. He had to control that. It had got worse since they had joined the ship in India. He had to learn to blank it out. The past must be buried or it would bury him. He took a deep breath.

'Come on marra!'

Jackie's use of the warm local dialect word for friend helped unlock him. He licked his palm. Pin-pricks.

On top of Howrigg bank, Sam stopped to look across the town, from the mock-Venetian bell-tower on Highmoor on the south side to the tall, grim chimney clearing chemical smoke from the factory on the north, and between those two the huddle and accretion of centuries. Narrow, twisting alleys, weavers' cottages, medieval archways, runnels slit between unsteady houses, Nonconformist sandstone chapels, the church in which his son had been baptised, quaint Victorian shops and hidden strips of land whose lie and use pre-dated the Conquest. The lives of near on five thousand souls, many from families dug in for generations, were penned together in the small fertile bowl less than a mile from the remains of the most remote military road in the Roman Empire.

With the barest of farewells the others hurried past him as the sun rose and warmed their backs. It was the completion of the circle which had plucked them out and taken them halfway across the world to fight in a place and against a people they had scarcely heard of.

Sam hesitated, trying to settle in himself the disturbing confusions of his return. The dreams of home were tinged with dread. The place below could suck him in, the old world close over him. Nothing had changed in the town that he could see. Yet his whole world had changed.

He looked to his left—

'They're building new houses,' he said to Jackie, who had sat down on a low garden wall.

'They won't be for the likes of thee and me, Sam. They've forgot about us.'

Sam looked at Jackie and saw the old terror. But they were back now and he had carried him for long enough.

'Let's move on, Jackie.'

'We're not due 'til breakfast time.'

'C'mon, Jackie. We'll surprise them.'

'Not before I'm due. I'll bide here.'

To emphasise his resolution he took out a cigarette.

Sam paused and then, suddenly, he had not a second more to waste. It was as if he were being reeled in, furiously, down past St

Cuthbert's church, over the bridge at Burnfoot, across Market Hill and there, the early sun flat on the whole terrace of tall houses, there at last and for sure would be his wife and son, waiting for him.

—⁂—

There were five steps up to the front door. He took them in two bounds and hammered against the brown painted door with his fist. He stood back, smiling apologetically. That knock could have raised the dead.

What if one of the others answered? He had never imagined that. But it was Ellen who threw back the door, knowing it was him, it had to be him, four years, more than four years, how many letters? The loneliness, the fear, there he was, brown and smart in his demob suit, his arms reaching out the moment he saw her, the strain of wonder and such a smile on his face. She in the plum dressing-gown, no time to get ready, looking so lovely, he thought, how could he have forgotten how lovely? The eyes dark, almost as black as the hair which smothered his face as he closed his eyes though he wanted to see all of her, touch all of her, knowing he would remember for ever the force of those arms flung around his neck. Only this could block out everything bad, the wetness of her few tears, squeezing the life out of each other on top of the five steps with no one to see, thank God, she thought, holding without even murmuring, scarcely breathing, just standing welded as so long ago in their first months when they were not much more than children, but Ellen now such a woman, so much time to mend, absence like a wound.

Joe in his pyjamas scrambled and squirmed among their legs, fighting to part them, wanting his share, straining his neck, his face pivoted up at the double-headed swaying couple locked above him. 'Daddy! Daddy!'

Sam pulled himself away from Ellen, almost dazed from the crush of her body against his. He went back down the steps and held out his arms. 'Jump,' he said. 'Jump!'

Joe looked at his mother, who nodded. He looked at his father, fractionally hesitating.

'Jump!'

And then the boy launched himself, arms spread like wings. Sam caught him, a small bundle of boy, under the shoulders, taking the contact gently, and with one easy spring of movement, he flung his son high into the air. The boy's arms and legs splayed out, the pyjamas flowed and he yelled aloud with fearful pleasure and down and once more the strong hands – the feel of them imprinted in memory – caught him and hurled him high, so that the boy remembered being suspended for an instant, perfectly still in the sky in the white morning light with his mother waving at the top of the steps and his father looking up, laughing, ready to catch him safely, and the world, at long last, as it should be.

CHAPTER TWO

The house they entered was at one end of a row of six, a cliff-faced block looking east and fronted by the downward slope of Market Hill, which still saw traders and where the fair set up for its last stop of the autumn before wintering in a field beyond the cemetery.

Ellen's Aunt Grace let out rooms, but hers were a distinct cut above the usual. The house had been inherited by Leonard, her husband, and many thought she had married him for it. Ellen had landed there at the age of nine and been something of a maid-of-all-work ever since. Her father, Grace's brother, had disappeared soon after her birth and the scandal was rarely alluded to in Ellen's presence, not even after she married. Her mother had died of tuberculosis. Grace and Leonard had no children.

When Ellen left school and insisted on going to work in the clothing factory which employed more than a hundred town girls, Grace was disappointed. Common work, she thought. She had hoped for better and Ellen was capable of better. Her final school report was clear on that subject – but the girl was pig-headed. Even more disappointing was her refusal to take up with John Eliot, who would certainly inherit his father's shoe shop. Instead she let herself down, as Grace saw it, by preferring Sam Richardson, whose father had nothing and came from nothing. Ellen's willingness to help in the house despite her factory work did not fully compensate for these failings.

Following Joe's birth, Ellen was not allowed to continue to work in the factory. That was the rule. She and Sam had taken rooms in Church Street after their marriage. Sam's departure for war brought her back to Grace's house. When Joe was two, tormented by loneliness and on bare pickings from what Sam sent her, she had found work as a cleaner for two sisters in a fine old house. Once the biggest in town. Soon she was cleaning in three houses and later, when Joe went to school, she also helped out in Eves' the Chemist on market day and Friday from one thirty to five thirty.

She had taken the boy with her on the cleaning jobs, first popping him in the basket in front of her bicycle and then, as he grew, planting him on the back seat. Sadie, who had worked on the bench with her in the factory, now lived in the basement three doors down, and she would always have Joe if Grace was in one of her moods. The house inhabited by Sadie had been broken up into rooms, like all the others in the row except for Grace's, the only one intact in the sense that the owners also lived there.

There were two rooms for commercial travellers – described by Grace as her 'guests' – together with the small back bedroom for Ellen and Joe, and the attic rooms, referred to by Grace as her 'rooms at the top'.

These, once rather scorned, had become her pride. Mr Kneale, senior history master at the grammar school, had taken them three years before, after the death of his wife. It had been a temporary measure, but the two rooms which commanded, as he told Grace, a most splendid view (which he had photographed more than once) and the small cellar which Grace allowed him to use as a dark room, made him reluctant to move on. Grace's cooking was as good as you could expect with the ingredients available, the location was central, and to have his own dark room was a singular luxury. As time went on, the rather lonely, middle-aged widower grew very fond of Ellen in particular and listened out for her and enjoyed the guileless and indiscriminate affection of Joe.

Mr Kneale was Grace's big catch. He had a married sister, she would tell her few friends, down in Chester, whose husband was a bank manager. Mr Kneale would spend a week with them over Christmas, and a fortnight in the summer. Before the war he and his wife had always gone abroad at Easter. He was very particular about his shirts, a clean one on Sundays, then every two days, same with undergarments, and he had offered to pay extra for the added laundry burden. After the first six months he had asked permission to get some of his own furniture out of storage – Grace had agreed, although it was irregular. But, as she told friends, she appreciated its sentimental value to Mr Kneale. Some of his pieces were beyond words, handed down on his wife's side, he'd told her. His manners were out of this world.

The engine room of the house was the semi-basement, full of light in the morning and easy to make cosy when the light moved off the front. Here meals were served, cellars and cubby-holes stored the fuels and utensils necessary for the running of the house, and it was kept warm. Grace's court, for occasional tea in the week and always on Sundays, was the chilly upstairs front room into which she would stray several times a day to admire its high-ceilinged proportions, to look over the heavy expensive furniture Leonard's parents had purchased on their twentieth wedding anniversary and to see what was going on outside. The bay window gave her an expansive field of vision and few of the comings and goings of neighbours or traders on market day or the rare strangers escaped her surveillance. She stored information about their movements as if she were compiling dossiers designed, one day, to bring them to judgement.

It was into this superior room on that first morning, after a little weighing up, that she invited Sam and Ellen and Joe with Leonard for a cup of pre-breakfast tea. The deciding factor was that the kitchen had been laid for breakfast the previous night for Leonard and her two commercial travellers and though she had about half an hour in hand, she feared the family gathering might interfere with the arrangements. Mr Kneale had his breakfast in his rooms: Ellen served that after she had laid the fires and seen to the other guests.

Sadie came round uninvited. She had heard the arrival on the steps. For Grace, her presence knocked the edge off it because Sadie was just about as common as you could get and had never been officially introduced to the front room. Grace put a brave face on it. She had been unexpectedly moved to see the young couple so intensely pleased to meet again. She had never known Ellen smile so much and the boy was beside himself and whatever she thought of Sam, he looked a fine handsome man now, almost, she had to admit, distinguished.

For everyone but Grace and the boy, the room was awkward. Grace sat in her usual armchair, so angled that she could survey the Hill and also look directly at the door. The boy, whom she indulged next only to Mr Kneale, squatted on the floor in front of her and leaned back into her heavy skirts. Even at that hour of the morning, her hair was majestic. Thick and grey, it swept loosely but under exact control from the upper half of her face to be gathered in a bun where it was stabbed with a large pin. It framed her still handsome face, giving it an indisputable dignity. It was her feature. Only twice in her life had Ellen seen her hair loose and on neither occasion had it been mentioned.

Sam felt unsettled. It was not as he had imagined it. He had hoped for Ellen, Joe and himself, just the three of them. It was not much to endure, he told himself. And why did such a small thing bother him so much, when only a couple of months ago, real danger had been met with far less agitation?

'Let's see if I can find any presents!'

He had the kitbag and the parcels. They stood in the middle of the carpet, as if they had dropped from the ceiling, moated by respectful space.

'Two for Joe. Number one for your birthdays – sorry I couldn't be here but I will be for your seventh.'

Out of the kitbag, unwrapped, came a magnificent ruby leather satchel embossed on the back with six tiny yellow elephants walking in line, trunk curled around tail. He watched the boy reach out and recognised the gesture as Ellen's. Yet the boy resembled him too, she had said that in her letters, and looking closely he could see that.

'There now,' said Grace. 'You can put all your things in that. Nobody else in Wigton will have one of those.'

'Did you see any elephants, Daddy?'

'Hundreds. I rode on one once or twice. They helped us build a bridge. They pick up the logs with their trunks.'

'They don't.'

'Oh yes.' Sam put his kitbag lengthways on the floor, knelt down and with his right arm miming a trunk, he lifted it up. Joe laughed and clapped and made him do it again.

'Now,' said Sam, 'your "coming-home" present.'

The parcel was bulky and well tied with coarse string, but the knots were easy and within moments Joe had destroyed the wrapping to discover a small wooden train, painted black and red, with four carriages and a guard's van, the doors and windows picked out

17

precisely, wheels perfectly smooth on the carpet. He looked at his father in adoration.

'What d'you say then?' said Grace, visibly pleased for him.

'Thank you, Daddy.' The words were dutiful and flat.

'It doesn't matter,' said Sam, storing up that look from his son, hoping that the print of it would not fade.

Joe slung the satchel around his neck and then concentrated on puff-puff-puffing the train around the room.

'It's very well made,' said Leonard, offering Sam a cigarette.

'Have one of mine.' Sam handed him a tightly packed drum of Players No. 1.

'Well, I don't mind if I do.'

'Take the lot.'

'No, no,' said Leonard, longingly. He had always liked Sam. Apart from everything else, both of them enjoyed a flutter on the horses and Sam had never given him away to Grace. He took the drum.

'Now then. Grace's present.'

Her shoulders stiffened.

'What about this?'

It was a double-stranded ivory necklace with a cameo of Queen Victoria as a centrepiece. He held it out. She took it, after a pause, almost as a tribute from a defeated foe.

'You shouldn't have bothered.'

'Try it on, Aunty Grace,' said Ellen. 'It'll suit you.'

It did. Grace's style was big and the white ivory sat imperially above her serious bosom. She fingered it as if considering whether she might buy it.

'It's very kind of you, Sam,' she said slowly.

'Makes you look like a duchess!' Sadie had restrained herself and even waited to be offered a cigarette instead of just cadging one, but now she had to speak out. 'Dead posh!'

'Ivory?' said Grace, probingly, her thumb and forefinger lightly caressing the cameo.

'Straight from the tusk. And hand-made, every bit.'

Grace nodded, carefully disturbing not a hair.

'I'll keep it for best,' she said and took it off and scrutinised it carefully.

He had bought several sandalwood boxes and he handed one out to Sadie. She held up her hands.

'You can't give me a present, Sam!'

'Go on, Sadie.'

'I didn't come here for a present.'

She would be lucky, Sam knew, to get one present a year.

'Smell it, Sadie.'

The small woman, light brown hair in curlers topped by a turban of scarf, face pinched but eyes twinkling like an imp, one stocking already at half-mast, pom-pom-less slippers shuffled paper-thin, took the exotic wood, pressed it to her sharp nose and filled her lungs.

'Now then,' she said, as she let out the air, 'that beats perfume hollow!'

Again she sucked in the scent before passing it round. All of them smelled approvingly.

Sam wanted to give Ellen her present in private. It was rather a strange present anyway. He had imagined the two of them, alone, perhaps even in bed, and the present flowing around and about them, weaving them together.

But everyone – save Joe, chugging into the hall – was expecting it.

'There we are,' he said, clumsily.

Ellen took off the brown sugar paper and was puzzled at first by the compressed layers of material. She looked enquiringly at Sam. He held her gaze longingly: she blushed, scooped up the material and pressed it into her face, pretending to smell it. Their exchange had not gone unnoticed by Sadie and Grace and both women felt like intruders. Joe chugged the train back into the room.

'They're what they call "saris",' Sam spoke shyly.

'What are they for?'

He looked at Ellen helplessly.

'Indian women wrap them around themselves for dresses.' He saw their plumed and gracious bearing in the highly coloured saris, their bodies undulating, and he remembered the times of his own longing for the body of his wife.

'How do you know they wrap them round?' said Ellen.

'Guesswork!'

Thank God, he thought, he had kept away from all that.

Ellen nodded and that nod was a rebetrothal, a second wedding band, the full stop to an inevitable suspicion – and quite suddenly she tugged at the tightly folded saris and flung them like streamers over the room, their colours gorgeous, high yellows, Prussian blues, green, orange, violent, burnt-oak reds, a swirl of colours like her dreams, the room exotic and alive with happiness.

CHAPTER THREE

The warm morning sunlight seeped through the cheap curtains and Ellen carefully propped her head up on her elbow to look at him closely.

He had changed. Not just the tan and the few flecks of grey hair in the red, nor the body, much stronger now, lean with muscle. It was the whole expression. She needed time to worry it out.

In the cobbled yard below, footsteps clacked on the stone and Ellen imagined glances thrown up towards the bedroom still curtained in mid-morning. She felt uncomfortable being so public.

It was not grim, exactly, his expression, but it did have a severity which had not been there before. It seemed set, whereas she was sure she remembered a softer face, much more fluid, changing almost from one minute to the next; that was one of the best things about him, the energy, always on to the next thing. But now it was set and his lips seemed thinner, clamped together in a way she had not seen before. Of course he was asleep and exhausted and you could only tell the real man by looking at his eyes and catching the smile – and the eyes still smiled and the smile still felled her – but as an involuntary spasm, a deep shudder, went through him for the third time since they had come to bed, Ellen was a little apprehensive about this man who was different in ways she did not want to recognise from the man who had marched away those years ago.

Sam had told her, in diffident, fractured sentences, that she looked 'just the same', 'even better than he remembered', and from such clichés, she had known the full strength of his feelings. He had, in truth, been almost winded by her beauty when she had undressed. That slender body, candle white and quick, had slipped into the hastily made bed, grateful that the first encounter for so long had been without embarrassment, with a clear reminder of the passion between them. Her face, he swore, had got younger, the hair even blacker, more luxuriant, the oval shape more defined, the deep brown eyes more teasing, the rather full lips softer.

Ellen coughed, barely audibly, and was relieved to see that Sam did not stir. They could not inhabit the room for too long, even on such a day. But there was still time to look and listen to his slow breathing and watch the mid-morning light dappling patterns through the curtains on to the bare white walls. He had been back for four hours and still it was not real.

Sadie had engineered Joe out of the way, up street, with many promises and heavy bargaining on his side – his right to take the elephant satchel and the train (the carriages made too much bulk). She had also volunteered to give word to Mrs Alfreds that Ellen would not be turning up for cleaning that morning. Sadie did not like Mrs Alfreds, who looked right through her when they met in the street, and she looked forward to delivering the inconveniencing message. Then she would take Joe on to school, the last day of the term.

Ellen did not see why she should miss her work at Eves' chemist shop that afternoon and though Sam would have preferred her not to go, he was not quick enough to propose an alternative. Once he himself was out of the house in the summer temperature of that early spring, he realised that they could have gone for a walk together – through the Show Fields, along the banks of the River Wiza, around Cuddy Lonnings or the Syke, any one of the trails along which they and so many others had pursued a long, thrifty and constrained courtship.

At the end of Market Hill, Sam turned left, west, and faced up the length of King Street which, with High Street, formed the axis of the town. Nothing, it seemed at first, nothing at all had changed. He strolled as slowly as he could, the leisurely progress and his rather smart light grey double-breasted demob suit giving him the air of a stranger, a visitor keen to absorb the atmosphere.

The place pushed at him wave after wave of his old life, his lives, all but stopping him in his tracks, the names themselves almost suffocating him with memories. On the right side Plasket's Lane where John Willy Stewart kept his ponies and sometimes let boys have a free ride. Tickle's Lane teeming with cottages where as a boy a friend had shown him, proudly, a floor carpeted in cockroaches. Station Road, New Street, Meeting House Lane: the weight and detail of the past seemed to press physically on his neck, bearing him down as the town had always threatened to do after the birth of Joe: most possibilities tested, life just begun. Soon the first of the pubs, the Blue Bell big as a railway station, then the narrow, sly Vaults, the Vic, the dominating King's Arms. Nineteen pubs and pothouses in the town. In Burma he had totted them up more than once. And those small-paned windows in the same old shops, one or two with awnings out against the unseasonal sun; and faces, faces all of which, it seemed, he recognised. When the first one or two stopped to say hello or waved 'Hiya Sam', then everyone appeared to notice him, 'How do, Sam?', and it was like pushing up an Everest of the past, grand, dislocating, stirring and somehow new, bewildering, this place of peace.

He went for refuge into the bar of the Vic at the end of Water Street, no more than a hundred yards from his starting point, grateful for its stale emptiness.

There was a young boy behind the bar.

'Is your dad in?'

'He's just gone up street.'

The first drink in Wigton. He had planned it would be with Ian. He shook off the thought, physically, like a dog shaking off water. He had to stop all that . . .

'Pint of bitter.'

The boy pulled it deftly enough.

'One and two, please.'

Sam had the exact change. The boy put it in the open wooden till and left.

He let the bitter settle before he drank.

It was a small bar, men only, just an old oak bench against the window, most stood against the bar itself. A door in the corner led to the billiard room. Sam enjoyed listening to the chinking of the ivory balls and the preoccupied murmurings of the players but had no wish to go in and be drawn into the game.

He wet his lips, paused and then downed a third of it and held the glass up, just a touch. A toast. Home. He stood square at the bar, facing the shelves, and took out a cigarette. His feet had still not touched the bottom.

He had a few minutes alone.

Henry Allen poked his head around the door and was just about to retreat when he spotted Sam. His hand went out like a piston, the smile genuine but well worn. Sam had been a steady customer.

'You look well, Sam. Nice tan.'

'I can think of easier ways to get it.'

'Look at today. You could top it up. Have one with me.'

'I've just got one in.'

The boy came into the bar.

'Just a tonic for me, Billy.' To Sam, 'Still bothered with my stomach, Sam. Never got past the medical. And fill up that glass of Sam's.' He slapped a half crown on to the polished walnut bar.

'Welcome back.' He sipped at the tonic, pulling a face.

Sam made a second toast and, to head off any talk about himself, he said, 'How are they running, then, Henry?'

'No faster, Sam.'

'Business?'

'Never complain, Sam, lads in Wigton've never been too skint for a bet. They're very reliable that way.'

Henry was the most prosperous bookmaker in the town and this was part of his midday run, picking up bets, illegally, in the pubs.

'Was it terrible over there?'

Sam nodded.

'So we heard. Mind you, it was terrible all over. Tales of woe wherever you turn. Your lot'll be about the last back. The bunting's long gone, I'm afraid, Sam. Everybody wants to get back to normal.'

'Include me in.' Sam offered Henry a cigarette. 'What was it like here?'

'In the war?' Henry drew in the cigarette greedily, his pale sallow face seeming to need the warmth. 'Heaving, Sam! We had the soldiers, and the RAF, they came from far and near, Fridays and Saturdays the streets were littered.' He looked about suspiciously, out of habit. 'You know what they called the King's Arms?' Sam shook his head. 'The cock-loft,' he said, softly, and repeated it with a dirty chuckle, much

25

more loudly, tilting his hat back, debonair in his Prince of Wales check suit. 'The cock-loft! And, Sam: it *was*!'

Sam's smile was a little uneasy.

'And I'll tell you, Sam,' said Henry, inspired by a new listener and excited by the gossip of the bawdy life he would never dare lead, 'there are women in this town with little kiddies whose fathers have nothing to do with Wigton and have moved on to faraway places! Say nothing.' He tossed back his tonic. 'You know – well, you won't of course – what the new Father down at St Cuthbert's said? "Well," he said, "I have travelled the world, I have penetrated the darkest parts of Africa, but I have never come across as wicked a little hole as Wigton"!' Henry's grin was wide, proud and delighted. He slapped the bar top with his palm. 'As wicked a little hole as Wigton,' he repeated. 'And he had penetrated darkest Africa. How's that for a testimonial! Billy!' The boy had gone out again, but returned instantly. 'Did Dad leave a little package for Mr Allen?'

The boy came back with a thin wad of notepaper and a clinking envelope which, after a doubtful look at Sam, he handed over.

Sam and Leonard had managed to exchange a few words at the house after breakfast and he had his bet ready. 'Lovely Cottage,' he said, pulling out, he did not know why, twice as much as he had intended to bet on the next day's Grand National. Henry pocketed the money with furtive swiftness.

'A few of the lads is on that,' he said. 'I suspect the influence of the ladies. You won't be wanting a ticket, Sam, you never did.'

'I'll be round for the winnings after the race.'

'Well,' Henry secured his brown trilby which had become a little rakish, 'I'll be on my travels. Time and Tide, Sam, the old proverb. Ellen's been looking very good, Sam. She's a smasher. She makes old

Eves' shop glow like a Christmas tree. Lucky man.' Although it was a compliment, Sam would rather not have heard it.

Sam decided not to visit his father that day. The old man worked as a gardener in a big house a few miles away and Sam had looked forward to the walk, but a sudden mood came on him which made him want to avoid any more intimacy. First though he had to buy the stamps.

'Penny stamps is now a penny ha'penny,' said Albert, behind the counter. Sam and Albert had been at school together, only two years apart. Albert had greeted him as if he had been coming in every day uninterruptedly since war broke out.

Sam pulled out the extra four pence and slid the stamps into his inside pocket.

'Mother well, Albert?'

'A miracle for her age. Very demanding.'

Albert looked away, distracted, as he always had been but by what no one had ever found out. His eyes had failed the medical. His glasses were as thick as bottle bottoms.

Just along the street was the George Moore Memorial Fountain which had replaced the Parish Pump in the latter part of the nineteenth century. It was thirty-three feet high, as all Wigton children were told, and topped by a cross. At its base there was a platform stepping up to four bronze panels – North, South, East, West – and then the spire. Drinking fountains were furnished on all four sides but recently they had been barred off by grim iron railings which were redeemed by four elaborate gas lamps, night sentries to the memory of the wife of George Moore.

As ever was, the men were there, killing time, loitering, pushed out or glad to be out of cramped houses, leaning against the railings, watching and marking the town go by and now and then squirting out a spit, sometimes hitting one of the dogs which lurched all about. They knew Sam and nodded or greeted him – unexcitedly – most of them remarking on how well he looked, as if he had come back from a holiday. Their indifference to his war made him smile to himself. There was a kind of settlement in it, perhaps even a wisdom.

This was the fulcrum of the town. He took his place. To the west was the sea and under the sea the coalmines in which his father had once worked: some of his family still worked there now. To the east was Carlisle where he had gone to volunteer what seemed a lifetime ago – and from there, east to service in North Africa, east to India, east again to Burma.

Ahead of him was High Street. He had walked it thousands of times, still jewelled with small useful shops, many of them with workshops behind making boots, making clocks and watches, butching, baking bread and cakes. Still there. Untouched though the world had gone mad: their complete survival made him smile. As he had done so often as a young man, skint, watching the world go by for his entertainment, he leaned his back against the railings among the poor-suited, mostly unskilled, usually broke, often eccentric and curious men long of the town who gave the place its character.

Sam offered cigarettes freely. He knew it was expected of him. The Salvation Army had not yet stopped dishing out free rations to ex-servicemen. He looked up at the bronze panels which, as he remembered from having it drummed into him at school, represented the Four Acts of Mercy.

Beautifully draped, graceful and serene women and children more handsome and certainly plumper than almost anyone in the town, represented Visiting the Afflicted, Instructing the Ignorant, Feeding the Hungry and Clothing the Naked. They moved him not at all – that was not what it was like. Suffering, Hunger, Affliction,

Nakedness were not like that. He had seen it real. He remembered their teacher, Miss Steel, had insisted that these figures were real. In the morning after their official expedition to the fountain she had asked the children to bring at least twopence to school to contribute to an appeal she ran for orphaned African babies. Those who could not afford it were shamed.

Halfway through his second cigarette, he moved off. No one took much notice – and again he felt as though he were going head on into a force, a high wind which made him want to bend his head and butt his way through. Yet the day was calm and warm, High Street quiet enough, with a few cattle being driven down the cowpat-splattered street to the railway station for shipment, fresh from the small Friday auction. Only one car on the street, parked outside the Lion and Lamb. He even knew who it belonged to.

The curious sensation persisted, as if he were walking waist deep in the sea, pushing against a tide, even a hint of panic in his breath. Hello Sam, yes, grand, glad to be back, lovely day . . . it never changes, the town . . . but in some way he could not define, it had. Or he had? Why did what was so familiar suddenly flip over into what seemed new? 'How do, Sam?'

He began to feel claustrophobic. Just a street in a small Northern market town. Hello Sam, Hiya Sam, lovely day. He saw nobody from the war. Some at work – the non-Burma lads – or didn't make it back. He would soon find out, Leonard would give him the list. He walked faster, past the Anglican church, past the Girls' Grammar School, forcing the pace over yet another of the streams which trickled through the town, heading south towards Longthwaite and open land, unbuttoning his collar, loosening the tie, taking off his jacket, faster up the hill, lovely day, it never changes, the town, hounding himself out of it and then – a vale of calm – nothing but fields, friendly lush fields with sheep and cattle grazing lazily as ever, rooted there. English fields free from war for more than three hundred years, stunning and soothing him with the power of their peace.

He wiped the sweat from his brow and gave the town a brief, almost furtive backward glance before moving on.

The fountain, memorial to one woman, there forever planted, part of what the town was. On the outskirts in the new cemetery the memorial to the First World War with the name 'Richardson' inscribed two times. What would there be for those who had not come back this time? Again he shook his head with that sharp movement which sought to shake off unwelcome thoughts as if they were raindrops. But it was not so easy. A nice tan? Lovely day? Yes, I'll take a fag off you, Sam, smoke it later, stick it behind the ear. No bunting. The German conflict had ended almost a year ago now. The war had gone cold.

Just as well, he reasoned, as he went through the kissing gate that led into the well-walked common land which wended by the river along the edge of the town. For many generations these fields had been a lure for children's play, for the saunterings of courtship and the placid strolls of the old. Budding, some trees greening, the fields had the deep security of familiarity and yet to Sam a friction of unease. The place looked not as once it had been. Yet surely it was exactly the same. It must be the peace which was unsettling.

He found a willow in a shaded place and sat against it, a few feet from the river. Through the water, clear and cold from the fells which rose up a few miles to the south, he saw a large school of minnows, darting and switching in impeccable, well-drilled formation.

No bunting. Better like that. But what would be their memorial, those who had not returned from Burma, from what was called the Forgotten Army? Men, he could let his mind whisper it now he was alone and unconstrained, men who had some of them been heroes and died to keep such bedded peace as this, in fields like these, to be passed on to their children. Who would build a fountain for them? His head jolted back at the 'image' of a child. It banged against the tree.

CHAPTER FOUR

He had put the pad in one of the capacious side pockets of his suit, the envelopes in the other, not thinking he would have time to write the letters on this first day but instinctively sensing that the right moment might come at any time. He had written during the campaign to the relations of everyone he knew, but that was not enough for close friends.

Sam put his cigarettes beside him, closed his eyes and in a moment he was many thousands of miles away. The run of the small stream was the drum of monsoon. The hedgerow fencing the quiet fields, the trees planted for shade, grass ready to grow yet another intricate carpet sweet with meadow flowers whose names promised comfort – all became jungle to be hacked through, dense with the dread experienced by those men he had heard of who had been driven crazy when left alone even for an hour in that alien, fearful place. A place of ambush, bullet and shell expected at every step, until the fear was sharpened into an alert tension so highly strung it sang in your mind and became a terrible joy.

He opened his eyes and looked at the peace and heard such stillness, hardly a bird call. The soft gurgle of the stream was the loudest sound. He began to write. He would not have admitted it, but part of the reason for his urgency was an apprehension, growing almost daily since he had landed back in England, that Burma would ambush him, shell him down, take him back there and abandon him unless he beat it down.

The letters, he hoped, would draw a line.

They were already written in his head. He had only to copy them down. On the long journey back, thinking about them, he had worked them out. He wrote steadily, giving to each one the two or three sides of paper he had decided was the least he could do. He paused only to drag himself out of the atmosphere they evoked so powerfully.

Those he wrote about had been in his section. One had led him. The others he had led. His section had been one of those right at the front, no shield, no advance force in front of them, they were the advance force. Sections were made up of ten men, led by a corporal: three sections to a platoon, three platoons to a company, four companies to a battalion and so up to the regiment and on to the Allied army in Burma described by Churchill (Sam had written it down) as 'an army the like of which had not been seen since Xerxes crossed the Hellespont'. He intended to look up Xerxes and Helle-spont. But however grand the names, it always came back to the section.

It was those ten men multiplied who had met the full fury of the Japanese army bayonet to bayonet. More than twenty men had passed through that section in Sam's time.

Sam would stop now and then to brush aside memories too savage to be sent into any of these homes. That ambush when almost a third of the company had been slaughtered was just a long scream of shock and blood, spilled guts, helplessness, confusion, retreat, bodies left for ever to rot away in what had seemed a quiet patch of jungle. Yoke and Buster, two of the nicest lads you could meet, dead within a

34

foot of each other, both bayoneted, clearly one had come to help the other. He said nothing of the malaria or the dysentery or the pains of terrible diarrhoea or the emaciation and exhaustion. His stories were drawn from another truth, that despite the punishments and wounds of battle, the tattered uniforms, the sores and private agonies un-spoken, these men were a disciplined army, prepared to fight, ready to die for each other and also, though this was never boasted, mostly ignored and sometimes mocked, for their country. However deeply buried and cynically dismissed their cause was, they had volunteered to serve it.

He did not write of the puddle of brains seeping out of the skull of Andy, who had been less than a yard away when he had caught it. He blocked out the final crescendo of martial curses when one hardened miner, caught too far forward, surrounded by the Japanese, had decided to take as many as he could with him rather than surrender and die Tojo's way. After two days of being holed up, he had gone out to bury the man's body and found him already buried up to his neck, the head crawling with maggots. One of Tojo's ways. And what did you say of Alan, who had gone to clear a nest of enemy machine-gunners whose bullets hit his body so hard, so many, so fast, that it stuttered and jived for what seemed like minutes on end until it folded like a jackknife?

What he wrote was, 'Conditions were sometimes very bad but he never complained. He made a joke of it and helped us all along.' He wrote, 'Things could get very rough but he would always be relied on to see any bright side.' In every letter, true or not, he wrote, 'He always spoke warmly of his home and his family and missed them a lot. There was never any doubt where his feelings lay and he wanted to get home and see you all again but it was not to be.'

Once or twice he introduced some of the new words they had

picked up out there – char for tea and dekko for have a look, pani for water and doolally for mad, believing that this would make it more convincing. Perhaps also it revealed his own still undigested and puzzled wonder that it had all happened so far away in so foreign a place.

The last letter of all was the hardest, as he had known it would be. As soon as they invited him he would have to face Ian's parents.

When he finished he felt stiff. Almost two hours had gone by. His packet of cigarettes was empty. The heat had gone out of the sun and he shivered. He put on the stamps very carefully and precisely so that the perforations ran along the edges of the envelope. He looked around. It was somehow miraculous that these fields, this clear brook, this deep silence had remained undisturbed. Miraculous and, for a dazed few moments, inexplicable.

He would post the letters on his way to pick up Ellen at Eves' the Chemist.

He stood up and felt giddy as the blood seemed to drain out of him. He steadied himself for a while. This, he thought, was how very old and exhausted and sick people felt. Then he began to walk almost reluctantly back into the town.

CHAPTER FIVE

'Did you ever go out to a pub on your own?'

'What?'

'Or with Sadie? Just the two of you?'

'Why are you asking?' Ellen had been slowly drowning into sleep. Now she was fully alert but she kept still.

'I was just thinking about what you did. They called the King's Arms "the cock-loft". Did you know that?'

'They said all sorts of things.'

'Wigton was very crowded, though, wasn't it? People coming from far and near. At night.'

'Who've you been talking to?'

'Henry Allen.'

'Henry makes half of it up. He was the same at school.'

'Well, did you?'

'No I didn't and you needn't have asked.'

'I know.'

'You're tired.'

'I know but I'm wide awake as well. Not even once? It would be understandable. You and Sadie?'

'Sadie went. A lot of women did. If they could do men's jobs they could go into a pub – that was the way they saw it. There was no harm in it, Sam.'

'Why didn't you go then?'

'I didn't fancy it. I didn't like leaving Joe.'

'Joe?'

'And I knew you wouldn't like it. Got the answer you want?'

Sam nodded. That was fair. He was propped up against the pillows, smoking, the window open on the spring night. Ellen was deep under the blankets, only part of her face visible. Joe had been in their bed a couple of hours before when they had come up but he had been easy to carry out, bonelessly soft with sleep, to the cubby hole along the corridor which Ellen had turned into a bedroom. As long as he could keep the train with him – the satchel had slipped to a poor second – he seemed content. Despite Grace's reservations, Ellen had insisted that the gaslight in the corridor be kept on, throughout the night, for a few days at least.

'You need sleep.'

'I know.'

How could you ache with tiredness and be so alert? He had known the answer not long ago. Fear and duty fast locked. But here, he was at home, in his own bed, with his wife, his son asleep, the town pacifically unconscious in the dark, no terror in the silence, no alarm in a sound, any sound.

The candle fluttered, the long yellow flame licked out towards him. He stubbed out the cigarette in the saucer which held it.

'Goodnight,' Ellen said, hoping to encourage him.

She snuggled herself deeper into the bed. He watched her settle down. 'I want you to give up that job at Eves'.'

Ellen waited for more to be said. There was no more.

'Why?'

He could not or he would not articulate the jealous truth.

'There's no need now. I'll have a wage coming in soon.'

'I like working there.'

'I saw that when I picked you up.'

'What do you mean?'

He had no answer. What had he seen in the shop? Ellen, happy, bright-eyed, lovely, quick, pleasant, independent, in charge, behind the counter, darting to fulfil the requests, fast with figures. And available for just anyone and everyone to admire.

'You could be back in time for Joe.' Sam's tone was critical.

'He thought you might pick him up at school this afternoon,' she retaliated. 'He'd got his pals together to meet his dad.'

Ellen sat up. She had vowed not to tell him that. Joe's upset had been smoothed over.

'I was . . .' Writing letters.

'I'll give up the cleaning jobs. Two days at Mr Eves' pays as much as all the cleaning.'

'Why do you want to cling to it?'

'It takes me out of myself. I meet everybody.'

Sam turned away, already exhausted by their brief argument. It was so complicated.

'Why can't you just *do* it? Just give it up.'

'Let's talk about it tomorrow. It's nearly one o'clock, Sam.'

She knew what his fears were. It was difficult to find the right words. Expressions of love and affection were hard to dig out. In their near silent love-making, in the complexion of everyday loyalties, in glance and in small gesture, she knew that Sam was aware of her deepest feelings as she was of his. Or had been. That had been the character of their bond before he went away. Tonight it was not there.

Ellen was not over-anxious. It would take time. They had time.

39

'You're tired, Sam,' she said, eventually. She leaned over and kissed him quickly on the mouth. 'I've missed you terribly,' she said.

He wanted to repeat the phrase back to her but could not. She must know.

Later in the night, Joe crept into their bed, bringing his train. He clambered over his father, transfixed in profound sleep, and took his usual place alongside his mother. Ellen felt the edges of the train dent her back and her thighs but she wanted no disturbance and so she put up with it.

When Sam woke, he was alone in the bed, the morning was half gone, his body was damp with sweat and for a few alien moments he had no idea where he was.

Grace called it 'the Holy of Holies'. She was slightly discountenanced that her first social invitation into that sacred room had come about because of Sam's return. Mr Kneale had never organised such an event for her. Still, she wore the ivory necklace. Later, Mr Kneale complimented her on it and reassuringly commended its quality.

Mr Kneale's sitting room at the top of the house was loaded with his late wife's fine furniture – high-polished by Ellen. Its style and age made the furniture in Grace's front room two floors below – so carefully selected by Leonard's mother – seem rather lacking. In the clamped, secret chamber of her mind, Grace might have breathed the painful thought that it was in a different class.

She breasted the way in, heavily pleated black satin blouse displaying its air of pre-war opulence. Joe in his one suit was next, clutching the train. The carriages had been forbidden. Ellen felt awkward: she cleaned the room, laid the fire in the room and served breakfast in the room. It was odd to be off-duty there, odd too to be wearing her good dress inside the house on a Wednesday evening. Sam wore the brown sports jacket and grey flannels he had bought for their honeymoon: the jacket hung rather loosely on him.

Leonard had 'slipped up street' and Grace had no choice but to accept that as a full and sufficient excuse for his absence. On a few seemingly marginal matters Leonard was immovable and his right to 'slip up street' was one of them. He had gone to play billiards and it had taken serious persuasion for Ellen to stop Sam joining him. The clincher was that 'Mr Kneale has laid all this on especially for you.'

All this was sherry, biscuits and photographs at seven.

In the week since his return, Sam had seen Mr Kneale three or four times. After their first introduction, the two men had greeted each other in perfectly satisfactory clichés about the unusual good weather, the inconvenience of queues, the scarcity of fresh fruit and, once, had a real conversation on the mooted introduction of the National Health Service which one eminent local doctor had described at a public meeting as the sort of thing Britain had fought the Germans to prevent happening.

Sam liked the schoolteacher well enough. Mr Kneale was rather short and very round with delicate hands and small feet; his hair was curly and still thick, though grey, and his tortoiseshell spectacles gave his rather bland features some definition. His manner, by contrast, was gentle, almost fluid in his compliant swaying and expressive gesticulating.

'Sherry?'

There was a mutter of assent. He poured it with extreme care out of a heavy cutglass decanter.

'For you, young man, cherryade.'

'Say "thank you, Mr Kneale".'

41

'Thank you, Mr Kneale.'

Mr Kneale patted Joe's head with a familiar affection not unnoticed by Sam. There had been quite a lot of 'Mr Kneale this' and 'Mr Kneale that' from Joe over the week, including 'Mr Kneale knows everything' and 'Mr Kneale sometimes tells me stories at bedtime'. Bedtime with Joe was becoming a problem. And Sam was still disconcerted at Joe kissing his photo on the first few nights and saying, 'Night night, Daddy. God Bless' to the eager young private spruce in his first uniform.

Sam had never been keen on sherry.

Ellen handed out the biscuits and Sam noticed how easily she and Mr Kneale seemed to get on with one another. It was not that there was, or could ever possibly have been, anything between them. But in his acute state of seeing so much twice over, as old and familiar and yet as new and unnerving, Sam registered their collusion and did not know what to make of it. She's just handing out the biscuits, he told himself!

Grace led the charge with a compliment on the sherry. Mr Kneale gave easy permission for Joe to chug the train around the fine furniture. Joe was far keener, though, to listen in to the talk, and the comics (confiscated at school) provided by Mr Kneale enabled him to return smartly to the company and eavesdrop.

The conversation did not flow. After a while, Mr Kneale got out a selection of the photographs he had taken of the town over the years and to begin with all three adult visitors were genuinely absorbed. The town was their home, their life and the source of so many continuing stories.

Mr Kneale first showed photographs taken a mile to the south of the town at the Roman Cavalry Camp known locally as Old Carlisle. He had labelled various mounds and hummocks of grass as 'possibly stables' or 'could be the kitchens'. His prize exhibits were from the town itself, where a few of the Roman stones and statues were bedded in the walls of the church and other buildings.

Grace nodded and listened with model attention but eventually her thoughts slipped away, as Leonard had slipped up street. They did not seem up to much, these Romans, she thought, no wonder they had died out, if they had died out, she did not like to ask. She settled back and began a systematic appraisal of the furniture.

Ellen always enjoyed Mr Kneale's enthusiasm and she smiled at his knowledge. It sounded funny – although she was sure it shouldn't – when he spoke of Head Pots and Steelyard Weights, of pagan altars, and showed ugly pictures of what he called Local Celtic Deities. It was difficult to imagine these people so long ago, so foreign, in the town which had mothered and fathered her in a way even Sam could not comprehend, even though he himself had arrived there as a young boy.

Sam spent little energy on the photographs. He watched Joe, peeping over the comics to observe Mr Kneale, the centre of attention, and when Mr Kneale caught Joe's gaze and nodded kindly, Sam's heart prickled at the boy's instantly affectionate response. He looked at Ellen too, how unrestrained she was in her appreciation, how quick with questions, how flushed when Mr Kneale described them as 'very good' questions or 'intelligent comments' or 'that's a question that has me stumped, Ellen'. They were so very nice and easy with each other. He began to resent the fluttering of the schoolteacher's delicate hands.

It was all opportunity, Sam thought, rather bitterly. He had passed the scholarship for the grammar school and been denied the place because money could not be found for uniforms and books and the other extras. Whereas Ellen never expressed regret about her brief education and relished being just one of the town-girls, over the years

Sam had often mourned his lost chance. Especially in the army when he had come across educated men – in the ranks as well as officers – and been dismayed that although he knew he could join in the discussions, words and knowledge so often failed him. He had been imprisoned in ignorance. He had not known, until he met these men, how much he had missed.

'Aerial photography would make all the difference,' Mr Kneale sighed, shaking his grey curls. It was a full, dramatic sigh, meant to show how much he cared for his art, which indeed he did. 'We could see the whole camp then, laid like that carpet.'

Grace smiled and thought the chaise longue could be into three figures. The carpet too was no ordinary carpet. Sam noted that Joe, it seemed automatically, asked what 'aerial' meant and Mr Kneale, equally practised, told him.

'For the Crofts, too,' he continued, 'aerial photography would be a revelation!'

The Crofts was the name of a lane at the back of long strips of working gardens leading from High Street. They had been carved out by the Saxons who had settled in the town at least two hundred years before William the Conqueror, Mr Kneale said. That so much of what had been should still today be evident and put to the same use excited Mr Kneale greatly. It left Ellen, for once, a little dubious as the Crofts were so undistinguished, and left Sam rueful that somewhere he knew so well he knew so little.

Mr Kneale showed his photographs of the church and here he came as near to anger as he got when he explained how a church built in the twelfth century and outlasting even the ravages of the violent Border Wars, had been razed to the ground utterly to build the present church in 1785. The orders were – not a stone to be reused. 'Vandalism,' he exclaimed. 'As bad as Oliver Cromwell. As bad as

Henry VIII, neither of whom – monstrous wreckers of fine buildings – had ruined Wigton. It was,' he said, rather solemnly, 'by Wigton hands alone that Wigton's past had been destroyed.'

Ellen tried not to smile at the little scowl on his moonish face. Grace tut-tutted sincerely at the terrible waste of it all. Sam remembered the day of their marriage in the church. A day he could see clearly but one which seemed so very distant.

He was made conscious, by the glance from Ellen, that he had said nothing at all. He stared down at the latest photograph being passed round, which was Mr Kneale's study of the Parish Pump, now chained in the public park.

'This is a good photo, Mr Kneale. Do you have a special camera?'

'That's a very good question. You can tell, I suppose, by the shadows.'

Sam looked again and nodded at the clear shadows.

'Of course I have a little Brownie,' said Mr Kneale, 'but this . . .' he reached behind him and produced the camera, 'is the real McCoy.'

He took the Leica out of its box and passed it to Sam, who handled it with respect.

'Is it German?'

'It is.' Mr Kneale pursed his lips and nodded gravely. 'I bought it in 1938 – you can't get them today of course – but it is German. I can't deny it.'

All of them looked at it closely.

'German,' said Grace, with just a colouring of criticism.

'1938,' repeated Mr Kneale, grimly, 'before the war.'

There was a brief silence.

'It looks very well made,' said Grace, judiciously. 'And I'm sure it can't have been cheap.'

'I did not think of using it for the duration.'

'No point,' said Sam, easily, and handed it back.

'He has things to stick on it as well, don't you, Mr Kneale? Nobody else in Wigton has things like Mr Kneale, do they, Mr Kneale?'

Joe's remark was quite neutral, but his treble voice and his innocent boast nipped the bud of embarrassment.

'What might they be?' Sam addressed his question to Joe.

'Show him, Mr Kneale.'

Joe went and stood by the teacher who, a little bashfully, brought out a wide-angled lens.

'And you should see the equipment he has in the cellar downstairs,' said Grace, fully restored to pride in her prize tenant.

'My own dark room,' said Mr Kneale, admitting privilege.

'You let some other people use it,' said Grace, somehow combining praise for his generosity with criticism at letting other people into her house.

'It's not a thing you can hog.'

Sam laughed aloud. Maybe it was the word 'hog'. He just laughed – and then Joe joined in, and Ellen (who had waited some time for the opportunity). Grace smiled, taking credit. Mr Kneale offered a final glass of sherry, but there were no takers.

When they left, Mr Kneale held the door open – all but bowed them out, thanking them more than once.

'We should be thanking *you*,' said Grace, but Mr Kneale would have none of it and he stood at the top of the stairs as if watching them set out on a long journey, still thanking them and saying they should do it again before too long.

He was deeply relieved that there was enough time to tidy up and change for bed and listen, as usual, in his dressing-gown, to the nine o'clock news.

'I think I'll have a dekko up street,' said Sam, when they reached the kitchen. 'Want to come?'

'I'm not going into a pub on a Wednesday.'

'I can't seem to get you there any day of the week.'

'You go ahead,' said Grace, rather unexpectedly. 'Ellen and me have plenty to talk about.'

Sam paused, just for a moment hoping that Ellen would change her mind and come with him.

'Enjoy yourself,' she said, 'your holiday's nearly over.'

'Mr Kneale liked the necklace.' Grace made it plain that the necklace had cleared an important hurdle.

'Can I eat them now?' Joe looked to Ellen to return to him the two toffees which he had been given and which he had immediately put into his mother's keeping.

'One,' she said and handed it over. She smiled at Sam, who seemed to stand uncertainly. 'Go on then,' she said, 'the sooner you're away the quicker you'll be back. I'll read Joe his story.'

'I need to get rid of the taste of that sherry,' he said.

'It was very good sherry,' said Grace. 'And the sheer weight of that decanter!'

He came back from the pub later than he had intended. The women were in bed. Leonard, alone in the kitchen, offered him a drink of port, a full bottle left over from Christmas. He pointed out that they had not yet enjoyed a welcome-back glass together.

Leonard was no bother to talk to. Despite coming from a well-off family he had no side and he was quite content with the undemanding occupation of chief clerk in a solicitor's office. One of his jobs was collecting rents from property which included the cottages in the yard behind the house. Sam was interested and asked about the state and availability of places in the town.

Very few, said Leonard, pouring another glass apiece, and none of it very attractive. The landlords had done nothing to the buildings for years on end. But the rents were low. New houses? Sam enquired, he had strolled back up to Kirkland – they looked good. Without question, said Leonard, proposing they should finish the bottle, and more to be built with all mod cons. But stiff rents. Bottoms up. Back from the wars. I bet there are some real stories . . . Muzzy, happy in a fashion, Sam had met three old pals who had been in the RAF, played darts for pints, no good on sherry . . . The women in India? said Leonard probingly, lowering his voice though Grace was two floors up and battened in sleep, in those saris, bet that was something . . . Lovely women. Sam nodded and nodded, lovely women, sold you cheroots . . . The last drop. Jungle Juice, Sam said, that was what we called it. All drink Jungle Juice.

It was not simple going up steep narrow stairs with arms around each other's shoulders but they made the attempt.

Joe was in the bed. Sam picked him up rather roughly and the boy woke up. 'C'mon.' Sam's voice was louder than he intended.

'Where are we going?'

'Back to your bed.'

He went along the short corridor, bouncing Joe a little, wanting the child to be as cheerful as he himself felt.

'Here we are.'

He dumped the boy on the narrow little camp bed which practically filled the cubby hole.

'I want to sleep with Mammy.'

'This is where you sleep now.'

48

Joe sniffed. He did not like the smell that came off his father. 'Why can't I sleep with Mammy?'

'Don't be such a baby.'

The words were harsh. Joe cringed and lay tactically still.

'We used to sleep in mud, sometimes,' said Sam, by way of reparation.

'In mud?' Despite his confusion, Joe was intrigued. 'Real mud?'

'Real soft brown wet deep dirty sticky mud so we woke up caked!' He laughed. 'We looked like chocolate men!'

'Why did you sleep in mud?'

'Because we had to.'

Believing his father now, and fully awake, Joe grimaced.

'It wasn't that bad. Looking back, it's funny!' He laughed, rather loudly. Joe joined in.

'I'll sing you a song.'

'No you won't.' Ellen was firm, though her voice was soft. 'You'll wake up the whole house. Come to bed,' she said.

Joe made a move but Sam put out a rather too heavy hand, pressing him down.

'Joe stops here.'

'Mammy?'

Ellen tried not to pause.

'Do as your Daddy says. You're a big boy now. I'll follow you,' she said, unobtrusively ushering Sam out of the cubby hole.

She stayed with Joe until he was settled. By the time she returned to their room, Sam was well away and snoring steadily. Ellen nipped his nose lightly and he turned on his side. The snoring ceased. She waved her hand in front of her face to waft away the breath of him and stared at the blank ceiling for some troubled time before being taken into a shallow doze.

CHAPTER SIX

He caught the bus to Carlisle in the late morning. It was almost empty. He sat upstairs, as he had always done as a boy, wanting to see over the hedges. The green mild fields stretched from one horizon to the other, horses, cattle and sheep cropping the new grass, one or two tractors. The eleven totally uneventful miles refreshed him.

He intended to shop and potter around in Carlisle for an hour or so. His extravagant bet on the Grand National had come off and Lovely Cottage had won. His winnings were, by his lights, big. He wanted to buy something special for Ellen.

He was soon frazzled. He had not the clothing coupons necessary for the coat he fancied her in. In the shop which sold handbags he lost patience with the la-di-da shop assistant who made such a performance over every one he wanted to look at. The small jewellery shop, so well stocked in the window, was empty when he went inside. The little bell tinkled and grew cold but nobody came. Sam almost tiptoed out. He would let her choose.

He walked towards the factory and stopped, abruptly, at the sign The Regimental Arms. Set in the old wall of the town, this was the pub they had come to after they had volunteered and signed on. He went inside. Nothing had altered. Iron bow-legged tables, old settles, red and yellow squared lino, fading photographs of local regiments on the walls. The bar was lit up by the sunlight which came through the big windows. Four men were having a quiet drink. He ordered a pint and took it to the corner where they had sat on that winter afternoon years before and where they had drunk until closing time.

He sipped the beer slowly and smoked a couple of cigarettes and smiled as that careless, crucial afternoon returned to his mind with nothing but warm memories. As he lifted the glass, the sun stroked through it, making the beer sparkle, golden, floating free as they had been then. Happy days.

It took an effort for him to leave the place.

He arrived at dinner-time as he had planned and went straight to the office. This was a wooden cabin which held a table, two wooden chairs, a stack of black files, a two-bar electric fire and the obese figure of Arthur Nicholson, sole proprietor of Nicholson & Sons.

'Sam! I heard you were back.' He wheezed and sucked harder on his pencil. 'Take a seat.'

Sam edged himself in.

'You look well.'

'You haven't changed much yourself.'

Arthur beat his chest with a pudgy fist. 'The old asthma won't leave me alone, Sam. Terrible thing, asthma. Underrated.'

He coughed a little, gaining time, Sam thought. Still those little raisin eyes in the expressionless face, hard to read. Though it was warm outside, Arthur was burning one bar of the fire and his head was insulated by a heavy cloth cap. A brown woolly muffler was knotted tight around his neck. Sam was sure it was the same muffler Arthur had worn the day he had got the job there before the war.

'You'll be looking for your old job.'

'That's right.'

Arthur wheezed, his eyes shifting rapidly.

'We're forced to take conscripts back. But not volunteers. There's no obligation. You know that.'

'I know that.'

'You were a volunteer.'

Sam nodded. Arthur leaned back. The chair creaked. He spread out his hands, indicating 'case proved'.

'You've no vacancies?'

'We've had a struggle, Sam. You had a struggle out there. We had a struggle back here.'

Sam let that pass. And he let the message sink in. He took his time.

'Fag?'

He offered one. Arthur reached out eagerly for it. He had always cadged cigarettes. Sam waited, obliging Arthur to reach for the matches. When he held out the flame, Sam took his wrist, hard, and tugged, just a little, so that Arthur's lardy face came close to his own.

'You made me a solemn promise, Arthur.' He grasped the wrist even tighter. The flame licked steadily down the match. 'Remember?'

Arthur's little black eyes twitched and darted as if they were being hunted down.

'Remember, Arthur?'

The flame was nearing Arthur's fingers. Sam's grip slid up from the wrist and clamped the fingers fast.

'Things changed, Sam. They changed.'

'So they did.'

He never blinked when the flame touched Arthur's fingertips. Arthur yelped.

'I think I'll save the fag for later,' Sam said and blew out the flame.

The next week there was an opening for a semi-skilled worker at the paper factory in Wigton. The work was hard but undemanding. It took no time at all to set up a card school. The majority vote was for solo whist.

—m—

Sadie came round as they were getting ready. Her right eye was red with new bruising. There was a small track of blood at the corner of her mouth.

Ellen took her into the back kitchen and dabbed the wounds in cold water. It was lucky that this was one of Grace and Leonard's Sunday mornings at the Methodist chapel.

'I want Sadie to come with us to Silloth,' Ellen announced when Sam came down. Sadie had gone to get changed.

'Why?'

'She never gets anywhere.'

Sam had been looking forward to just the three of them going to the seaside resort for the day. 'Has he had another go at her?' He knew that Ellen did not want him to raise the subject.

'He got into bad company last night.' Ellen took up Sadie's position. 'Alec's easily led. He always has been.'

Sam looked at her closely but she shook her head. This had been going on, at intervals, since Sadie's marriage. Sam had offered to sort it out at the beginning. He repeated the offer. Ellen turned it down.

'He'll just use it as an excuse to have another go at her.'

Sam had accepted that argument years before. He found it more difficult now.

'If he got a fright, he'd lay off her soon enough.'

'She doesn't want attention drawn to it. Mostly he's quiet.'

'He shouldn't be let get away with it.'

'She won't hear anything against him.'

'So Sadie comes with us to Silloth.'

Ellen nodded, unhappy at the fact but bound to her new promise, even though she knew what Sam had hoped for from the day.

Sam bought Sadie's ticket with the rest, but she insisted on paying her own fare and pressed the 1s. 10d. into his hand firmly, a lump of money, mostly coppers.

'Everybody in Wigton's here.' Sadie's exaggeration was pardonable. The fine spring weather was holding up and the queue for the buses to the seaside resort was a gathering. Relief buses had been ordered up and as the ancient double-deckers cranked uphill from the garage, the crowd cheered.

The journey was like an outing.

'We used to have to get out here and walk up,' someone said, at the bottom of the hill at Waver Bridge. 'To save the horses.' On the school outing, the annual holiday, the one day trip to Silloth. 'On Tommy Miller's wagons.'

When the bus driver took the hump into Abbeytown at a fair speed and the bus seemed to fly for a second, there was a loud 'whooaa' of appreciation.

Joe was excited at seeing the aeroplanes, scores of them, all damaged, though he did not know that, hedgehopped to this remote airfield for repair.

'You should have been a fighter pilot, Daddy.'

Sam smiled.

'Next time,' he said. 'What's that one – over there – just in front of the hangar?'

'A bomber.'

'Good. A Lancaster.'

They cheered when the bus came to its destination in Silloth, and then, with sandwiches and coats just in case, the more fussy or experienced with groundsheets against the sand, with buckets and spades and bats and balls, they went on to the wide spring-turfed green which lay like a stage between the stately Victorian front and the rough and treacherous Firth of sea which separates England from Scotland.

They made for the donkey-rides and all of them had a go, including Sadie, whose reservation (undeclared) was lack of money, but from now on Sam ignored that and paid and said nothing about it. It was Sadie who was assigned the only lively donkey and her loud yells of delighted panic cracked across the turf. On to the putting green, up into the little wood of pines and across to the salt baths and the amusement arcade. Joe handed the elephant satchel to Ellen and gave what to him was Ali Baba's cave his full attention.

Sadie's pennies came in handy there. Joe pressed his nose to the glass and strained to manoeuvre the three shiny claws of a crane on to one of the dusty treats cocked on the faded velvet. Ellen and Sadie rolled pennies, Joe raced across to a machine which tempted you to spring a ballbearing into tiny cups marked 3d., 2d., 1d. He had three unsuccessful attempts.

The firing range was for fun only. No prizes.

'Go on, Daddy.'

Sam put down 6d. for nine pellets. The gun was well worn but the sights were straight enough.

He shot six of the pellets and then plucked Joe up on to the counter and put his arms around him.

'Close your left eye tight shut. See that little pin thing sticking up at the end of the barrel?' Joe nodded. 'And see the black in the middle of the target?' Another movement indicated yes. 'Now point that little pin straight at the black ring.' Sam was supporting both the rifle and Joe and he put his hand over the boy's hand, taking it to the trigger. 'Nice and steady. Keep them in line. Now, don't jerk it, squeeze the trigger gently.'

Bullseye!

'Again! Again!'

As they looked for a place on the beach, Joe put his hand in Sam's hand more warmly, Sam thought, than at any time since his return.

A wave of love and hope seemed to beat into him. Clouds scudded across the sky but they were light and unthreatening and the sun got through. The sea rolled eagerly up the sand. The beach was full but not crowded, and at the water's edge there were sandcastles and ball-games. There were a few bathers and men paddling with trousers rolled, women calf-deep gazing over to Scotland in tucked-up skirts, greys and blacks and browns, a soaking of happiness, a congregation for simple pleasure. Sam quite suddenly rolled his head around as if easing a stiffness but the action was just to mark the deep ordinary undemanding pleasantness of it all.

'Did you shoot many Japs, Daddy?'

'That was why we went. Come on – I'll race you to the sea.'

Joe darted ahead, instantly competitive, and Sam let him lead, pretending now and then to pass the boy but letting him win.

'We could have a game of cricket over there.'

They found their patch and the afternoon settled in. With a child's cricket bat bought by Ellen in the Christmas rummage sale, a jacket for the wicket, and a tennis ball, Joe and Sam played cricket on the hard sand just above the tide line.

Ellen was glad of Sadie's company. She could listen and watch the cricketers more closely than if she had been on her own. She would have felt too self-conscious.

'Did you see they warned you to bring your own soap if you come here on holiday?' Sadie grinned toothily, her bruises looking quite gallant as she puffed mightily at the Craven 'A' Sam had given her. 'And now they say, now this is true,' Sadie's voice carried, 'in the paper last week, you must have seen it, that people in Carlisle is getting "telephone conscious"! How can they want telephones one minute in Carlisle and not have any soap the next day in Silloth? Telephone conscious my eye!' Others besides Ellen smiled. Sadie picked up on it and began to sing 'Chickery Chick' – Ellen joined in. Nearby two or three of the women hummed along. One of them had a look of Celia Johnson.

Ellen smiled to herself as she sang along. A few days earlier, while Sam had been visiting his father, she had slipped down to Carlisle to see *Brief Encounter*. Celia Johnson was an idol. She would never have sung 'Chickery Chick' on a beach! How beautifully she spoke. Ellen enjoyed the thought of Celia Johnson and Sadie together.

Sadie followed up with 'Cruising Down the River on a Sunday Afternoon' and this time more of those around joined in, rocking gently as they crooned the gentle song. A song of recovery, not of triumph. A song of people back to normal. A tranquil song of people who had come through. The sounds mingled with the wash from the sea and were swept inland.

Sam, too, as he lobbed the ball to Joe, picked up the song and the gentle sway of the tune mixed soothingly with the steady pace of the game.

'Give me Frank Sinatra any day,' Sadie announced – and there was a scattered cheer. Ellen liked the way Sadie could always get a sing-song going. It had been the same in the factory when the supervisor had let them and again after work going home up Station Road, arms linked.

All four then built a sandcastle, with proper walls and a moat, and all four defended it against the waves before standing back in surrender, despite last-minute scrabbling by Sadie and Joe, watching it seep away, dissolved by the waves. For a few moments Sam felt mesmerised by the sight.

Sadie took Joe along the shore to where there were pebbles, betting him that she could do better skimmers than he and flicking her head at Sam and Ellen to take advantage and go for a stroll together.

They went into the pines and tasted the smell of pine and salt as they ambled through the little pathways, passing other couples arm in arm or with arms around each other's waists as they had.

Sam saw again Ellen's attractiveness, by comparison. There were several couples like them, young, lean, beginning again. Some holding each other as much for comfort as for love, as if coming out of an illness. Tentative, rather uncertain, but with laughter breaking through and eyes alert for a private place to sit together. Sam felt that he was truly back and together with Ellen. They had wandered along these paths before. He pressed her to him as they walked side by side and, as there were not too many people about and no one she recognised, Ellen yielded tenderly.

There was a little kiosk. Sam bought two bottles of ginger beer. They sat in the shade, looking towards the sea, saying nothing, needing to say nothing.

It was a good time.

When Sadie arrived with a flustered Joe, Sam had fallen asleep and Ellen was curled around him as if protecting him.

'He thought his Mammy and Daddy had left him.'

Joe threw himself passionately on to Ellen. His fretting threatened tears. She hugged him close and soon enough he was calm. Sam, who had been woken up by the boy's whimpering, looked angry, Ellen noticed, and she repositioned her body slightly, instinctively, shielding the child.

'Isn't the smell good?' Ellen asked.

'Nothing smells as nice as my box Sam fetched from India.' Sadie was in full earnest. 'I have that on the mantelpiece. Alec says its my altar.'

'Let's have a paddle.'

Sam was on his feet and they were off towards the sea. The quickness and energy of him as he raced into the water, swung and flung Joe about and then darted off for the tennis ball and drew them into silly games like Donkey and geed up the day to something way beyond its previous level brought home to Ellen, fully, touchingly, the man she had fancied and courted and married.

A ride in the sway boats, Sam and Joe cheering in one, Ellen with Sadie shrieking in the other, a last ride on the donkeys, ice-cream all round, the church clock facing the green striking six, the last buses at twenty past, the exodus beginning.

On the way to the bus stop, sat propped against the lavatories, there was a tramp. He was bundled in smotherings of old clothes, bearded like Old Father Time, each big filthy hand clutching a bulging potato sack crammed presumably with his worldly goods. Sam looked around quickly to see that no one was watching and held out a shilling.

'Here you are, marra.'

'Thanks, pal.'

Sam walked on briskly to catch up to the others.

'Why did you give him that money, Daddy?'

'Did I?'

'I saw.'

'Curiosity killed the cat!' he said, and bent down and swept Joe up in a somersault which landed him plump on his shoulders.

———

There was a letter from Mr Kneale waiting for Sam. While Ellen prepared a weary but protesting Joe for bed and Sadie stuck around helping, determined to pay off what she saw as the debt and also to delay as long as possible going back to Alec, Sam read the letter in the kitchen.

He had been forced to write to Mr Kneale because he could not pronounce Xerxes or Hellespont. He had copied out the words of Churchill but never heard them spoken aloud. Shyness was not a characteristic of his, but with Mr Kneale Sam did not quite trust himself. He knew it was stupid to be jealous of the portly, kindly, harmless, little schoolteacher, but there was no doubt that his feelings towards the man who had seen Joe grow from near baby to boy and helped Ellen along the way while he was absent, were ambivalent. So he had written.

And now he was only half better off because although he might know more he still did not know how to pronounce Xerxes and Hellespont. It annoyed him because it exposed a lack of nerve on his part. Why had he not just gone and asked?

'The Hellespont,' Mr Kneale wrote in meticulous sloping copperplate, 'now known as the Dardanelles, connects the Aegean Sea to the Sea of Marmara and controls navigation between the Black Sea and the Mediterranean. Though almost forty miles long, it is as narrow as half a mile in parts and in 481 BC, Xerxes crossed it by constructing a bridge of boats. Xerxes, son of Darius, was King of the Ancient Persians and his mission was to destroy the Greek State – an objective in which he almost succeeded. Winston Churchill was referring to the many peoples and different tribes in his army. Just as in Burma the Allied army came from (if I am not mistaken) forty countries. Incidentally, I am determined to find out more about that Burma campaign: Imphala and Kohima are names and battles which I think might rank high in British battle honours. So Xerxes brought out of Asia many different tribes and peoples . . .'

A list of names followed, none of which meant a thing to Sam. The letter exasperated him. For a passing moment he thought of putting it in the fire.

'What's bothering you?'

Ellen's voice was light and happy, full of affection, just as he had called to mind often enough far away. He tried to pull out of his unexpected lurch into irritation.

'It's that letter. Let me see.'

She took it from a reluctant Sam.

'He sounds very helpful.'

'He's going to find out about . . .' Burma? The war? What I did? Sam could not bring himself to complete the sentence. His objection seemed so unreasonable.

'I don't want him involved.'

'It'll be nice for you to have somebody to talk to about it.'

'Not him.'

'You're jealous,' Ellen laughed, reached out and tousled his hair, 'of Mr Kneale.'

The accusation was true and he resented her for the truth of it. 'It's not that. It isn't that, Ellen.'

His voice was hoarse. His use of her name in that tone indicated that he was serious. 'What is it, then?'

His look was almost wild. How could he be seized like this, he thought, after a day which had returned to the very heart of their normality?

He wanted to talk. He could not talk to Ellen, it was too terrible. More than that. You just did not talk about it, except privately and rarely with those who had been through it with you. And never to admit pain.

Ellen sat in the chair opposite. She could see that he was in trouble and she could help only by being there.

After a while he took back the letter from her and glanced at it. 'It was kind of him to bother,' he said.

'You can't be worried about Mr Kneale.'

'I'm not.'

Sam turned his face to the fire, ashamed to look her in the eye. He shook his head, to rid himself of all this. 'What does Mr Kneale know?' he said.

Ellen felt her throat go dry at the savagery of his tone. It was new and it was disturbing. By the sea, in the pine wood, on the green, on the bus he had been like his former self.

'What does he really know?'

She wanted to say something to help but words failed her. Maybe he should get it all off his chest to her. But how could she encourage him to do that? He would always work out hard decisions for himself. And she was not able to say – Why not talk to me, why not tell me?

They sat and between them the silence was like a wall.

'I'm ready!'

Joe careered into the kitchen, united with the train which had been denied a journey to Silloth. Sadie had washed him down and put him in his pyjamas and scraped his thick red hair into a good imitation of his father's neat flat military style.

He all but leapt on to Sam's knee, jolting his father, who took a fast breath to steady himself for the demanded instant change of mood.

'Up carpet hill!'

'Down sheet lane.'

'And into the blanket shop.'

The child smelled so fresh and clean, so soaped with newness, that Sam felt a disturbing prickle of tears.

'Off we go!'

He stood with the boy in his arms and first Ellen and then Sadie came across for a goodnight kiss. Joe no longer kissed the photograph.

Up the dimly-lighted stairs, up again and into Joe's room.

'Can't I go in Mammy's bed until you come up?'

'This is your bed.' Sam found that he was having to strain to speak calmly.

'Just 'til Mammy and you come up, then I'll come back here.'

'You're a boy now, Joe. Not a baby. Boys have their own beds.'

'Please.'

The plea had an edge of fear in it. But the boy had to learn.

'You've been in Mammy's bed for the last time, Joe. That's final.'

'No.'

'That's final.'

'Not the last time.'

'The very last. Now say your prayers.'

'No story?'

'I'm sorry. I'm a bit tired, Joe. I'll give you two tomorrow night. After the seaside, you'll sleep like a top.'

'Please, Daddy.'

Why was it such an effort? So weary at the simple request.

'Tell us about the donkeys.'

'The mules.'

'When Jaspar ran away into the jungle.'

The soap smell was strong. The boy's face flushed from the sun and the sea air was like Ellen's, strikingly so at the moment, his smile was hers, his eyes were hers.

'Jaspar was the oldest mule we had and he had a mind of his own . . .'

The repetition of the story had drained it of all significance and Sam himself now saw Jaspar much, he imagined, as Joe did. Jaspar was a funny old mule, always into mischief, and the hinterland of Asia over which he had carried his mountainous load was a magical land without fear, without hurt. Sam whispered the stories and Joe smiled and, smiling, fell asleep.

Sam hesitated a moment. The child was so unmarked, so peaceful in sleep. Just like Ellen.

He kissed him on the forehead. As he went out he reminded himself that he must fit a bolt to the door of his own bedroom.

CHAPTER SEVEN

Jackie's wife sent word for Sam and he went right after his dinner. He had been on the morning shift – from six to two – and he had relished the newness of having a leisurely meal. Now he gobbled through the Irish stew. Grace had kept it warm in the oven. Ellen was out cleaning. She had not surrendered any of her jobs. The subject had been shelved.

It was a Monday and the washing was out in yards and sidestreets everywhere. As he hurried up the street Sam thought – this is our bunting. He enjoyed the thought and smiled at the sheets and pillowcases, the shirts and underwear, snapping in the dry brisk wind. The sky had turned grey, scudding with clouds. Sam preferred it that way. It felt more like Wigton should be.

Jackie lived in two rooms in a damp semi-basement two doors up from 'King' Haney the mushroom and soft fruit dealer, who also dabbled in scrap. His wife stood in the middle of the front room, stock still as if she had been waiting since sending the message. Sam had never seen such poor and bare accommodation in the town. There were two mattresses, a couple of worn blankets strewn on them. A rough bare table was served by a wooden bench and three assorted chairs. A cupboard stood on a slant. There was nothing on the floor, not even linoleum. The walls were bare. Annie herself was short, broad, her coarse hair cruelly cut, a long green pinny half covering a cheap flimsy summer dress. Bare legs and feet; old sandals.

'He's in the back,' she said. 'I can't do anything with him, Sam. The boys just laugh at him now.'

There were three sons, always on the loose around the town, half-hungered, scavenging.

Sam went through. The back room was a smaller, darker, even bleaker version of the room he had left. There was a sink, like a trough, against the back wall. Jackie was squatting in a corner. He seemed asleep.

'He sits like that when he eats,' she said. 'He's given up talking. He can go crazy halfway through the night, running about shouting. I'm at my wits' end, Sam.'

The grief and her tone made him turn to look at her closely. No one had ever once called her pretty or even presentable. She had lived on as little as got you by in that town. Her skin was poor and spot-infested, and she had always been at the bottom of the heap, but the loving anguish in her words moved Sam.

'We'll see what we can do, Annie.'

He went up to Jackie, whose eyes flicked open, scared. Then smiled.

'Me old marra,' he said. 'Sam.'

'Hello, Jackie.'

'How's Sam?'

'Fair to middling. What about you?'

'I'm jiggered, Sam. I'm doolally half the time. Did she send for you?'

'Yes.'

'She's very good, Sam. But she doesn't know, does she?'

'You're a lucky man, Jackie, with her.'

Jackie looked away, vaguely, and Sam had an eerie feeling that the conversation had not taken place.

'Fancy a walk?'

'Aye. Grand.'

He was up immediately. He had been sitting on his jacket. He put it on.

'When will we be back, Sam?'

'Oh, an hour or two.'

'An hour or two, Annie.'

'It'll do him good, Sam.'

'We'll go up the Lonnings.'

They went up Water Street, left past the burned-out site of the tanning factory, past the lemonade works and into the narrow lane which led to a bigger lane, the Lonnings, which in turn led to a village of allotments, pigeon sheds and the town rubbish dump.

As in the town there were sheets and pillowcases, shirts and blouses pegged out, flapping against the iron railings which flanked one side of the Lonnings. Women who had no yards brought their washing to dry here and sent children along to shoo off the cattle which threatened to nibble it or brush against it.

'I can't get them Japs out of my mind, see,' said Jackie, hitting a fast pace, 'especially when it gets dark, Sam. There's thousands of them.'

The shorter man stared hard ahead, never once turning to Sam. 'I can't go out on my own. My lads are no good. They're not bad lads, Sam, but they can't know. It's Annie I feel for. What can I tell her, eh? Japs everywhere? She'd have me put away.'

They went past the allotments and into open fields.

'Fag?'

Jackie stopped, turned to Sam and took one.

'Take a couple for later on.'

Sam lit both their cigarettes and stood quietly, looking across the fields. 'I think an uncle of mine was hired over there for a few years.'

'Maybe I should take up farm work. Animals keep your mind off things.'

'You were at Pringle's, weren't you? You were conscripted. They'll have you back.'

'I couldn't hold the job down, Sam.' Jackie drew cadaverously on the cigarette.

'I couldn't hold it down,' he repeated. 'I'm jiggered, Sam. They're everywhere.'

'Here?'

Jackie sucked the last quarter inch of cigarette and then heeled it into the grass.

'Everywhere.'

'Let's get them!'

'What?'

'Let's get them, Jackie, you and me. Now! C'mon!'

Sam dropped on one knee and mimicked holding his Lee Enfield. 'Come on, Jackie!'

'You daft bugger.'

'Come on, Jackie. They're in that copse. Fire! Fire! Keep down!'

'Fire!' Jackie said, 'You bastards! You bastards! Fire! Fire!'

'Keep it low. A bit to the left. Fire!'

'Got one! Got one, Sam!'

'Let's rush them. We'll be covered. C'mon, Jackie.'

Sam sprung up and, ducking and weaving, he raced across to the copse with Jackie at his heels. 'Fire! Fire! Bayonets, Jackie. Use bayonets.'

Into the meagre copse they went, stabbing, shooting, yelling. Then they were through.

'Cleared it.'

'We did, didn't we?'

'Got the lot.'

'Got the lot.

'Well done, Jackie.'

Jackie beamed with pride: for a moment he was back there. Then he laughed. 'We must've looked a right pair of clowns.'

'Round the bend,' said Sam, laughing with him.

'They'll think we were plastered. Anybody that saw us.'

'Somebody always does. Never mind.'

They lit up again and smoked squatting against a tree.

'You daft bugger,' said Jackie and as they walked back through the Lonnings, he seemed to have lost some of that crippling tension. But as they swung into Water Street and came nearer his house, Sam could see the fear take a grip again, see it as clearly as if the man had started to stagger.

'Come in for a cup of char.'

'I'll have to get back, Annie.'

'I've just boiled the kettle.'

The plea in Annie's voice could not be ignored.

The three of them sat at the table. Two of the boys bolted in, ravenous. Annie gave them a slice of bread scraped with jam. Every now and then, Jackie laughed aloud, but he would not tell Annie what had happened. 'You're a daft bugger, Sam,' he said, when they parted.

—⟋⟋—

Sam hesitated at the entrance to the yard and watched them. They were completely absorbed. Joe had been back from school for an hour or so and Ellen had just finished a cleaning job and they met as, it seemed to Sam, they had done often, to complete the day's washing. There was the last lot to be unpegged from the rope lines which had been strung up criss-cross in the early morning.

It was a little performance, he thought, and he was the audience. He edged back so that he was hidden behind a buttress. Joe would lower the prop so that Ellen could unpeg a sheet. The boy concentrated so that the rope was low enough for his mother to reach but not so low as to dip the sheets on to the cobbles.

Then they would stand, the two of them, each with two corners, and flap the sheet so that it snapped in the air. Joe's arms were fully extended. Flap, snap, snap, the rectangle of white lit up the yard. Then, rather solemnly, they closed the sheet in half, lengthways. Flap, snap and snap again and then they advanced on each other as if in a country dance, each holding high the edges of the sheet, and when they met, Ellen took Joe's portion and the sheet was quartered. Joe held out his arms, palms upwards, like a page boy waiting for a tray or a cushion, and after Ellen had laid the sheet across them, he all but marched to the mangle in the corner. Ellen always passed them through the mangle a second time. It was not necessary but she liked to see Joe enjoying it.

Quite expertly, the small boy fed the thick folded end between the two wooden rollers, took the iron handle and heaved it through, squeezing out any last moisture. Three times he did this until the sheet was flat and stiff as a board. It would then be placed in the large swill basket, one woven by the gypsies who came through the town every year. That done, he went back to fold again.

Ellen had not told Sam that the boy had begun to wet his bed.

It was so well drilled, Sam thought, so well practised, they were so close, those two. Sometimes he knew that Ellen sensed his jealousy of their intimacy and tried to cover up, pretend indifference, even scold the boy. But Sam was not easily deceived.

Another sheet, then another, now the pillowcases – Joe did two of these himself – all well worked out, nothing hurried. Finally, with the basket full, Joe manoeuvred the long wooden prop back into the wash-house while Ellen unhooked the line, the last in the yard, leaving it clear again as it was the other six days of the week.

Sam, feeling a little embarrassed, walked towards them over-heartily and picked up the swill basket, taking it back to the house. It began to rain.

—ᴟᴜ—

They always had tea in the kitchen before the commercial travellers came back. Sometimes Mr Kneale preferred an early tea and joined the family rather than waiting for his fellow lodgers.

He brought a square biscuit tin, with blowsy red roses painted all over it. His sister had sent him a fruit cake. 'Where she would get the ingredients,' said Grace, shaking her head in wonder, 'I do not know.'

'I want everybody to have a good slice.' Mr Kneale twinkled with benevolence and his little hands floated over the cake as if he were about to turn it into a rabbit. There was even a layer of icing on the top, thin, very thin, but still a layer. 'And put a slice aside for Leonard,' said Mr Kneale.

'Bank managers,' said Grace, nodding at Ellen, 'these bank managers.'

The cake was sliced into two and then into four and then the quarter was cut into six portions.

Joe licked the icing, took a nibble at the cake and quietly put it back on his plate.

'It's beautifully light,' said Grace, who knew about these things. 'I haven't had my hands on ingredients like this since I don't know when.'

'Delicious.' Ellen's reaction was genuine, but the emphasis was designed to encourage Joe, who felt the force of it, had another nibble and spat it out.

Sam was not displeased. It was not nice but there it was. So the boy hated Mr Kneale's cake. Grace, very ostentatiously, said nothing. Ellen looked at Sam, read him, felt an urge to smile, resisted and told Joe to say he was sorry to Mr Kneale.

'Sorry, Mr Kneale.'

'Too rich, I suppose,' said Mr Kneale, being strictly fair. 'Too rich.'

'It is rich,' Grace concurred, pleased that Joe was being let off lightly. 'But some like it rich, Mr Kneale. Me for one.' She popped in the last chunk of her portion and with an easy gesture reached out to take what Joe had rejected.

'Can I get down?'

Ellen glanced at Mr Kneale before answering Joe's request. Why the hell, Sam thought, did she have to look at him? Did she need the schoolteacher's permission for his son to leave the table?

'Let him go out and play,' said the schoolteacher and Joe was released.

'Back before dark.'

Joe heard the words but pretended not to, which, he thought, gave him some leeway.

Sam considered his options. He would be welcome to sit quietly in the kitchen, reading or even listening to the wireless until and while the commercial travellers had dinner. He could go to the bedroom or he could go out.

Ellen would be busy about the place. Leonard might suggest they slip up street together. Whatever it was he felt dependent. It was time to look for a place of their own but this, like her work, was not a subject which could attract much of Ellen's attention. Perhaps she was the sensible one. Just do things slowly.

'Imphala,' said Mr Kneale, announcing the subject. 'Now, how much did you get to know about that, Sam?'

A lot. From men who had been there. Imphala and Kohima where the full force of Japan had finally been stopped. Why was it that yet again he could not respond to Mr Kneale's genuine and kindly curiosity?

'Not much. We went in later.'

'I'm thinking of making a study of Burma. So many people are just interested in Germany.'

'I wish everybody could just forget about it,' said Ellen. She got up abruptly and began clearing the table. 'It's over now.'

'We have to record it, we historians. That's what we do. It has to be put down for the future.'

'It does no good picking away at it.'

'Do you agree, Sam?'

'You both have a point,' he said, wishing he could be like Ellen, knowing he was with Mr Kneale.

'I'll leave you both to it.'

Ellen began to set up the ironing board in the back kitchen which announced her retreat from the conversation.

Sam swallowed the weariness which swept into him at this prospect, this quasi-examination, this remembrance on demand. He would have to offer information for the sake of politeness.

'I spent a few weeks with some lads who had been with the Kents at Kohima,' he began.

—⁂—

He was in the Crown and Mitre with Leonard later on when one of Jackie's boys sought him out. It was late evening. The gas lamps had been lit in the main streets.

The alleys and runnels and passages and yards were inky with occasional dabs of the yellow street light flickering through.

Water Street had only four gas lamps the length of it, but one was near Jackie's cellar. Annie stood in the doorway, the light just reached her. From inside came the weak illumination of a small paraffin lamp.

'He's got worse, Sam,' she said, 'since you took him out.'

'He's gone daft,' the boy – Jackie's youngest – had said nothing since asking Sam to come down. His head was a stubble of hair, recently shaven. The pullover was full of holes, the trousers too long and patched, hand-me-downs. He wore plimsolls long since white, no laces. His face was hurt and taut, his tone pitiless. 'He's a dead loss.'

Sam ignored him. This was not the time.

In the back room the two other, older sons were sat against the wall, eyes fixed on their father, who was crouched in the corner. Ready to pounce, Sam thought, if their father moved.

'He's round the bend,' one of them said as Sam came in. He was more excited than upset. 'He thinks we're all Japs.'

'He keeps trying to get us,' said his brother. 'He's doolally.'

'Sam?'

'Jackie.'

Sam sat down beside him and indicated to the boys to leave. They were reluctant. He looked at Annie, who had followed him in.

76

'Out!' she said. Still they sat. 'Out! Out!! She laid into them, slapping out at their heads as if they were surly dogs and they moved next door.

'He should never have gone out,' she said.

'They're all over the spot, Sam. You and me, eh? You and me.'

'That's it.'

He handed Jackie two cigarettes. One went behind his right ear, the other was cocked up for a light. Jackie inhaled very deeply and shuddered.

'It's no use, Sam.'

'It'll be all right.'

'They've got us, man.'

'What about the doctor? He should know a bit about this sort of thing.'

'No doctor,' said Annie. 'They'll lock him away. No doctor. Anyways, he won't come here for nothing.'

'Maybe he would.' Sam wanted to be fair and to show that the whole world was not against her. 'Anyway, that can be managed.'

'They've finished me off,' said Jackie. 'They were here. They were in this room.'

'You just need a bit of time, Jackie.'

Sam stood up and moved over to Annie. She had brought a candle in a saucer and it flared up her unfairly plain face, making it ghostly. In its light her eyes seemed enlarged, velvet black.

'I'm not having him locked up, Sam. I'll never get him back again.'

Sam sensed the effort she was making not to let any emotion show.

The boys crowded behind the door, snuffling, hovering.

'I can look after him,' she said.

Sam looked around. They had nothing. Jackie had nipped the cigarette and tucked the butt behind his other ear and dropped his head forward onto his arms which rested on his knees. He made a very small and ragged bundle. They had nothing.

A doctor would definitely put him away, Sam saw that. He heard the boys laughing, not making a great effort to conceal it. He saw the short, all but totally impoverished figure of Annie, survivor on scraps and hand-me-downs and favours and pity and little nagging debts and he looked directly at her.

'They'll just lock him away,' she said.

He was on her side. And he knew what she wanted him to do now. Why she had called him back.

'All Jackie needs is a bit of time,' he said, raising his voice. 'We were in a lot of terrible fighting together.' He heard the silence settle in the next room. 'Jackie went straight at them.' The lie ought to have been easy but his mouth was dry. He had never seen Jackie in Burma. Which action could he call up? 'Straight at a nest of Japanese machine-gunners.' That was Alan; that was Alan's story. 'It was madness but Jackie just went for them. We thought he'd be shot to bits.' That was all he could manage. 'There's a lot of them taken time to get over it. He just needs time.' He paused: then added clearly and strongly, 'He was a hero.'

Annie clenched her lips to trap the emotion. She raised a hand, just a little, to indicate her thanks.

'Hey!' Sam's curt syllable, directed at the next room, brought in the boys, all three of whom looked sternly but no longer contemptuously at their father.

'You'll have to help your mother until he gets a bit better.'

There was no acknowledgement but there was no resistance. Sam pulled out two half crowns. 'Get yourselves some fish and chips. And bring some back for your Mam and Dad.'

When they had gone, he said, 'I'll come tomorrow.'

'No! No thanks, Sam. I don't want him seen outside in this state. He's better just with me. I shouldn't have weakened.'

The surge of respect he felt for this woman almost overwhelmed him. 'You just have to send word.'

'I know. I think he's asleep,' said Annie. 'How he can sleep sat up like that, I'll never know.'

He left her, gazing down on her husband, guarding him.

When he saw the boys on the street he would go out of his way to be friendly – unusual treatment for them: even among the hard cases in the town they were hard. Now and then he gave them a shilling or pointed them in the way of a bit of work. One of them would leave school soon.

It was time for him to attack his own past. Jackie had helped him. It was time to make a new start.

CHAPTER EIGHT

Ellen did not feel easy in the pub. The King's Arms, mid Saturday night, was bulging. Sam had secured a couple of seats for them earlier on and she was soon in detailed conversation with her neighbour, as she could have been with every person in that saloon bar.

As a child, a girl and a woman, Ellen had known Wigton and been known by it so well and been bound in so tightly that even an afternoon's trip away would find her heart whole again only at first sight on her return of that beacon of the town, the mock-Venetian tower. The families never seemed to change in character, in location or in attitude. She knew more about many of them than they wanted known or she herself cared to know; as they about her.

There were more women in the bar than usual because of the dance in the Market Hall. Their laughter and the higher pitch of their voices gave the crushed sound a pleasant excitement. Some wore the long dresses they had sported before the war. Others were decked out in a patchwork of styles, making the best, as they admitted, of a bad job with so few clothing coupons. Brown lotion had been rubbed into white legs and in some cases a seam line drawn down the back. Ellen had guarded a pair of stockings since her honeymoon. The darns just tolerable to her, were invisible to Sam.

She kept glancing at him. He stopped to talk on the way to the bar. She was proud of him, a popular man, with that straight army back, strong shoulders filling out his light grey demob suit, copper-coloured hair glistening with a lick of Brylcreem. He always stood out, Ellen thought, but then, she corrected herself, she was bound to think that. No boasting. In the high white gaslight he looked more like his old self again, less strained. Since his return she had worried about the strain but said nothing and tried to understand and given him time.

Ellen had not yet got over how strange it was to see him again. He was quite foreign sometimes, little ways and sayings and gestures changed or gone. Such a new spine of life in him, a life which had scored into him and one which he spoke about so rarely and then either jokingly to Joe or elliptically to her, clamming up if she asked for details. His nightmares were vivid. So much alarm. He always swore he could not remember a thing about them. But he looked more like his old self tonight and she felt her heart relax.

God alone knew what he had done and what had happened to him in that war. The bits she had seen on the newsreels in the Palace Picture House were enough to terrify anyone. Who could know what effect such experiences could have on somebody? Now and then she felt that he had become a complete stranger, not a man she could have loved or married. But these moments passed and she told herself not to be silly.

He was easy, here, with the other men, all crowded together but no trouble. And to women he had always been polite. But she had seen his edge with Mr Kneale and she knew the root of it, how galled he was to have to seek out information which an education ought to have given him. He was bothered about Mr Kneale's friendship with her, she recognised that too, though she could not take it seriously. It was more serious with Joe, it was upsetting, the rivalry that was developing between father and son. It was not what son and husband should be like.

'Here we are!'

Sam looked down on her beaming, open with his feelings for her. Her hair was piled high – Hollywood style he called it – and it fell thickly over her shoulders. The dress was cheap but fitted her well, green with white polka dots, a wide white collar, a slim plastic belt which pincered her small waist. She caught his look for a second only and winced because what it said was too public.

'I asked for lemonade.'

'Another port and lemon won't do you any harm.'

'I'll only leave it.' She frowned at the waste.

'I'll polish it off for you.'

Sam was drinking a favourite mix, a pint of ale and porter. He took a serious swallow, tilting back the glass, leaving a thick cream froth of moustache on his upper lip. Ellen tapped her own upper lip. Sam licked off the froth appreciatively, rolling his eyes in pleasure, a pleasure which ran like a current into Ellen and joined them.

'Let's off upstairs. It used to be called the cock-loft,' he said, waving his glass.

'Sam!'

'Sorry.'

'Mrs Fisher's always kept a decent house,' said Ellen, stiffly, using the landlady's indisputable reputation for severity as a way to block off Sam's line of thought.

'How would you know?' He was still beaming. 'You're hardly ever in a pub.'

'Everybody knows Enid Fisher,' said Ellen and, against her previous intention, she took a sip of her drink. She did not like to go dancing feeling light-headed and it took very little alcohol to make her giddy.

'Sam! You old son-of-a-gun!'

He turned and his free hand was seized by Johnny Glaister, who had been working down south for a few months. They had been in the Wigton cycling club together.

'Ellen! She can still put the glamour on, eh, Sam?'

'Hello, Johnny,' Ellen said and then she looked around at two of her friends, Marion and Lil, who were two tables away. She did not much care for Johnny. She pointed at her watch. The women stood up instantly, as did Ellen.

'What's this?'

'We're going on ahead.' Ellen's tone was brisk.

'Minds of their own,' said Johnny, admiringly. It was a phrase he liked and used a lot. 'You haven't finished your drink.'

Ellen picked it up and smiled.

'Here we go,' she said, and downed it.

'Good for you,' said Sam, softly, and he leaned out to touch her cheek.

'Don't blame you, Sam,' said Johnny, who flirted with them all. Every man's eyes, Sam thought, flicked towards Ellen as she moved off.

The women pushed their way out of the pub and on to the street, lapping up the air. The four gas lamps were lit around the fountain, not quite illuminating the Acts of Mercy but light enough to attract the lads gathered there, as at the entrance to a cave, to keep a close account of the Saturday-night history of the place. So far, no significant news; Arthur Hall, the policeman, sighted twice; no disturbances, disappointingly, in any of the pubs; Kettler already drunk; Archie given his mother the slip again; and a growing move-

84

ment towards the old Market Hall now decked out for the dance. Jimmie Tate and his All Stars were about to begin their first session. The women had timed their arrival to a 't'. This was the time of the women.

There were some couples there of course. All the Turnbulls, who would have been at the door at eight thirty prompt not to be done out of a penny's worth of their ticket. And the teetotallers, who felt that at least they were in the action. Lawrence's bar only sold soft drinks but it was a bar and there were records playing at eight thirty to warm up the place. There were the serious dancers as always, who knew that only at the beginning of the evening would they have the space to show off their full spectrum of skills, scissoring from wall to wall in flash quickstep, getting a real touch of Valentino in the tango, whirling unimpeded in the Viennese waltz.

The Saturday-night dance catered for the old and the new, the foxtrot and the Dashing White Sergeant, the modern waltz and the Canadian Three-step, although the country dances faded as the hall gathered its post-pub harvest. There were the Studholme lads, of course, each one taught by Queenie, their mother, each one, as were almost all the men, smart in a two piece suit, white shirt, tie, gleaming shoes, swooping and gliding across the floor as elegant as dolphins. Putting on the Ritz.

When they arrived, Jimmie Tate and his All Stars were already on the makeshift platform which backed on to the partition shutting off the wet fish market. However hard the floor was scrubbed, the sickly smell of lingering wet fish percolated through the partition and it was widely known to bands that a strong stomach was needed for a Wigton dance. Smoke and drink helped to keep it down.

Ellen and her friends exchanged their coats for a raffle ticket. Ellen went to the Market Hall every Tuesday when it was full of stalls and bargains and men with oiled tongues from as far away as Newcastle parleying their wares with patter it was a joy to hear. In the Market Hall she had been to children's treats and dog shows, seen plays, listened to brass bands and concert parties, even gone to the local Hunt Balls and Police Balls in her long dress before the war, and turned up at church functions thought too popular to be confined to the church hall. Its transformation for a Saturday-night dance was simply done. Some streamers, a few coloured light bulbs. It was surprising how alluring they made it look.

Ellen began to dance with Lil. This was the time of night when women danced together without feeling like gooseberries. The men would be in from the pub after ten, closing time. It was a very relaxing way to get into the evening and there was room to move, not too much noise so that you could talk, the band saving itself for later. The keen men occasionally gave you a dance which latecoming husbands could never match.

Ellen went for a glass of water after the first dance and sat out the next couple to steady herself. She would be perfectly all right, she told herself, as long as she steadied herself now, early on.

'Country hicks!' Sadie pronounced, plumping on the bench beside her. 'Hicksville! Do you think they'll be doing all this hick stuff in London tonight, Ellen? Don't you believe it!'

'We can't all live in London.'

'Give me Ambrose.' Sadie stood up and swayed a little and looked with unambiguous disgust at the placid formations executing the Palais Glide. 'It's past, Ellen! Where's the jitterbugging? We could get jitterbugging in the war on the aerodromes. You can still get it in Carlisle, but Wigton? No chance.'

'Not everybody likes the same thing.' Ellen always felt obliged to defend the town, whatever the charges against it, though, secretly, she too would have loved to be dancing to one of the big bands, sixteen or twenty men in tuxedos, a row of saxophones, a beautiful singer in a sparkling long dress and a crooner imitating Bing Crosby or Frank Sinatra in the quiet numbers.

Sadie all but threw herself back on the bench. 'What was your Sam doing playing Cowboys and Indians in the Lonnings with daft Jackie last Monday?'

'Was he?'

'They never grow up, do they?' Sadie said. 'Men.'

Sam had told her something about Jackie's circumstances, but Ellen did not pass it on.

'All Stars?' Sadie's glance at the band was contemptuous. 'Fred's never been any use on that trumpet since he had all his teeth pulled out in Egypt. And a banjo might be good enough for a kiddies' Christmas party, but can you imagine Ambrose with a banjo? Dorothy, on that second accordion, that's just taking advantage of his sister. She can't manage the buttons and the load of that thing on her chest – it's a wonder she isn't as flat as a board.'

'Dorothy has quite a nice figure,' said Ellen.

'No thanks to that accordion.'

A quickstep was announced and with a dramatic sigh Sadie hauled Ellen to her feet and nimbly, skilfully, they swished around the well-sprung floor.

Sam was good enough as a dancer and though Ellen was glad that she had enjoyed being at full stretch with Lil and Sadie and a couple of the Studholme lads, she was pleased that there was no show about him. His shoulders were square, the right hand firm on her waist, the left signalling out left with her right arm, her left lightly on his shoulder. He moved steadily and there were no frills.

In their second dance together, a headiness swept into Ellen. This was their life! This was her and Sam. She squeezed his hand. He smiled.

'Nice to be back?'

'It is,' he said. He manoeuvred her towards the edge of the floor where there was more space, quieter.

On the crowded dance floor, surrounded by people who consciously and unconsciously ticked off every move and nuance of the behaviour of those whose lives were literally crammed so close together, Ellen felt that she and Sam were serenely on their own. It was as it had been. A cascade of joy went through her and she smiled as she had not smiled for years. She went closer to him, holding on tighter so that this cascade, this sudden sweeping away of the years, did not drive her wild. And she knew that he felt the same.

She knew that was what she most deeply wanted of Sam. That he feel the same as her and be just the same as he had been. Here, carefully foxtrotting towards the bandstand, she felt for the first time since his return, that he was.

The band played 'I Can't Begin To Tell You' and first Sam and then Ellen mouthed the words to each other until they caught the dreamy chorus building up around them and began to sing aloud, but softly.

Now and then he would catch a voice and strain, strain to hear it. Was it his Daddy's or his Mammy's? A door banged. His house? Strain again and wait, motionless in the cold wet bed, overcome by tiredness, holding out, sleep just under the surface but finally unconscious. He did not hear the loud goodnight of Sadie and the door bang and his longed for parents come into the house.

Yet something may have percolated into his small room because soon enough he was half-awake and as if guided by a homing device, on course for the kitchen, down the two flights of stairs, silent as a cat.

He blinked though the gaslight was low and stood quiet.

Sam and Ellen were dancing. Both were humming the tune quietly and they were pressed close together, the rug in front of the fire pulled back, the fire itself just rescued from its embers. They swayed, they clung together.

Joe felt a ripple of cold shiver through him. He walked in and was almost on them before they realised he was there. He pushed his head between their bodies, all but waist high. For a split second he was charged with such warmth, such comfort of smell and closeness and being part of them, his arms feeling still soft with tiredness, reaching out to embrace their thighs. For a moment the three of them melded together and Joe closed his eyes and felt their swaying take him with them and knew the fathomless security of being part of them.

The three of them broke apart.

Sam, benign, leaned down to pick him up, but Joe dodged out of range. He did not want to be grabbed too tightly and squeezed too hard. He did not want the wet bottom of his pyjamas to be discovered. He was now fully alert.

'You should be in bed,' said Sam, his geniality a little crushed by Joe's dodging away.

Joe looked to Ellen.

'I'll take you up,' she said.

'I bet,' said Sam, encouragingly, 'that he could go back up on his own just as easily as he came down on his own. Couldn't you? You're not frightened of the dark, are you?'

Joe shook his head. Then he shivered. Ellen tugged him towards the fire.

'He should be in bed.'

'Let him warm up.'

Ellen rubbed Joe's back. Her hand hit on the damp patch at the bottom of his pyjama jacket. Joe tensed. If he was still enough, perhaps she would not notice. Ellen patted him and said nothing.

'Right.' Sam sat down at the breakfast table already laid for the next morning and guzzled from the cup of tea Ellen had made.

'I'll just take a minute.'

Ellen held out her hand. Joe took it but as he passed Sam, he found himself hoisted, suddenly, but not fiercely, his face rubbed against the roughening bristle on Sam's cheek, a routine which usually made him scream with affectionate protest.

'Piss-a-bed!' said Sam.

He held out in front of him, like an exhibit, the hand which had received the full damp print from Joe's pyjama bottoms.

Joe looked at his Daddy's mock – was it mock? – disgusted expression and began to cry.

'Don't be a cry baby.' Sam had promised himself not to use that taunt again. He could see how it hurt.

Joe tried to brake his sobs, to heed that terrible rebuke, but the more he tried to stop, the more convulsive he became, and the more the confusion which had been building up for some time found its release.

Sam was first sympathetic and then, when Joe violently resisted his rather clumsy attempt at a cuddle, annoyed. 'Give him back to his Mammy! Here.'

He held out the boy and Ellen enfolded him. Out of some raw memory, Sam said, 'Mammy's boy. He's been spoilt!'

'He has not!'

Ellen tried to soothe Joe, irritated with him for breaking the evening's spell yet unable to bear the sobs.

Sam tried to shake off the imp which pushed him on. The boy's sobs disturbed him. The sound was distressing. He had heard it but rarely and in extremis and from gravely stricken men. That anyone should just sob, for no great reason. But he was a child. 'Quieten down, Joe. You're all in one piece.' The effort to speak kindly did not eradicate as much of the roughness of tone as he would have wished.

The boy began to cough, cough and sob and stutter words, red-faced, eyes pools of water, twisting in his mother's arms. Ellen began to joggle him, as if he were still a baby. Sam watched in dismay.

'He's a boy, Ellen. Let him cry it out.'

'Just, just, there you are, there you are, it's all right, just, leave us alone, Sam.'

It was as if a flash went across Sam's mind at these words and he raised his hand in a gesture which made Ellen sway back protectively, out of his reach. Then the hand smacked down flat and hard on the table, lifting the breakfast placings.

Joe was quiet, instantly, a quick scared intake of breath, a transfixed look at his father.

Ellen took him away.

Sam, alone, felt caged. He wanted to charge after them or rush outside but neither course was open. One would cause more uneasy tumult; the other could create a small scandal in the town because he would be spotted. However late, you always were.

It was utterly stupid and inexplicable, he thought, that such a minor exchange, and with the two people he loved beyond all others, should cause so much turbulence. He had hoped he was pulling through that. And the faces of those boys were on his mind again. He thought that they had begun to fade.

He stood up and breathed in deeply and told himself he had taken a pint too many and there was nothing to fuss about.

But Joe's transfixed look had been no slight exchange. The boy had locked horns. Yet how could he? A boy, his boy, his son – but Sam remembered the look as if he were studying a photograph and he knew that in some part of himself, perhaps only for that moment, Joe had turned.

Ellen changed the sheets and put Joe in his spare pair of pyjamas and then gave in to his pleas to stay until he went to sleep. She lay beside him, outside the blankets, jarred after the upheaval. Until then the night had been so good. Joe asked her to sing and she half murmured, half chanted, 'I Can't Begin To Tell You' and soon both of them slept.

When she found her way back to her own bedroom, cold, and unhappy, Sam was tight-curled, foetal, dead to the world.

CHAPTER NINE

The days were drawing out. After Joe had been put to bed, they went for a walk. Ellen shied away from the more popular routes and steered Sam along the Lowmoor Road and up to Forrester Fold. They took the bridle path across the fields and stopped at an old bench, well placed high on the bank above a deeply-gorged stream.

Sam pulled out a cigarette. Sometimes Ellen disliked the smell but she rarely commented. Now was not the moment. She kept her voice low even though she had scanned the fields to confirm that they were well alone.

It was difficult to know how to begin. She took a deep breath and looked away.

'Joe,' she said, and her tone in that one syllable made Sam instantly suspicious.

'Maybe Joe isn't as – what is it? As rough? As tough? – as you'd like him to be. But you have to remember that you haven't been here for him.'

The implication that he had been missed by his son, that his absence had created a gap and a problem for his son, though obvious enough, touched Sam and his resentment subsided.

'I'm too sharp with him. I know that.'

'He worships you.' She turned to him.

The extravagance of phrase was so unexpected that Sam looked fully at Ellen to see if she meant it. His scrutiny was steadily returned.

'So,' she said, and paused. 'So you won't hit him, will you?'

Sam jerked back his head as if he himself had been hit and his eyes flared in anger. 'I've never laid a hand on him!'

That was true. As a boy, Sam had been hit, deliberately and casually, like every other boy he knew. Men hit boys. Fathers hit sons. Other men felt they, too, could act as the father and deliver a smack or a blow. Sons were supposed to thank their fathers for it, later in life. In Sam's world of tough physical work it was seen as the short road to discipline, the proven method of control.

'It'll do him no good to be wrapped in cotton wool.'

'I'm not saying he should be wrapped in cotton wool.'

Sam had promised to himself since Joe's birth that he would never strike the boy. The war had frozen his resolution. He must not think of that: it was a scar he could never pick. But could she not tell? Ellen? He resented her for not understanding, despite the fact that he had never told her of that horror. Once she would have known: just known. Once, a glance would have done. Her words provoked him terribly.

'What makes you think I would hit him?'

'I saw the look on your face the other night.'

Ellen spoke severely. Despite his anger, he rated her guts. Ellen had always had more nerve than anyone else when it came to it.

'I didn't touch him.'

'No.'

'But you think I was near it?'

'I don't know, Sam. I won't have him hit, that's all.'

'What's so special about him?' Sam could have bitten his tongue, not only at the words but at the jeering sound of them, and yet he could not stop them, hurt and envious at the same time that this boy should be protected from what had bruised his own childhood.

'Who do you think I am?' he added, helplessly, thinking, in that moment, who do I think I am?

Ellen chose not to answer. Sam felt slapped down.

'He's got to toughen up, Ellen. He's nearly seven. If I don't harden him there's others'll do it and that'll be far worse for him. Boys soon know who's soft. He's got to stand up for himself.'

'He can do that. He won't be a cissy.'

Sam immediately thought of Ian. Why had his parents not yet replied to his letter? He stood up. The discussion was over.

'We need a place of our own,' he said, eventually.

'There's nothing worth looking at.'

'We'll have to take what we can get.'

Ellen stood and they began to walk.

'We should put our names down for the new houses,' she said. 'Just to be on the list.'

'At the bottom of the list! Leonard says the rents are going to be so high most folk won't be able to cope.'

'My wages will come in useful.'

She smiled. He had taken her point about Joe and taken it well. She could tease him a little now.

'There's still no need,' he said, but she had won.

'It's given us some savings. What are we going to use for furniture?'

They climbed a stile which marked the outward limit of their walk. Early summer was warming the land and despite a cold snap the fields and hedges, the trees and flowers were thrusting themselves out of the earth, towards the sun, breathing and in turn expelling scents

95

long absent. Across fields strewn with heavy Shire horses and frisky ponies, with stolid beef cattle and pendulous milkers, with the ever-grazing sheep and occasionally a few goats, they saw clearly their own Venetian tower standing on the hill to the south. Once it had boasted a bell, Big Tom, which could be heard ten miles away, but the weight of it had threatened the tower and it had been taken down. Ellen used to love listening to it and she missed its great sounds. It would have been good to hear it now, the familiar sounds trembling in her stomach.

She put her arm around Sam's waist and looped his arm around her shoulders. Once again she had stubbed against the stranger in him. She had not anticipated this. They walked back through fields and lanes, not reaching the house until it was quite dark, the streets almost empty.

'There's very little of any quality at all,' said Leonard. He took a deep pull of tea. 'Very little.'

'We'll have to start where we can, then.'

'It's a country wide problem.' Leonard kept up with events and on the housing situation he was a town expert. 'Bad as it is here, it's far worse where they had the bombing. As you would expect. Over four million came back from the services, Sam. That puts a strain on any system. A lot of them with not a sausage to their name.'

'The new houses up Howrigg Bank and Kirkland and Brindle-field?'

'Brindlefield's more or less reserved for Water Street. Over a hundred and fifteen families there, Sam, living in less than a hundred yards – a miracle in its way – homes chopped up how and which way. It'd never be believed. They'll be emptying them starting soon.

Howrigg Bank seems to be allocated to the lads who were in the RAF, which is an odd business but we can't seem to do anything about it. Kirkland's not much more than a twinkle in the planner's eyes, Sam, but it'll be hungry hill up there. The rents!'

Leonard put aside his professional character for a moment. 'You're very welcome here, you know. Grace,' he paused and the pause said enough between the two men, 'is very fond of Ellen and the kiddie.'

As I am, he failed to add and, again unspoken, I value you as an ally.

'We need a place of our own.'

Ellen had not really risen to the bait when he had suggested this. She had humoured him, he thought. She was well dug in and in no rush to leave. But Sam was determined.

Leonard listed the four places currently available. All were small properties tucked into the centre of the town. Leonard ruled out three for damp. There was one decent house he did not mention because he had decided that Ellen would not be easy there. The house was sound but it was next door to the house of the family of the young ex-soldier just hanged for shooting the sister of his girlfriend by mistake. Leonard excised it.

'So that leaves Scott's Yard,' said Sam.

'It's not in the yard itself. There's a little tunnel affair leads off it and into another small yard with four dwellings. Old Billy Robertson still lives in it since his wife was taken, but one of the daughters is having him. He's clean and tidy enough, is Billy. There'll not be much needs doing to it. Six and nine a week.'

'How many properties does your man have? You must rake in a fortune.'

Leonard was impassive.

97

What he had not mentioned was the first thing Ellen noticed. That there was only one lavatory and one tap serving the four dwellings.

Billy Robertson was a faded little fellow who had worked for most of his life in the flour mills. His unexpected fleece of white hair seemed like a badge of service. Ellen's instinct to rush off was ambushed by her manners – the old man had placed three rock buns on the table and the kettle was simmering on the hob. What was an inspection for them was something of a party for Billy and there was nothing to be done but sit and wait for the tea and take a rock bun and talk. Mostly Billy talked, cataloguing his misfortunes in cheerful sentences.

Eventually the house was looked over. The room downstairs would struggle to be half of the size of the kitchen at Grace's. The extra space for the sink and the gas rings was not much more than a dent in the wall. Upstairs there was the main bedroom. That was it. They would need a sofa bed downstairs. Wardrobe, cupboards and Joe could be upstairs.

Scott's Yard was off Water Street, which was the main drive for cattle and pigs and horses up and down to the markets and the slaughterhouse. The place on offer was in a tiny sunless space, backed on one side by the high wall of the dirty brick warehouse which held cattle feed, on another by the little used rooms of a failing draper's shop. The lavatory was next to the tunnel which led through to Scott's Yard, which held a dozen dwellings of all shapes and sizes. Billy's house was in moderately good repair.

'Well,' said Ellen, as they walked down High Street, 'that's easily decided.'

'It's the best there is.'

'Then we'll have to wait for a better.'

Sam said nothing until they got in and then he asked Ellen to come up to their bedroom to talk things over. His request was made in front of Grace, who was annoyed with him for making her feel an intruder at her own hearth. Ellen could not refuse without seeming to put him down.

He bolted the bedroom door rather deliberately although it was afternoon and Joe was out playing. Ellen sat uncertainly on the side of the bed. Sam stood, his back against the door.

'This is the only place we get any privacy here.'

'We do not! We can be in the kitchen any time.'

'It's not our kitchen.'

'You like talking to Leonard.' Ellen tried to be lighthearted.

'That's not the point and you know it.'

'What's wrong with here?' Ellen started, then checked herself. Billy Robertson's was so cramped and confined compared with Grace's house; and it was so beseiged by others. Though less than a couple of hundred yards away it would take her into a different clique, and although she knew them all and had worked with some of them and been at school with some and danced with them and sung in the streets and played, talked with them, they were not *her* clique. But how could she say all that without seeming spoiled? Women were supposed to follow men when the final decision came. Young couples were supposed to accept whatever was on offer. Being choosy was putting on airs.

'I couldn't stand that – privy – only the one.'

'There's probably fewer using it than use the one in Grace's backyard here.'

That was not true. Both of them knew that the spillover – especially the kids from Scott's Yard which was a nest of big families – would inevitably use 'their' lavatory.

'They're decent enough people,' he said.

'It isn't the people I'm worried about! There's very nice people in Water Street.'

'What is it then?'

Change? Change. Here, with Grace and Leonard in the refuge of her childhood and in the house which had protected Joe when Sam was in the war, she felt safe. Anywhere else and with Sam still far from his old self, was unsure. They had not found each other again, not yet.

'It's not like you to be frightened,' he said.

'I'm not frightened.'

But she was and he was right and both of them knew it.

'We'll not get anything better. Leonard's given us a leg up for this one as it is.'

'Why can't we wait for one of the new houses?'

'We could be old and grey.'

'I don't know what it is, Sam.'

Ellen was not proud of herself. Clammy fear sickened her stomach.

'You'll be all right once we're in.'

'I don't want to go, Sam.'

'I've had it here. I want us to get going on our own. This is the best we'll get.'

'Can we not look around for a bit longer?'

'You'll have to leave here some time. I don't want to be in rooms again. Neither of us liked that. This is a start. For God's sake, Ellen! It's just up street! It's just a house! What about us?'

The loudness and hoarseness of his voice impressed her. He leaned back against the door and she could almost see the colour draining out of his cheeks. His hands closed into fists. She felt more strongly than ever before the strangeness of him. The man who had lived and been fashioned by such extreme forces when she was not there had taken total possession. He was in pain, far away.

She had no choice. She would never like the place or feel settled. She must try not to hate it.

———Ω———

Sam took to the theme tune of *Have A Go*. Ellen enjoyed the wireless programme well enough, but Sam's compulsive humming, and whistling and muttering of the signature tune and the words threatened to get on her nerves. Yet it also made her smile. He sounded cheerful. So she could moan happily which cheered him up even more.

'You would think we'd come into Buckingham Palace,' she said to Grace, who was not pleased to see Ellen go, despite the younger woman's assurance that she would come back and 'lend a hand'. A hand was a poor substitute for being on call. The extra bedroom could be an extra lodger but that, of course, would be even more work about the house. It was not convenient. And though she would not care to admit it, she would miss them, even Sam, much improved, she thought, by the army.

'You'll find the place very poky after this,' said Grace. They were in the kitchen, curtains drawn, polishing Leonard's late mother's modest collection of horse brasses.

'Plenty manage.' Ellen would not give Grace the satisfaction although she agreed with her.

'Water Street's always been a rough place.'

'I know most of them there.'

'Knowing them's not living among them.'

'You have to make a start somewhere, Aunty Grace.'

101

Grace was about to remark that it was a pretty poor start but she saw the tension in Ellen's expression and managed to hold her tongue. Ellen did not need Grace's view spelt out.

They polished in silence. Ellen attacked the brass strenuously as if she were attempting to rub out the lump of apprehension which lay so cold and obstinate in her stomach. She had tried to disguise her feelings, it was something she was good at. The old Sam might have spotted it.

But when Sam came in from the late shift just after ten and began to whistle that blasted tune again, Ellen's spirits lifted. He looked happier than she had seen him for weeks!

'Right.' He sat down immediately and Ellen took his dinner out of the oven. 'Alf's going to help me to decorate – he's the professional! Billy gets out on Friday, we start on Saturday, I'm on the morning shift all next week. Allowing for it to dry out, we could be in maybe ten days at most from then, so if we can get hold of that furniture . . .'

How could she be so reluctant when he was so full of hope? She joined in. The Utility Furniture had been available on two years' payments, but Ellen would not have it. Debt worried her. The weekly furniture sale in the Market Hall would provide – she would go there. One of the women she worked for had offered her some, rather worn, curtains which could be cut down. Ellen was uncomfortably grateful. She still had the prodded rug, a gift when she had left the factory. They spent all their savings. It could be pulled together into a cosy home – and blessedly for this purpose, the room was small.

They would borrow a handcart to take the few things they had in Grace's house. Grace herself began to help, thawed by the warmth of their talk. 'There's that little cupboard in the back kitchen,' she said, casually, though the matter had been considered painstakingly. 'You can have that. Until you get a better.'

Sam smiled and Grace experienced an unusual blush of charity. 'Mr Kneale wants a photograph on the steps,' said Grace. 'You three and then the lot of us.'

'The usual suspects,' said Sam. He had taken Ellen to Carlisle to see *Casablanca* and that was one of the phrases which had caught his fancy. The other was 'a hill of beans'. Joe had liked that too. For a couple of days the expressions peppered his conversation. Like *Have A Go*, the words somehow gave him a grip on being back home.

'Suspects?' said Grace, feeling left out.

'Just ignore him,' said Ellen.

Sam could have kissed her for that! Instead, he went upstairs to the bedroom to make some notes on what needed doing.

The house had organised him. He had tried and failed to re-attach himself to the routine and some of his interests pre-war, but he had not been very successful. He still had a flutter two or three times a week but he no longer played football and the fantasy of long evenings of uninterrupted snooker had not stood up to the reality. Of his close town friends, one had chosen to stay in the army, one had come back only to move to his wife's birthplace in Scotland where there was work in her father's garage, the third was absorbed in an allotment and had taken up pigeons. Sam's course had been haphazard. Now he had the house.

When Ellen came into the bedroom, he said, 'We mustn't do too much to it. I want to move on.'

'If you want to move on, why don't we wait until what we want to move on to comes up?' She was undressing, rather hurriedly, in a corner, as always her back to him.

'We've been through that.'

'There's still time!' She smiled as best she could, knowing well that now there was no time.

Sam opened his arms. ' "Have a go",' he began to sing. ' "Come and have a go"!'

Ellen picked up a pillow and swiped it at him. He caught it and used it to tug her onto the bed.

—⁓—

'Water Street,' said Sadie, 'is paradise on earth.' It was near the end of the morning and she had run out of games and treats.

Joe still drew the train, with full complement of carriages, along the lino, but he stopped the chuff-chuff-chuffing noises and Sadie knew she had his attention. He, too, was a little bored and anxious.

She had been his guard and then the stationmaster. Sam had knocked up a very primitive tunnel, a bridge, which was already on the tilt, and a platform. These, together with the handful of lead soldiers given him with no little ceremony by Mr Kneale, had greatly extended the life and attraction of the train. Soldiers and a train! Sadie was as absorbed in the toys as the boy, but still it had been a long morning.

She had offered to look after Joe while they moved in.

'Now then,' said Sadie, 'you didn't know you were going to live in paradise, did you?'

Joe shook his head. He had his father's thick copper-coloured hair but his features were all Ellen's. He looked very small, Sadie thought, down on the lino beside that big busted sofa, price two shillings and ninepence, which Alec had hauled back from an auction of the 'entire possessions of the house of Miss Ellerby'. It dominated the dark room, whose walls festered with damp. The only colour was provided by the green alarm clock and the Indian sandalwood box on the mantelpiece.

'I was born in Water Street,' Sadie continued in her headline fashion. 'Did you know that?'

Again, Joe shook his head. Sadie settled in to her monologue. It was grey outside and only a dim light crept into the dismal basement, but such as it was it caught her thin face which was filled with the pleasure of recovering happy memories.

'There's royalty in Water Street,' she said, and indeed the long habit of nicknames had dealt a royal flush to what was the poorest street in the town, 'with "King" Haney and Dusky Prince and Queenie Studholme, Queenie Fisher as was, and Duke Laws who plays the piano in the Vic at weekends. Never had a lesson.' These were rhymed off and embellished and in Joe's imagination the street which he had seen a few times, practically alive with excrement and bluebottles on summer days and always swarming with children, began a transformation. Sadie saw the interest in his eyes and built on it.

'Dusky Prince,' she said, 'has the smartest little pony and trap in Wigton. He might let you have a ride in it. He let me. And Queenie Studholme will do anything for anybody. You ask your Mam. She's as royal as the real thing.'

'They call it the Rabbit Warren,' she went on. 'That's how many lives there! You know about rabbits!'

There was a sort of triumph in the declaration which infected Joe with ignorant pride. He nodded. He knew that rabbits were crowded in hutches and seemed happy to nibble dockings. Rabbits made you smile.

'We'll start at the bottom of the street,' she said, 'just off King Street, on the corner where the Sally Army plays on Saturday nights and Jack McGee tells you to give up drink which he can't. He plays the melodeon like nobody's business. There used to be an archway there when I was a girl. There's the Vic where your Dad'll have a drink so that's handy for him, isn't it? With a billiard room where your Uncle Leonard'll come and play and pop in and see you. And when I've got my mushrooms or my rose-hips or my raspberries, I'll be round at King Haney's like a shot and I'll pop in as well. Any excuse for me! I'll be there. King Haney or no King Haney!'

She smiled and her thin brown gypsyish face lit up, forcing a return smile from the gullible boy.

'There's Scopie Pearson's bakehouse for them with no ovens and your Mam'll be asking you to take her bread there and maybe a big tatie-pot. Scopie could have been a chef on the Railway but he wouldn't leave his mother. And – listen to this! – Water Street has its own barber. Arnold Fisher, clips you with sheep shears the lads say. And there's Tommy Abut – that's not his real name, but he says "Abut" a lot so we gave him Abut. Tommy Abut can get you anything in the world. Just you ask. Polly Bowman sells lemonade and candles and such and wears slippers day in, day out, a bit like me, and sings to herself, the old songs, and you can get your clogs recaulkered any time, day or night, at Polly Bowman's. You've seen the lads play football, haven't you?'

Joe nodded – it did not matter whether he had or not, somehow he knew that. The force and excitement of Sadie's description had driven him towards her and now he squatted at her feet, gazing up as if he were being tossed his daily feed.

'Well, Piggy Sharp in the auction dries out the bladders and so you're never short of a football in Water Street. There's nowhere in this world like Water Street for games for kids. I'll back it against the lot. We have the best hide and seeks, the best chaseys, the best hares and hounds – nobody can beat us. There was a little place I could hide in I would never be caught! If I didn't give myself up, nobody would have found me 'til this day. I could have died in it. That's Water Street for you.'

All the happiness in Sadie's harsh life had been bottled on Water Street and now she siphoned it freely to Joe.

'There's a tailor, Mr Harris, takes tick, very useful, and a builder, Stan Armstrong, soft Stan, won't send bills, there's a fish and chip shop where you can get scrams for free, and an ironmonger. Maggie Carson makes ice-cream in summer and Sammy Bowes sweeps chimneys; Queenie lays people out and never takes her coat off, Mr Chicken and Mr Wiggins is carters, he has a handlebar moustache like a bicycle and Pringles has the garage next to the lemonade beyond the Masonic opposite the Sands where the tanning factory burned down – what a fire! And I know who set it off! – and at the end there's the Congregational church with manse and a man in the manse and a dance hall underneath and a nice big graveyard to play in, and beasts – hundreds of cows and bullocks and sheep up and down Water Street on market days, it's like the Wild West. You're a lucky little lad to be going to live in Water Street, Joe, I wish I was you so I could do it all again.'

As she finished her rhapsody on a sudden wistful note, the weak sun seemed to stir itself and Sadie's face irradiated a glow, her turbaned head looked royal and the pom-pom-less pink slippers tapped the lino with a patter of applause.

Sadie did not know that almost as she spoke the exodus from Water Street was about to begin and the inhabitants of the Rabbit Warren at the very centre of the town were to be sent almost a mile away, to the south, into houses with three, sometimes four, bedrooms and an indoor lavatory and even a bath, with gardens front and back and no damp, no TB, no rats, no cockroaches, no chesty coughs, no beatings and worse, no stench of beasts and excrement in the street:

and yet those who had grown up in the Rabbit Warren would always in some part pine for it like Sadie and freely declare that nothing was the same, nothing was as good or exciting since they had been put out of Water Street.

'We'll go there now,' said Sadie, after looking at the clock, and they set off together for the promised land.

CHAPTER TEN

There were bad houses in the town, but theirs was not a bad house. The damp only threatened. It was largely vermin-free. The fire warmed it through. Sam, who had slept single in a bed for the first time on his first night in the army, was well pleased. He had been brought up in a big family, packed to the walls. This was plenty good enough for three. It was their own and it was private.

It was not private enough for Ellen. Their immediate neighbours could practically reach through the window. On one side there was Madge Hartley, widowed, and Bella her daughter, who was not quite right and never would be, harmless enough, always smiling, and always in the small yard just hanging about. Mr and Mrs Rook on the other side had the best house. They were strict Primitive Methodists. Ellen always felt she had to be solemn in front of them. Their children had left home. They were polite but not neighbourly, keeping themselves to themselves and all in all a relief for that.

Across the yard the final house, a hovel, was inhabited by an old Wigton idler and cadger nicknamed Kettler, who wandered through the day on stout and tripe and dodges which entertained Sam greatly.

The privy was at the corner of the alley next to the tap. As Ellen had anticipated, it was much used by the overspill from Scott's Yard where several big families shared the one lavatory, proudly declared to be 'always warm'. The privy was also a hidey hole, a secret chamber for illicit cigarettes or a few minutes' peace and a site for mighty battles with constipation. The children would scurry up the tunnel and be in and out of the forbidden privy faster than they could be caught. They were messy. Ellen became the one who kept it clean.

Sam was at the factory for eight hour shifts. Ellen was in and out all day and, whereas she had found many ways of disappearing in Grace's house, here she felt wholly exposed. Even when the door was closed, she could see Bella Harvey in the yard or hear the slam of the lavatory door and the scuddy speed of the kids' feet. Her own yard and Scott's Yard and Water Street itself were always so active with people and noise. On Market Hill there were periods of activity but also intervals of peace. And there was space and it was where she had dug into her life and settled her fear of losing Sam for ever and built up her days.

It was, she knew – and she was angry with herself for it – ridiculous to be upended by moving such a short distance. Especially when Sam was so pleased with it, with the new wallpaper and the jumble of furniture – he had never taken an interest before. And Joe, who had gone down with a nasty cough and had to sleep with her for a few nights, did not seem to miss the old house.

She let the first week go by and then asked Grace and Leonard and Mr Kneale to come around for the inspection she knew they wanted and in a way, she thought, were entitled to. She wanted to get it over with. Sunday afternoon was the right time.

Sam chose the day to go and visit the parents of Ian. They had not replied to his letter but then some people were shy of letters. Sunday was a day when visitors were expected. Ellen was not best pleased and wondered if his departure was related to Joe's clinging to her. He was over the worst of the cough now but for three days they had been as bound together as they were when Sam was in the army. Come the day, though, she was relieved that Sam was not there. The room would have been intolerably crammed. She fought successfully against being embarrassed by it before the invasion of two such house-proud people.

They still kept their bikes down at Grace's house in the shed. Sam went straight into the backyard without first calling to see them. Ian's parents lived about sixteen miles away. It would give the bike its first half-decent outing since his return.

He headed towards the sea and Silloth. He could cut across country just before he reached that town and make for the little seaside village of Allonby, a few miles down the coast. It was a cool day, a light wind coming in from the sea but nothing to struggle against. He pushed down hard on the pedals, enjoying the flow of the bike, the easy control of it, the freedom, the lash of air into factory lungs. There were a few small hills and twists in the narrow road until he settled on the broad flat Solway Plain where you could spin along almost without effort. He could see, like mirror images, both the Scottish hills north across the Firth of sea and the Cumbrian fells, sentries of the Lakes. Hedges and trees were now fully out in new green, fields fat with livestock. The road itself was virtually empty, troubled only by rare cars and rarer buses and a few other bicycles.

He had never met Ian's parents. Ian, though, had talked about them at length and on two or three occasions lovingly, and Sam had been struck by the openness with which the boy felt able to discuss his feelings for his family. He had always thought of him as the boy.

Ian had started as an oddity in their section. Among the tough working-class Cumbrians, Ian had appeared too fastidious, soft. He was teased, and though he took it good-naturedly, which helped, still he was teased and almost bullied.

Sam was landed with him. The ten-man section would split by tradition and instinct into pairs, each man having his friend, his mucker, his marra. The pair made tea for each other, looked out for each other, shared the load. Sam lost two such and found himself stuck with Ian. No one else wanted him and Sam was in charge.

It did not go well for some time. Sam was irked at what he saw as Ian's fussing: he would be so over-elaborate when packing his kit or washing their gear. Sam's method was the common way – fast, direct, no frills. Ian seemed to have all the time in the world to do things, well, more in a womanly manner. Certain gestures lay in that direction too. And Ian silently expressed a close sympathy towards Sam which he found uncomfortably a little reminiscent of Ellen, though more often like the oldest of his sisters, Ruth, who had mothered him when he was a toddler.

Ian's reputation had stabilised after he'd first seen action. He did not flinch. When bayonets were fixed and they went into a direct assault, he was not found wanting, and that was noted. Noted, too, was the way his willingness to be helpful extended to anyone in the section who would let him. His gossipy, rather mothering talk became mocked only lightly. He survived further actions in which his courage had been fully tested. One image which remained with Sam was of Ian's bayoneting a Japanese soldier with such force that the bayonet when pulled out was bent almost at a right angle.

Everybody in turn became fond of Ian and new recruits to the section who tried to grease their initiation by making game of the boy were given short shrift. Especially by Sam.

His death had been hard to bear. It was still hard to bear. As he went to face Ian's parents, the wound at the loss of his friend opened once more.

The last few miles ran alongside the dunes. The tall marram grasses waved like corn in the wind from the sea. The tide was well out, Scotland within touching distance, and it was easy to imagine why so many armies over the centuries had been beguiled into thinking they could march across to the enemy's flank. For four hundred years, these flatlands had been a war zone.

Allonby was quite busy, but the greyness of the day had kept away the big crowds. He asked for precise directions at the Tea Rooms. The house of Ian's parents turned out to be one of a small terrace built right against the dunes so that it appeared almost as a defence wall against the sea. Number Five.

He leaned his bike against the wall, steadied himself and knocked briskly.

He was welcomed. The kettle was put on. The daughter who still lived at home busied herself laying the table. Ian's father and mother gave him their full attention. His letter was mentioned but no reason was given for the failure to reply.

Sam found it difficult to speak and he was grateful that Mrs Bell took the lead and talked about this and that. He was shocked at how closely she resembled Ian, or vice versa, he thought, would be more accurate. The same loose, rather gangly build. The same very white skin and deep brown hair, in Mrs Bell's case parted in the middle and drawn back though not as elaborately as Grace's hair.

Most uncannily, there were the same mannerisms. The arching

of her right hand when she was explaining something was so precisely like Ian's gesture that for a moment Sam stared at the hand as if mesmerised, as if Ian himself, somehow, had re-entered the room. And her tone, her choice of words, her phrasing – it was all Ian.

The room itself – he had been ushered into the parlour – was burnished. No speck of dust dared settle, no untidy wrinkle found a home. This, thought Sam, was Ian's school of fussiness. His heavily framed photograph had pride of place. Sam tried not to look at it. It was Ian in his new uniform, soon after he had joined the regiment.

Mr Bell was shorter than his wife. Though she was dressed as if anticipating visitors, he was more relaxed, a brass stud on the top of his collarless shirt, a waistcoat but no jacket and no attempt to put it on, despite his wife's unequivocal stare. He watched Sam very closely but said enough to be sociable.

Over tea, very awkwardly, but that was appropriate, Sam told them what a good soldier Ian had been. He told them how much he had talked about his family and how much he cared about them and missed them. He told them that Ian was brave and popular and helped others when they needed it. And finally he confirmed what he had written in his letter, that Ian had been shot by a sniper, an unexpected, instant death. 'He can't have felt a thing,' Sam concluded, and the silence was like a prayer. It was broken only when Mrs Bell quietly left the room.

They finished their tea.

'I'll get a bit of air with you.' Mr Bell pulled on his jacket and screwed a hat on to his balding head.

They talked a little, Sam wheeling the bike. Once through the small village, Mr Bell swung away on to one of the many narrow, hard-packed tracks which led into the dunes. Sam had no option but to follow him.

They stood side by side on a tiny hill of sand, Sam holding his bike beside him, Mr Bell looking intently across the water to Scotland. He offered Sam a Woodbine and the two men lit up.

'I was in the First War,' the older man said, 'with the medical lads. I told the recruitment I wasn't going to kill anybody, but I wasn't going to let them think I was frightened either. Our job was to go into no-man's land and bring back what was left to our own trenches.'

He spoke unemotionally. They were isolated on the dune. The tide had turned and was racing in with treacherous speed. He paused before continuing. 'You've never seen such messes. You can't imagine. What can be done to a man, especially to his face. You get used to heaving up. I didn't eat the morning of an attack. It was just a waste.' He paused again. 'So you see, Sam, you can tell me exactly what did happen to our Ian.'

He did not turn around to look at the younger man.

Sam, already tired by the strain of meeting Ian's parents, was jolted by his intuition. He collected himself. The wind appeared to pick up. Its moan grew louder in the telephone wires on the road just behind them.

'It was a fine day,' he began, 'and we were in a safe clearing. Hundreds of us,' and the large clearing in Burma was as visible as the beach before him. 'We were in no sort of danger. We'd been through a bad patch but the Japs had pulled right back. We were checking on our equipment and making good what had been damaged and resting up – you'll know about that. You know how tidy Ian was. Well—'

Sam had been no more than three or four feet away from Ian. Other men from the section were strewn around almost as near, oiling their rifles, polishing the bayonets, repairing the ravages of combat. Close beyond them were scores of others about the same business.

'It was a good time. The Japs were nowhere near. We were on a sort of break. For a day or two, maybe more.'

Ian. He could remember every moment. Ian had been smiling, a cigarette dangling from the corner of his mouth, his equipment laid neatly around him. He wore that rather balmy, contented expression which Sam had come to like – Ian's off again, he would say to himself, off into a world of his own. Ian had caught Sam's smile and understood, fully, its meaning and thrown him the pack of cigarettes as a sort of acknowledgement. Then he went back to his dreaming and his fastidious cleaning.

'I can see it now. He was cleaning a grenade. I'll never know why as long as I live.' Sam swallowed. His throat was dry. 'He pulled the pin before removing the fuse. What was he thinking? So,' Sam paused, 'he had a count of five before it blew up.'

That look. Sam could not, would not want to forget that look. For both had known, instantaneously, that there was nowhere to throw the grenade without killing some of the others. There was nowhere at all to throw it. Ian's look had been of wonder and then, this was scored on Sam's mind although he could scarcely credit it, Ian had smiled, gently, sweetly, like he did sometimes and he had tried to say something before he violently twisted himself over and flattened himself on to the grenade, taking the full weight of the blast into his own body. He did not die for almost two hours. He had tried so hard to stop himself from crying out. Every so often he said, 'Sorry'. *Sorry!* You never walked away from that.

Somehow, wholly understated, Sam conveyed the essence of that to Mr Bell. The older man took a half-step forward as if hit and his shoulders slumped, his head bent forward as if he were bowing. A spasm, a retch of shock went through him and he wiped his lips. 'I'll not tell his mother,' he said eventually. 'She can't fully cope as it is.'

He indicated he wanted to be alone. Sam left him without a word, wheeling his bike carefully as if afraid he might damage it. When he came to the road, he looked back. The old man stood firm, unbowed now, enduring.

PART TWO

CHAPTER ELEVEN

Sam was exhausted. He wanted to sling the bike down, find a level bed of turf and sleep. The growing wind was at his back and it seemed that only the force of its invisible pressure pushed him inland, back home. If he had hoped that the meeting with Ian's parents would help relieve him of another burden, he had been wrong. Talking to Ian's father had not helped. Ian had been resurrected.

It was as well the roads were all but empty of traffic as Sam slowly swayed and zig-zagged. He even got off for the small hills and pushed the bike up the inclines with difficulty. The weariness drenched him. He knew about weariness. He knew about exhaustion. He knew, as well, about how you fought them. But this had ambushed him. It was worse because it had no physical cause. No long night standing-to. No hacking of routes through jungle. Nothing but tea and talk.

Slow as his pace was, the Venetian tower rose before him too soon. Whatever it was that had a grip on him, he wanted to nurse it. Ian, whom he had tried to dam out of his mind, now flooded his thoughts. His smile, his gestures, the fling of a handful of tea, the boyish earnestness on his face as he set about a task, the slightly over-large bush hat which made others look like film stars but Ian rather clueless, his pleasure in the phrases 'what's cooking?' and 'right up my street', the serene sweet boyishness in sleep: the last hours.

After Waver Bridge he switched left to go back the longer way, to give himself more time alone. It took him past the cemetery. Beyond the fine wrought-iron gates was the War Memorial to those who had died in the Great War. He got off the bike and stood, looking at it, through the open gates. The evening was cool and grey but beyond the Memorial he saw a few people among the graves, standing still as he was or walking slowly, serving the dead.

He turned from the Memorial and looked across the darkening town and remembered how he had seen it from the east, so recently, on that first morning back. The fear then that it would suck him in. For the first time he felt a chill, an uncertainty, about Ellen and Joe, about himself, about the world he had come back to. Too much of him did not belong here. Too much of him was still with Ian, and beyond Ian, a darkness that must never be disturbed.

Ellen was pleased to have the house to herself. When Grace had announced she was going to make some treacle toffee on her return, Joe had leapt out of his Sunday-best boredom. Helping Grace with the treacle toffee had become one of his jobs and for his help he could lick the pan with his finger and later expect a slab of the dark treat. Ellen was glad to see them all go. Grace, Leonard, Mr Kneale, Joe, herself – it was too many in that room and everybody had been too polite about it. She wished someone – not herself because that would have been complaining – had said 'What a crush!' or 'How are you going to cope in something this size?' But they had sat uncomplainingly crammed, had tea and some newly-baked scones, and chatted easily enough and pleasantly enough but Ellen was glad to see them go. Perhaps time would get her used to it.

For now, she was confused. She did not like the feeling of embarrassment which threatened her. There was nothing to be ashamed of. Who did she think she was, being fussed by a perfectly normal little home for starting off in? Grace was not critical, indeed she passed no single remark which could be misinterpreted. Leonard, a little like Sam, was genuinely blasé about such matters. Mr Kneale was more of a problem. He was meticulous in his appreciation and it was he who confused Ellen, because she did not know why it made her want to scream. It was such a disproportionate relief when they went and she tidied up like lightning.

Then she sat in one of the chairs and took up her magazine and tried and failed to read. Without self-pity she suddenly thought how good it would be one day to have a new chair, a chair no one but her had sat in. She stirred the fire unnecessarily.

How could she feel so lonely in such a cosy place? With Joe and Sam due back soon, the place ship-shape, warm, her own. She heard some girls in the big yard and smiled as she recognised the skipping song. They were lively enough around here. She would have her work cut out defending the lavatory and that too made her smile as much as grimace. You could not be over-fussy where kids were concerned.

It was not the place, the place would do. The place was a good start. It was Sam, of course. He was still not hers, not his old self, not easy with himself. He still clashed himself in nightmares and cried and woke up Joe and claimed he never remembered a thing. And when he looked at her sometimes it was as if he looked through her, clean

123

through her, as if she were not there, not there at all, and the chill went to her bones.

—⁄⁄⁄—

Joe insisted on going back himself and Grace made no fuss. The boy was nearly seven and he had all his wits about him and the way was simple.

First he ran around Market Hill, his old playground, like a puppy trying to pick up smells. Down to the row of black railings and the stone steps which dropped you into Tenters, along to Minnie's House which was half on the hill and half below, sniffing for old friends. He thought it would not do to knock on anyone's door and ask if they could come out to play. Not on a Sunday evening. Not when it was getting dark enough for the street light at the corner to have popped on.

He gave up his recce and set about mapping his way to his new home. The quickest, most obvious route, was back on to King Street, up past Tickle's Lane and the bus office and some shops and there was Water Street. He rejected that. He could go to the very end of Market Hill, up the steps next to Henry Sharpe's field and loop around the lane at the back to come in at the top of Water Street and take it by surprise. Or there was the way which passed the building in which his mother had gone to school – now a warehouse – down past the Temperance Hall, along the back of the Spotted Cow Dairy and the Parish Rooms and then either into a slit in the wall back on to King Street or down past Hudson's buildings to the wash-houses which flanked one side of Water Street. Joe did not know all the names of these small squares and lanes and runnels and alleyways but games of war and pursuit had made them familiar.

He chose the longest route and decided that he would clear out the Japs along the way. Every corner was a full stop, a careful peer around, a sudden dash and a deadly burst of fire – 'da-da-da-da-da-da-da!' When someone from the adult world suddenly loomed, he would stand still and look at a wall and put his hands in his pockets. At the back of the dairy he decided that there was a mass of Japs and so he scraped up some pebbles for hand-grenades and lobbed them over the wall – 'Eeow-boom! Eeow-boom! Boom! Boom!'

There was an exposed dash down a tunnel of an alley which led to the wash-houses and he decided there was nothing for it but to fix his bayonet and run like hell, head down, as he had been told, yelling at the top of his voice fit to scare them to death.

Some of the Water Street gang were playing around the wash-houses which stood halfway up the slope on the Waste. A few lads were swinging on an old tyre they had rigged up from the only tree. A handful of the bigger boys were huddled together, hidden from Water Street but in clear view of Joe, sharing a hard-gotten Woodbine. Five girls were squatted in a circle, talking away. A small fire burned, unattended. In the dimming light, in the rather steep open space overlooked by high windows now glimmering with candles and paraffin lamps, it looked like the temporary settlement of scavengers. Perhaps it was.

Joe thrust his hands deeply into his pockets and walked carefully. He was still very much a newcomer. He was aware instantly that his clothes – his best, uniformed for the visitors at afternoon tea – were smarter than those of the other boys. He had had time to learn a few faces only and as yet had made no friends. Most of them went to the Catholic school while he went to the Church of England Primary and that was a schism. He knew enough to walk steadily.

'Richardson!'

He stopped, abruptly. He looked around in the twilight. No one seemed to claim the voice. He walked on, feeling uneasy.

'Richardson!'

This time his name was followed by a few sounds, caws, calls, pack sounds meant to unnerve, and they did. He stopped again and looked about him, furtively. What did they want him to do?

'Mammy's boy!'

The insult sped out of the semi-darkness and his eyes smarted. Once more the caws and calls and pack sounds. What he could not have named as fear took its grip. He swallowed to ease the dryness of his throat and moved forward slowly again up the final few yards of the unmade path which would wriggle between two large gloomy buildings and into Water Street.

'Mammy's boy!'

He bolted up the final incline, out into the street, swung right and down towards his house as fast as he could go. A scuffle of feet followed him some of the way and then stopped and a few small pebbles flew by, some close.

But the caws and calls grew louder and they stung his ears and did not stop until he had crashed through the door and into safety.

'What's wrong?'

'Nothing.'

'What happened?'

'Nothing.'

'Where have you been?'

'Coming back.'

His chest heaved from the pain inside it. His expression was wild.

'Who was chasing you?'

'Nobody.'

Ellen went out into the yard and then into the street. A couple of young men were leaning on the wall of the shop, smoking. She knew full well what had happened. She knew where they would be and her anger almost took her there but she paused. Better to talk to Sam. These things could get very tangled. Bottling her vengeance with some difficulty, she went back into the cosy core of her house and found Joe warming his hands before the fire, shivering.

'You didn't come back by the street, did you?'

No reply.

'Time for bed.'

He stood up and the blank look of uncomprehending fear in his eyes cut into her.

'Clothes off,' she said over-roughly. 'Daddy'll be home soon to read a story.'

—ꝏ—

But Sam did not come home until later. He had cycled aimlessly around the edges of the town, not wishing to expose or to unburden this heavy feeling. He went into a pub which he hoped would be empty this time of the evening and he was in luck. The landlord served him and returned to the other bar. Sam drank two pints of bitter, slowly, and smoked, practically chain-smoked.

When he got home, Joe was asleep and Ellen disinclined to say much, which he took, gratefully, as a recognition of his mood. He was right. Sam's mood was so unmistakably unhappy that instantly she decided to seek a better opportunity to tell him about Joe's state. And anyway, that was boys, it could be forgotten the next day.

Sam acted, she thought, as if he were sleepwalking and unless she asked him a question, he said nothing. Yet he did not rebuff her. His concentration was deep and binding and elsewhere.

Later, upstairs, Joe awoke to a comforting rush of warmth between his legs, followed by a pleasant clamminess and then the shame of wet pyjamas. He hoped that God would not let his Daddy find out and be angry with him. He did not know what to do when his Daddy was angry. Perhaps, he thought, somehow, it would all dry by the morning. He listened hard for the murmurings of his father and mother and did not like it when he heard them unfold the bed. He shivered in his bed, his fears like cries in the forest of dark. Ellen lay awake listening out for him. But he was silent.

CHAPTER TWELVE

For some time he kept well clear of the Water Street gang and took no more short cuts after dark. The gang on Market Hill still accepted him and after his tea he would go back to his old haunts. With its two flights of stone steps down to the Tenters, with the yards and runnels and the open space of the sloping hill, there was nothing that could not be attempted. There were also twin girls – the Harrisons – two years older than him, who made him feel excitingly uncomfortable. They knew he was their slave. And he could always slip into his old house. Mr Kneale even told him that he did not come often enough.

Ellen watched him carefully for some days and then relaxed. Shift work and Sam's growing restlessness meant that father and son built up no regular habits together.

On Mondays Ellen came to the old house to clean through and do the washing, her own as well as Grace's pile. Joe would go straight there from school. Sadie would come to the yard for a talk. These were the best days for Joe. Just as they were before Daddy came back. He said that out loud at home and Sam smiled. Just as he did when Joe would ask if he and Mammy could go out, to Carlisle, on walks, up street, just the two of them, as they had done before Daddy came home. Joe seemed to choose raw moments to say such things and it was Ellen who chided him, but mildly.

Sam would bring him tales of the Water Street gang. He called them 'real little warriors'. It became one of his favoured expressions. Joe felt obscurely criticised by it.

Joe began to watch and take note.

On that market day during the holidays, when the Hirings brought even more people into the town, and his father was at work, he sailed out to play mid-morning when his mother had gone to one of her cleaning jobs.

First, though, Bella had to be dodged. His mother insisted fiercely that she could not help how she was and you had to treat her normally, say hello and a few words, but Bella always tried to grab Joe. He had been taken by surprise two or three times in the early days and she had caught him and held him hard against her and sort of joggled against him. She was very strong, bigger and older than Joe, and his yelling was tinged with genuine alarm. Bella became someone to be negotiated. Best of all if she was not there but that was rare. Even in the mornings on his way to school she would be beating a rug against a wall or trailing to the tap or the dustbin or just prowling in the dark yard, waiting for him.

On school mornings he had the excuse 'Got to get to school!' as he fled past. She followed him down the alley but rarely went into the big yard and never out into Water Street. The worst was when he went to the lavatory. She would wait outside and sometimes lean on the door to keep him in longer. It was his Dad who helped him deal with that: he suggested that Joe take advantage of Bella's strict mealtimes, and it worked some of the time. Joe also tried to do it at school or he would go home by way of Aunty Grace and do it there. But it was not easy to schedule.

Sometimes he would be made to try to play with her – the simplest games like throwing and catching an old tennis ball – but she was hopeless and it always ended with her grabbing him. She was ponderous though and Joe was fast on his feet and now she rarely got within striking distance, which frustrated her.

When Kettler watched the performance he would shout, 'My odds is on the boy! Five to two on the boy!' 'Daft baggage,' he called her. 'You're a big daft baggage, Bella,' he would call out as he stumbled from his slum of a room late morning to find the first drink. 'Daft baggage you, Mr Kettler,' Bella would reply, shaking her finger.

Mr and Mrs Rook always kept walking but asked her how she was and she always shook her head. Bella liked Sam who would stop and talk to her or give her a sweet. Ellen tried not to feel too responsible for her. Whenever she went shopping she asked Bella's mother whether she could get anything for her. She had allowed Joe off the task of doing the same. He would go to one shop or other most days.

On this holiday morning he waited until she was at the dustbin and then hurtled out of the door and bombed down the alley shouting 'Hello Bella! Sorry! Hello!' while she cried 'Joe! Play! Joe!' in a voice which did not sound quite right.

The girls skipping held him in the big yard.

'You did you did you silly kid

'You broke your mother's teapot lid

'How much will it cost to mend?

'One penny, two pennies, three pennies.'

After a certain number was reached, the two girls holding the skipping rope swung it harder and faster and called out handicaps – 'one leg!' 'put your arms behind your back!' 'eyes shut!' – as the counting went on and the flimsy skirts flew into the air and the voices went shriller with excitement.

'Have a go, Joe,' they began to sing. 'Come and have a go!'

They were easy on him. Kept the rope low and slow. He got up to eight pence on his third try.

'Can we use your lavvy, Joe?'

'Ours gets too full.'

'We can't wait.'

'Can we use your lavvy, Joe?'

'Ask your Mammy. Promise, Joe.'

'Promise, Joe.'

Their voices chittered like starlings in the cold brick yard. Their old knowing looks and laughs flew high over his head and he promised all they wanted.

'You promised, Joe.'

'You've promised now.'

'Heaven or hell

'Heaven or hell

'How many prayers?

'Who can tell?

'One, two, three, four, five, six, seven . . .'

The skipping hit speed again and after watching a while, Joe swung into Water Street.

The high noon of beast traffic was imminent and Water Street was already splattered with varieties of excrement. The sun was getting to it. He heard the high fast drone of the auctioneer from the pig market along the way and out in the main street he saw a pony and trap parked outside the jeweller's shop. In Water Street itself, a few of the inhabitants so rapturously referred to by Sadie were visible – he had already picked up many of their names. A horse was tied to the railings outside the barber's shop and two boys were stroking it. As he stood and scanned, he weighed up the options. A whooping hollering from the far end, beyond the Congregational graveyard, announced the passage of beasts – a few beef cattle – being driven down through the town to be penned beside the railway station until their train came in.

Three of the Water Street boys were helping Patchy do the drive, hoping to pick up a bob or two at the end of the day. They loped alongside the small herd, slapping the flanks, hollering at the top of their voices, now ahead to block off a yard or an alley, now behind to whoop on the amiable beasts, creating their own Wild West.

Joe pushed himself against the wall and felt grateful when one of the boys nodded to him.

The cattle had left a new surface glistening on the street. Joe found that he was sloping towards the pig market. Drawn by the high monotone of the auctioneer, he snuggled his way through stout and worn jackets and trousers. The pigs squealed into the sawdust ring and trotted about erratically. Their fate was sealed by the bids of grave-faced butchers. Beyond the ring were scores of empty pens and he picked up the sounds of boys playing. He went over.

After waiting for a while he was allowed to be part of the game. The first rule was never to let your feet touch the ground. The pens were the only way to travel. The second rule was to evade the boy who was 'it', who tried to tag you and get you on his side. Joe was the smallest and soon he was 'it'.

He could scuttle crabwise along the pens but the other boys flew. Skinny legs, holes in old pullovers, patched pants, broken-down shoes; movement as elegant as gibbons. He had no chance but he was game and he loved it.

They came closer to him. Sitting side-saddle on top of a pen until Joe puffed up to within a few feet, they would suddenly swing away. They did this for some time until they got bored.

133

'You're a dead loss!'

It was said without much malice and it galvanised him but the older, bigger boys were too good for him.

He did not want to give up.

They lost interest in teasing him and congregated in the far corner high on a window ledge above the pens. He clambered his way there, rather laboriously now. He could not make the leap up to the ledge and so he perched below like an outcast.

'Richardson.'

He looked up.

The oldest boy spat down directly into his face – a long dangle of sticky spit. The others screeched and rocked on their seats. Joe wiped it off with his sleeve.

He gave it another minute or two to avoid, as he thought, any charge of backing off. Then he made for the way out. He looked back once – the boys were gazing out over the business of the morning, looking for pickings from their safe perch.

Back in the sunlight, Joe scrubbed at his face with his sleeve and then licked his fingers and wiped his face and scrubbed again. He did not quite feel the chill of fear which had frightened him that evening in the wasteland by the wash-houses. There had been no menace in the spit, he thought. That was what older boys did to you.

He spat hard to relieve his feelings and walked up towards the big market, ignoring the safe option of Market Hill.

It was here that the older boys found bits of jobs – looking after horses, seeing cattle in and out of pens, fetching and carrying, scavenging. But it was too big and busy for Joe and although he saw faces he knew, they were intent on some project to hand. Sometimes a barter or searching for a bargain, months of husbandry would be slapped away with a deal stuck with a spit, hand to hand.

Leonard took a long dinner break to be at the big auction on Tuesdays, but even he had no real time for Joe, though he gave him twopence for an ice-cream. Joe had hoped to see his Dad, who had told him he had gone to see a man about a dog, and for a short while he beavered through the crowds but there was no sign. Not a real dog, his mother had said, a way of talking.

He went out on to High Street, just below his school, and considered which ice-cream shop to patronise. The nearest won the argument and he took his cornet and sat on the edge of the pavement, his clogs in the gutter. A dog came sniffing around and he broke off a bit from the bottom of the cone, dipped it in the ice-cream and gave it to the dog, and the dog pestered him until he was finished.

Further down the street, around the fountain where the men stood around and smoked and spat, there was a much larger crowd than usual because of the Hirings, but Joe had passed the church clock and knew it was time for his dinner. He left the crowds and nipped up the alley next to the Market Hall, then through a runnel into Church Street. Instead of following the street round, he dared himself to cut through the pig auction, over the pens, looking for the gang he had played with, wanting to show that he was not afraid of them, just wanting to be with them.

He had envied so much the way those pinch-faced boys had leaped from rail to rail.

—⟋⟋⟍—

On the following Saturday Joe came back from Market Hill while it was still light. King Street was crowded, early evening, dry, grey but warm enough. People going for a walk up and down the street, sometimes an entire family, mowing up and down the two main

135

streets, looking at the shop windows which would soon be in competition with displays at carnival time, or striking out to the Show Fields to walk by the river. Men slouched against the walls and spat now and then, calculating when they could afford to start on the drink; a queue beginning in Meeting House Lane for the second house at the pictures – *The Corn Is Green*, well talked about. Boys were swerving in and out of the crowds, expertly steering iron hoops – old bicycle wheels mostly, controlled with short batons – or striking sparks on the brown pavement edge with the caulkers of their clogs.

This ferment, registered from below by Joe, was no more than a sketch to those like Ellen who really knew the town. To those embedded there, such a Saturday night was deeply detailed, multiple stories interlocked and eternal yet in constant flux.

Jack McGee and his group from the Salvation Mission had finished their weekly attempt to convert the sinners of Wigton at the end of Water Street and marched down to their hall in Station Road with empty-handed dignity and the drum beating. There was still a crowd. Jack played the melodeon well, the songs were free entertainment and the older men liked to heckle when Jack got on his high horse, reminding him of what a drinker and a brawler he had been in his time and how rough on Sally his wife.

It was too exciting for Joe to settle for home and it was not yet dark, which was his curfew. Irresistibly, it seemed, without knowingly thinking about it, he was drawn up the paradise street to Polly Bowman's, where he turned down the short steep hill and on to the Waste. He felt a little tightness in his chest and hovered. He saw three women, in their large pinnies. One was Polly Bowman herself, smoking. They were sitting on some steps, taking the air, and they gave Joe confidence.

He went on to the wasteland to sniff around and was soon

helping a boy his own age and two of the older girls from the yard build a dam across the trickle of stream which flowed diagonally down the derelict space.

The bigger boys were squatted on the roof of the wash-houses, playing chucks with pebbles. Two of the bigger girls had got hold of a ramshackle bike with no mudguards, no seat and no brakes and careered down the hill yelling loudly. It was a message for the bigger boys to join them but the game of chucks absorbed all concentration.

After a time he edged across to the wash-houses, keeping out of spitting distance, but stalking it, pretending to be on the lookout for oddly-shaped stones. The boys ignored him.

He veered over to the girls on the bike and watched, mesmerised by their boldness, by the long legs and flashing knickers, and flying hair, by the abandon of their yelling, by the undertone in the coarse unanswered calls for help. The allure of the Harrison twins from Market Hill began to fade.

'Want a go?'

'Come on!'

'Hold him on first time!' Polly Bowman's voice carried. The sentence was spoken without, it seemed, dropping a stitch in the conference she was holding with her peers.

'We will!'

Joe was grateful. He had never ridden a two-wheeler. He had grown out of his three-wheeler which had been given away to a cousin. The two girls hoicked him on to the skeletal vehicle so that he sat astride the crossbar just in front of the sad stump of seat.

'He's not a scaredy cat anyway.'

'Hold on tight!'

He gripped the handlebars, long stripped of their rubber grips.

'Hold on tight now!'

'Whooaa!'

The girls held on to the handlebars and the seat stump, one on either side, and flew him down the hill. Joe's heart leapt into his mouth and the exhilaration was almost unbearable.

'Good lad!'

'Another go?'

'Yes please.'

' "Please" – that's a good lad! "Please yes"!'

Again they raced down as escorts, their bodies close on him, their breath on his face, the same uplift of the heart.

Joe wanted this to go on for all time. Just this.

They did it a third time, the same.

'Now you try on your own.'

'Go on.'

'We'll watch you.'

'Mind you do!' said Mrs Bowman, as, with the other two short-pinnied women, she felt the first brush of evening coolness and rose to adjourn for some tea ever-stewing in her back kitchen just around the corner.

Joe had not the courage to refuse.

They held him very steadily, murmuring encouragement, and then 'One, two – three!'

He wobbled, moved forward a yard or two, wobbled again, stiffened, looked back at the girls and fell off. His knee was not too badly grazed. 'One, two – three!'

This time he did not survive the first wobble. There was a scrape up the outside thigh, riding under his short pants, and it stung but he could not cry in front of these girls.

'Again?'

He nodded, even though he had lost the taste for it.

This time he whizzed down a dozen or so yards, swerved violently, forged up a small bank and found himself decked with the bike pinning him to the ground.

'Smashing! Smashing!'

All sorts of bits of him hurt now, but he took the compliment with an attempt at a grin.

'Again?'

The lump in his throat was suddenly as big as a duck's egg but he managed to nod and trailed back up the hill, a small mangled figure in the dangerous encroachment of twilight.

He fell off immediately.

'Next time!'

'He got stuck in.'

'Another go?'

He really did not feel at all like it. But some obscure impulse told him that he had to have another go. He looked around to the steps so recently vacated by Polly Bowman. He could have found help there.

'His pants is ripped! Look!'

'You won't tell your Mam it was us, will you? She'll kill us.'

Joe shook his head, overwhelmed to be doing them a favour.

'Cross your heart and hope to die. She'll murder us!'

He crossed his heart.

'And hope to die?'

'And hope to die.'

'Spit.'

He spat.

They left, taking the bike. Joe limped over to the stream where two dogged little ones were still at the dam. He let the darkness wrap around him for comfort and the little ones let him join in without fuss.

When the gaslight popped on at the bottom of the Waste, it was time to go and he moved rather unsteadily across to one of the slits which led back into Water Street. His head was whirling. He should have followed the girls with the bike, but they had made it clear they were done with him for the day. His pants were hardly ripped at all, he thought.

'Want a fight?'

He was in Water Street and under the gaslight and the words came out of the gang of all sizes gathered in its weak yellow circle.

Who with? Why? It was time to go home. He was very tired. He stood still.

'I'll fight him first.'

One boy stepped forward. Joe knew him. He was the youngest of Jackie's sons – the Jackie his Daddy had told him to say hello to if ever he saw him out and about. This was Alan, nicknamed Speed, about nine, dressed in ragged clothes, recently scalped for lice. His head seemed very small.

Joe had been in plenty of battles, hurling and charging against other bodies, and once or twice there had been real blows, but not until now a formal fight.

He did not want to fight.

'Come on then.'

Speed came closer and Joe registered a look of piercing, reckless hatred. It was so direct and he found it utterly baffling.

Out of the dark came the words as swift and unexpected as bats.

'He's yellow.'

'Scaredy buzzard.'

'He's a mammy's boy.'

'He's yellow. Give him first bat.'

'Have first bat.'

Speed dropped his arms.

Everything went slow. The gaslight cast a pool over a gang of barely moving beings who inched their way towards him, spreading out like a slow stain, beginning to encircle him, and the boy looked on foggily, trying to understand what was going on so slowly.

Suddenly, Speed's small hard fist hit him in the face, high on the cheekbone, jolting him hard. It hurt. He hurled himself towards the older bigger boy and Speed grabbed him, wrestled him to the ground and pounded him.

'Give in?'

Joe began to cry. He tried, very hard, not to. But he began to cry. The boys who had cheered when Speed had thrown him to the ground now crowed with raw triumph. A Cry-baby!'

'Cry-baby!'

'Cry-baby!'

Speed sprang away from Joe as suddenly as he had sprung on him. A door had opened across the street and the voice of Queenie Studholme called out – 'What's going on?'

The boys dissolved into the black patches of the street.

Queenie Studholme came across but by the time she reached him Joe was on his feet.

'What've you been up to?'

He choked on the sobs and looked up at her in misery. Surely she would not make it even worse by asking him questions.

'Get along back home. I'll watch you down the street.'

She flicked his shoulder to set him on his way. Then she turned to the empty darkness and announced, 'And if I catch any of you little beggars I'll skin you alive!'

Joe went to the lavatory where he could stop himself crying in peace.

—◆—

Ellen waited until Sam had finished his food.

The two to ten shift on Saturday was never popular but the overtime made it worth it and Sam's funds had been depleted by the move. He was silent and into himself and she knew to leave him alone at such times, but what she had to say would not be repressed.

'Joe came back in a terrible state tonight.'

Sam had lit up and was hunched over the fire. He scarcely seemed to take in her words.

'His clothes were torn, his face was bleeding, his legs were grazed and he'd been crying his heart out, I could tell.'

'Well.' Sam tried to summon up the attention. He wanted nothing more than to sink into his own wearily ill-defined, brooding thoughts, letting himself be drawn down deeper and deeper, seeking to touch bottom. 'Boys are like that.'

'He's being bullied.'

'How do you know that?'

'I know.'

'Did he say?'

'No. But I know.'

'He'll want to sort it out himself.'

'He's only little.'

'They all have to start some time. It'll blow over.'

'He's being bullied, Sam. He's scared stiff. You just have to look at him.'

Sam regarded Ellen's anger with some surprise. It seemed such a lot of energy to spend on such an everyday matter.

'He isn't being bullied, Ellen, they're just giving him a bit of a rough ride to begin with. That's what happens when you move in somewhere new.'

'So we do nothing!'

'I'll keep an eye out.'

'What good will that do? The boy's terrified.'

'Don't exaggerate, Ellen. He'll have been in a fight, that's all.'

'You didn't see his face.' His eyes, she meant, his stricken eyes, that the world was so.

She sat in the chair opposite his, obdurate.

'You never see him.'

Sam looked at her directly for the first time.

'What's that supposed to mean?'

Ellen paused. It meant so much. Yet now was not the time to let go her feelings about Sam. Joe needed help first.

'It wasn't just a fight, Sam,' she said, 'I can tell. He's being bullied.'

'You shouldn't dress him up.'

'I do not!'

'For this street you do.'

'This street isn't the whole of Wigton!'

'This street is all right,' said Sam, doggedly, dipping his memory into a much leaner childhood than Joe's.

'They're little warriors out there,' he added.

'If you won't stop their bullying, I will.'

'You mustn't interfere.' Sam was peremptory.

'If I see one of them so much as touch him, I'll not be responsible.'

143

Sam smiled at her ferocity. Her cheeks were flushed. The hair, coal-black, was glowing under the gaslight. Her white skin seemed to shine like armour. He reached out a hand to her. Ellen saw a gesture for which she had waited for some time but spurned it. Sam was hurt.

'You can't coddle him up for ever.'

'I don't want to coddle him. I want to stop him being bullied.'

'Maybe it's because you do coddle him.'

'What?'

'That it's happening. Maybe,' he said, 'they think he's a mammy's boy.'

Blood rushed to Ellen's face and for an instant Sam thought she would leap at him.

Instead she grabbed the coal scuttle and went out, across the yard to the hutch which held their fuel. She stood quietly for a few moments, pulling herself together. Was this what she had waited for?

On the streets in the town they were rolling home from the pubs. In the small yard Ellen felt as trapped as if she were at the bottom of a deep well.

The coal scuttle was already all but full.

Joe, in bed, heard bits of the talk but the words did not matter, he knew his Mammy and Daddy were angry.

When he heard the door bang he pushed aside the curtain, just a little, and saw the shape that must be his mother standing over the coal hutch. He felt a ripple of cold run over his body, a goose-pimpling rash of fear that she would not come back in. His mouth opened wide and he breathed as softly as he could so as not to alarm her. Eventually, eventually, she scraped at the coal heap with the lip of the scuttle and came back in.

The boy flung himself back on the bed, swallowing hard. She had not left him.

The hard lump had not gone from his stomach. He knew exactly what it was. It was the lump which said that although he could go to school and up street shopping, although he would go to Market Hill and Aunty Grace's house and Aunty Sadie's and on walks now and then with Mammy and Daddy and maybe trips and even to church, the gang would always, from the next morning, be out there, waiting for him. There was nothing he could do about it. It was hopeless.

CHAPTER THIRTEEN

Annie waved him down. She had been waiting for him on his way back from the morning shift. She smiled and Sam noticed how very small her yellowing teeth were. But she was smiling, and the smile on that stoic, unblessed, hard face was a ray of sunshine.

She led him down the steps without a word, went into the house, stood in the middle of the room and pointed at the table.

Jackie was having a cup of tea.

Sam looked at her. The smile was now radiant.

Well done, he thought to himself, but repressed the words. Well done you.

'Are you going to have a cup?'

'He'll be late for his dinner.'

'What's he come in for then?'

Jackie cocked his head to one side, even playfully, knowing full well that Sam was viewing a man who had recovered.

'I will have a cup.'

'Bring the man a cup of char!' Jackie paused and then added, 'There's nobody makes better!'

Sam nodded. He was moved. In a world sterile of compliments

this was an open declaration of love. Annie grimaced and turned away to get another cup.

'So what's cooking?' said Jackie.

The easy question left him blank.

'Not a lot.'

'A lot of building. A lot of new houses, Sam.'

'That's true.'

'I'm trying for a start next week. Up at Brindlefield.'

'That's where we're all being shifted,' said Annie.

'I'll believe that when it happens. But they need brickies. Back with the lads.'

'Maybe you'll end up building your own house.'

'That's what the old lass said! Fight on, eh, Sam?'

Jackie nodded at the pair of them as if they had pulled off a conjuring trick and he was the rabbit who had come out of the hat. He poured his tea into the saucer and blew on it gently.

As Sam went up the steps back into the street and the warm summer rain began to fall, Jackie's youngest son, Speed, arrived out of the blue and banged into him.

'Steady on.'

The boy looked up at the man, his shaven head poised to dodge the blow.

'Good to see your Dad on his feet again.'

Speed stood, alert, frozen, suspicious.

'Here.'

Sam took a sixpence out of his pocket.

The boy's small hand sped out like a lizard's tongue.

'Thanks.'

Released, he shot down the steps.

Sam's step lightened as he walked across to his house. Jackie had come through! It was curious but Sam felt as if his own condition had been directly improved by Jackie's success.

He glanced up and down the street being hosed down by the rain and saw in his mind the parnee sluicing him sodden in the jungle and enjoyed the sight of a gang of the Water Street lads suddenly catapulting from the pig market, no doubt being pursued by oaths and threats. Sam liked the roughness of the boys and, as he remembered his conversation with Ellen, stood even firmer in his conviction that it would do Joe no harm to have to settle in among them. Bullying was a different matter but it had not to be confused with roughing it. Joe would get stuck in. However illogically, Jackie's recovery had given him confidence in that belief.

'Hello, Bella. You'll get wet.'

'Nice rain, Mr Richardson.'

'What's so nice about it, Bella?'

'Nice and wet, Mr Richardson.'

Sam laughed out aloud.

'You're a comedian, Bella, that's what you are. You're a comedian.'

'Thank you, Mr Richardson. Will Joe come back here today, Mr Richardson?'

'You never can tell. Mind you don't catch cold.'

He went into the house and his high mood, so different from that of the preceding days, was instantly recognised by Ellen.

'You look very pleased with yourself.'

'Give us a kiss.'

'What's wrong with you?' she said. He locked the door while she swiftly drew the curtains.

Afterwards though, when Ellen had left to go shopping, he could not hold on to the mood. She had consented but there was a reluctance which had not dissolved. The brief flurry of affection had emphasised how rarely they were affectionate with each other these days. But Sam could not confront this. Not yet. Just as he did not want to admit to himself that his homecoming was so much less than he had anticipated. That would be to complain and he did not want to be of that party of ex-servicemen who complained – about lack of housing and job promises broken, of lack of recognition or funds, of the apparent preferment given those who had stayed behind and the sense of wasted time. Sam had been told early and often by a father who had no religion that God only helped those who helped themselves.

Alone in the small house of which he was already fond, he was soon nipped by the restlessness, like a physical itch, which overcame him so often now. His work brought home the bacon but it was repetitive and tiring. However astutely it was garnished – with jokes and quick, surreptitious card games, and the gossip of the day – it exercised only what least interested him. There had to be more than that. He had felt a fuller man in uniform. He had felt more certain of himself even in those long boring stretches between actions. Something else he did not want to admit to himself was that he had felt a purpose and known what he valued then much more clearly over in Burma than back in Blighty.

He was too weary to do even the simplest tasks. Joe's train was under the table, broken, the back two wheels finally dislodged after weeks of hard pounding. It had been there, waiting to be mended, for two or three days. The boy had not nagged him overmuch. Maybe he had lost interest in it. Maybe it was a test. All it needed was a decent screwdriver.

He reached out for the *News Chronicle* and picked the couple of horses he would back when he strolled up street, and then he thought about Jackie and his wife. That had been a victory. 'Fight on,' Jackie had said. But there could be a relapse – he had seen men supposedly recovered crack again quickly once the strain took hold. He had heard talk about cases like Jackie from the First War, now and then. A cup of tea was no more than a beginning. But still, it was a beginning and a victory of sorts. Jackie had crawled towards the light. Fight on Sam? Compared with Jackie what had he done?

He could not focus his thinking. Waves of unaccountable lethargy immersed him in a kind of blackness. It was not the boredom of waiting which he had experienced in war. It was a nothing. As if the only way he had found to cope, to rid himself of the tensions of war, was to collapse into an emptiness.

But Jackie, perky, overconfident, admirable Jackie had tweaked his conscience. Sam was a young man of energy, intelligence, some anger, thwarted education, and a determination which other soldiers had come to rely on. Surely he could do better than this.

He met Leonard, later that afternoon. Their meeting had become regular at opening time, five thirty, in the tiny back snug of the Hare and Hounds, when Sam was on the morning shift. They could be guaranteed privacy in that room, at that time. 'The trouble is,' he said, 'that, it seems stupid, this –' he avoided Leonard's interested gaze '– how can I put it?' Sam took a sip from his pint of bitter and lit up again. He had opened up to no one since his return.

He trusted him – partly perhaps because Leonard had missed the war and so had no stake. And he had not been a particular friend before Sam went away and so was a clean slate. Or maybe it was the age difference or the calm of the older man, always secure, never having had to scrape, always well enough placed. Leonard was the sort of listener who left you free to talk openly. Sam had come across two or three men like that in the army – you would start the conversation out of nothing and before you knew it was going where you had never been before. It seemed strange but in the distant marooned battlefields of Burma, he had opened up his heart and mind more than in any other place at any other time in his life. Even with Ellen when they were courting and he had admitted his hopes for their future, he had been guarded. She would not let him get away with much romancing about that and besides such talk could seem like boasting or, just as bad, dwelling too much on yourself.

Leonard listened, hinged as a shadow. He had always liked the way Sam looked and in the false twilight of the snug he studied the younger man admiringly. The hair was such a deep copper, cut short in the military fashion but still threatening a thick burnish of Celtic colour. His face, much paled since his return, was cut clean as an axe head, the few brown speckles softening glints. The blue eyes were so direct when turned on you they could make you wince. There was a soft ginger down on his cheeks, caught now in the occasional intrusion of the sun.

'It might be all right if you had something to do that stretched you a bit,' Sam began, eventually, coming crabwise to his point. 'But what I do . . .'

Leonard nodded, tapped a growth of ash neatly into the big red pub ashtray and waited. Sam was evidently struggling.

'The army was an education for me,' Sam said. 'You think the army's where they treat you like a number, but that's only one side of it. The people you came across, and talked to, some of them had been to university and they would just talk to you, some of them, with no side. They knew all these things!'

He took a particularly deep drag on the cigarette, coughed, heavily, drank.

'That wasn't it, though.' He wiped from his eyes the little spring of tears brought on by the coughing. 'There was a . . . It all meant something. Everything you did. The dead boring bits as well and God knows there were plenty of dead boring bits.'

Leonard sipped his beer and seemed to dissolve in the deep brown summer warmth of the small snug with its two oak settles face to face over an imitation marble-topped table.

'Even that isn't the most important.'

Sam seemed to drift away and Leonard made no attempt to prompt. Between them the silence feathered out. It seemed that the town was poised on its late daytime hinge: shops closed, work done for most and back home, auctions cleared, even children taking breath between tides, the day dying in the fingering shadows of the summer evening.

'What am I trained to do, Leonard? I can bivouac in mud. I can get by on slim rations, for weeks if I have to. I can hump my kit wherever I'm pointed.'

He paused. He felt as if he were hitting a barrier but he had to go on.

'I can keep a rifle clean and hit somebody at three hundred yards; more if I concentrate a bit. And . . . keep going, you know, and take men along with me – and all that is to do with being drilled for fighting a war and I loved it, you see. Maybe that was the problem, it was what I could do. It was what I could do better than anything I'd done before and however much we all carped on and moaned, it was worth it, especially when you saw what I saw, what the Japs did, when you saw that. So there's all that – and there's more, really . . .'

He stubbed out his cigarette carefully until the last wisps of smoke had been extinguished. 'So what can you do with all that? There's no answer is there? It just has to be locked away and forgotten. And it's no use, is it?'

The pitch of his voice had heightened and his breathing was tight. He fell silent. Suddenly embarrassed he grinned, reached out and tapped Leonard on the shoulder.

'Poor old Leonard, having to sit through all this. Same again?'

He knew that Leonard only allowed himself the one pint at this time of day. Grace would already be fidgeting. Tea would be on the table.

'Just the half,' said Leonard, after consulting his watch and making calculations. He added, 'And there'll be nothing as exciting again, I expect, will there?'

The tone was envious. How unlived his own life by comparison.

'That's another point,' Sam replied and he went out to the bar to fetch the drinks. And maybe that was the real point.

He sent word by Leonard to Ellen that he would be home late and went off to see his father. He wanted to walk himself into the ground. After that encounter with Leonard, he felt both useless and angry. And the combination activated a loneliness he had felt, keenly, several times since his return despite the foolishness of feeling lonely when he was back among friends and family. Sam tried to dismiss all unhappy states as foolish, seeing them as weaknesses best ignored, soonest mended. He feared that his confession to Leonard had been a gross act of weakness. What did he want with confessing? What was gained by confession compared with what was lost? Now he would have to live with the knowledge that Leonard knew how weak he was.

He could not think what had come over him.

He walked fast, settling into a forced march rhythm which devoured the distance and soon shifted him out of the final cottaged bounds of the town and into the countryside largely unchanged for a century, centuries even. He took the longer road, plunging into a network of ancient paths and narrow twisting roads already bulging with hedge and tunnelled with trees leaning over to meet and touch and break up the evening light into a patternless dance overhead.

He would see someone in a field now and then and raise a hand in greeting whether he knew the man or not, but he did not break his step. He wanted to drive himself as hard as he could on this mild Northern summer evening, in landscape tamed and placid, seeking exorcism through action. Only twice in the five mile walk did he encounter anyone: a boy wearily taking three cows back to the fields after a late milking and a young woman, still dressed for winter, a black headscarf wrapped tight, who scurried past with the barest acknowledgement, an expression on her face, he thought, which clearly indicated private pain, do not enter.

He burrowed further into the country in this remote, unvisited, unexploited area, some of it uncharted still, and he felt it close around him. At first that was a comfort and then the hug of the slender lanes, the mating trees, the full-breasted hedgerows became oppressive. He had always hated being closed in. It had taxed his willpower to endure it abroad. He had not anticipated the same literally choking sensation back home. The unexpected attack of claustrophobia clammed him in cool sweat, sent him searching for a gap in the too busy, burgeoning hedges, looking for a way out of this rat run: open fields. He burst through and stood for a moment panting as if he had just bobbed to the surface after too long under water.

He fixed his direction and walked on.

The cottage was in the gloomiest, least attractive part of large grounds belonging to Miss Jennings, now in her seventies. A beech wood more than half circled it and shade was all but constant. Damp was permanent. The cottage had been shovelled up at the end of the nineteenth century with leftovers from an extension to the stables. It had two rooms upstairs, two down. Water came from a tap in the

155

corner of the garden, next to the privy. Sam's father thought he had fallen on his feet. He was nearly seventy.

Since his wife's death he had lived with his daughter, Ruth, unmarried and now in her early thirties, thought by everyone including herself to be for ever on the shelf. She was maid of all work up at the house. When they were young she had been good to Sam. He was the youngest and had arrived unplanned, the last of six, way past his father's limited interest in children.

The two other sisters were married and in another part of the county, visiting rarely. The eldest son had been killed in France soon after the outbreak of war. The second, wounded, had landed up in a hospital in Cornwall. He had recovered, and he wrote now and then but he had drifted away.

Now that Sam had arrived he did not know why he had come. Ruth's wide loving smile and her instant flit to boil the kettle and find food in itself might have made it worthwhile, had Sam not been so driven into himself.

His father sat in a large floral patterned chair – a gift, a throw-out, from his employer – smoking black twist in a small-bowled pipe. Inside the fender beside a fire which was needed in that cottage despite summer, was a dish of tea. He was a small man but he held himself well. His thinning hair was merely sandy, his wife had carried the copper crown, but Sam took his hard blue eyes from his father.

Sam sat down opposite him and immediately felt himself in opposition. There was so much he wanted to ask this man. He felt dizzy with a rush of questions he had rehearsed so often in Burma. Good questions about his experiences in the First War – to discuss war together, to be on common footing for once and with something to say to each other. He had thought that would bring them together but even at their first meeting soon after his return, his father had not wanted to talk about it. Hard questions like why could he not have somehow scraped up the little money to let him stay on at school? Unaskable questions – why had he been hit so often for so little trespass? Unthinkable questions – was his memory true, had his mother also been struck until David, the oldest, had intervened? Unanswerable questions – how do I, Sam, avoid ending up imprisoned like you, my father, like this?

Ruth brought him tea and a couple of scones. He saw his father's eyes flick to the scones and guessed that they were being checked for butter.

'Is Monty Fisher being moved up to Highfield?' his father asked. Highfield was the workhouse, but that word was avoided, especially by those who feared ending up there.

'I've heard talk, yes.'

'I worked with Monty in Number 9 Pit after the war.'

'He's told me that himself.'

'He was always terrible thin. We gave him "Drainpipe".'

'He's thin enough now.'

'I used to see him now and then. Not lately. Why would they send him up there?'

'It's not such a bad place, Dad.' Ruth, still standing by the sink, kept her voice neutral.

'She went up,' said the old man. 'To see Jane Tyson, she said, but I knew why she went up.'

He laughed but there was no warmth in it.

'You have no worries, Dad,' she said, and Sam was moved by the sorrow in her tone.

In the gloom of the shaded cottage – the lamp was not yet lit – the talk shunted along such rails for a quarter of an hour or so. Sam was not impatient with it. This was what there was, this catching up on the news of others, this occasional revelation of private fears, these smallest of pebbles added to the cairn of what they already knew. And yet, Sam thought as he decided to leave, how much was left out.

'We never talk about what matters,' he said to Ruth as she walked him across the grounds and into the lane.

'He's never been much of a talker.'

'But you would think. Even when Mother died.'

'It was such a shock. I think he grieves even after all these years, but he would never let on.'

Nor would you, Sam thought, as he opened the gate which led out of the grounds. Ruth had a look of their mother, everyone said so, particularly the hair of course, like his own, copper beech, dark and in her case long and coiled and bunned into subservience, into plainness, into deliberate unattractiveness.

She sensed his thoughts. She had always known him best.

'We manage well enough,' she said as they walked, her arm in his, under the canopy of fresh leaves. 'Miss Jennings pays badly and she's a bit of a devil but Dad's his own worst enemy. The lawns have to be like billiard tables. And no weed dares show its face. But we have the vegetables and she's good with game and meat sometimes. And there are her dogs.' Ruth smiled with pure joy. 'The dogs keep me going.'

Ruth inclined her head just a little on to her favourite brother's shoulder. They were about the same height. After their mother's death, it was Ruth who had mothered him although so few years separated them.

'It can't be much of a life for you out here.'

'We manage.' Her tone ended that line of enquiry. 'And I'm kept busy at the house. Then there's Dad.' The sadness could not be wholly ironed out of her voice.

'Have you ever thought . . . ?'

158

'Of going away? Oh yes. Even now. I'd like to be one of those Land Girls. They have an independence about them. We have two round here. They're so lively.'

She laughed, a gentle, admiring laugh.

Sam stopped and turned to her.

'You should get away, you know. You know you should.'

Ruth nodded.

'I can't leave him.'

'What about the rest of us taking a turn?'

'They won't,' referring to her sisters. 'And you? You and Ellen and Joe? You'll have enough to do keeping afloat between the three of you, I'll be bound.'

All was simply said and simply true.

He gave Ruth a brief impulsive hug and a starved flush of gratitude went through her body.

'I'm all right, Sam,' she said. 'It's you who shouldn't clash yourself.' She paused, but he would not talk and Ruth pushed no further.

'I'd better go back,' she said. 'He'll start to fret. Tell Ellen I'll be through not next market day, the one after, and give Joe this.'

From the deep pocket of her long coarse pinny she produced a burnished sixpence; its silvery sheen caught the long weakening rays of the sun and sparkled between her finger and thumb, like a smile.

She watched him set off, straight-backed, at a smart pace and waited until, as she knew he would, he turned and waved, and then she tacked her way back home, worrying about Sam's inner conflict so transparent to her, pausing every now and then to look about her, to breathe in the deep calm of evening, to repair the scars of longings that Sam's too plain questions had unwittingly but painfully reopened.

Ruth shivered a little as the damp came from the ground and

159

finally, all excuses spent, she hurried over the shaven lawns, pulling her shawl tightly round her shoulders, to where her father waited in the dark in the cottage.

The darkness wrapped around Sam as he walked back and now he welcomed it. These Lonnings, so narrow and dense and claustrophobic in the light, seemed like helpful secret passageways in the dark. The munching and cropping of incessantly feeding animals in the fields were the only sounds on that still night when even the light new leaves lay undisturbed. His own step sounded heavy and sure: it felt eerie moving in solitude in such a solitary place. He had known it before, more menacingly. Here it was not worrying but perhaps stranger, this body which was his striding through the unmooned lanes, guided by the merest gradations of shadowy dark colourings in the landscape. He felt surely alone and freed by that feeling.

As the town drew nearer, like a kite being drawn in, he played with the idea of extending this walk. He could cut down into the Show Fields and follow the River Wiza or hike back towards Pot Mettle Bridge and through to the cemetery and over to Standing Stone and loop the town in this cool velvet-dark comfort. Or, for a wild moment, he considered swinging away from the town altogether, making for the old high Roman Road and stretching his legs on that until real tiredness forced a halt. The trouble now was that the walk had not wearied but aroused him.

Yet, fair was fair, and like a homing pigeon, he forced himself to bear down on his own loft. The town was quiet, not yet closing time, the second house of pictures not yet out, chip shops empty, more dogs than men. The few street lights spluttering as if nervous after years of blackout.

The fire was low but still burning. The gas lamp above the mantelpiece was full on. Steam was coming out of the kettle on the hob and he tugged his sleeves to make a glove before lifting it away from the fire. Then he went upstairs.

A thick candle in a safe holder burned a perfectly still flame. Ellen, fully dressed, was in bed with Joe, the boy's arms around her neck, his face nesting on hers, half obscuring it from Sam's view. They seemed melted together and the sound of their breath was one.

He wanted to smile and feel tender. A sight such as this, his son, his wife. He should steal away; Ellen would wake in good time, there was no need to disturb her. And this, perhaps, was the picture he had imagined during desperate times apart. What better could there be? All that was best in him wanted him to play his proper part. But the very perfection of the two of them, their loving docility and help-lessness, the intertwined dependence, all haloed in the candlelight which cast him as a monstrous shadow on the farther wall, this closeness between them ignited a powder of unhappiness which led so swiftly to a scorch of jealousy that when he pulled back the blankets and shook Ellen too roughly on the shoulder, he was as much taken aback as she was.

'What's wrong?'

'Why are you up here?'

'Ssshh, you'll wake him.'

'I can speak, can't I?' His voice sounded like a klaxon in the small still room.

'I'll come down. Just give me a minute.'

'Why can't you come down now?'

Joe stirred. His eyes propped open. They fixed on Sam and he did not smile. He tightened his grip on Ellen.

'Leave her be, can't you?'

The sentence was like a slap.

'He was . . .' Ellen did not finish the sentence. She did not want to betray Joe by telling Sam that he had shouted out and cried and wheedled her into staying with him until he got off to sleep.

'He's never done crying!' Sam felt too big in this room, with the two of them curled in the narrow camp bed. 'He'll have to grow up!'

'He'll grow up in good time.' Ellen's measured whisper, as much for the neighbours as anything, only incited Sam further.

'Why can't you speak normally?'

'Why can't you go downstairs?'

'Let him fight his own battles, Ellen.'

'I'll be down in a minute.' She turned her face away from Sam and began to rock Joe, just a little. The boy had been very upset. Now he was just as tense as before.

'Joe.' Sam's voice assumed a half-whisper and sounded hoarse, harsh. 'Joe – you don't want to be a cry-baby, do you?'

Joe's return look was full of reproach.

'Go *away*,' said Ellen firmly.

'Go away,' echoed Joe.

'What did you say?'

Ellen recognised the rise of Sam's anger and made no reply. Joe held on even more tightly. Sam swayed above them, his shadow all but covering the wall behind.

'I wish I could,' he said, only half to himself; the words coming from a torment of disquiet out of his control, not knowing and, worse, in some way not caring what he meant.

He went down the stairs as carefully as a very old man.

CHAPTER FOURTEEN

Sadie sang 'Into Each Life Some Rain Must Fall' to cheer Ellen up.

Ellen hummed along, concentrating on the rapid machine-fire of the sewing machine. They were in Grace's kitchen. Ellen was making white dresses for some of the young dancers who would be in the Carnival. The work had been scaled out among a few volunteers.

'Just imagine if it's a day like this.'

Warm summer rain was sheeting down.

'They had the dog show in the Market Hall but they couldn't fit a carnival in.' Sadie sought no response. 'Dogs is one thing. Seven hundred kids is another.'

It had been announced that the children of Wigton – about seven hundred – would march behind the two bands and the floats and the forty girls in white dresses who would dance with bells elasticated around their wrists and ankles and on each corner of a white handkerchief. All the children would receive a new threepenny piece and free tea in the Park.

'Just as well the evacuees is gone back,' Sadie chattered on. 'I miss them, mind. Poor little mites. Remember when we all went down to meet them off the train? I think they thought they'd been sent to jail. How many more threepences would that have been?'

The noise of the machine was continuous as Ellen pedalled steadily and scrutinised the columns of stitching which suddenly marched onto the cotton.

'It was happier then in some ways, wasn't it?' said Sadie. 'I know it's a funny thing to say but there was more life about. And the rationing is worse now – how can that be? Things is scarcer all round. How do they manage that?'

Ellen had brought Joe with her. He was out playing on Market Hill so she felt he was safe. She could even hear the shouts now and then, ringing across the space as the children flocked and switched direction like swallows practising for migration.

Sadie began to sing again.

Ellen finished some intricate manoeuvring around the sleeves and held up the dress to the light.

'Lizzie will be one happy little lass,' said Sadie.

Ellen nodded and then, as from nowhere, she heard her voice say, 'I can't make him out any more, Sadie.' She held the dress still. It was a shield between her face and her friend. 'I don't know what it is he wants.'

Sadie looked at the white dress in silence. There was a catch in Ellen's voice which she had never heard before, not even that time when letters had not come for weeks during the war.

'It wasn't better for everybody in the war,' said Ellen and she lowered the dress and Sadie could see the strain of holding back tears. 'I missed him all the time, you know.' Ellen nodded rather rapidly, as if blinking. 'I don't know how I managed to hold it all in.'

In the dying light of evening the silence between them seemed infinitely deep.

'My big mouth,' said Sadie, quietly.

'So,' said Ellen, 'there we are. Just the hem to finish off.'
The machine drummed into the silence.

—⁂—

Sadie took the dresses to her place to iron them. Ellen was disinclined to go back home just yet and went to the upstairs room to look out of the window. Grace and Leonard had gone for a drive in the car, second hand, which Leonard had finally negotiated. The lodgers were quiet or out. There was a stillness in the large gloomy house which felt heavy, pressing down on her.

She could have cut out her tongue for being so unguarded with Sadie, although she was certain that Sadie would not gossip about her. Sadie had a terrible, grateful loyalty to Ellen, who had friends all over the town and yet stuck by Sadie, who was not much sought out. But it was an awful thing, Ellen thought, to give in like that and discuss personal matters.

Ellen tried to concentrate on what was disturbing her but her mind seemed unwilling or unable to grapple with it. Her attention would be caught by something going on outside the window, by a flurry of memories, and images, fugitive, irrelevant. The more she attempted to compose her thoughts, the more discordant they became. When she tried to shepherd them, they scattered. Standing lonely and still at the window, she thought she would burst with the difficulty of it.

What was she to do? It was as it always had been – accept and carry on. Sam now turned his back on her in bed, not out of anger and not out of distaste, but from a weariness, a consuming innerness which could radiate from him like a warning – keep out. Joe, who had idolised the photograph of his father in uniform and clearly loved him, was also at odds with him, straining his patience and using her as a refuge and an ally too often. She would see obstinacy in the boy's eyes and the fierceness, normally held well in check by Sam, and they disturbed her. However skilfully she tried to chivvy things along, there was no getting at the root of it. And Joe, she was convinced, was still being bullied and Sam was still determined that the boy fight his own battles.

She ought not to feel like this. Not at all. Sam had survived. He had returned. The pain of continuous worry which had had to be endured, a rope twisted tight around her head and tightened with every grave news bulletin, every sight of the boy on the post-office bicycle who brought the telegram of death, had gone. She could still be taken by surprise at the lightness, the freedom. What were these murmurings of unease compared with that? What did it matter that she could no longer float into that inner dream which had given her a curious comfort? They were the lucky ones, weren't they? Between them they earned enough money. They had their own house – even if she did not feel settled there, but it was a whole house when so many lodged or lived in or shared. It was ungrateful to feel unhappy and yet the unhappiness was intensifying.

Why had she wanted to talk about it?

She saw Joe looking across at the window and she stepped forward so that she could be seen and waved at him. He stared at her for a few moments and then gave a brief wave in return as if the contact barely mattered to him. His pretence tugged at her heart. It seemed he needed her to be there for him now much more than at any time since he was a baby.

'I was hoping I'd catch you,' said Mr Kneale. Ellen was startled. 'I've been looking at you for a while.' His solemn round features mooned into a smile. 'You were in another world, a world of your own.'

'I must be getting old.'

'Not a bit of it.' Mr Kneale was earnest. 'You never change.'

'Away with you.' Ellen folded her arms. There was a pause which was not quite comfortable.

'Will Sam be coming down?'

She shook her head. He was on the two to ten shift. She and Joe had left the house before he had got up and not been back.

'It was just something we were talking about the other day. Last Saturday when he came down to see me.'

Ellen nodded as if she knew about it.

'Perhaps photography might be an option.' Ellen waited. 'He could use the dark room, until he got started. I know we have two professionals in the town as it is, but where there's two there's usually room for a third. And it's much more the sort of business the British Legion would look kindly on than being a bookmaker. I'm afraid he was disappointed when I gave him that piece of advice, but I stand by it. Do you think he might like photography?'

'He's never talked about it.'

'Some young men could think it was a bit routine. Portraits and weddings. But there is a call for it.'

'I can't see Sam being very good at weddings.'

'It does take a knack, yes. It must be very difficult for these young men. That's why I'm in favour of the British Legion's scheme. By all means give them a loan to start up for themselves. What better investment in these post-war years than to invest in the youth of the country?'

He sounded a little Churchillian, which was intended.

Ellen worked it out.

'Don't misunderstand me,' said Mr Kneale. 'There's nothing at all wrong with being a bookmaker. But a photographer is more likely to attract the Legion.'

'I'll pass it on.'

'There would be no charge for the dark room. I emphasise that. Not until he found his feet.'

'That's very kind of you, Mr Kneale.'

'We have to help these young lads back from the war. I'm taking an interest in the war, in the campaign in the East, you know. Terrible stories are coming out. Terrible stories.'

'What sort of stories?'

'I don't know whether I should repeat them.' Mr Kneale shook his head, upset at man's inhumanity to man. 'Atrocious is all I'd care to say at the moment. What these young men went through.'

Ellen felt herself blush at the shame of not understanding enough.

'I've been talking to some of them. Just to get a feel of the subject, you know. We'll have to wait a while for the official accounts but I think of myself as stealing rather a march, talking to the men on the ground. I think they like to have somebody to talk to about it. Sam's good at describing conditions but you feel he's still keeping a lot to himself. These things can't be rushed. Well now. I just wanted to suggest photography. And if he cares to pursue it, tell him I'd be glad to take it further.'

He smiled at the young woman shadowed against the window.

'I'm very glad to see you and Joe, you know. We got to be quite a little family, didn't we? Give him this.'

He handed Ellen a short stick of barleysugar.

'Thank you. He'll thank you himself when he sees you.'

'I'm not much of a sweets man. I dare say if I didn't feel you had to use up the coupons I wouldn't bother at all. Well now. I'd better be off about my business.'

—⁓—

'Why didn't you tell me about this British Legion scheme?' she said as soon as Sam came in from work, despite having schooled herself to keep it until after he had eaten his meal.

'You've been talking to Mr Kneale.'

'He just came out with it. He says you might think of photography. You can use his dark room he said, no charge until you get on your feet.'

'What would I look like taking photographs at weddings?'

The question, and more the tone, spelled out the flat impossibility of such a project. Ellen wished that she had not leapt in. She had wanted to express in some way the warm feelings stirred by Mr Kneale's words about what the soldiers had gone through. Now the room was charged with tension, which more and more frequently characterised their moments together.

But she was not so easily quelled. She poured out a cup of tea for both of them and sat with him at the table, although she had eaten earlier with Joe. 'Mr Kneale said you talked to him about the war.'

'I wish to God I'd never opened my mouth!'

He crashed the cup down on the saucer and in the small still room the sound was fierce. Ellen's glance fled upstairs and Sam caught it.

'He'll be all right.' The tinge of bitterness was unmistakable.

Ellen had not planned it like this. She wanted to employ the mood of tenderness which had filled her in the hours since her meeting with Mr Kneale. The thoughtful words of the schoolteacher had made her feel ashamed of the shortcomings of her own sympathy and she wanted Sam to know that.

'It was interesting,' she said, rather dry-throated, ignoring the jibe, 'what Mr Kneale said about the war. He's making a study of it.'

'I wish he'd make his study somewhere else.' Sam's manners coarsened as if to emphasise the trapped strength of his feelings. He bent the blade of his knife into the plate, scooped up a few peas and put them straight into his mouth. Ellen remembered how rough his manners had been when first they met, how Grace had sniffed at the commonness of his ways, how obstinately Sam had stuck to them until he had tired of it and, overnight it seemed, taken on the manners of Grace and Leonard. Now he glowered, in the gaslit kitchen, a fury in him, fists holding the knife and fork upright.

'I would like to know.'

'What would you like to know?'

'What happened.' Ellen would not be browbeaten. She had seen Sam's temper erupt and although he had never threatened to hit her, here was no place for a coward.

'I'd like to know what happened,' she repeated. 'What you were going through all that time.'

Sam glared at her as if she had grossly insulted him. His grip on the knife and fork tightened. The room seemed airless, contracting, everything being sucked in to the sudden rush of violence which was pressing him.

'Whenever you want,' she said.

Instead of flinching, she sought out his eyes with her own and looked steadily at him. His anger was savage. The eyes seemed to have lost shades of blueness and paled. By his eyes she did not know him. But she held his gaze and even when she felt herself being physically drained away, a sense so palpable that her hands gripped the edge of

170

the table as if to prevent herself being pulled down an abyss, even then she did not look away.

'Some time,' he said. 'Not yet.'

He leaned back in his chair and put down his knife and fork. He had scarcely begun and yet he would eat no more. He saw that Ellen's hand was shaking a little as she lifted her cup to take a sip of tea. In the yard the lavatory door banged as someone left it. Sam took out a cigarette and went across to the mantelpiece to get a match. When he turned, he saw the broken train. He felt weak, even as if he might pass out and fall down. He steadied himself.

'I must fix that train,' he said. 'It's a small enough job.'

CHAPTER FIFTEEN

'I suggested they should get in touch with you.'

'Why?'

'They needed somebody.'

And it might help take you out of yourself, she thought.

'Where'll they get the tents?'

'George Harrison has the details.' She paused. 'I thought you might enjoy it.'

He did. The tents were rented at nominal cost from the regiment in Carlisle. Tommy Miller went down in his cart with Sam and a couple of others. There were three tents. Two, very large, for the children's free teas: one, smaller, for the distribution of the three-penny bits and the prizes and rosettes from the sports. It would be a big day.

For two weeks in late summer before the Carnival, the shop-keepers cleared their windows and put in displays. Not necessarily and not often of the goods they sold, but Displays, works of art, some of them, Mr Kneale said. In Parks' shoeshop there was a grotto – it must have taken weeks – the rocks skilfully fashioned from cardboard and embellished with real moss and pebbles beside water made from Cellophane paper and somehow manufactured from the real thing were mini-trees. Toy sheep grazed everywhere. How clever, people said – you could never have told those rocks were cardboard. Mr Snaith displayed the liner he had made and also laid out examples of his watch and clockmaking craft – the innards as well as the finished articles. What skill, they said, all so very small and marvellous.

George Johnston devoted one of his two large windows to a history of Wigton – photographs, old maps, posters, bills of sale, sports teams. Nobody would have thought, they said, there was so much history to such a little town. In the saddle shop there was a spectacular collection of horse brasses, polished clear as mirrors and reckoned to be worth a small fortune. Grace looked appraisingly, as did the lads from Vinegar Hill. Most impressive of all (it was agreed) was the Snow White and Seven Dwarfs in Robinson's the Bakery. How Polly had managed to get all the material. And they were all the spitting image. With the faces made out of icing. Sadie made a point of seeing it every day – the work that went into it! The work!

With forty-eight shops entered, for a shilling you could buy a card and judge the Displays. The first three got certificates and small cash prizes and seven others received certificates only. The bulk of the entry money went into the Carnival Fund. Every fine night – and the weather was holding up – couples and families walked the trafficless evening streets, studying the windows, the artefacts and the fantasies, consulting with each other now and then, taking their time. Joe had done the rounds with Ellen and grown bored after half an hour, but she kept him in tow as she did when she took him to Carlisle for a treat and some window-shopping first to make the most of the time.

Joe wanted to be in the park to watch its transformation entirely under the direction of his father, or so it seemed to Joe, who circled him now shyly, now proudly, unable either way to come to terms with this man, who was organising the raising of those great romantic khaki tents which, he was told, had been on battlefields all over – Africa, India, Burma, deserts, mountains – all over the world.

First they were spread out on the fresh-cut, sweet-stinking grass like gigantic cowpats dropped from the Milky Way. Then, under Sam's unfussy direction, the volunteers began to burrow and peg and fasten and hammer until the spread of khaki rose steepling from the ground and where there had been nothing there was a barn of shelter. The sudden coolness and eerie emptiness of the new space sucked in the little boys, who buzzed around the poles like wasps trapped in a jam jar. When the men were gone some of the older, bolder boys used the guy ropes to scale up to the roof of a tent and then they slid down on their bums, yelling. As soon as an adult appeared, they scarpered. The three tents were stately and grand as liners, moored in the quiet park.

Joe was in a flux of all but uncontainable excitement. There was so much going on and nothing must be missed. Should he go and take advantage of his mother teaching the Carnival Dance to mingle with the chirruping chorus of excited town-girls skipping in unison in rehearsal down a back lane? Or be near his father in the park and again and again enjoy the heady unadmitted superiority of seeing his own father at the heart of things? Both, both. And then scud around the town up the alleys into the yards where the floats were being dressed; shooed away as secrecy was preserved but catching enough glimpses behind high doors, over walls, in open sheds, of the invention and beautiful decoration going into the floats. The Carnival Queen and her attendants had been chosen two weeks before and there was for the first time – though not without some raised eyebrows – a Labour Party float. They put up the bunting, made out of pre-war flags, in all the streets – Water Street most decorated of all – and the boys were allowed to help, sometimes even being permitted to climb a ladder.

175

Joe stood outside the Congregational hall at the end of his street and the sound of the silver band in rehearsal slithered down his nerves and seemed to possess him, stun him to stillness and prime gunpowder in all his limbs. There was an army band coming to lead the parade and his father had told him stories of boy buglers and drummers leading men into war and Joe's dreams went to war with marching music. In all this time he managed to avoid Speed and the others and suffered nothing but the occasional knuckle on the arm. He had begun to nest inside a group of his own in the street and although most of them were girls it afforded a measure of security.

On the morning itself he dashed hither and yon like a mad puppy until Ellen leashed him in, scrubbed him down and put a clean shirt on his back. Sam had gone down to the park to help with the trestle tables and to mark up the distances for the sports. Sacks, eggs and spoons had all been assembled and the baking ladies and the committee were working on their quota in their own homes and would bring to the tents food which would be divided into seven hundred free plates for the children and others at 1s. 3d. per head for adults.

'Brilliant weather favoured Wigton's Children's Carnival,' said the *Cumberland News* the following Monday. Crowds collected from all over the county and the narrow streets were crushed with people. Ponies and donkeys for the free rides were drafted in from seaside towns. Mr Hadwyn from Martin's Bank took the seven hundred new threepenny pieces down to the park in the back of his car, alone. He had considered asking for a policeman to accompany him but then thought that would be far too dramatic.

The Ismay sisters rode their Penny Farthings as they had done in the last carnival before the war. The regimental bandsmen were dressed in scarlet and gold and their black boots glittered. 'You could shave in them,' people said. The brass instruments shone as bright as the sun. They marched in slow time and the precision was a matter of pride all round. Leonard said that nobody else in the world could march like that. The corps of white-dressed, bell-jingling girl dancers followed the regimental band and then came the town band, which halted at set points and played for the girls to dance, taking care not to drown the sweet jingling of the bells. The individual entries followed and the floats and finally seven hundred tidy children, most of them grimacingly self-conscious, were shepherded down the narrow courses of the old market town, in the hope and celebration of peace.

Joe was electrified with excitement. On the way to the start of the procession, he had eyed every float in wonder. The costumes! The wigwams and huts and cardboard tanks, the caves and jungles they had built on the lorries! He recognised almost everyone – except the Minstrels with banjos from New Street on Sheddy Pape's lorry – yet they waved at him and he blushed at the honour. He felt altogether strange for a Saturday afternoon: his best shirt, green and white stripes, his best short pants, navy blue (the bottom half of his Sunday suit) with the braces and a new pair of shiny, bright brown sandals which were already hurting his feet. Despite the heat of the day he wore grey woollen stockings up to his knees, carefully folded over a loop of thin white elastic, the same make as that which looped the wrists and ankles of the girl dancers and held the bells. It was more a Sunday than a Saturday outfit and it was an outfit which told him to be on his best behaviour. Life as usual.

But in the Carnival everybody was unusual, everyone was dressed up as if they were in the pictures. In the grey, rather bleak little Northern town, rationed and drawn and still mourning after the war, this gaiety and colour and the splashes of imagination were like a constellation of rainbows. Joe thought that his head was going to burst just trying to take it all in and when the procession passed the crowds in the street and the people clapped and even cheered, he did not know where to look. It was all so unnaturally magnificent.

The day flashed by, the day dragged deliciously through a thousand branded moments. The two poles were his mother and father. His father, loved beyond measure as his son had watched and 'helped' with the tents, seemed now to be the steadiness at the centre of the tumultuous park, now as crowded as the makeshift town of a medieval army. He was there holding one end of the tape at the finishing line for the sports. He was chatting to the soldiers in the band and now he whistled Joe over and one of the soldiers let him try on his hat and blow in the mouthpiece of the tuba. Other men called out to him and grave messages were quietly exchanged. The night before, risking a lot, Joe had been drawn into a spin of boasting about the number of Japs his father had killed in the war and that was the only anxiety: that one of the boys he had told would walk up to his father and challenge him and he would be found out.

His mother stuck with the dancers until they did their final performance right down the middle of the big stretch of grass where the sports had been held. This time, both the regimental band and the town band combined and the crowds clapped and clapped as the simple brass and silver sounds spread into the brilliant summer day and the forty girls in white danced in sweet amateur formation on the glossy cropped turf. Ellen walked quietly beside them. She had been in their number before the war, as had so many of the women looking on, and now she had trained a new generation, passing it on. Joe could scarcely bear to look at her, he was so breathless with pride.

Along with the others he was ushered in for his free tea and the same pink raffle ticket got him his shimmering new threepenny bit. He joined up with his father beyond the swings where the donkeys and ponies were saddled up. There, Sam recognised Ian's father and put a hand on Joe's shoulder to indicate that he should stay where he was while he went across to him. They shook hands self-consciously. After remarking on the luck of such a fine day, the older man said: 'It must be a record turn-out.'

'It feels that way,' Sam replied, trying hard to slough off the sense of awkwardness which had suddenly gripped him.

'I've had kiddies here from all art and parts.'

'Ian,' Sam felt he had to say the name, quickly, but the name stumbled through his lips, 'said nothing about ponies.'

'I help him out when he's short-handed. Since he lost his wife a month or two since.'

The man he was speaking of, a swarthy, thick-set, gypsy-looking fellow with a polka-dot red kerchief around his throat and a broad brimmed brown velvet hat, was leading one of the bigger ponies down towards the fence. Two little girls in white from the dancing were huddled together on the saddle.

Sam was stuck for words.

'Things working out?'

'Could be worse,' said Sam.

Did that seem ungrateful? To the father of Ian?

'It isn't easy for anybody.' He nodded in the direction of Joe. 'That yours?'

'Yes.'

'I'll give him Lightning.'

Lightning was rather bigger than the other ponies and the only piebald, which gave him flair. His reins were red and there was a red rosette in his mane.

'Come on, young fella-me-lad.'

Joe obeyed the summons. The day was now spiralling into

fantasy. Like a cowboy, he managed to put one foot in the stirrup and then, with a helpful push, he swung into the saddle and the shocking height and the smell of horse invaded him with a wholly new excitement. He turned to his father and grinned as widely as his mouth would go.

'It's seeing the kiddies' faces,' Ian's father said, only half looking at Sam, 'seeing them smile.' He clicked his tongue and led Lightning on the trodden path to the fence.

After the children had been fed, the tents were open to the adults: Full Tea 1s. 3d. – sandwiches, teacake, sausage roll, choice of a cake. Grace had performed miracles of baking and basked through an afternoon of compliments. Ellen did her shift and then took a cup herself when Ruth came in. She got on well with her sister-in-law and starved Ruth loved company. There was not a woman helping in the tent whom Ellen did not know well: some were known to Ruth but Ellen's unobtrusive inclusiveness was a benison. They unpicked the day with praise. Sadie, who had spent much of the time selling raffle tickets for prizes donated by the shopkeepers, came in to the cry that her feet were killing her and had anybody a dog end? Ellen laughed. The Carnival itself, and Sam nearby and Joe scampering around in pleasure, warmed and reassured her. She began to sing.

Shaken by the unexpected meeting with Ian's father, Sam wandered down towards the bowling green and found a patch empty of crowd. He sat against a sycamore and lit up, remembering and remembering again with painful vividness the number of times in this posture leaning against the trunk of a tree he had offered, been offered, a cigarette. By Ian. 'Seeing the kiddies' faces.' The phrase had got to Sam and he drew in deeply and the smoke set off a cannonade of coughing. Tears sprang to his eyes. He looked around furtively.

Nobody must assume he was crying: 'It was just the smoke,' he said to himself, as if excusing the tears to someone else.

After the sports had ended, the regimental band gave a last display, marching and counter-marching, drumsticks twirling, the sergeant major hurling his mace into the air, children strutting alongside, memories of setting out for war, of returning, of those who had not returned, all mingled in the crisp harmonies of brass which clarioned across the park. 'God Save The King' was played. The men took off their hats or caps and ex-servicemen automatically clicked to attention. The women sang full throatedly and there was one final unbidden cheer.

The crowds ebbed away through the park gates, back into the town, costumes bedraggled now, some of the floats half dismantled though a few were unblemished, preserved for competition in other carnivals throughout the summer. The scarlet regimental band clambered into a battered bus.

Sam had asked a few of them to help him take down the tents there and then and to Joe's dismay the castles of canvas pancaked to the ground in minutes and in no time at all they were packed and stacked in the shelter ready for collecting the next morning.

Some of the children, like Joe, were still so charged up that they could not bear to leave and as the park resumed its old contour, like a shore restored when the tide goes out, the swings and roundabouts and banana slide made their appeal. The Water Street gang, not great enthusiasts for the park as a rule, decided to stay and dominate proceedings. They hogged the American swing and then when they saw a happy crowd queuing up the steps for the banana slide they abandoned the big plank of swing and hunted across to walk up the front of the slide itself, smear it to speed with the stump of a candle someone had and climb up the stilts to the cabin at the top, thus bypassing the patient crowd on the steps. Soon they drove everyone away.

Joe felt that he was under examination. Whose side was he on? The scavengers, the terrorists who had made extra profit out of the day by devoting much of it to the collecting of empty lemonade bottles and claiming the halfpenny deposit back on each one and sometimes stealing the empties to have another bite; or the law-abiding, those willing to queue, true to the age and habit of queuing? By temperament, Joe was the latter; by desire and imagination, the former, but he was too small, not ready, and his longing only confused matters. When they laughed, they laughed at him especially, he thought, and sometimes he was right. But Sam and Ellen were nearby and apart from a few shoulderings there was no direct challenge. Until they had grown bored with the easy prey and switched their focus to the river and what could be done to make disturbance there, he felt clouded with misery, the misery that was always at hand.

Yet, young, out of sight was soon out of mind and there was half an hour at least for the mopping up of the pleasures of the day with other children also nearing euphoric exhaustion. The park keeper asked for volunteers to help pick up the litter and Joe set out eagerly with others, snapping it up with the zeal of terriers in a barn of rats. His father was folding the tents. His mother was wrapping crockery and loading it into the tea chests. His Aunty Ruth and Aunty Sadie were lending a hand with the trestle tables. It was all done calmly, even slowly, as the children snapped across the park sniffing out litter.

There was a moment, just before they left, when the three of them, Sam, Ellen and Joe, were walking together, the child between the two adults, each holding a hand, as the sun began to colour with blood in its setting and there was the sound of bowls clicking on the green, the crystal chirrup of children's voices mixed with the bird-songs of evening, and finally the Carnival was over, when they swung him high, high in the air.

CHAPTER SIXTEEN

'Bad?'

'Bad.'

'How bad?'

'Still plastered, Sam. Bad night.'

Kettler was held upright by leaning hard against the wall of the Vic at the end of Water Street. His rough-skinned, stubbled face with the large purpling nose almost distracting from the pain of the piggy, bloodshot eyes looked so sorry for itself that Sam had to laugh.

'Come on, I'll get you one.'

'I'm skint, Sam. Not a sausage.'

Fair warning. Sam nodded. They walked across to the Blue Bell. Kettler took his first few sips of the pint of mild – the cheapest drink – with both hands, carrying the rim of the glass prayerfully to his parched mouth. They took out a set of dominoes and began to play fives and threes, a penny a game, Kettler's losses on the slate.

It was the middle of the day. Ellen was out working, Joe at school, the town quiet and lazing in the hot sun, no market or auctions that day, long fatalistic queues on the streets for bread and flour, just rationed, the gutters being swept by Joe Stoddart. Sam was on the two to ten shift.

They were alone in the bar and the landlord left them to it.

They were well matched in the game and when that became clear, they gave up and sat back to talk. Sam offered Kettler a cigarette and Kettler, who rarely smoked but never refused any gift, took it gratefully. He smoked rather airily, as if through a cigarette holder. He eased himself in his seat to let the wind go free. The mild was doing the business.

Kettler's clothes fell, by a hair, the positive side of rags. He wore, he possessed, nothing that had been bought new: most had not been bought at all but handed on or rescued. His chief need of the day was a large helping of tripe from one of the seven butchers in the town. He alternated. Some of them, at the right time of day, would give it him for nothing. At the end of an afternoon, now and then, he would go to Joseph Johnston's for a loaf of stale bread which cost him a halfpenny. He might take a slice of cheese with it if he was in funds. Funds were primarily the dole, secondarily the occasional pick and shovel employment (although he claimed a weak back and Dr Dolan would often play along with it). Most of all, though, he scrounged. Bits of easy work on market days with half a crown for his pains, 'helping out' here and there – taking a hound dog to the trails, keeping an eye on a pony and trap. Kettler had found many minuscule gaps in the local economy which were made for his always available and always brief attention. Then there was the occasional fiddle.

He nipped the cigarette halfway down and popped the stump behind his ear. He had pushed back his cap and the surprisingly luxuriant but greasy black hair gave him rather a dashing appearance. He could charm some of the ladies: Ellen was not one of them.

He sipped carefully now. The pint glass was half empty and there would just be the one. He had no credit in the Blue Bell.

Kettler let the conversation lapse. It was an effort to talk and he'd got his drink. Besides, listening mostly paid off best. The sun came through the grimy windows throwing small pools of yellow, like doubloons, on the dark stained wooden floor. There was a dog, a collie, curled in front of the empty fire. No sounds came from the streets.

'Where'll you be going,' Kettler asked eventually in his broad accent, 'when they start shifting Water Street to Brindlefield?'

'Haven't thought. Are you going?'

'Me?' Kettler revealed his dogged remaining teeth. 'Up there? That's for millionaires.'

'We aren't down for a house.' Sam smiled. 'I should never have gone away. I lost my place in the queue.'

'Water Street'll be dead.'

'There'll be you and me, Kettler.'

'I'm back off to Vinegar Hill.'

'Why's that?'

'The lads is down there. They have a bit of fun.'

'Vinegar Hill.'

When Sam's father had brought them inland from the coalfields along the coast, Vinegar Hill was all they could afford. It lay just beyond Water Street, between the Rabbit Warren and narrow defile called the Straits. It was a huddled, in-built, ramshackle, chronically overcrowded little world of its own, with steps up to single rooms occupied by a large family or a survivor from a previous goitred age. There were three patches of ground where a few ponies grazed and junk rusted and often at an open fire the two tinker families who dominated Vinegar Hill would bake hedgehogs and entertain visiting traders with a potion gathered at low cost late at night from the dregs buckets of the pubs. The little thieving there was in a town with little to steal would find its way to Vinegar Hill and work as the world knew it was a word unknown.

'I mind you coming there,' said Kettler, who was a good dozen years older than Sam. 'Little bit of a thing. Game enough.'

'So that's where you're going.'

Sam did not want Kettler to say any more. He had not thought of Vinegar Hill for many years. He had stayed there through his schooldays and took it as his home as children do. His mother had contracted TB there and one of his sisters had a scar patch on her lung. His father had fought for years to get out of it and getting out of Vinegar Hill had been the first step up from the Nothing that Grace had so woundingly accused him of being.

But now, as if he had suddenly come across a hidden waterfall, Vinegar Hill poured into his mind and the torrent spoke of ease: of taking the day as it came; of a calmer pace, your own pace. All the stinks and intolerable crush of the place (which, in truth, as a child, had not struck him as anything but the way life was) dissolved in this selective memory of a place where you lived life on your own terms.

'Ellen would never tolerate it,' said Kettler, who was wise enough to pick up on Sam's expression. 'She'll want one of them new houses.'

'They all still down at Vinegar Hill? The same lot?'

'You'll never shift them, Sam.'

'I wonder,' Sam said, 'if they ever noticed there was a war on?'

'Diddler,' Kettler was speaking of a cousin, 'said things had never been better in the little town. Not in Vinegar Hill.'

Sam laughed out loud. Threw back his head and laughed and laughed – not wanting, not able to stop himself.

The landlord walked in and stood behind the bar with a crooked smile, waiting to be let in on the joke. 'Give the man a half,' said Sam, and he went to the bar, fishing in his pockets for change. 'Nothing for me. I'm off.'

He put the sixpence on the bar and turned to Kettler. 'So things had never been better in the little town!' he said and, laughing again, he went out to collect his bait and go to work.

CHAPTER SEVENTEEN

She did not know what she wanted to say and who to light on but she had to talk. The Carnival had been an interlude. She was still drifting away from Sam: Joe was becoming fearful and unlike himself. Maybe it would all pass. Given time. But she had used up all her waiting time while Sam had been away.

Ellen knew that it was not easy to talk about a marriage. Talk was disloyal. It was loose. Talk showed weakness. You could not be certain it would not spread. It was always better not to talk, especially about marriage. Marriage was the end of openness unless you were one of those who did their dirty washing in public and Ellen was not. Husbands could be joked about, caricatured, and even, in the right voice, criticised, but not betrayed.

It was known that there was bad feeling between certain couples: extremes were also registered – this couple had not spoken to each other for a dozen years, this man or those men beat their wives, this man or those men gambled or drank away the money, the wife flirted or worse. There were a couple of open scandals – a virtual bigamy, an obvious incest, one or two deeply plotted affairs and the increasingly common separation or divorce.

But the norm was endurance and silence and often enough

contentment reached by humour and underpinned by modest expectation. Ellen cleaved to the norm in all things and until Sam had gone off to the war, she had been as reticent about her unusual good fortune and happiness as she was now about this pressure of anxiety. But now she simply had to talk or she would burst.

Who to turn to?

Sadie was not close enough, much as they spent time together, and she was wary of Grace. It would have been out of the question to talk to the people she worked for in the houses or in the chemist's and men, even Mr Kneale, or Leonard, or Mr Scott, her old teacher who had always taken an interest in her, were off the agenda.

Ellen had a large range of friendships with women. Her circumstances made her more eager to reach out than most but there were in the town about two score women around her own age whom she knew well. This did not include the older women, whose interest and recognition still made a walk up the street a passage through a family. Nor were those younger, who being siblings or relatives of friends or girls she had seen through the carnival dances, any less part of the network, but it was those of her own age who formed the group. At school together, in the Guides or the cycling club or church organisations together, in the factory together and at the dances and socials, helping out with this or that in the town – tea after the football, setting out the chairs for concerts in the Market Hall, loafing around the streets, skint together and herding off for walks, all within a narrow, similar band of income and possessions. There were factions of course and quarrels or splits and cliques, but always the gang of them, always there.

Most of them were married, fourteen had been widowed by the war, many had worked on after marriage because of the opportunities presented by the war and were dropping out of work reluctantly now the men were back home. They seized on part-time jobs. A favourite was in the canteens at the schools. Or like Ellen they cleaned the larger houses – most often three-or four-bedroomed, plain, not rich. None was skilled. Hollywood was Heaven. American kitchens were paradise. Film glamour was copied instantly and with reasonable ingenuity on spectacularly small budgets: clothing coupons were not allowed to dominate the reality. If their husbands took them to the pubs on a Saturday night, it was they who led the singing and knew all the words, as they did on the bus trips when the songs would never cease. This was the first normal summer for seven years. They were approaching it carefully.

When both their husbands were on the afternoon and evening shift, she went for a walk up Longthwaite Road and into the Show Fields with Moira. It was a warm evening and others had had the same idea, but you could always draw away from the path and be private. Moira was a little older than Ellen. She had lived next door to her on Market Hill throughout their childhood. She had no children – the gossip was that she 'couldn't' have any, but Ellen would not have dreamed of enquiring further. Moira was private: and also discreet.

Although she too had worked in the factory and in the war found a job delivering mail, there seemed to Ellen to be a distinction about Moira. She was taller than all the others and with that willowy figure Ellen admired in the aristocratic women and models who were in the newspapers. Her face was rather long, her hair always beautifully done, her expression a little distant as if she were seeing further than most. With many of her friends, Ellen would have crooked arm in arm, but not with Moira.

Both the young women wore summer dresses bought before the war and reshaped to meet the modern look. Their open shoes slushed through the long grasses as they moved away from the wending path

193

and took the barely used track some distance from the river. They found a convenient hummock. For a while they chatted, rather nostalgically for such young women, about times past. Of the other life before the war – prompted by the hill beyond the river, known as Pasce Egg Hill, where they had all come after church on Easter Sunday morning to roll the hand-coloured eggs and where in a winter of snow, the boys made icy runs for their sledges and the girls came to watch, trying to cadge a go.

Moira's husband, Alan, who worked in the booking office at the railway station, had not been in the war. A childhood bout of tuberculosis had ruled him out.

How to begin? The evening was so calm and pleasant, the deepening blue benevolent sky, the stalk of grass Ellen sucked so sweet, the wild flowers embroidering the lush pasture field so restful, it seemed inappropriate to introduce her small grief. Better surely to drift into the mood of the evening and become part of its harmony.

It was Moira who began.

'—but it must be very hard,' she said and Ellen's attention was snagged back. 'Look at poor Jackie.'

'Sam thought he was on the mend.'

'He just couldn't keep up. Even when they gave him the lightest jobs. They say he went back too soon.'

Moira looked away and Ellen feared that this opening might be lost in contemplation of Jackie's relapse, which had been dramatic.

'They must,' said Ellen, suddenly determined not to duck it, 'have gone through a lot out there. A lot they don't tell us about.'

Moira nodded. Her eyes still sought out a distant horizon and did not turn to Ellen in sympathy. This made it easier. Ellen went further.

'I suppose it's harder because I thought I knew everything about him before he went away. He used to say I could read his mind.'

'You can't hide much,' said Moira wistfully, 'in a place like this.'

'No. But more than that – I *knew* him. All about him.' She paused, thinking hard, how to express this without complaint or betrayal. 'Now, though, he's had this other life.' It sounded so lame. 'He's a bit strange: sometimes. Nothing funny. But . . . I can't seem to recognise him. Sometimes.' Her voice had grown softer.

There was a pause. Moira always sat very still. Then she said, evenly, but in a charged way which pierced her friend's heart, 'That must be terrible for you, Ellen . . . I can't think of anything worse.'

Now she did turn and Ellen wanted to run from the pity she saw in Moira's expression. She should not have talked.

'It's getting damp,' she said, made to stand up, to move on.

'Don't go yet.' Moira's pity turned into a plea, which rather embarrassed Ellen, but embarrassment was much better than the knife of pity. She put her hand over Ellen's wrist and she let it lie there, exerting no pressure.

'I've always been rather ashamed that Alan didn't go,' Moira said, eventually. She turned away: in anyone else it could have been a gesture to encourage admiration of the fine profile but Ellen knew the effort that was being made. 'It's not something you want to talk about,' she stole a quick glance at Ellen and smiled. 'He couldn't help it, of course, and he would have gone – he tried, he went back three times but they wouldn't take him. They said his lungs were a "patchwork of scars". But I still felt rather ashamed that he wasn't doing his bit and sometimes he picked that up which was no good for either of us.'

'Everybody knew he wasn't well. They sent him away to South-port, didn't they? For the sea air.'

Moira nodded. Her divergence into the confessional was over.

195

Her poise was back. The moment had been addressed. An exchange had been made. The conversation moved on.

Down on the river path they met up with a few others and together they strolled through the three fields, slowing their walk in the last and biggest field where so many events had taken place both big – the agricultural show – and small. It was on this stretch of river that most of the men who fished introduced their sons to the sport and there were deep pools to gaze in and now and then a trout flicked itself out from under the bank. Moira invited Ellen in for a cup of tea but Ellen pleaded Joe's supper and bedtime.

'Joe's crying, Mrs Richardson.'

Bella announced this solemnly, nodding with every word. She stood like a sentry at the entrance to the yard.

'He's crying, Mrs Richardson.'

Joe was curled up in the armchair, small inside it, knees up to his chin, face tear-stained, wretched, and at his feet the railway engine and carriages, recently repaired by Sam, now utterly destroyed.

'What is it then?' More strongly. 'Who did it?'

He cowered, as if the question were a slap.

Ellen pressed down her impatience and her anger and sat on the armchair, putting him on her knees and cradling him as if he were even more of a child. His quiet unhappiness crept into her like cold. Why had she been out, self-indulgent, when this was going on?

'What is it, then?'

He burrowed more closely into her.

She could work out clearly what had gone on. They had teased him and started to pick on him and taken a kick at the painted wooden engine with its trim little carriages and then it had spun out of control and they had kicked it to bits and run away leaving Joe, desolate, to carry home the pieces.

At that moment Ellen would happily have thrashed the lot of them and had she known their names she would have sought them out and let loose. It was much more difficult to sit still and rock Joe back to some sort of calm.

'I've got some cocoa,' she said. 'Would you like that?'

He wanted the cocoa but he did not want his mother to move away. Not just yet. Not when the warmth from her body, as on their nights in bed before his Daddy came home, was flowing through him, filling him slowly but surely with drowsy, happy comfort. He made no answer. Ellen understood.

She rocked him and hummed quietly and did not even move to light the gas, though the fading light from the gloomy yard darkened the room relentlessly. The mild sunny evening in the Show Fields and her conversation with Moira seemed far distant in the silence wrapping itself around the small bounded house.

'What happened, then?'

All but imperceptibly he shook his head. His eyes tracked down to the splintered, broken toy. Already he knew enough to say nothing.

'If I catch them,' said Ellen, thoughtfully, 'I'll murder them.' Joe smiled, for the first time, and pressed his face into the soft warm body of his mother and somehow contrived to indicate that cocoa would be welcome.

She put him to bed and went on with the story but only for a page or two because he soon dropped into sleep. She watched his sleeping face, hurt and fear dissolved, now, the unlined, unblemished, unwritten face of a child and wondered how she could ever protect him from what would surely come.

Downstairs, the light now on, she began preparations for supper but her movements were slow. There was a distraction at the heart of her. She was confined in such a small space. Beyond that the street which in summer stank, no other word, and the bluebottles settled on the excrement and the hosing was never enough. Beyond that, the town, but a town now changed since Sam had come back from the war and she had been forced in part to see it through his restless eyes. She had to work to hold on to her town and since the move away from Grace and Leonard and Mr Kneale, she herself had been restless, but maybe that was all caught from Sam.

There was loneliness, though, that inner distraction which threatened a return of the unhappiness she had endured as a child after her mother had died. She took up a magazine and flicked through to find the serial. She was so feeble! Why, in her own house, her son upstairs in a healing sleep, her husband whom she loved and who loved her about to return home; why, in health and luck and so full of life, did she want to scream aloud?

'Just hit it,' said Sam. 'Don't be frightened.'

Joe swung out his left fist.

'No. It's got to come straight from your shoulder. Straight out.'

Sam demonstrated. They were in the yard. Sam was kneeling on a folded piece of brown sugar paper. Joe was self-consciously trying to follow instructions. Bella was one of the problems. Though she kept her distance, she was still there, blotting him up with her eyes.

Sam held up his right hand, palm facing Joe, and encouraged him to hit out. It was not easy to get the hang of a straight left. Sam brought the small boy to him, turned him round (they were the same height with the man kneeling), took Joe's left arm with his hand and pumped it out a few times.

'Don't stand so square. Left foot a little bit forward.' He shifted his son's left foot. 'Right foot a little bit back. Try to balance on the balls of your feet. Straight left and move to one side. Straight left and move again. Straight left and move to one side. That's it. Put a bit of oom-pa-pa into it – that's better. Straight left and move to one side. Hit him on the nose and he won't be very keen to come back. Just keep that left hand going. Straight left solves your problems. It doesn't come easy. Now then. Have another go. Have a go, Joe, come and have a go. Hit my hand. That's better. Go on, hit it as hard as you like. That's better. Straight left. That's the ticket. And again. Joe Louis. That's what he does. And again.'

In Water Street, Ellen tracked down Lizzie who had been suspiciously elusive. She was one of the 'big' girls who was in the gang around Joe. She lived in the adjacent yard and had stopped raiding Ellen's lavatory since Ellen had made her white carnival dress. She had also stopped the others.

Her summer hand-me-down dress was cheap and skimpy, ill-fitting. The sandals were badly scuffed. She was thin and malnutrition played its part in that. But her slim face was spotless, the hair clean and plaited into perfect pigtails. Everything that soap and water could do had been done. She was on the Sands, opposite the Congregational church, slowly pacing her way, head bent to the ground in concentration.

'Lizzie?'

The girl looked up with a frown at being disturbed. Then she recognised Ellen and pleasure struggled with guilt. 'Mrs Richardson?'

'Come here, Lizzie.'

The reluctance was all the proof Ellen needed. 'What are you doing?'

Lizzie opened her left hand. There were several pebbles clumped together.

'I'm collecting for the boys,' she said. 'They're going to have a fight with Church Street tonight.' She smiled. 'Beside the Baths.'

Ellen put that to one side.

'You know what I want to know, Lizzie. Don't you?'

Lizzie looked left, right, up, down, then repeated the sequence and finally settled for down.

'It's bullying, Lizzie, and I'm not having it. He's smaller than the others. I thought you would look after him.' Lizzie's face looked even more steeply down. 'You won't tell me who it was?'

Lizzie shook her head, just enough to see.

'I can guess.'

Not a tremor.

'I relied on you, Lizzie.'

The head sank so low that Ellen could see the pinched white nape of neck where the plaits parted to swing penitently down past the small ears.

She murmured.

'I can't hear.'

'I told them to stop, Mrs Richardson,' said Lizzie.

She had. But the few moments' flash of destructive frenzy were beyond her. And then it was done. And then the boys were all fled leaving Joe on his knees trying to put the train together again and Lizzie boiling with so many contradictory fears and feelings that she too had fled.

'Well, tell them,' said Ellen, 'that one day, and one day soon, I'll catch them. I have a good idea who they are. I'll catch them. And they won't forget it.'

'Yes, Mrs Richardson.'

Ellen was finished. But it all seemed too much. This girl from a big rough family struggling just to get by was crushed.

'You were very good in the Carnival, Lizzie. You're a good dancer.'

At this unaccustomed compliment, the head bobbed up.

'Was I, Mrs Richardson?'

The pinched face shone with pleasure. Ellen had to smile in return.

'The others followed you,' she said. It was true. Ellen should have told her earlier. 'You were the leader.'

Lizzie's smile split her face.

'Those stones could be dangerous,' Ellen said.

'Oh, the boys,' said Lizzie, vaguely.

'Keep an eye on him, Lizzie.'

'I will, Mrs Richardson. I will.'

Her expression tightened earnestly and Ellen left her feeling a little comforted.

Along the street the boys swooped and tacked, deep in plots and games but uneasy, one or two, Ellen noticed, as she walked at a deliberate pace, back to her own house.

'I'm taking Joe up the town,' said Sam as soon as she got back. 'I thought I'd see if Norrie can use us for his pony and trap. He delivers on a Saturday morning.' He nodded – the common purpose unstated between them. 'Joe's coming on,' he put a hand on his son's shoulder. 'We'll make him World Champion in no time.'

And, like Ellen, Sam walked along Water Street very deliberately, looking about him, Joe close by his side. It was the second clear warning.

Joe was proud of himself beside his father and excited after the boxing lesson. In his mind he was climbing into the ring, waiting for the bell, putting on the gloves, knocking everyone out, raising his hand in victory, hearing the applause. It had been precious, this intimate attention from his father, this encouragement to be a boxer, the care taken, the focus on him. It carried on from the Carnival. The fear which had grown was overlaid. He wanted to please his Dad. He wanted to show that he was not a cry-baby. He wanted to prove he could stand up for himself.

In the evening after the Salvation Army band had marched back once again without a single convert, Sam and Ellen took Joe for a walk.

They went out towards Carlisle, over Howrigg Bank from which Sam had first seen Wigton on the final leg home. So long ago now, it seemed. They paused to look down on the town and again Sam felt the grip of dismay that his life was bottled up there and as always Ellen felt herself soften into the mould of the place. Joe, who had heard of the stone fight but not been asked to join in, not even to collect up the spent stones of the Church Street gang, had gathered a few for himself and pitched them with determination but little art against the big oak tree in Robinson's field.

'Like this,' said Sam. He took a stone and his arm whiplashed. The small object hurtled through the air and smacked plum in the centre of the trunk. 'You snap your arm,' said Sam. He demonstrated. Then he laughed. 'First it's one arm and then it's the other, eh?' Joe did not quite understand but he understood profoundly that his Daddy was in a very good mood and so was his Mammy and both together and the exhilaration of it acid-burned away some of the stomach lump of fear. He threw again and almost got the trick of it.

Ellen strayed on ahead. They were building more houses here. The town was growing, though not in population, for these too would serve for the decanting of families from the fast nucleus in which Wigton had been concentrated for more than two centuries. Ellen was a little distressed at this loosening, at this dilution, even though it was only a spreading of space. The intense cohabitation would ebb, she sensed, and it was that which had supported her so much.

'They'll be a good-looking size,' said Sam, nodding at the new foundations. Joe was straddled across his shoulders.

'Shouldn't we put our names down?' Ellen's question came unplanned. She did not even know whether she wanted a house on the very edge of town.

'There's no rush, the rents are twice Brindlefield.'

'You keep saying you'd like a garden.'

'Let's talk about it.'

He meant the opposite and walked on.

Before them the rich Solway Plain stretched towards the Borders, deceptively amiable – on this Saturday evening, fine, warm, undisturbed. The biggest intrusion was the double-decker bus panting up the hill. Everywhere Sam looked there was a sense of effortless peace. Farms scattered apparently haphazardly across the Plain. The beasts in the fields moving so slowly. Missing nothing as they chewed up the lush pasture. Hedgerows thickening with fruit and berries.

There were two men out walking their hound dogs and that was all their company until they turned off just before the bridge and strolled down the lane which had been a courting lane to Sam and Ellen; and so it was still to another young blushing couple hopelessly pretending to be interested in what was around them instead of what was in them and written all over them. Joe was looking for rose-hips which could fetch a good price, but it was too early for them to be worth picking. Ellen had brought a tennis ball and they played catch as they walked under the undramatic sky. Joe scampered after the ball like a happy puppy.

They went under the railway line and turned back up a lane which came out near one of the houses which Ellen cleaned. It was a place of some local splendour, defended by worked wrought-iron railings, a place of big rooms, rich objects, untroubled wealth and the kindly hospitality of the two ageing sisters – one a widow, one a spinster – who had been born there. They would have welcomed an unannounced visit by Ellen, whom they cherished, but they would also have been rather surprised had she made the call. It never occurred to Ellen to do so.

At the railway station Sam yielded easily to Joe's request to climb the steps beside the high sandstone wall and wait to see a train.

The station looked at its best. The gardens were in bloom; and there were six hanging baskets. The platforms had been freshly swept and the sandstone of the classically-inspired main building was picked out in a deep iron ore red as the sunset struck it square on.

They went along the platform which led to Carlisle and walked up the bridge to cross to the main building. Joe lingered on the bridge and let his parents get ahead. While they were walking down the other side, even when they were on the far platform, he was still on the bridge itself, looking up and down the line, watching out for the white puff of smoke, signal of joy, and the unmistakable rhythm which pulsed through the veins.

Straight left. Whiplash with the right arm. Safe up and down Water Street with Mammy and Daddy. Seeing them below. Talking to a man in a dark uniform, an important man.

Three people now, two grown-ups and a girl, near his age, came out of the waiting room anticipating the Carlisle train. The girl stared up at him and then turned her head away, swinging her long plaits. His mother looked up and waved at him and he waved and then his father turned and gave him a thumbs up and Joe knew what he had to do. He had to do. The excitement and fear whipped up an ecstasy in his mind and he had to do it. Looking down at the two of them important on the platform, straight left, his feet were on the outside ledge of the sandstone-built bridge, the ledge below which was a sheer drop on to the shining railway lines. He had seen the big boys do this once when all of them had strayed way out of their territory down from Market Hill to the station to watch the trains. The big boys had gone across the bridge by the ledge, somehow keeping a grip on the perilously narrow ledge which jutted an inch or two from the foot of the bridge and clinging on with their hands to the pocked sandstone top of the bridge, inching across like crabs. He was smaller than they were and he had to reach up for the top to grip and shuffle his hands along and his new sandals still hurt a little, being a little too big, bought for him to grow in to. He felt brave.

His face was very close to a sooty wall. He turned to shout down to them but turned back quickly as the twist in his body had caused a wobble in his feet. A little wave of chill fluttered through his stomach and the palms of his hands, sweating helpfully, seemed stuck. He moved along slowly.

'Don't say a word.' Sam put out his arms to bar Ellen from rushing forward. He spoke quietly.

Ellen stayed where she was, wide-eyed, rooted, mesmerised at the sight of the small body crawling along what seemed the sheer face of the bridge. The sunset was lighting up the reds in the sandstone and in the boy's red hair, giving him a halo effect. For a moment the boy seemed unreal. It must all be happening to someone else, Ellen thought. That was not Joe, her beloved son, awkwardly, anxiously aping his big heroes and literally one false footstep from certain serious injury. This was not her, not his mother, watching immobile, not saying, not doing anything at all, not even praying, frozen in time and place.

'Good lad!' Sam shouted. 'Don't look round now. Good lad! You just keep on. You're a good lad! Don't look round.'

Three options. Stay. Somehow get onto the line beneath him or go up the steps and along the bridge and grab those hands clinging onto the top of the wall. That would take too long. Best to stay, but he could not stay because Ellen might not be able to tolerate it if he stayed. He began to move forward, calmly, swiftly, his eyes beamed into the back of his son's head as if by force of gaze alone he could and would pin him and fix him safely on that ledge.

On the other platform, the three passengers who had come out of the small waiting room looked up the track for the imminent train and saw the boy and they too gazed at the spectacle, especially because the boy seemed in some trouble.

Sam eased himself down on to the track. He was about ten yards away from the bridge. He kept talking, not incessantly but regularly. 'Good lad! Take a rest if you feel like it! Nearly there.'

Joe was barely halfway across and becoming more cautious by the step. The ledge beneath the soles of the sandals seemed to be narrowing. He was cheered by what his Daddy was saying. He could tell from the way he said it that this was what his Daddy wanted him to do. The top of the wall was a bit too high and his hands were scuffed.

As Sam picked his way over the lines, the train from the West puffed steadily around the bend at the bottom of Station Hill. White smoke, perfect little white clouds, piping up towards the darkening blue sky which was now shot with blood red.

Ellen took it in but she did not take her eyes off the boy. About five yards to go. Sam was on the suddenly fatal railway line and the train was headed towards him. Joe was clearly in trouble on the bridge. She scarcely saw Sam. She looked at Joe. At *Joe*.

Ellen opened her mouth to shout, because of the train, but a sense of greater danger alchemised the shout into a whisper of his name.

Joe began to whimper. He heard the train. He knew he was over the line the train was using. He wanted to go faster so that he was not there when the train pulled in, was not there when the big engine filled the space under the bridge and emerged black and steaming, braking for the platform, shuddering under him. One foot accidentally touched the other and he felt a lurch of terror.

'Good lad. Nearly there.'

Joe looked round and down and saw his Daddy below but something else, the spin in his head and it was cold on his forehead, sick in his throat, the noise of the train braking hard was a squeal, like a squeal inside him. Sam now in the middle of the line as the fireman saw that it was serious and pulled harder on the brake, leaned back on it, giving it his full weight while the driver hung out one side of the cab and shouted. But the noise drowned his shout – for Sam to get off the line – the people on the platform caught up in it, Ellen dry-lipped, dry-throated, chest tight, so hard to breathe.

Sam was directly underneath him. 'A bit faster now, Joe,' he yelled, ignoring the black blunt face of the engine screeching slowly towards him. 'A little bit faster now, Joe. You can do it. That's a good lad. You can do it.'

Fear, encouragement, the noise, survival fused in the child and he scuttled the last few feet and found refuge in the corner where the ledge was bigger and where he cowered while Sam leapt on to the platform and up the steps to hand him over the wall and the engine sank hissing to a stop just before the bridge.

Ellen ran to them. The stationmaster went to the train to explain and Joe was in his father's arms checked from sobbing by the praise.

207

'You're a little warrior! That's what you are, eh? A real little warrior!'

He carried the boy on to the bridge where Ellen flew into them and claimed him. She almost winded the boy with the first fierce force of the hug she gave him. 'Don't do that,' she said. 'Don't do that ever again.'

Joe looked at Sam who was smiling at him and he smiled in return, but Ellen tugged back his attention and looked at him with her full strength.

'Don't do that ever again,' she repeated, only pretending to smile. Joe quailed at the fierceness of her.

'He did well.'

Ellen's intensity neither lessened nor swerved. 'Never again,' she said and lightly but with intention and despite all her better feelings, she cuffed Joe on the back of the head.

It did not hurt. It scarcely registered. He looked out to his father but Sam was not smiling. And back to his mother and she too was unsmiling. They were looking at each other and not at him. He began to cry a little and, when Ellen pressed his face into her shoulder, he sobbed more painfully.

'Well, I'm proud of him,' said Sam and he walked ahead, to square things with the stationmaster. Slowly, Ellen followed, feeling so much unravel inside her, a sudden knowledge, in that moment, of what could fall apart.

PART THREE

CHAPTER EIGHTEEN

Bella's crying disturbed Joe. He wanted her to stop but he understood her distress.

'Please, Mr Kettler, don't, Mr Kettler, please.'

It was mid-afternoon, a drizzly summer afternoon, and Kettler was mellow from the pub, otherwise Bella's dramatic stand in the corner of the yard, ever-incessant sobbing and the endlessly-repeated pleas might have got on his nerves. Despite his easy manner, the key to his survival, Kettler could be nasty.

'Go inside if you don't want to watch, you daft ha'porth.'

'I'm not daft, Mr Kettler. You daft, Mr Kettler. Please don't do that. Please don't.'

Her words sawed through Joe and yet he stayed at his post, helping Kettler, considering it a privilege to be invited to assist.

The big tin bucket was almost full of water. Five kittens, soot-black, splashes of white, only a few hours old, blindly squirmed and pawed and nuzzled each other on the rough tear of blanket. Their two dead siblings lay wet, immobile, dead, on the other side of the bucket. Kettler was doing a publican a favour.

He had taken off his jacket and rolled up the ragged shirt sleeve almost to the shoulder. He picked up one of the tiny kittens pawing for succour, held it firmly and pushed his arm deep down into the bucket. As he held it there he smiled at Joe, an amiable, man-to-man smile, flicking his eyes towards Bella, rolling his eyes a little.

'Round the bend,' he said. 'Doolally.'

Joe smiled complicitly, but the wailing of Bella touched his heart and his mouth was open partly in horror. The kitten came out, drowned dead, smooth-soaked, all cuddliness and charm and life gone in that short time. Kettler chucked it on to the pile.

'Want a go?'

Joe's throat panicked. His tongue seemed to slither all around his mouth, out between his lips, down his throat. His face froze in an expression of fear.

Kettler laughed, a little cruelly.

'Roll your sleeve up,' he said.

Joe did as he was told.

'This is the boy for you.'

He picked up the kitten and put it in Joe's hand, where it felt big, warm, lovely. He looked at it. He wanted it. He wanted to stroke its little furry chest, see its sticky blind eyes open, press it to his face.

'Please, Mr Kettler. Please, Mr Kettler.'

'Big daft Bella. Eh Joe? Big daft Bella.'

Joe felt that he had to nod in agreement. The life in the palm of his hand now wriggled a little and he all but dropped it.

'Now then,' said Kettler.

He took Joe's hand in his own and closed his fist over the child's hand and the kitten and lifted both over the lip of the bucket and held them down. Joe felt the kitten move and then twist and he felt the paws. He tried to let go. Kettler held on tightly, grinning down at the boy, the beer smell coming strongly off him, the purple nose only inches away, the locks of greasy hair dangling down from under the grubby cap. Joe went blank and when Kettler lifted out his arm he was glad that it was over, even though the kitten was dead.

'Good lad,' said Kettler. 'Have a rest.'

'Joe,' Bella cried. 'No, Joe. No, Joe.'

She was banging her back against the wall in the corner furthest from them. No one paid her any heed. Her mother only ever came out to call her in for a meal. Sam and Ellen were at work. The Rooks were away on their week's holiday to Bridlington.

Joe's stomach felt queasy with excitement and dread, the sight of the soaked black kittens, the fluffy white patches somehow disappeared in the water, the fur so very thick and smooth, pasty. He glanced at Bella to laugh her away as Kettler did, but he was not successful. Her spiritless black hair, forever lank, had escaped the clasp of her big clip and fallen over her lumpy white face on which the mouth was working away in a torment. Her right hand churned the hem of her cheap print summer cotton dress and pulled it up, showing the big green knickers which made Joe hot to see and her left hand was clenched into a fist, pounding the air in front of her.

'Shut up you daft noggin!' Kettler was becoming irritated and he proceeded quickly with the remaining kittens until there was only one.

'Your shout,' he said to Joe. He handed it over.

Once again Joe loved the warm life in his hand. Once again he wanted to pet it and keep it. Could he keep it? The idea flooded his mind with the fullness of it. Everything stopped while he looked at the blind kitten filling his small boy's hand. If only he could keep it. If only he could keep it.

He looked at Kettler – the mottled and sly old face, broken-veined, world-knowing and cynical – and panted at the courage required to ask.

'No, Joe. No, Joe. Tell him no, Mr Kettler. Mr Kettler!'

'Can I keep it?' Joe whispered, but so low that the words did not come out. He sucked his dry throat and looked straight at Kettler and somehow managed to say, 'Can I keep it?'

'Now then.'

'Can I? Please.'

Kettler shoved his tongue into his cheek so that it bulged as big as a plum. There could be profit in it. Sam was an open-handed type and he could well see a pint or two coming from it. Ellen had no time for him – they were both clear on that – but this could be a difficult one for her, which would do no harm; he would welcome a smile from her, a pleasant word.

'Oh, now then. I don't know. What'll your Mammy and Daddy say?'

Joe looked miserable. How could he know? If only he could stop this panting in his chest.

'They'll maybe say they can't be doing with a kitten. Not everybody likes kittens. They may be mad at poor old Kettler for being soft-hearted.'

Joe shook his head. The kitten was almost inert in his hand, calm, not trembling at all. Joe took strength from it.

'They won't, Mr Kettler. Promise. They won't. They won't.'

They couldn't. The tears that pricked his eyes told him the truth of it. They wouldn't.

'All right then,' said Kettler, with a big sigh of reluctance. 'Just tell them if they can't cope, then Kettler'll deal with it. What'll you tell them?'

'If they can't cope,' said Joe earnestly, fervently, not understanding, 'then Kettler'll deal with it.'

'Say it again.'

Joe obeyed.

'Away you go. It needs a bit of milk. In a saucer. Put a bit of water with it, mix it together – and keep it warm till your Mammy gets back.'

Wild-eyed at his good fortune, Joe darted across to his house, holding the kitten in front of him as if it were a bowl brimful of precious liquid.

Kettler sluiced the water from the bucket and tied up the dead in the blanket. He would take them along the Lonnings to the tip and stay for a word with the pigeon men, sure of a fag or two there, maybe a bit of a job, back for opening time.

Bella was now squatting in the corner worn out, sobbing noisily, her dress wide open, dangerously strewn up her fat adolescent thighs.

'Get yourself decent, Bella,' said Kettler, as he swung the knotted blanket over his shoulder. 'You clueless tart.'

His joy had transmitted itself instantly to Ellen, who thanked Kettler for this unexpected benison – why had she not thought of it? Blackie was the perfect lightning conductor for the turbulence of Joe's feelings. She brought a box from Eves' the Chemist and lined it and put it in Joe's room, pretending that Blackie would treat it as a kennel, knowing that Joe sneaked the kitten into bed and knowing, too, that Blackie had a mind foreign even to the besotted commands of a child and would soon walk free and alone.

Joe loved with the eye of passionate indulgence. He stood now, immobile, to watch it play with the material at the bottom of the easy chair, stab at it with tiny spindly paws, light as fluff.

'We have to go or we'll never get back.'

'Will Blackie be all right?'

'He'll be fine.'

'He won't get hurt?'

'There's no fire on. We'll shut the door. He won't get hurt.'

Still staring at the kitten, he backed to the door and watched carefully while Ellen over-elaborately pulled it tight shut.

'Can I stroke Blackie, Mrs Richardson? Can I, Joe?'

'Not tonight,' he said and then, because his mother was there, 'Sorry, Bella.'

'Tomorrow then, Joe?'

'Yes,' said Ellen. 'You can stroke Blackie tomorrow, Bella.'

'Thank you, Mrs Richardson.'

And she let them pass. Since the adoption of Blackie, Joe's terms with Bella had altered dramatically. The promise of a stroke of the kitten or a holding of him (very rarely granted) was enough for safe passage to and from the lavatory and the threat of withdrawal of the favours secured liberty in all other journeys.

It was a summer's evening in the middle of the school holidays and the town was largely full of children. The weather had not been kind – rain, light rain, intermittent rain, but still, rain most days. Now there was a break and mother and son put their raincoats over their arms as they set off for more water at the Town Baths.

This was a handsome sandstone building in a lane at the bottom of the field behind the main auction. Ellen had been a competitive swimmer as a girl and Joe had already been taught. He could manage a couple of breadths and provided he stuck to the shallow end he was safe.

Ellen played with him for a while, saw that he was settled enough – there were half a dozen others of his age, the inner tubes were in the pool, there were no adolescent boys exercising a reign of terror – and swam a few lengths, feeling as she always did the sensuous freedom of water, her movement through it, the body flowing and fluid. She lay on her back and floated for a while and let the feeling of lightness penetrate her. Her body lost all weight and her mind seemed to follow and lose all care. It was truly a world of her own as the gentle eddies of the pool lapped her. While Sam had been away, over those years, this, in a way she could not explain, was the closest she had been to him. She floated voluptuously, consumed with the luxury as long as she could until she was forced to come back and remember how little time she had. Then she went for a bath.

The zinc bath they had been given by Grace did well enough, but once a week Ellen had to have the full treatment. The dream was the bubble bath of Hollywood with all the trimmings of glittering taps and carpeted floors, a chaise longue, gilded mirrors, perfumes, space, lamps, an orchestra in the background. The reality was a plain white bath in a raw narrow room, a thin towel, a wafer of soap and a time limit for your ticket. Still, once stretched out with hot water brimming up to the chin, the rubber bathing cap still stuck on tight, there was real pleasure in it. If she levered herself up even very slightly on the pads of her finger tips, she could seem to float again.

So when would she tackle Sam? How would she say and do what she wanted without making it worse? How could she make it better, like it was before? Before he went away. Before he changed. Perhaps she too had changed but that thought was no more than a flicker on the margin. He was the stranger.

Joe was there, a boy, seven years old in a few weeks, and she knew that Sam found him a check, even an obstacle between them: how to right that? And to reach Sam – it seemed less possible by the moment. After that first confluence, their streams had diverged and the gap was widening. The only way was to act. It would not change by wishing. Neither of them seemed capable of those easeful confessions which can bring reparation. It was by action alone that this rift, this wholly unexpected, strange, unacknowledged, unseen, unforeseen rift between them could be mended.

The attendant knocked on the door. Her time was up.

Joe was hopeless at drying himself properly and Ellen went into the blue-doored cubicle to rub him down as he shivered back to warmth.

The rain, more drizzle, was waiting for them, but they buttoned up the raincoats and stepped out. Ellen felt buoyant and optimistic, as she so often did after a visit to the Baths. She had Joe take her arm and they sang, softly, 'It's a Long Way to Tipperary' and 'Goodbye Dolly' and other marching songs from the First World War, as they followed the narrow wending path back into the centre of the town.

Time had sweetened the songs. Joe had picked up the words and loved them, because they were sung by his mother, because they were so cheerful and the names so big and ripe and meaningless. And it was good to be alone, unchallenged, with his Mammy.

'Goodbye, Piccadilly, farewell, Leicester Square,

'It's a long, long way to Tipperary

'But my heart lies there.'

Sung on the way to the Somme and Passchendaele and by men still active in the town.

'Goodbye, Dolly, I must leave you,

'Though it breaks my heart to go.

'Something tells me I am needed

'O'er the hills to fight the foe.'

Joe, his arm linked with his mother, dreamed of fighting the foe as he stepped out with this troubled, attractive young woman, his mother, believing her to be immortal and unchangeable.

They skirted Vinegar Hill. Ellen had never liked it. Although Joe had hovered around its edges and shivered at the stories that came from the place, he too was glad to avoid it. Most people did.

The fine rain settled on them like a gentle net. It glistened on Ellen's dry hair and wiped Joe's face with its pleasant soft moisture.

They found Lizzie and her sister in Scott's Yard, oblivious to the drizzle, beside themselves with excitement. 'We've got one, Mrs Richardson! The one what we wanted.'

Joe glanced at his mother to see if he had to stay and listen to this. The urge to see Blackie was almost a lust. A gesture released him and he arrowed down the narrow runnel, flew past a flailing Bella and into the house to find the kitten on the table scratching the dark green cover so vigorously that the heaped-up material almost buried it.

'We went up last week,' said Lizzie. To Brindlefield, the new estate.

Her sister, younger by a year, watched Lizzie carefully, checking every word for its amazing truth.

'And we picked one out. That we wanted. Didn't we, Mary-Jane?' A measured nod. 'And I said – that's ours – didn't I? I said – that's ours, Mrs Richardson – and it is!'

The pinched girl's face creased in such joy that Ellen felt her heart lift.

'It is!' and the tone rose up the scale almost to a squeak of pleasure. 'Number Eleven. And – and – the Graveses –' their neighbours in Scott's Yard, 'Graveses is next door. Next door!'

Mary-Jane nodded with vigour.

Ellen felt her smile matching that of the delirious girls.

'It's got,' said Lizzie slowly, 'three bedrooms. Every one bigger than all our downstairs. It's got a front room, a back room and a kitchen and another little room downstairs. And,' here she paused and stared, knowing that the next revelation lay beyond belief and yet

219

desperate to be believed, 'and it's got a room with a bath and sink in and an indoor lavatory.'

Her face became quite solemn.

'Indoor lavatory,' echoed her sister. 'I had a sit on it.'

Lizzie was silenced by the thought of the splendour that would soon be hers. Ellen wanted to give them each a sixpence but did not quite know why and felt a flush of shyness – men gave money away – and so the moment passed.

'Well, you'll all be very pleased. I'm very pleased for you.'

'And two gardens,' said Mary-Jane, nudging her sister. 'One at the front and one at the back.'

'Daddy says he'll build a shed.'

'It sounds like a palace,' said Ellen and she heard the wistfulness in her tone. 'When will you move?'

'In less than a month,' said Lizzie, promptly.

'Well,' Ellen repeated, 'I'm very pleased for all of you.'

'Water Street is on the move our Mammy says.' Mary-Jane liked that idea and issued her first smile. The hardness of life which had produced an inextinguishable zest in Lizzie had crushed her into a premature but permanent cringe of anxiety. Happiness was a rarity.

'It will be,' said Ellen.

And already she saw the handcarts with the few bits of furniture strapped on with baling twine, the prams full of clothes and knick-knacks, cutlery, crockery, the small accumulation of a lifetime drawn along the back streets as they would be until forced into the main Southend road and then up the hill which led to Brindlefield, the new Council estate, crowning the southern rim of the town and looking out clear towards the mountains of the Lake District. Her confidence drained away as she saw the people draining away. They had proved, as she knew they would, decent neighbours, decent people, despite her own and Grace's foreboding, and who would take their place? She shivered in the wet cool air. Would squatters come? She saw the Water Street houses empty. She had heard talk of them being boarded up. She had read reports of people desperate for any roof over their heads. Who would the squatters be?

'You can come and see us, Mrs Richardson,' said Lizzie boldly, 'whenever you want. And you can bring Joe.'

'Well then, I will. Thank you, Lizzie. I'll do that.'

Joe was lying on the floor encouraging Blackie to box with him. Ellen tidied up the tablecloth. The house felt damp and confined. More than anything, she wanted to get out of it, get out and somehow start again. But how could you start again? She heard Lizzie and the girls chanting a skipping song and nodded to herself. All it needed was the determination.

'Blackie's hungry,' said Joe, 'aren't you, Blackie?'

CHAPTER NINETEEN

Leonard was not a religious man nor was he a musical man but he had taken to the new song 'Money Is The Root Of All Evil'. Once he had grasped the tune he would hum it or whistle it but most of all he liked to sing it aloud, not very loud but audibly, which he did morning, afternoon and evening, even on the streets, cheered by the repetition of that single sentence 'Money is the root of all evil'. Dead right, he would mutter to himself, bang on the button.

He weighed up Grace in the light of that line. She was pouring tea from a teapot inherited from his mother but owning it now as she did all the inheritance so hard accumulated. Grace had been a smasher, a bit of a pin-up in her way, and Leonard had been unashamed to throw the inheritance into the balance. It had worked. She was still a handsome woman and since they had got the car she had become more responsive again. It was all, he thought, that really made her tick. The house, the family chattels, the car – the tune hummed inside his head clear and free floating. He wondered that Grace could not hear it.

Mr Kneale was sitting beside Joe catching up, it seemed to Leonard. After all, for nearly three years he had been in close contact with the boy and he had sometimes seemed to make a well-meant attempt to take Joe over. Leonard had observed Ellen's anxiety and occasionally felt a proprietorial pang of his own over the fatherless child with the attractive young solitary mother.

The schoolteacher was reading to Joe from the local newspaper: ' "Business Announcement. Rose-hips will provide much needed Vitamin C for children and invalids next winter." Vitamin C is the source of life, Joe. It's in apples.' He waited for a response, but Joe kept quiet. He did not want to join in with Mr Kneale this time. After a disappointed pause, the teacher continued. ' "Almost every town and village in the North has a depot where threepence a pound will be paid for rose-hips freshly picked when red or turning red. Collecting Rose-hips is a Healthy way to Contribute to the National Health." Now that,' said Mr Kneale, patting Joe's head, 'is a worthwhile way to make some pocket money.'

'Nobody can beat me at collecting rose-hips,' said Sadie, who had crept into the kitchen uninvited and stuck there regardless. It was true. Certain of the poorer women and the tinker women were expert at hoovering the hedges of rose-hips, blackberries and wild strawberries, bringing overflowing baskets to King Haney's in Water Street. 'I'll take him with me next time.'

'I was thinking to taking him myself, Sadie.' Mr Kneale's accent was in itself a criticism of broad-speaking Sadie and the implied reproof was unmistakable.

'Sorry, Mr Kneale,' she said.

'I was thinking of going round by the Syke road,' he said.

'That was stripped long since,' said Sadie. 'Sorry.'

'Longthwaite?' said Mr Kneale.

'As long as you're prepared to walk on.'

'We'll find some, Joe, won't we?'

No you won't, thought Sadie, with satisfaction.

'If we do decide to go around the Syke,' said Mr Kneale, in a tone which Ellen recognised as condescending and Sadie enjoyed as pique, 'then I'll take the camera. You can get some unusual views across the Deer Park.'

'I saw them deer,' said Sadie.

'Really? I thought they were all disposed of after the bankruptcy.' Mr Kneale was growing icy towards her.

'That bankruptcy as you call it,' said Leonard sharply, 'was brought on poor Mr Banks by the citizens of Wigton. If they had bided their time they would all be millionaires by now.'

'And there would still be the Big House,' said Ellen.

'They must have kept the deer on, then, because I saw them,' Sadie persisted. She enlisted Ellen. 'So did you.'

'Yes.' Ellen felt it was almost a disloyal confession and glanced apologetically at Mr Kneale. 'The deer were there when I was a little girl. The Storeys had the Big House after the Banks left and they kept the deer on for a time.'

'Poor little Mr Banks was drummed out of Wigton,' said Leonard, indignantly. 'And see what he did for the town. He built the Baths. He built the Kildare because Wigton needed a good-class hotel. He maintained the church. He built that Italian tower – a landmark, a monument for miles around. A true gentleman.'

Mr Kneale cocked his round and curly head, indicating that he needed to be filled in, but did not care, in this company, to admit ignorance.

'Mr Banks had agreed to invest some money in shares for Wigton tradesmen,' said Leonard. 'They came to him. He didn't seek them out. He had been very lucky on the stock markets of Europe.' Leonard almost sighed with the pleasure that exotic and gilded phrase, that image of distinguished, unimaginable wealth brought him. 'Finally he gave in and invested it for them. But in 1917 there was some sort of crash and the tradesmen of Wigton wanted their money back quick. You see, he'd given them guarantees being the gentleman. But he couldn't find it quick. To sell – so I've heard quoted – was lunacy – and he was right – if they had held on—'

'They would all have been millionaires,' concluded Grace, reverently.

'So he paid up.'

'Like a gentleman.'

'And he was bankrupted. He left the town by train and when he drove through the town in a carriage, they said he was jeered at.'

'He was just a little sort of a man,' said Grace. 'Beautiful clothes. Beautiful manners. Smoked with an ivory holder.'

'They followed him to the station and saw him on to the train.'

'Broken-hearted.'

'He died soon after in a London club.'

'He never came back to Wigton.'

'Leonard feels it,' said Grace, 'because his father did some work for Mr Banks and Mr Banks took something of a shine to Leonard and used to give him a silver threepence when he saw him.'

'He was a real gentleman,' said Leonard, firmly.

Mr Kneale nodded, sympathetically.

'There's never been a house like that,' Sadie announced, drawn into the tragedy.

Ellen nodded and while the conversation about Mr Banks continued, she slipped into a reverie about the Big House on Highmoor.

It belonged in the same part of her mind that was full of awe at the glamour of Hollywood. As a Girl Guide, she had marched with the troop up the great beech avenue to the Big House for the fête. Tea was set out on the long trestle tables, draped in fine white linen tablecloths, and they were waited on by maids, some of whom Ellen knew. Miss Storey would emerge with a small group, all wonderfully dressed, and walk about with such elegance and amiability. They could go to the private zoo or wander in the Deer Park, not getting too close to the deer, and not feel that they were trespassing when they tiptoed closer to the house and discovered the vast vegetable plot or the small walled rose garden and even peeped through the windows (hoisting each other up in turn) to see the gilded mirrors and furniture they had never seen before and long curtains, mounds of cushions. The house to Ellen had been the Aladdin's cave of Wigton, and now that the Storeys could not keep it going she lamented its passing as if she had been part of it. It had been, it was still, it would for ever be the perfect and unattainable house.

'Them railings around the Deer Park,' said Sadie, grown cocky, 'they were stopped from melting them down in the War. For bullets. That's how important it was.'

Mr Kneale chose not to demur. It was unfortunate that on the increasingly rare days Ellen and Joe came down together the cameo, he thought peevishly, should be turned into a gargoyle by the slippered and slatternly Sadie.

To regain the initiative, he passed around his most recent photographs, which were of the Nonconformist chapels and meeting houses in the town.

At a predetermined moment, with the blessing of Grace's knowing smile but to the slight bemusement of Mr Kneale and Sadie, Leonard murmured that he was taking Ellen 'up street' for a few minutes. They were gone before questions could be politely formulated.

Leonard felt braced after his aria on Mr Banks. He took Ellen's arm – he was, after all, more than old enough to be her father and he had, for many years, stood in for her absent father – and felt the swish that comes when a fine-looking young woman walks up street under your protection. His greetings were a little louder than usual, Ellen's a little more subdued; and though he whistled 'Money' once or twice, it was all but noiselessly.

They were making for a small, discreet alleyway very near the middle of the town which led into a big cobbled yard. There was only one house there – which was partly why the yard was so rarely visited. A second reason for its neglect was that it had been until lately the house of a spinster whose life had been blighted by the death of her fiancé in the First World War and who had inherited the house from her parents and become more and more of a recluse. At her death she was practically a hermit, still pining to be rejoined with the fair-haired young lieutenant of the almost faded photograph beside her bed.

Though the house was double-fronted, it was shallow, with only a narrow strip of garden at the rear: land had been sold off and a high wall darkened the back rooms. There were four bedrooms – one of which had served as a storeroom. Downstairs the two drawing rooms were identical – over-furnished, under-aired, scarcely used. There was a kitchen which over the years had become not only the centre but for weeks on end the sole part of the house to be utilised and then there were 'the usual offices' said Leonard, a little grandly.

The house brought out that little grandness. Though shabby, though worn and desolate, it still spoke of a former style where money could be spent without fretting and objects gathered with discrimination. Even the peeling wallpaper seeping from the walls had that air about it – that air, to Ellen, of the unattainable by her and her kind.

'When the old furniture is cleared out it will look a tidy old mess,' said Leonard, banging a chaise longue to make the dust rise. 'And there's some damp – needs painting throughout. God alone knows what's under those old carpets. But in the right hands . . .'

Ellen felt nervous just looking at it. How could she consider it? How could she aspire? How could she even afford just to look at it? It was such a leap. Yet there was something which had tempted her from the moment that Leonard had mentioned it and she had found herself darting into the almost secret yard on her way back from her stint at the chemist's. It looked so secure. For all of them. For ever more. Deep in the centre of the town which had brought her up. With style but hidden away so that it could not excite comment. It would take years to put right, it would look a mess for months at least, how could they furnish it, though decayed, it might be thought too posh for them. The negatives built up as a way of making her positive.

More than anything else, Ellen felt that it could be her private fortress. Put her there and she could take on whatever Sam in his newness, his strangeness, had to throw at her. There, she could build a family. There she could dig in for a life which she would not regret.

This was the first time she had been inside and it was gloomy, even a little weird in its dated stillness, something of a mausoleum. But all that could be blown away like the dust. She felt herself grow to fit it. The longer she stayed the more dry-throated she became at the thought that she might not be able to manage it.

'Sit down,' said Leonard, and Ellen perched on the dusty edge of a deeply-cushioned armchair. Leonard relaxed in its faded velvet opposite. It seemed rather unreal to Ellen to do something as normal as hold a conversation in the dead woman's room, crammed as it was with her life – the lamps and rugs, watercolours, photographs, knick-knacks now out of fashion, ornate clustered chairs, a big mahogany oval table, an empty, once-white birdcage, vases of dried flowers, a glass-fronted bookcase holding uniform volumes in dark-blue bindings. In part Ellen was reminded of what she had glimpsed as a girl through the window at the Big House, and in part it resembled the house belonging to the two sisters on Standing Stone. The one she dreamed about, the other she cleaned.

'Now then,' Leonard continued, 'what I'm telling you I'm telling you in advance of others and so treat it as confidential. Miss Ivinson's income fell below par some time ago and Willie Barwise, who had been a friend of the family and his father before him, being then Chairman of the Parish Council, exercised a perfectly legal right – with the Clerk to the Council – to purchase the house for the Council and let Miss Ivinson live in it at a peppercorn rent until her day was done. She took a bit longer than the estimate but that's all in the game. So this, Ellen,' Leonard smiled as a bringer of good news, 'is, strictly speaking, a council house.' Leonard glowed, he shone: it was not often since her childhood that he had been in a position to dazzle and impress Ellen and her concentrated attention had a stirring effect on him.

It mattered that it was a council house, Ellen thought: that meant it was not special. But she could not yet see why Leonard wanted her to be so pleased.

'Speaking simply,' said Leonard, unconscious of being patron-ising, 'it comes down to this. Because of the peculiar but not irregular circumstances,' he broke down every last syllable, 'a £50 down payment is necessary, after which rent will be levied on the current council house scale, which I would guess for this size is somewhere between £1 10s. and £2 a week.'

Ellen nodded. The rent could be met. How could they raise the £50?

'What is in your favour,' Leonard said, smiling, 'is that with these new council houses already built and being built and just about as big as this and with no £50 needed for a down payment and no restoration and general cleaning up to be done – I think you'll have a clear field. At least for a while.'

To talk Sam into it: Ellen nodded.

'Now then,' Leonard concluded, and he looked around as if he feared he was being overheard, 'I'll take this one step further . . . I'll give you first refusal. That is to say, if anybody else shows serious interest, I'll let it be known there was a previous enquiry which takes precedence and come to you first.'

He had thought it all through. Ellen was moved by that. He had taken on board her enthusiasm, seen her love for the place, under-stood her circumstances and the potential difficulty with Sam. Thank you would sound inadequate and yet she had never been able to hug him. The memory of her father had made it awkward and even now that memory checked her impulse.

'You've been very good,' was all she said.

Leonard knew the feeling behind the remark and smiled, widely. 'It's nothing,' he said, 'and tell Sam – if he gives it the go-ahead – that there are ways of getting that £50. Just tell him that.'

'I don't know if Sam'll want it.'

'That's between the two of you. I'm saying no more. Grace wanted to have a say but I said – say nothing. They have to decide this one for themselves. This is a turning point, I said.'

'Thank you.'

'Now then,' he stood up and turned around, 'dust me off, will you?'

As Ellen did so, he hummed his favourite tune.

The wallpaper, she thought, should be light-coloured through-out. Even yellow.

CHAPTER TWENTY

'I won't ask you to do this again,' said Annie as they drew out of Wigton.

'Don't worry yourself.'

'Just this first time. Just to get myself used to it.'

'You don't smoke, do you?' Sam offered her a cigarette.

'No. Jackie does enough for the two of us.'

She gave the faintest smile as she mentioned her husband's name but that was the only smile.

Annie's unsunned broad spotted face was clamped in concern. Throughout the bus ride to Carlisle she gazed out of the window, partly because the scenery was not all that familiar – she made few journeys – partly because she did not want to meet Sam's sympathetic eye. It was a hot day and the bus stank of nicotine.

From the Carlisle bus station which served south and west Cumberland, they walked the couple of hundred yards to the bus station which served the north and east. Annie looked out most carefully along their route and Sam helped her identify the chief landmarks: HRH Majestic Theatre and, across the road, just before the turning, the Barley Mow. Annie stood stock-still before both, until she was sure they would not slip from memory.

The next bus they caught had the humiliating, dread name 'Garlands' on its list of destinations. This was a single-decker bus and fuller, in mid-afternoon, than the Wigton bus had been. Annie had kept her head bent as she had arrived in the new station and she kept it low throughout the journey. This time she did not object when Sam paid both fares, too ashamed to look up even at the conductor.

They walked the last half-mile to the lunatic asylum they called Garlands. Sam took Annie by the elbow as they went through the big iron gates and spoke for her at Reception. They had come from the bus, with others, self-absorbed, like a congregation. Visiting hours were narrow and strict. They had arrived a few minutes early and found a seat on a narrow bench with others huddled in a misery of silence.

'You can go in now.' A crisp Sister made the announcement and the visitors heaved themselves resolutely off the benches and made for the ward.

'Ward C,' Sam murmured, just for the sake of saying something.

The disinfectant smelled to high heaven. Depressing dark green tiles. Footsteps on the wooden floors sounded threatening. The beds in the wards close together and spartan. Only about half the inmates had visitors.

Jackie was sitting up, his hair freshly combed, his slim neck looking even smaller in the oversize brown and white striped pyjamas. He gave them a drugged but warm smile.

'There,' Sam whispered, 'he does recognise you.'

That had been one of Annie's greatest fears.

'Now then,' he said.

'Hello, Jackie.'

Annie went first and stood by him, not knowing whether it was allowed to give him a kiss, not accustomed to public show and distrustful of it. So she simply stood her ground and looked down on him.

'Top feed,' he said, looking up at her. 'Three times a day.'

'I've brought two plate cakes. One's from Francis.'

Annie drew the cakes out of a white paper bag, looked for a place to put them, saw the empty, minute side table and put them there.

Then she stood once more in silence.

Jackie looked and then swerved away and caught Sam's eye.

'Ah. That's my pal!'

'That's right, Jackie.'

'That's my marra.'

'That's it.'

'That's my pal.'

'It is.'

'Well. You old bugger.'

Sam took a step forward, bringing him beside Annie. 'I've brought you some fags.'

'Woody Woodbines?'

'Woody Woodbines.'

'We're not allowed to smoke, in here, except under supervision. That's it. All a fiddle.'

Jackie looked from left to right and then a hand darted out for the cigarettes which were pushed deep under the sheets.

'Right up my street,' he said.

'How are you?'

'I just kip, Sam. Mostly I try to kip. Don't stick your neck out in here, you know.'

'Do they look after you?'

'Top feed. Three times a day.'

'You're looking well.'

'That right? Lots of our lads in here, you know. Lots worse than me. Terrible at night time, Sam, when I try to kip. Terrible at night time.'

His worn face, until then so eager and pleased to see his visitors, crumpled in exhausted fear. 'Terrible at night time in here.'

There was a single metal folding chair, green, beside each bed. Sam motioned to Annie to sit down. As she did so, he noticed that her lower lip jutted in front of the upper lip and her eyes glistened from withheld tears. Though the heat was oppressive, she had not un-buttoned her navy-blue coat, loaned her by Mrs Charters and rather too small. In her hands she clasped the empty paper bag which had held the cakes.

'I'll leave you,' said Sam. 'I'll be back before time's up.'

Neither of them registered much. Annie's nod was all but imperceptible. Jackie's head had gone back on his pillow, his mouth had opened, he looked at the ceiling.

Sam strode rather quickly through the low intermittent mur-muring in the ward, down the pungent corridors, back through Reception and out into the grounds – green and flowered and expansive – which would have brought credit to the small country house Garlands had once been. He counted eight men working in the gardens, in the heat, and wondered how many of them were inmates. There was a shaded bench beside a huge burgeoning bush of rhododendrons whose foreign luxuriance and deep and certain reds seemed to flaunt themselves in such a place. He took out a cigarette and tried not to think.

Not to think of the history behind the men confined here. Not to think of those who had cracked up over there. Not to think of Ian, of the children in that village, of the cries, of the wounds, the wounded, the dead. He had to fix his barrier against that and he had thought he was succeeding.

In the distance, two men in army greatcoats, despite the heat, were walking very slowly, very close to each other as if so afraid to walk alone that they had to grasp tight. One of them wore a bush hat. Sam had once thought he might use that dashing Australian hat in civvy street or give it to Joe, but he had done neither. It was still at the bottom of his kitbag. But the romance of it, as he saw now, broad-brimmed, risibly useless for modern combat but fiercely cherished, perfect against the sun as it had been against the tropical downpour, adding glamour to the meanest. The hat itself, never mind the sad ex-soldier supporting it as he edged around the gardens, triggered a cloudburst of memories, so that, for a few moments, Sam felt that he was losing his self-control. Something about the bush hat undammed him.

He stood up and moved away, feeling a coward that he did not go over and talk to the pair so painfully walking and that he did not stay where they would surely pass.

He kept to the paths, although there were no signs about keeping off the grass. He walked quickly and chain-smoked: both helped.

The bell went – a big old school-handbell that rang out the five-minute warning. Half an hour was the allotted time. With the two bus journeys and the waiting between it had taken Annie and Sam the best part of an hour and a half to get there.

He went in as the Sister clanged the bell even more forcefully to announce two minutes to go. Already as he went into Ward C most of the visitors were leaving; more keenly, he noticed – or was he mistaken? – than they had arrived.

There was a slice taken from one of the cakes. Annie pointed to it. Sam smiled. It was some sort of victory.

Jackie now looked fretful. His talk was near babble. Whispered. 'I'm clapped out,' he said, several times. 'Blisters. I'll give you blisters. Big as pancakes. I'm a dead loss.'

'No you're not,' said Annie, without a tremor. 'No you're not.'

The Sister's baying voice replaced the bell and the command had to be obeyed.

'I'll be back next week,' said Annie emphatically. 'This time. Same day. I know the way now.' She reached out her short stubby arm and he grasped it with both of his thin hands. The pyjama sleeves fell back and Sam saw how terribly thin his arms were. Jackie began to shake his head. The Sister was right behind them now.

'Time to go home,' she said. 'Sorry. Time's up. Time to go.'

Sam turned around angrily, but the Sister's smile was full of understanding.

CHAPTER TWENTY-ONE

Joe took careful aim at the solitary tree in the Waste, a narrow spindly thing twisted and slanted and no use for play but a good target for an arrow. He missed and the arrow sped on the bounce into the steps which led up to the house which sold lemonade and made clogs. He tried and failed again with his second arrow. For his final attempt he allowed himself three, quite big, steps forward. This time the arrow glanced off one side of the trunk and Joe felt that Robin Hood was looking down on him with pride.

Sam had taken him to see *The Bandit of Sherwood Forest* and Joe had been Robin Hood and all his Merry Men ever since. Even Blackie had been relegated, though not neglected.

He went to collect the arrows and looked around. He had chosen a good time. Three small girls were playing in the stream. No one else was using this patch this late Saturday afternoon just into the school term. Joe knew that he couldn't be too circumspect now that his protector, Lizzie, had departed for Brindlefield in excitement and tears. He picked up all the arrows and decided to test distance. From the wall at one end of the Waste he shot high towards the wash-houses and with his first arrow he almost made it. The second fell short, but by the third attempt he had taken account and the arrow satisfactorily clattered against the wash-houses, or the walls of Nottingham Castle as they had become.

Happily self-consumed, dodging between the mighty oaks of Sherwood Forest and keeping a sharp eye out for the deer and the Sheriff's men, he trudged across the barren ground, his bow safely slung across his chest. His father had made it for him. He had bought the cane at Stoddarts. He had shown Joe how to slit the ends and bind them with thin string.

The arrows were made from slimmer shafts of cane, again neatly slit at the ends to fit into the bowstring with a twist of wire on the head to give balance. Feathers, Sam said, would make no difference but he had got hold of four from an old set of darts and two of the arrows were plumed in black and gold. Watching his father do this for him, out in the yard, Bella at bay, Kettler passing a word of admiration, had been a good time for Joe, a time which melted some of the fear of his father.

The fear of Speed rose in his gorge like nausea when he saw the older boy saunter onto the Waste, look around, spot one of the arrows by the wash-houses and pick it up. Joe's heart gathered pace. His feet trailed and his legs were watery but he trudged on. Speed noted him and then spied the other two arrows and gathered them up. Joe's head was bowed but he could think of nothing else to do but walk on.

Stand up to him his Daddy had said, whoever it is, stand up to him, you'll only have to do it the once, straight left, catch him on the nose. That'll do it.

Speed was examining the arrows closely. Would he suddenly snap them in two? He was looking even harder than usual. His hair had been convict cut; his pullover was riddled with holes and one of the sleeves barely survived. His pants were patched all over and the big patch on the bum was loose. The shoes were too big. He still looked as angry as a wasp.

'Who made these?' he demanded when Joe stopped a few yards away.

'My Daddy.'

'Let's see that bow.'

Joe took it off and handed it over, which meant he had to draw nearer because Speed did not budge an inch.

Speed studied it minutely. 'It's great,' he said.

He slotted in an arrow and shot it almost directly above him, high in the air, so that the boys screwed up their eyes to follow it, and then it turned and flew down and by a miracle stuck upright and quivering in the mud beside the stream.

Speed turned to Joe and his smile was seraphic. Joe was almost jolted by it, by the surprise of it, by the strength of it. 'Your turn,' said Speed.

Joe's lips were dry. He licked them and took his bow. Speed offered him a feathered arrow. Like Speed, Joe shot directly upwards, into the sky, up towards the clouds, streaking for the blue. And then the arrow turned and sped down and this time it bounced on hard ground and did not stick.

Speed grinned again. 'My turn.'

This time he shot as far as he could across the Waste and the arrow hit the wall at the other side. Again, Speed smiled and picked up an arrow for Joe. 'You,' he commanded.

Joe did not disgrace himself but he did not hit the wall. Speed's next arrow threatened to penetrate it.

The boys set off, Speed going at a trot, to pick up the fallen arrows. Speed collected all three. He looked at Joe, his sharp and pinched features pointed by the force of what he had to say. Joe flinched. Straight left, then move. Don't flinch.

'I wish thy Dad was my Dad,' Speed said. 'You first this time.'

CHAPTER TWENTY-TWO

She was in bed, alone. Sam was on the morning shift. She was in the house alone. Joe and Blackie had gone to spend the weekend with Ruth and his grandfather. He had been engineered there by Ellen. It was past eight o'clock and she had drawn back the curtains to avoid comment. The light was weak. A drizzle had set in. The yard was silent and even beyond: she had to strain to catch a sound from a Water Street now being steadily depleted.

Ellen lay in the middle of the bed and spread out, luxuriating in sole possession, visited by that swirl of sensations, full of colours and warmth, that universe of impressions and fragments of thoughts which at one time – during Sam's absence, while guarding Joe in her bed – had been a steady refuge. Since Sam's return, that dream time had all but disappeared and Ellen had felt the loss of it. Nothing had ever been resolved in those moments as far as she could tell, and she had sought for nothing to be resolved, but she had felt a cradling, a sense of disappearing without terror, a sense of peace.

On this damp, important day, the feeling had come back and she stretched herself slowly, with infinite time, it seemed, rich in drowsiness, hoping this state would not end too soon. Then she fell asleep for a short while and woke up to find it gone. She closed her eyes and stretched again but the mood could not be summoned back. It had visited her and now it had left her and she moved out of the bed reluctantly, as if leaving Joe or Sam unwillingly, and closed the curtains tight, even though her nightdress swept from neck to ankle.

She filled in the nervousness of the morning by going to Grace's house and giving the drawing room an unnecessary, thorough clean.

Sam arrived just after two for his dinner but the afternoon was the wrong time to speak. They had, most unusually, the day to themselves. Sam was tired after his sixth morning shift of the week and Ellen went down to Carlisle with a couple of friends to see *The Blue Dahlia*, while he occupied the bed lately vacated by her. When she returned he was not there but she knew that he was out for a drink or two and would be back for supper. There was a dance on at Thursby and some of their friends were making up a taxi, but Ellen had expressed no eagerness to join them.

Ellen had got hold of two fresh eggs from an old farmer who used the chemist's and had taken something of a fancy to her. There was a sausage each, bought in Carlisle, and a black pudding for Sam only – she hated them. Then there was rice pudding. The conversation did no more than tick along. They drank tea.

She washed and dried and put away a little less rapidly than usual. She had thought about it too much now and she felt apprehensive, though why she should feel like that, part of her thought, when all she was going to do was to talk to her own husband about the future of their lives together now that he had been back a few months and settled in – why she should feel dry-mouthed was silly!

He was reading the paper. She knew that he would put the wireless on soon to hear the Saturday play. She sat across the empty grate from him. Sam's back was to the window and though it was only early evening in early September, the continuing drizzle and the gloom of the yard made the outside almost dark.

She drew the curtains and lit the gas lamp.

The room seemed suddenly very cosy. However cramped and unsettled she felt and always would, there were moments like this when it was theirs, and Ellen wondered why that feeling of possession had to occur at this, precisely the wrong, even the worst, time.

Sam read studiously. Had he sat like that, looked like that, read like that before he went away? Had they talked so little? Had she ever been apprehensive? Never. But had he been like that? As far away at times as Burma itself. Tired, too; gripped by it.

'Now,' he put the paper down and smiled, which wiped the tiredness off his face and brought him back home to her instantly, 'what were you feeding me up for?'

'I'm glad you noticed.'

They smiled at each other. An old familiar smile. Tender courting, the power of physical love. Secret places they had found on their walks. Dances galore. Private jokes. Bicycle rides. Silly quarrels. It was all captured in that smile, but they knew also that the game was on.

His smile broadened. 'And no dance – Joe out and no dance? You? With who is it playing?'

'Billy Bowman.'

'The one and only Billy Bowman! At Thursby. On a Saturday. With a taxi or two being made up. And me caught up on sleep. I don't have to be Sherlock Holmes.'

She took a deep breath and told him about the house. She was scrupulous. The disadvantages had been well-rehearsed and were spelled out, if anything, over-emphatically. The advantages seemed

245

harder to offer. She could not say, there was no way of articulating, that this place in the centre of the old town, built of stone a hundred and fifty years before and built to last more hundreds of years, this solid, solid house had become in her imagination and in her deepest hopes, the very centre of the life she wanted to live as long as she did live. How could a mere building stand for all that? Yet it did. More – should it not be hers, Ellen felt there would be danger: a danger which she would not, could not have described, but which was to her as clear as the expressionless face of Sam himself. He heard her out with no interruption.

'I can't have been in that yard more than two or three times,' he said. 'If that. I remember her. When she used to come shopping. The old style. You felt you had to bow.'

'She was very pleasant.'

'How could you tell?'

'She might have been old style but she was old Wigton as well. It would be a pity if they all died out.'

'Would it?'

'I felt sorry for her. In that house. There weren't cobwebs everywhere but it felt as if there could have been cobwebs everywhere and she was all on her own. For so long. She had a broken heart,' Ellen concluded, rather firmly.

Sam nodded and folded the paper into four and put it beside the fire. 'It's too much,' he said.

'We could borrow.'

'I never thought I'd hear you say that.'

Ellen licked her dry lips. It was a justified comment. 'I could take more on. Leonard seemed to think it would hang around for some time.'

'I bet it will. God knows what's behind that peeling wallpaper.'

246

'We've already something put by, haven't we? From your extra shifts. And my work.'

'I want that to be . . .' Sam faltered. What? At root, a small promise of independence, but from what and how did you explain it? 'That house would eat money.'

'But it would be for something, wouldn't it? It would be for a home.' She wanted him to want it as much as she did but he did not. 'Once we'd got a house like that we would never need anywhere else, never.'

Sam took out a cigarette, lit it and then very quietly said, 'You mean we'd be stuck in Wigton for good.'

'What's wrong with that?'

Could she not tell? Could she not tell from every sign he had given over the past months? So uneasy in his own skin. So stretched beyond endurance by the predictable, repetitious job: with no change in sight, no advancement, no expansion, nothing but the same, flat as an iron, the same. Being the same, doing the same in the same place in the same way with the same men and the same talk and the same lack of expectation and why not if the same was what you wanted, but if not, if you had seen and smelled other worlds, then this same, however friendly and comforting, this every day every way same meant you might as well be dead.

'It's too much,' was all he said. 'Why should we pay £50 to get into an old house when half of Water Street is walking into new homes free?'

'Our names aren't down. Anyway, it's nicer than the new houses,' Ellen said and although she meant it, her words carried little authority.

'It'll cost a fortune to put right.'

'There's no rush. I've said I'll get more work.'

'I don't want you to get more work.'

247

'Until we get settled.'

'It's just a waste of money.'

'Let's put ourselves down for a new council house then.'

'OK, if that's what you want.'

She didn't and both of them knew it.

'I really want this place, Sam,' she said, invoking his Christian name as a sign of her seriousness. 'I really want it.'

She looked at the floor as she repeated the sentence and her hair fell forward, that thick dark hair he loved to touch yet had found few occasions to do so recently, but now he wanted to reach out and stroke it as a way of saying 'I understand'. Because he did understand to his soul the hold this town had on her and her almost helpless need for it, a need greater, perhaps, than for him. Perhaps it was that light stroke of jealous realisation which held back his hand and left the rich glossy hair untouched.

'It's too big,' he said, loudly, kicking his objections back into life by trying a new tack. 'It's far too big for us. We would just rattle around in it. And I'm not taking lodgers. Or travelling salesmen. Grace is as Grace does, but that's no way for me.'

'It's only too big . . .' Ellen hesitated, because there was something forward in what she was about to say, 'if we stay as we are.'

Sam fixed her with blue eyes which had always, when at ease, moved her: but now there was a glint which she did not recognise and, in that slenderest moment, feared. 'You mean have another?'

'Maybe more than one.' She threw her fear back at him.

'I see.'

He bent forward, elbows on knees, hands propping up his head, the hair deep copper in the gaslight. The hiss from that light made the only sound in the room. The pubs were not yet closed and the drizzle had kept the streets empty. Ellen saw that his eyes were tight shut. She noticed, though she had always known, that his hands were quite small for such a strong man. There were freckles on the back of them. It was lucky his face was not freckled, she found herself thinking, so many with red hair suffered from a freckled face.

'I can't do that.'

The words were guttural, as if they all but choked him. Ellen did not recognise where the tone or the sentiment came from. She had never anticipated such beaten, implacable, undiscussed opposition.

'I can't do that, Ellen,' he repeated the words as if to make sure they were heard but the tone and the force stayed the same.

'We'll have to sooner or later.'

'No.'

'Why not?'

Still not looking at her, he rubbed the back of his neck with his left hand, rubbed it hard as if there were a knot of spasmed muscle which had to be loosened. 'Just don't ask,' he whispered.

Ellen tried to sit perfectly still.

Sam sat up, still rubbing his neck, and then his hand dropped. His eyes went right past her.

'I want to,' she said, eventually, the words sounding loud and intrusive. 'And I think we could be happy in that house.'

'Who cares about a house?'

The question came out like a cry.

'Who cares about one place or another? They're just spots to live in. What are we going to do, Ellen, you, me, you and me? That's what matters. Not a house. Not even a town. Not even children!'

His words were increasingly violent, bucking the sentences, but Ellen would not be thrown.

'I say the house would be a fresh start. And I think we should have another child.'

'No!' he said, and he stood up as he spoke, and the single syllable rose with him into a shout. He looked quite wild. He grabbed his jacket and Ellen saw that his arms were trembling as he pushed them into the sleeves.

'Tell me why.'

'No. I can't. No.'

His body seemed to flinch with each word spoken as if a devil were inside him.

'You can't go out.'

'I just – just walk around – no drink. I'll be back. Sorry. Sorry, Ellen. It's not right. I know.'

The look on his face was stricken and desperate and she got up to hold him and chase away all talk of house and money and children and all that ached so invisibly inside him, so visible in his eyes, but he lifted his arm to warn her off before she got near him and hurried for the door, leaving it open as he strode across to the tunnel that would take him away.

Ellen waited. After a while she put on the wireless but both the words and then the music were an interference. She had seen into a blankness of the man she loved and she had no purchase on it. She thought of him raging in his own silence around the dark side alleys and out to the unlit walks he knew well, and she could see the paleness of his face forging through the dark. A chill settled on her which she made no attempt to throw off.

When he did come back she was asleep. So deeply that he boiled the kettle and made tea without disturbing her but woke her up for the tea and they drank it almost scalding hot, commenting on how hot it was. Sam saying he had met only two or three on the streets and they would think he was off to a pub and Ellen wondering aloud if Joe was enjoying his first weekend away.

CHAPTER TWENTY-THREE

August had been the wettest month of 1946 the newspapers had said and September had started no better. At first, Sam had relished the damp overcast summer days, feeling at home, admiring the bloody-mindedness, the sullen independence of a region so long renowned as Arcadia, a honeypot for tourists and yet so unobliging. But the rain could become oppressive and as he looked out of the window of the bus winding between lush hedgerows to Carlisle, he would have traded one or two of the famous Lakes for a week of strong sunshine. He looked south out of the trundling old bus and saw the mountains on the northern frontier of the Lake District pressed down by clouds, the sky unrelieved grey, the fields glittering green, but even the fields prey to low drifting cloud and soaked by the unremitting drizzle. The harvest was feared for, he had read, and it was no wonder. Sam hated this sulk of summer, hated the sense of being trapped under those big loose-bellied clouds which sucked up Atlantic waters and sagged over western Britain, giving no respite.

Sam had been undecided about the Reunion but as the bus crawled into Carlisle, he knew that it was right to come. He had thought that he had had enough of the war. Now, as the bus stopped opposite the museum in Castle Street, he realised that in peaceful ways he wanted it to continue.

He walked up towards the castle almost adopting a brisk march. Carlisle Castle had a picture-book aspect, set on a hill as it had been since Roman times, facing north over the River Eden to confront the barbarous Picts, the Scots, the enemy. Roman captains had fought there and legions from all over Europe had cursed the weather, marooned on this key fortress on the Great Wall, the northernmost limit of the Roman Empire. When Rome fell, Dark Age chieftains, Arthur perhaps among them, used the remains and ruins for their own wars. Later, William the Conqueror's son rebuilt the castle, which became a focus of bloody warfare between the English and the Scots for more than five hundred years. Part of the training had been regimental history and castle history and Sam could still remember it, six years on.

Kings of Scotland had been crowned there and legendary warriors executed there, the ballads recording their bravery and recklessness still sung in Burma. Richard the Lionheart used those Northern Marshes as his training ground and for Wallace and Robert the Bruce and last of all Bonnie Prince Charlie, Carlisle Castle was the first great prize of England. In those wasting wars, the character of the Border warrior had created his own myth and history, one of thieving and torching, of vendetta and treachery but also of loyalty and a terrible harshness. For Border men, fighting was the only life available for centuries. Sam was proud still that Carlisle Castle had sent out regiments all over the Empire trained to engage in battle without cowardice, men and boys, and win or die in the very thick of it as they had, as was testified by banner after tattered banner in the medieval cathedral built partly out of stones from the Roman fortress.

There were others moving towards the castle, but for a few

moments Sam kept to himself. He picked up the march coming from the regimental band inside the walls and time went on hold. He knew, and years in the army had ground it into him, that warfare was boredom and waiting for weeks for a spasm of fear and desperate action. He knew that soldiering was tedious, knew homesickness and resentment at stupid decisions and foul conditions and that mindless nit-picking disciplines were endemic. He knew the weary load of war. But in that moment, on the way from the bus to the castle, with the regimental band sounding crisp in the damp air, he saw how much it had given him and how much he had so willingly given back. The bonding beyond friendship with men whom you might not even like very much but for whose life you would risk your life, knowing it would be done in return. The knowing without words that when split seconds mattered, utter reliance could be placed on the man beside you and should you fall he would stay with you. That loving, if he could use such a word, of those who had survived with you the slaughter of an encounter which you had survived only because of them. The being a unit, eight, nine or ten men intent on one object with a ferocity of purpose which could only come when sudden death was the imminent alternative.

And beyond that unit, other units, companies, battalions, the army, a mass of mankind, each man different yet sacrificing that difference to a greater purpose and, Sam thought, as he stretched his stride and remembered the deaths and remembered the evil, a fine purpose. He had been part of that. Grown, enlarged, crowned in that. No forgotten army here. A life which in some essential way it would be hard to measure up to outside. And there had been a liberty also. However unlikely and contradictory it seemed, he had at times felt a full free man for the first time in his life.

'You old bugger!'

'Doug!'

'You were off with the fairies.'

'I was.'

The Reunion was under way.

The men had been asked to turn up at ten a.m. and the air was chill inside the solid sandstone walls. The band was playing non-stop as if music would warm the place up. Sam arrived some minutes ahead of time. He felt odd, in that place, out of uniform. Some men had brought their bush hats but, Sam noticed, one or two took them off and held them. Maybe later.

A sergeant major announced that breakfast was served and they trooped into the dining hall where the first treat met them. The meal was what they had eaten in Burma – bacon, beans, porridge, bread and unlimited tea. When the men saw this they cheered. After they had sat down at the trestle tables, each one was presented, by new recruits, with a plate on which was placed, like a delicacy, the timeless staple item of British fighting men – hard tack, a small, square half-biscuit, half-oatcake. On each square was a cube of bully beef. Scarcely one of the men had not vowed never to eat hard tack again, but scarcely one now resisted it. With hard tack the Reunion really began.

The Hindustani words which they had made their own were emphasised and over-employed. Who had any mallum these days? And how many bints had Dacre had – he had sworn he'd have a dozen before Christmas. That chota wallah over there had made the best char west of Rangoon but even char could not beat chaggle water, brackish, life-saving chaggle water. They ate their bait and took a dekko at the connor, lamented the pani and laughed at goolie stories and klifty stories and tik hai, they said, all right, good, tik hai. Words from halfway across the world latticed them together.

The day was, of course, organised to a 't', which most of the men took nostalgic enjoyment in. It was also made perfectly clear by those in charge that no one had to join in the activities, even though they were bullied into them in a friendly way. Tug-of-war teams were announced without consultation and a five-a-side football competition was set up – for this they were allowed to pick their own teams – and there were other games, but Sam drifted down to the shooting range, drawn by an urgent desire to get his hands on a Lee Enfield once again. Sam had been classified as a first class shot (the top-notch was one up – the marksman). He had loved his Lee Enfield. Ten rounds. Experienced men could fire at such speed that it was like automatic fire and yet every single shot was aimed and the extreme range was a mile. A few brave new recruits were throwing the plates into the air.

As Sam waited patiently for his turn, he felt released. It was topsy-turvy: in the civilian world, free to come and go as he pleased or could afford, endowed with all the opportunities Blighty had seemed so full of when viewed from beyond the Indian Ocean, he felt trapped; here, in the quasi-regimentation, he acknowledged that service had given him a certain freedom. His duty, his work, his goal – all these had been decided for him. There had been no options. Yet this straitjacket had liberated energies inside his mind. With the Lee Enfield snuggled into his shoulder and the intrepid young lads hurling plates into the air, he was brushed again by that inexplicable sense of freedom.

Sam's best show had been three out of five at a distance of two hundred yards. Three out of five. Still not a marksman.

'You won't recognise me.'

It was said almost with bravado.

Sam, invited to stare, stared. What he saw was a severely

emaciated man, cheekbones threatening the skin, his clothes so loose they were, painfully, like the oversized suit of a clown.

'There's others put it on. It doesn't seem to take with me. Doctor says time will cure all.'

He grinned and the skull seemed to dissolve the skin.

'It's Harry,' said Sam.

'Of course it's Harry.'

'I heard you'd been captured.'

'Surrendered. Not my decision.' Harry grinned again. Sam wished that he did not find it so disconcerting.

'We were—'

'Solo whist. I won a packet.'

'Fifteen quid?'

'Nearer seventeen.' Harry's saucer eyes rolled in their deep sockets. 'Never had a pay-day like it.'

'Early on, wasn't it?'

'Before Imphala. I was sorry to miss that. I'd liked to have laid it on the Japs. Invincible! Inhuman, Sam, sub-human you ask me, animals. I could tell you. I was four stone. Still only five and a half. And I was one of the lucky ones, Sam. I've seen things done.' He shook his head. 'You and me were pals.'

The statement was so forlorn that Sam had no idea how to reply. He looked at the suffering man before him and he could feel the residue of fear and humiliation and the injustice. To have held on for years in the brutality of a Japanese prisoner-of-war camp and to survive: to cross half the world and survive: and still, months on, to be this gaunt ghost of times best forgotten, a spectral reminder, marked out as the man who had been starved almost to death by the cruel thwarted soldiers of the Empire of the Rising Sun.

'I hope we still are pals.'

'Wigton's too far from Whitehaven,' Harry said. 'I kept meaning to come through. There's three of you out that way. But it seems to take such a lot to gather myself together.'

'TIFFIN!' called out the sergeant major.

'I eat,' said Harry. 'I can eat.'

They went in together. It was bully beef, biscuits and tinned fruit, but the bully beef was supplemented by potatoes and carrots and gravy and the biscuits, donated by a local firm, included creams, the tinned fruit came with condensed milk and there was beer and two packets of twenty Players' cigarettes neatly stacked by each plate.

The more Harry ate and talked, the less Sam could eat or talk. It was not only Harry's condition, not even his obsessive references to his condition and the cause of it, but there had been an aspect, perhaps a single movement of his skull, which had transferred Sam to the cinema in Meeting House Lane where, some weeks before, he had seen footage of the concentration camps. The sight had simply numbed and drowned his senses. That this had been done. He had heard something about it but they were so far away deep in their own battle, their own atrocities, and the Germans from the First World War had seemed not too terrible, clean deep trenches, singing carols, ordinary men like British ordinary men. But then they did this. Systematically. On that scale. He and Ellen had come out into the Lane as if into an unreal world because what they had seen was so real. How did you deal with that fact and that knowledge and with those who had with foreknowledge been party to that fact?

Harry had hooked on to Sam and monopolised him.

'You can have my beer,' said Harry. 'I can't get the taste for it back.'

'Thanks.'

The word came out as through cotton wool.

Sam drank for the two of them. The cadets serving the beer had been ordered to be generous.

Harry's talk was stopped when Colonel Oliphant – MC and Bar, twice wounded, much liked – rapped the table and said that he did not want to spoil their fun and there was more laid on including the tug-of-war and Housey-Housey, but he would just like to say a few words.

First, though, he was sure that before anything was said they would all want to observe a minute's silence for their comrades and friends who had been killed, who had not come back from Burma. The Kohima epitaph said it all:

'When you go home, tell them of us and say

'For your tomorrow we gave our today.'

The men stood. The instant massed silence was a sound of its own. Most bent their heads. Memories rose up like prayer. Time slowed, all but stopped.

'Thank you,' he said, and allowed the men to sit down and settle and the mood to ease. Then he began.

Important to keep in touch. Essential to look with pride on what we did together. Forgotten Army? Let history take care of that. They knew what they had done. Churchill's Hellespont. Attlee on Slim. (All cheered.) 'Slim was the chap . . . he made do with the scrapings of the barrel.' (More cheers.) Some scrapings – ask Jap! (Cheers and banging on tables.) Fourteenth Army had stopped in its tracks the great Japanese army which had swept through China and Malaya and Burma and was a whisker away from India, which it would have devoured. They were part of that. Others too. Many nationalities. Fair play. But this great county regiment from a remote island off the European mainland had taken the battle to the enemy on the main-land of Asia and won. Never forget that. Won. I salute you, he concluded.

And Colonel Oliphant together with the other officers who had quietly fallen in behind him, drew themselves to attention and saluted their men.

There was a pause, it was almost a shock, and then the men clapped and then stood and then someone called for three cheers and they cheered. Many thousands of miles away from the battlefields where so many of their comrades lay buried, they cheered what had passed and sang 'For he's a jolly good fellow'.

—⟋⟍—

The beer began to flow.

Harry latched on to someone else and Sam quelled his guilt at being relieved and, fortified by the beer, went to seek out Metcalfe.

Alex (for Alexander) Metcalfe was the son of a schoolteacher, who had himself just begun as a primary schoolteacher when war broke out. He was Sam's exact contemporary in Wigton, but he moved in a different circle, although they had met at the cycling club. Alex had failed to become an officer and dropped all ambition for authority. He was, Sam thought, the best-educated private east of Bombay. Although Alex was scrupulous in taking his orders from Sam and never let past familiarity muddy the military relationship, Sam could still find it a bit difficult, especially when things were slack, to give him commands. This was compounded by Alex's willingness to talk and to listen to what Sam felt were his uneducated, under-informed opinions and to reinterpret them and return them as new lamps for old.

Sam had spotted him at the Reunion early on but had been too diffident to seek him out. He had heard that Alex had taken up a post in a village school four miles out of Wigton but he had not come across him since his return. When he saw him, Sam realised how much he wanted to speak to him. It was almost like a yearning. Yet he felt diffident. He had always believed that Alex gave him much more than he had ever been able to give Alex in return. And their friendship – it could be called that – had been underpinned by necessity: that was now in the past.

'So what do you make of it all, Sam?'

Sam smiled. Typical. A question. Still the slim face, fair thin hair that looked rather foppish even though short, a beaky or, at a pinch, an aquiline nose and the cigarette held rather daintily.

What was the correct answer?

'I thought I wouldn't much care for it.'

'But you do?'

Sam nodded.

'Make you want to join up again?'

For a few moments back there, Sam had indeed entertained that idea. He shook his head.

'It did cross my mind. But – no. You?'

'Not for all the tea in China, old boy. Let's cut games and enjoy the view.'

He led, reversal of roles, and Sam followed, up one of the sets of steps which steeped up to the ramparts. The moist day was warm and a light haze veiled any long views but it was pleasant on the ramparts, it felt airy and commanding.

'What did you think of Oliphant's speech?'

'I liked it.' Sam knew that he sounded over-emphatic.

'So did I. Oliphant's one of the good eggs. Do you remember when he sang that dirty song at the concert? I like an officer who's prepared to make a fool of himself. It's important that those set in authority over us make fools of themselves. At one time, kings and noblemen would set aside a day when they were the servants and the servants their masters. We have a lot to learn.'

'Fag?'

Alex took a cigarette and the men cupped their hands to light up.

'I'm thinking of pushing off,' he said.

'It's a bit early.'

'From England. From Blighty. From here.'

'Where to?'

'Dunno. What I'd like to do is just swan around the world but that needs more pounds, shillings and pence than I can muster.'

'What's brought this on?'

'A severe case of the browned-off, but by what it's hard to say. A case for Professor Freud, I presume. Nothing specific; is anything ever specific? Country might be going in the right direction. Job's fine; kids half-civilised and parents pleasingly impressed by the little knowledge of a local schoolteacher. Love life a bit of a dud, but I suspect that's my fate, if we can use such a mighty word. Dunno. How have you settled back?'

'Not bad.'

Something in Sam's mind acted like a portcullis and slammed down instantly against the mass of disquiet which threatened to spill out. He had grown used to answering Alex's questions honestly.

'You're *married* of course. And Joe. The family bond. Can't beat it. Don't know you're born.'

'Sometimes, Metcalfe, I have my doubts about you.'

Alex smiled. His teeth were nicotine-stained, but the smile was infectious.

'Remember meeting those Australian lads?'

'Yes. There was one had come from round here.'

'Dixon. From Aikhead. Frank Dixon. I've been thinking about them.'

261

Sam conjured them up immediately. He had liked their similarity to the Border lads and yet their unmistakable difference. They were tough. They were humorous. They were every bit as cynical as the Cumbrian lot. But something else.

'There was something of the sun about them,' said Alex. 'Just as there is something of the cloud about us. Climate and character: could be connected. Did you talk to them much?'

'Not a lot.'

'I talked to a couple of them. I've been trying to put my finger on it. Everybody was "mate". Everybody with us was "marra". But we meant something personal. Only personal. They meant something political or social, I can't put my finger on it. Something much bigger. Don't you feel hemmed in here, Sam? I'm not talking about your family, excuse that, but just hemmed in? Despite the changes which we're told are going on, it's the same old grey weight pressing down on us and keeping us in our place and keeping us away from exercising any real influence. Oh, this is rot! Probably it's just the weather. Give me sun and sea and the devil take the hindmost.'

'There was something about them,' Sam said, carefully. 'I think it was that they felt they had a real stake. The sky was the limit. It was their place. It was a new place and they were going to get stuck into it and nothing would stop them.'

'What stops you?'

'What I don't know,' Sam replied, rather sadly, and Alex regretted his flippancy. 'What I never learned.'

'It wouldn't stop an Aussie. I mean it. They would say – well, that's the way I am, mate, and too bad if it doesn't suit the system. The system will have to change. That's what an Aussie would say. That's what anybody with gumption would say after travelling twelve thousand miles to set up a new life. Once you set off to start a new life – why should you rest until you've got the new life you want? The whole point is that you've cut yourself off from your old life, from everything about the old life, all the good stuff as well as all the bad stuff, all the tradition that's been hard won as well as all the inheritance that crushes the life out of you – you start again on a continent so big you could tuck England in a corner of it and never stumble across it again. You can be God. You can make your own life the way you want it. Out of Egypt!'

Alex stopped. He had been carried away – not something he cared for in others and a lack of control he positively detested in himself.

'I think I'm rather keen on this Australian business,' he said. 'We can get there free, which has to be attractive, hasn't it? Or ten pounds, is it? For all the family?'

Sam nodded. He knew about the assisted passage scheme to Australia. When it had been announced, it seemed almost half the ex-servicemen in the town were going – if not to Australia, then to Canada, New Zealand, Tasmania, anywhere far away, unknown, not England. Sam had never seriously entertained the idea, but Alex's words set him alight. It was staring him in the face.

'Quite a lot of the lads are doing it,' Alex said, burying his singularity. 'They tend, to my untutored eye, to be some of the boldest and best of our crop. Or maybe just want to run away from it all. You know? Live to fight another day. Slough off the old skin of corrupt old Europe. Fresh fields, Sam. How about you?'

'I'd have to think about it.'

He was too overwhelmed with the prospect to let any of it slip away in unprepared conversation.

'Thinking slows you down,' said Alex, looking north towards what for so long had been enemy territory. 'I should know. I fear I may have exhausted the Australian in myself by thinking. Or maybe thinking was enough. Still I intend to make the first moves next week.'

'Soon as that?'

Sam felt a pang of prospective regret. They had just met again after months apart. He had just begun the usual rather lengthy business of letting Alex have as much rope as he pleased before attempting to haul him in to some point on which he needed illumination. He would miss that.

'Maybe I'm dignifying the whole thing,' said Alex. 'Or romanticising, an old Northern fault. Maybe it is just running away.'

'There's a time for that,' Sam replied. 'Often enough you have to run away—'

'To fight another day.'

'We did.'

'We did.' Alex plucked out a cigarette from his packet and offered it to Sam. Again he lit both. 'It's over though, isn't it, surely, war? The bomb's done for it, don't you think?'

Sam took his time.

'Not as long as there's something to be gained by it.'

'Who wins when atom bombs wipe everybody out?'

'I remember those Japs charging at us covered all over in hand grenades. They knew they were going to blow themselves up. Didn't stop them.'

'War is madness, yes. Made by bad men. Hitler certainly. Mussolini. Tojo.'

'Tojo was a fanatic,' Sam said. 'Isn't there a difference?'

'It's a fine line,' Alex laughed. 'I'm damned if I can draw it. You'll have to consult a philosopher, Sam. But one thing is for sure – since those poor shivering Romans were stationed on this wall, war hasn't changed a lot. Sieges? Look at Stalingrad and Kohima. Lines of battle?

264

Well, look at the trenches and we were forever drawing lines in Burma, weren't we? Rivers were our lines. Bigger armies? Grant you that. And more of the population involved. Long-range weapons – guns and bombs – that's probably the only big difference. The fellows on these walls knew that all this equipment was just an introduction to the real business of hand to hand. That's changed.'

'Not in Burma it hadn't.'

'I realised that the moment the words came out of my mouth.' Alex looked directly into his former corporal's hard blue eyes and turned away.

'I never thanked you enough for that,' he said.

'It was over in a second. The whole thing was a shambles.'

'I still see the little bugger and his bayonet. I froze. I still wake up in a sweat. I'd had it. Yes.' He paused. 'Thanks for that.'

'It was a shambles. So where do you find out about this Australian caper?'

Alex told him. Sam made a note.

The band struck up again.

'The Last Waltz,' said Alex. 'Mustn't keep our public waiting.' After a final dainty drag on his cigarette, he threw it over the ramparts and accompanied Sam down the deep stone steps and onto the parade ground for the end of the Reunion.

It was Doug who started it all but nobody would admit that. Doug had never been easy. Sam and he had eyeballed each other several times in Burma before the fight which had seen Sam busted, but after that Doug had quietened down and taken Sam's orders.

The problem Doug had was that deep in his gut and his whole

being was the imperative to disobey. If anyone said, do this! – especially a command – then Doug's immediate responses were either, no, or why pick on me? Or a torrent of foul and abusive language. He was also a compulsive thief, second nature, no hard feelings and often of objects he had no use for and could not turn over. In the small town almost smack on the line of the English-Scottish Border in which he had been brought up – 'dragged up more like,' he boasted – he was feared when sober and best avoided when drunk, which was as often as he could lay his hands on cash. He had spent much of his training in the glasshouse for offences that several times threatened his ejection from the army, but they had held on to him and, as time went on, he held on to the regiment. He had not the slightest hesitation in going for his awesome Gurkha knife if anyone outside the regiment whispered a syllable of criticism of it. After their dust-up and when eventually Sam got his stripes back, he was asked whether he wanted Doug in his section. There was no question – you wanted Doug on your side.

Doug bought a loaf of bread. In fact he bought two rather stale end-of-the-day loaves, but the first one he tore through and wolfed down to soak up some of the beer. Most of that particular gang which had roared out of the castle and into the town were well-oiled. Sam's section was much in evidence: not only Doug but Titch (well over six feet tall), who had been with them during the last fifteen months of the war, and Spud (because his face looked like one), whose passion had been for cheroots. Alex had slid off towards the cathedral. 'Never miss an opportunity to see medieval misericords,' he had said as he had woven off into the Close. Sam had thought to follow him, but felt embarrassed to intrude and anyway what did he know and therefore care about medieval misericords and by that time the tide had carried him forward. They were headed for the town centre with its old cross and medieval town hall and the streets were still quite busy, late-afternoon shoppers and strollers and those with nowhere in particular to go and no money to spend.

Doug passed the loaf to the next man who had asked for a bite. But he passed it as if he were passing a rugby ball. That simple flick of the wrist went through the unit like an electric current. He in turn passed it to the next man, who broke into a run, dummied a smiling shopper and then passed on along what had developed into a line. And on to the next man, who was forced well into the road and swerved round a car before racing ahead past the august Crown and Mitre Hotel, lodging of judges for the Assizes and host to the gentry, and into the town centre where a large triangular patch of traffic-free pavement became, for a few minutes, a miniature rugby pitch. Two sides emerged and the game was on.

The tackles gave no quarter and the men crunched to the hard ground. The beer cushioned the bruises and whipped up the excitement. They yelled for the ball, the loaf, skidded, slipped and one or two could really play, dummied, scissored, forced their way over the line. The pedestrians scattered about good-naturedly and soon there was a small, cheering, clapping crowd and one policeman scratching his head – held back from a policing decision by his own interest in the match.

When it spread beyond the triangular patch it was clear that someone had to call a halt but no one wanted to. Sam, carrying an injured shoulder which he had collected in the road and which would stiffen up badly in the morning, was far too involved to care and yet someone must have sensed that they were turning into a riot because the game slowed down, the men looked up and saw a bus driver laughing at them but banging on his horn to get through and, in the other direction, almost half a dozen cars waiting, patiently enough, but waiting.

267

Scenting danger, Doug put two fingers in his mouth and let out a whistle which could have been heard back at the castle.

'Opening time!'

He led them across to the Crown and Mitre.

The loaf of bread, or what was left of it, lay in the gutter only for moments before stray dogs found it.

To the rear of the Crown and Mitre was a public bar, usually approached by the back entrance. It was the hotel's concession to the populace. For the Crown and Mitre, site of smart dinners and lavish coming-out parties, watering-hole of the county set and as liveried, embossed and enslaved in hotel pomp and ceremony as any grand hotel in the land, made it plain from scarlet doormen to a cute capped bellboy that this was not the place for the hoi poloi. The hoi poloi agreed.

Doug decided on the direct assault.

The doorman was about to offer a protest and then he caught Doug's eye and decided to concentrate on his feet as more than a dozen dishevelled men, who had been tidily dressed and sober citizens at the beginning of the day, walked in a well-behaved manner through the majestic lobby – portraits of judges, Lakeland landscapes, a wide burnished-oak staircase and an acreage of faded but still impressive maroon deep-piled carpet – conscious of being out of place but happy with the lark. Doug began to sing, 'See what the boys in the back room will have and tell them to bring me the same', and two or three others who had also seen the Marlene Dietrich film joined in, which was probably a mistake as it attracted the attention of those in the hushed tea room who would have been oblivious to them but now looked up and saw what they feared might be the Peasants' Revolt.

The men packed out the small, ill-furnished bar. The drinks rolled in, the stories unwound, the singing was just getting properly under way when three policemen arrived and took down everyone's name with much licking of the stubs of pencil.

Two weeks later they were fined, one pound.

Disorderly conduct.

The magistrate said he was being lenient because of the service these men had given to their country but they had to be reminded that they were now part of a civilian population in a peaceful country. He had been much impressed by the statement from Colonel Oliphant: otherwise the fine would have been far heavier.

It was a story Sam liked to tell over. He did not mind seeing his name in the papers in such gallant company and Grace's displeasure was, privately, enjoyed.

With growing eagerness, he was looking through the material on Australia, its newness, the sun.

CHAPTER TWENTY-FOUR

The squatters came to Scott's Yard in the half light and by the morning the boards had been ripped down, meagre furniture moved in and the smoke from the chimney confirmed defiant possession. There were four children in the family and they were soon in the small inner yard and in and out of the lavatory. Bella was frightened and retreated inside her house.

When Joe went through the yard on his way to school, the squatters' children stopped what they were doing, stood still and stared. No sound came from them until he had passed by. They treated Ellen in exactly the same way although she smiled and said hello. Sam had left for work before their arrival and when he came back early in the afternoon, the children were gone.

The next morning the two other empty and boarded houses in Scott's Yard were taken over by squatters, again with large families, again silent and antagonistic.

'No wonder,' Sam said. 'The poor beggars have been living like animals for months. No wonder.'

They were from a town almost twenty miles away and they had walked, pushing their goods on an improvised cart, having heard of the Water Street clearance. Over the next two weeks, as Water Street continued to filter up to Brindlefield, squatters struck down the flimsy council boards again and again. By the time the first batch of Water Street families – sixteen – had all moved and a halt was called until the next lot of houses was finished, they had been replaced and although the squatters were in a minority in the street, they were a world unto their own – outlawed, resentful, fearful that they would be thrown out.

Ellen was tormented by her reaction. She wanted to see everyone as nice, decent people, all with something to be said in their favour except in the most extreme cases. Here, though, she could not force down her alarm and her dislike. She disliked her new neighbours in Scott's Yard – all of them, parents and children both. It was not uncommon for people to be careless over cleanliness, but the squatters had a matted-haired, grime-ingrained-clothing, dirt-caked-limbed filth which it needed only water to remove. Nor did they ever yield to a friendly greeting. Silent animosity was their trademark.

Ellen had a new sense – which she fought, but unsuccessfully – that nothing was safe, that houses should be locked. The door of the lavatory was broken but it was no use trying to find the culprit, although it was obvious that the blame lay with the new families. Being themselves unsettled, they seemed to be hell-bent on unsettling others. Ellen felt the unaccustomed and disconcerting beat of envy – against her and Joe and Sam because of their 'real' home, and Sam's good job. The squatters themselves cut turf down on the moss.

Ellen could not deal with this corrosive envy. She had been fashioned by her anonymous ordinariness, her normality. She had shaped herself to that as a sapling is shaped straight being lashed to a pole. It disturbed her that she should be envied because that made her someone who stood out, which she had never wanted. How could she stand out, be superior even, be exposed as having advantages? She,

272

who in her heart had grounded her life in the religion of her unyielding ordinariness, in having 'nothing', like everybody else. Being exposed put her in some sort of danger which she could neither fathom nor articulate but only feel. She had always known where she stood, where she was. The squatters had upset all that, broken that compact between her self and the outside world.

The other almost shameful cause of her unease, which she could only half-admit even to herself but knew it and fought it and lost, was that they were strangers. It was culpably intolerant, but one of the things that had helped her survive her childhood lack of parents, which even now she could remember only with pain, had been to see the town and the people in it as the familiar security. Grace was rather cold, Leonard now and then full of rather uneasy play but much more often aloof, about his own business, taking his cue from Grace. But the town was always there. The town for Ellen was a secret addiction, a need, only revealed when it seemed in danger of being removed. Now that Water Street, her part of it, had become a foreign place, she wanted more each day to live in that big old house, secure in the cobbled yard, planted deep in the town.

Yes, said Leonard, when he saw her, it's still on the market.

She contrived to go and look at it, even just a quick furtive glimpse, on most days, as the weight of the squatters turned her hope into a lust for the place. It was terrible: she could think of nothing else.

Australia dominated Sam. He saw the beaches, he could smell the ocean, he breathed widely into that vast space, already he loved the sun and wanted to do battle with a new life in a country which could be his as England, he feared, would never be. If he felt more free, more energetic and full of greater hope just thinking about it – how much more was there to win by going there!

It would be action. It would be taking his life in his own hands and risking it for himself and for Ellen and Joe.

He recognised, after Alex had lit the blue touchpaper, that the Australian move had something of the same initial liberation about it he had felt on joining the army.

He wanted it so badly that he kept it from Ellen, hoarding it, guarding it, feeding it, waiting until it was ready and the moment was ripe.

Yet it was difficult not to talk about it to someone. He had biked through to Aikhead to see Alex but the schoolteacher had been out and the family he lodged with, a retired solicitor and his wife, had been a little supercilious, enough to deter Sam from a second visit. He would surely see him on the streets of Wigton at the weekend. But Alex failed to show on the Saturday afternoon when, he had told Sam at the Reunion, he sometimes came in for a game of billiards. Sam hung around the streets for almost an hour.

Mr Kneale spotted him and invited him back for tea. The younger man found it impossible to turn down the invitation even though the prospect rather depressed him. It was like a command. A social command but still a command and Sam responded obediently even though he had sworn that after the war he would be done with commands. He knew what Mr Kneale wanted and was not surprised when, after Alison, a new young girl Grace had taken on part-time, had brought them tea, the schoolteacher pulled out a notepad.

'I have a list here of several – not all – of the Wigton men who returned from Burma,' Mr Kneale announced, raising a large round teacup which almost obscured his small round face. His little finger stiffened upwards to attention as the cup met the mouth. 'Some of them are in quite a bad way as you know. Poor Mr Donnolly's consumption – they've put him in a bed on stilts so that he can see out of the window – the boys play football in the field. And Jackie you know about. Gilbert Little tells me . . .'

The voice went on and Sam switched off. Could Mr Kneale be someone to seek advice from about Australia? It was no good going to Leonard. He was a little soft on Ellen, Sam knew that well, and he would want to keep her in Wigton. Mr Kneale similarly was keen on Ellen but surely an educated man ought to be capable of a dispassionate view.

How could he frame the question?

'I'm in touch with the Castle of course and they tell me that there is already at least one book underway on the Campaign. That will be the strategy and tactics of it. I want a more human perspective.'

Could he ask – 'What do you think about Australia, Mr Kneale?' Or would it be better to be more direct. 'I've decided to go to Australia – what do you think?' Any question would do.

'When first we talked about your experiences,' Mr Kneale looked grave and behind the tortoiseshell spectacles the eyes softened with the sympathy of a mourner, 'and I know how painful it can be – but what you said was very graphic, Sam, you have a way of describing the really ordinary Tommy's point of view and that's what I'm after with you fellows. So—'

'Some of the lads were thinking of pushing off to Canada,' said Sam, picking up his cup. The tea was almost cold; he was embarrassed drinking it. 'Or New Zealand, or even Australia.' He drank the unappetising liquid, draining the cup in two gulps.

'Wholly mistaken in my view,' said Mr Kneale, severely. 'Nothing more than a romantic delusion. You'll see them haring back faster than they ran away. If they can't buckle down here, why should they buckle down in Canada – or in Timbuctoo for that matter?'

Sam nodded and replaced the cup in the saucer, taking inordinate care over this simple action.

'I have to push off soon,' he said.

'This needn't take long,' said Mr Kneale, and that beatific smile for Sam announced a sentence that had to be served. Courtesy was law. He took a clean sheet of paper.

Sam clenched his mind. No one would be told what had really happened. Not Mr Kneale. Not Ellen, and if he could help it, not even himself. The nightmares were less frequent. As long as he kept busy. Australia would see all that left behind. The sight of those bodies would not follow him there.

'It was the mud was the worst,' he began, thinking of golden beaches and blue oceans.

—⚬—

'I never approved of Water Street in the first place.' Grace felt vindicated.

'There's nothing wrong with Water Street,' Ellen countered. 'The squatters have changed it a bit but I'm sure there's nothing wrong with the squatters either.'

'Try sending any squatters down here to Market Hill and see what happens,' said Grace. 'The band will play, I'll tell you that. They should be sent back.'

'But they have nowhere.'

'That's no reason to break into houses and work on public sympathy.'

Ellen held her tongue. She had not sought out Grace to discuss squatters.

'All I said was that I thought the house might suit us.'

'I know you,' said Grace, triumphing in what she saw as Ellen's capitulation to reality. 'You want out of Water Street.' Grace smiled broadly. They were in her kitchen. It was a Sunday afternoon, but despite that Joe had been encouraged to go out to his old haunts and see if he could find one or two other lax Christian children to play with. His protracted absence indicated success.

'It's a fine house,' said Ellen.

'Leonard's told me all about it.' This was not altogether true but Grace had nosed out a secret pact and would not be seen to be left out. 'He says there's a bit of damp.'

'Not much. I'm sure it's neglect more than anything else.'

'It's very big.'

'Not as big as this.'

'This is exceptional,' said Grace. 'Leonard says it's gloomy.'

'It could be made lighter.'

'It's certainly better than anything Water Street has to offer.'

There's nothing wrong, Ellen said to herself, with Water Street, but she said it to herself.

'How will you get the money?'

'Uncle Leonard said it could drop a bit. There's been very little interest.'

'There's been none at all. Doesn't that worry you?'

'No.'

'It should. Never take tea in an empty café. Leonard's mother told me that.'

How can I tell her how much I want this place? When it came down to it, Grace was the only one she could talk to on such an emotional and family matter and yet she could not talk to Grace in any way approaching the way she felt. Would a mother have been

277

different? Surely. Surely. And a father? Even more so. Surely. You wouldn't even have to mention it. They would know. They would understand the real reason. Not a flight from Water Street, much as she still, despite all efforts, disliked her dark, poky, inconvenient and unprepossessing home there – one up one down leading to nowhere. It was a flight *to* somewhere. To a real future, uninterrupted, with her own place in the town for ever.

'Have you talked to Sam about it?'

'Once.'

'And?'

'He wasn't that keen.'

'Men know nothing about houses. Somewhere to eat, somewhere to sleep, somebody to cook and wash for them – it could be a palace, it could be a chicken shed, they'd notice no difference. Does the money bother him?'

'That's part of it.'

'It always is. But that asking price will come down – Leonard says that and I'll give Leonard this, he knows his Wigton property. But there's more than that, isn't there?'

Grace's tone softened in that last sentence. Ellen was caught off guard. For a moment she was about to confess everything. Such relief to describe the silences and clashes. The anger at not being able to talk openly even to each other. Neither of them, since Sam's return, had found it possible to talk about what mattered most to them. The recent past had padlocked the deepest emotions.

Ellen longed to break that lock.

'Marriage is not a bed of roses,' said Grace, encouragingly. 'I could tell you things. Take the lid off this town and you'll find damnation right left and centre. I could name names. You've always been too head-in-the-air. You don't like to believe the worst. I say the worst is what's what. I know a couple who've never exchanged a word for more than thirty years and there's others nearly as bad. I know women knocked about and things that would make your eyes pop out of your head even in the highest society, so the ups and downs of married life is not a secret.'

Ellen knew all that but she did not like to admit it. Even more when it concerned Sam. It would be letting him down. To talk about him truthfully would be to betray him. It was just not possible.

'It isn't that,' she said.

Grace's face registered disappointment. She had put out a hand, she thought. All that Ellen had to do was offer something up. A little would have done. Nothing at all was almost an insult.

'You can put the kettle on,' she said. 'Leonard and Mr Kneale should be back from their little outing about now.'

The squatters did not bother Joe. This might have been because of a visit to Scott's Yard the evening of their arrival by Speed and his two older brothers looking for a fight. Joe had been playing with Speed when the notion had come to Al, the eldest brother, now running wild since Jackie's incarceration and openly threatened with a spell in Borstal. The mother of one of the squatters' families had bidden her sons into the house. The last thing they wanted was trouble of any sort. But the territorial point had been made. The brothers ran around the yard whooping and yelling for a while to ram it in.

Perhaps, though, the children of the squatters were just not interested in fighting. They were rowdy and louder than the girls who had previously dominated the yard, yet they were easily called off with one shout from their perpetually angry mother. Certainly Joe walked through the yard with no fear, which was unusual for Joe.

Bella, though still a problem, was now much subdued. She did feel afraid of the squatters. Their newness and the new crop of jibes and taunts and insults upset her. And she was obsessed with Blackie, now growing rapidly and with every inch claiming just a little less attention from its owner. In order to see Blackie and to hold him and be allowed to cuddle him for a circuit of the tiny yard, she knew that she had to be careful with Joe; and cunning, because Joe could be cruel, she thought.

Twice already in that week he had refused to bring Blackie out for her to play with. It did not occur to Bella that the boy was in a hurry to be in the house for as quick a bite as possible and out again to be back on the Waste, which had become a real playground. For Joe, in that mood, every minute's hold-up was unacceptable.

But when he came back from picking rose-hips with Sadie he felt expansive. Sadie had borrowed his mother's bike, plonked him on the carrier seat and cycled deep into the Solway Moss to a place she had heard of through the sister of one of the turf cutters. Rose-hips galore, unlike, as Sadie reminded Joe more than once, his sterile outing with Mr Kneale, which showed that schoolteachers did not know everything. Laden with their booty, they came into King Haney's yard like chieftains bringing tribute and after due weighing and pondering, Sadie came away with four shillings and sixpence and Joe with one shilling and threepence. The money jangled in his pocket and he could not wait to add it to the money he had recently got for his seventh birthday. Leonard had given him a money box in the shape of a pig and he liked to rattle it and hear the coins clink together.

With money in his pocket and happily weary from the afternoon's work, he agreed that Bella could hold Blackie and brought him out right away.

Bella almost swooned to hold on to the pretty little creature. It scratched her neck as she nuzzled it to her but she did not mind and took care to be gentle in her handling. She asked Joe if she could walk around the yard and Joe said yes. He sat on the step and watched. Inside the house his mother was preparing the tea. His Daddy would be back from the football match soon.

When Bella asked, most humbly, for a second circuit, Joe acquiesced without hesitation. It was so comfortable on that step. The sound of crockery being laid out on the table, his Daddy coming back with news of the game. He had brought out his piggy bank and now and then he put it to his ear and shook it just a little and smiled drowsily at the clink-clink sound.

And a third circuit was allowed, taken languorously by Bella, swooning over the kitten, rocking as she went, stroking it so lovingly that the purr-purring of the creature expressed a completeness of contentment. When Bella came to the narrow passage beside the lavatory, she stopped and rocked to and fro, crooning a little, a noise without melody but soothing and sensuous, the lumpy, plain, ill-dressed girl made graceful, even attractive in this coupling with the kitten.

The air was turning chilly. Joe shivered.

'Time's up now, Bella.'

Bella took no notice, cradling the furry animal which stuck to her fast.

'Come on Bella. You've had three goes round.'

She looked lazily at the boy but ignored his words, wholly absorbed in her loving of the kitten.

Joe put the piggy bank inside the front door and went across the yard.

'Give it back, Bella.'

He held out his hands.

Still she ignored him.

He reached out to touch Blackie, to pluck him off her, but Bella swayed around and used her height to stay out of reach and Joe was frustrated.

'I won't lend him again, Bella.'

Bella smiled.

'One more go round, Joe. Please, Joe.'

'It's enough, Bella. Three's enough.'

'Please, Joe.'

'No. I'm going in now.'

He held out his arms.

'You can see my bottom, Joe.' She indicated the lavatory.

Joe stared at her, the arms still held out.

'You can prick it with a pin if you want to,' she said.

Joe was quite suddenly dry in the throat. His widened eyes looked around the empty yard. The door of his house was open.

'I want Blackie back,' he pleaded.

Her eyes seemed to mesmerise him and he felt a mild giddiness. 'Come on, Joe.'

She backed towards the lavatory door, still fondling the kitten. The little boy was immobile as the pillar of salt.

'I want Blackie back.' Now it was a whimper. 'Please, Bella.'

She shook her head slowly swaying and was about to step into the lavatory when Sam turned into the alley.

'I saw them walking down the street,' said Leonard, as he enjoyed the final cup of tea of the day. 'They make a handsome couple. You know, I think she's even bonnier since he's come back.'

'You've always rather exaggerated where Ellen's concerned,' said Grace. 'He's smartened up, I'll give you that. The war did wonders for his general appearance.'

'They looked as fine as any couple in Wigton,' said Leonard. 'All life before them.'

'We'll have to be like Mr Asquith and wait and see.'

'They'll get that house.' Leonard smiled. 'I'll put my money on Ellen for that.'

'Sam might have a say.'

'I'd back Ellen.' Leonard's smile softened.

'There might be more going on there than we know about.'

'The squatters turned the balance – that's what's new. Mind you, they're causing complications all round.'

'Where did you see them? Ellen and Sam.'

'Walking down High Street. He must have met her out of Eves'. Lucky Sam, that's what I thought.'

'We'll see,' said Grace, with unusual gentleness of tone.

She stood and leaned down to pour out another cup for Leonard and her bosom grazed his face.

When she sat down, she began to unpin her majestic hair. Leonard quickly took out a cigarette while there was time.

CHAPTER TWENTY-FIVE

Sam had sought ways to lead up to it but found none. It should have been easy enough. There should have been a casual way to introduce it but since the rift following Ellen's suggestion that they move house, both of them had trodden carefully. They were polite, they deferred, they were hesitant: an observer might have thought that they were distant cousins, recently reunited. But Sam knew that Ellen was only waiting before launching another attack and Ellen had picked up, in the way intimates do, that Sam was concealing something important.

He thought of introducing the topic on the Saturday night but Ellen looked so tired and Joe was restless, came down twice. So the opportunity did not arise.

He decided he would break the news on the Monday. He thought he was prepared for it to be sticky. The truth was that since Alex had planted the idea, it seemed obvious and irresistible. Two weeks had passed and every day had strengthened his faith in this dramatic move. He had no doubts. He saw their future as if written in columns of fire. The word 'Australia' made his spirits soar – so much of what had kept him down would be transcended, there was no apprehension, he would be unbound, unbounded, the words free and freedom flanked the name of the distant continent and he could not wait to go.

'But I'll never be able to get back.'

Ellen's first reaction made him smile. She was wearing the dark blue buttoned summer dress he liked and, with her hair down, she looked much like the near-girl he had married.

'We can save up.'

'No. They can never afford to come back. I've heard them talk about it.'

'I'm talking about going.' Sam kept his voice light. 'We can talk about coming back later.'

'No. We can't. It's too far, Sam.'

'I want it to be far.'

'Why? What for?'

Her earnest tone, the stricken look suppressed Sam's optimism. These questions, so simple but full of such force, checked any easy answer. The excitement and plans and union of this conversation, imagined so vividly and so often in the past fortnight, collapsed utterly.

'I want to start again.'

'You can start again here.'

'No. I've just gone back to much the same thing.'

'Well, find something else.'

'It'll still be there, won't it? I'll still be the same penned-in man.'

'Who's penning you in?'

'I feel penned in.'

'But somebody must be doing it.'

'Ellen, whatever I do in Wigton, I'll always be Sam Richardson who left school at fourteen and never got a trade and stuck in a dead-end job and,' he struggled to say what he meant without claiming too much for himself, 'and that's all I'll ever be. However long I live. However hard I work. I'm sorted out and labelled for life here, don't you see?'

'No.'

'You must.'

'No.' Ellen was curt. 'If you don't like your job you can change it. What makes you think you can get a better job in Australia?'

'I'm not going for a better job.'

Ellen waited.

'Although,' he lifted up the two brochures he had thought they would study together, 'there do seem to be much better openings over there.'

'That's just to get you to go.'

'It may very well be.' He paused only for a moment. 'But I believe them.'

'It's a long way to go to make a mistake.'

'It's new, Ellen. Over there they haven't got all this that holds us back. I've talked about it to other lads who are going – they're good lads, they're some of the best lads – and all of us want to get out and find a better life. There's got to be a better life than what we can have here.'

'Why has there to be?'

'Can't you see?'

'No.'

Sam attempted to stifle his growing frustration.

'Look, Ellen. I might not be much but I think I'm better than I'm ever going to get the chance to be here. I think you're just being obstinate. What can I make of myself in Wigton? What is there to do except the same old thing that I've been doing and my kind always does? I go down to that factory and the lads are good lads and the work – well, there's worse work – but more and more I feel suffocated. I can't explain it. I just seem to be in a thick fog that I'll never get out of – I can't explain it in words. It's so shut in. I'm completely shut in.'

As he struggled to convince Ellen the feeling he experienced at the factory crept up on him and he breathed with some difficulty, felt his body pinioned, wanted to break free.

'You'll have to change that job, then.' Ellen's tone was sympathetic. 'That can be no good for you.'

'I want to go away, Ellen.' His voice was low, his head sunk forward. It was a plea.

'I don't,' she said, not unkindly, almost helplessly. 'And what about Joe in Australia?'

'Kids settle anywhere.'

'Joe's been unsettled enough moving from Market Hill to Water Street without thinking about Australia.'

'Look how pinched and cramped we are here.' Sam felt a renewal of energy. 'There's more rationing than there was in the war. We have to take charity from America – and Australia by the way. Everything black or grey or clapped-out. Everybody has his place and that's it – you're marked down as a private in the pioneers for life. There'll always be the haves and the have-nots in England and we'll always be the have-nots.'

'What makes you think Australia will be different?'

Because of what I believe, he thought, and need to believe – that was the heart of it, but it was too emotional to be spoken aloud.

'I'm sorry.' Ellen felt Sam's yearning. The shock of his announcement had been absorbed somewhat and the strained, longing expression on her husband's face made her want to help him.

'I'm sorry,' she repeated. 'But I can't.'

'Why not?'

'I just . . . can't.'

She was so definite. The three syllables went into Sam like nails. 'But why not?'

Ellen opened her hands, palms upwards as if in supplication for an answer for herself.

'You can't leave Wigton. A fact.'

She shook her head. Did not trust herself to speak.

'Why not?'

Again, all that Ellen could manage was the dumb show of a shaken head.

'So all of us have to stick it out because of that. Something that you won't even talk about. You talked about Joe. Do you want him to be brought up where he'll be kept down? And yourself – is cleaning other people's houses as high as you can go?'

'We could have a good home here,' said Ellen. She swallowed as she found her voice but the words were firm.

'Not that again.'

Sam's puzzlement and disappointment funnelled into anger.

'You're not still on about that. We settled that.'

'You walked out, that was all.'

'We settled it!' His voice rose and Joe, who had been uneasy for some time as the intensity of their conversation had penetrated to his room, now woke up fully in alarm and curiosity.

'You might have settled it. It isn't settled for me!'

'I'm talking about Australia and you want to move up the street? It would be comical if it wasn't so bloody stupid.'

'Don't you swear at me, Sam Richardson.'

'What do you want?'

That house, thought Ellen, but said nothing. Sam's temper had always been short on occasion. She did not quail but neither did she want to provoke him. She kept her peace.

'You see? You have nothing to say.'

Oh yes I have, Ellen said to herself, but not now.

'You think that by sitting there like a sphinx I'll just give up. I won't, Ellen. I won't.'

And, as he said it he knew, neither would she.

'We can get there for nothing. Nothing! There'll never be another opportunity like it. Hundreds and thousands of our lads are going over, with their wives and families, taking their chances, looking to build a new life in a new world and get away from all *this*, all *this* – even just for the adventure, for the chance, Ellen.'

He was tormented now and her opposition began to melt, seeing the desperation on his face, hearing him fight for the words that would say what need not be said in words because it was so plain, the longing, the terrible longing on his face, how could she resist this when she loved him and she did love him as intensely now, in these moments of flat confrontation, as at any time and yet she did resist him, she hung on, she could not give in, she could not let go.

'Just for the chance.' On that last word his voice almost broke and almost did her resolve. 'I could be somebody different over there. I wouldn't need to feel inferior all the time or lacking or left behind because so many of us would be starting from the same base – from nothing much but all more or less the same and then it would be fair, don't you see? It would be fair in a way it can never be fair here however much we like it – it can never be fair. It isn't fair from the moment you're born and that's all right, I'm not complaining, but imagine what it would be like, just imagine, to have the same chance as everybody else, no excuses, no privileges, all of you off the same boat and may the best men win. Can't you see, Ellen, can't you see how much I want that?'

Ellen was silenced. On her tongue, in her head, in her heart. His force moved her so deeply she wanted to surrender. To throw her arms around him and say yes, I'll come with you, we will go together and come what may we will have taken our own lives in our own hands and made what we could of them as so few people do or have the chance to do. But an even greater pull held her back.

Sam had leaned back in the chair, eyes closed, not exhausted but done. He had said all that he could say. More than he could have dreamed of saying. He had found a way to say all that he meant.

'I'm sorry, Sam,' she began, eventually.

'No you're not. If you were sorry you would come with me.'

'It isn't a crime to want to stay here.'

'No.' He opened his eyes and looked at her so fiercely that it took all her nerve not to shiver. 'That's one way of getting out of it.' The small room began to close in on him. He pulled at his collar.

'I'm not trying to get out of it.'

'So what are you doing, Ellen? Just tell me. That's all.'

The harshness was turning bitter.

'It's just too far,' she said.

'That's pathetic.'

'Well. It's what I think. You asked me to tell you.'

'So you won't go.'

Ellen literally bit into her lip.

'Come on. You're saying – no – you won't go.' He paused. There was such a fury coming from his eyes. 'You're frightened to come out with it.'

'I'm not. No. I won't go.'

'Right!' The word smacked into her. 'I'll go on my own!' He sprang up and at that moment noticed Joe peeping round the corner of the stairs, his sleep-filled face quite terrified.

'Go on your own then. Just go!'

'What are you doing up? Back to bed!'

Joe did not move. The loud fierce words pinned him to where he was. Ellen turned and saw him and his terror flowed into her.

'Don't shout at him.'

'I'll shout as much as I damn well like. Bed!'

Still Joe would not, could not move, and Sam made a start to go across to him, but Ellen was out of her chair, blocking his path.

'Leave the boy alone,' she said.

'He'll do as he's told.'

'He's frightened. And no wonder.'

'No wonder what?'

'You'd scare the daylights out of anybody.' She turned her back and went across to Joe, arms beginning to open for him, soothing sounds in her throat, her whole posture telling him that he would be looked after and safe. Her loving, devoted, unquestioning attitude was so violently in contrast with how Sam thought she had appeared to him that he could not endure it.

He stepped forward, caught her by the shoulder and pulled her round, roughly.

'I'll deal with him,' he said. 'You've all but ruined him as it is.'

'Don't you push me like that.' Sam had unbalanced her and when she regained her balance she pushed him away. He retaliated and she stumbled backwards against the door.

Joe ran from the stairs and looked from one to the other in panic.

'You,' said Sam, bound in confusion. 'Get to bed.'

'Mammy!' Joe went to Ellen, who was a little dazed, not so much from the impact of what Sam had done but from the fact that he had done it. She gathered Joe up. Sam saw the boy's arms swiftly circle her neck, his head sink against her cheek, his small body press hard against her. He went to them and grabbed the neck of Joe's pyjama jacket, to rip him away.

'Leave him alone.'

'I've left him alone too long. He's for bed.'

'I'll take him.'

'He'll go on his own or I'll take him.'

Joe turned. Sam saw a wild little face, the smaller face of Ellen, screwed up in a frenzy.

'I want to be with Mammy. I don't want to be with you. I don't like you.'

Sam used both arms and levered the screaming boy off his mother murmuring, 'It'll be all right. It'll be all right.'

'No!' Joe kicked out, which Sam disregarded, but again he screamed, 'I don't like you! I just want to be with Mammy!' and deep in Sam there was a wrench of despair. His son. Their son. 'I don't like you!' The boy's tiny hand reached out to Sam's face and little nails raked down one cheek.

Sam hit him. The blow landed on the shoulder and the boy dropped to the ground and got up and turned back to his mother when another blow caught him across his back and spun him round. Again he fell. His legs and arms went in the air to defend himself as Sam moved forward, all but out of control now, bearing down on the boy, and he lashed out again, this time the blow catching Ellen who got between them. She straddled Joe and faced up to Sam, her eyes wild with despair, her arms raised in anger, and he could not bear it.

His arms fell to his sides and the past broke, broke in his mind. He was his father now.

Ellen was panting. Joe was whimpering, too stunned yet to cry.

'Go on your own then,' she said. 'The sooner the better.'

How could he say he was sorry when there was so much in the way? He could find no words for anything.

He took his jacket from the chair and saw his hand was trembling. He could not bear himself. He had failed and he had spoiled everything. But where could he go? How could he bear what possessed him? His violence had recoiled on him and finally there was no escape from that unimaginable darkness beside the white pagoda in Burma. He stood, his head hung down, as Ellen soothed the boy and took him upstairs. He sat and listened while she crooned to him and waited for her to come down, but she stayed with Joe. Then he braced himself.

CHAPTER TWENTY-SIX

It was past the middle of October but still raining and the humidity was high. More than three months now of damp tents, damp sleeping bags, wet clothes and no way of getting them dry. Their gear – the green uniform, green shirts, green socks, green pack, all items dyed green in the same vast vat – was as sodden as the tropical landscape through which they moved. It was now an advance of attrition against the long, fighting retreat of the Japanese, who would sooner commit hara-kiri than surrender.

The company was camped for the night in one of the burned-down areas which the Burmese would farm for a few years and then, when they had exhausted the soil, move on to burn down another patch. Yoke, the only farm labourer in the platoon, never got over the waste of good land. It was a running lament.

Sam remembered that evening in detail. Perhaps in pushing it so deeply to the bottom of his mind, by sealing it off so severely, he had preserved it whole like an object silted and complete, buried until now. They had made fair progress despite the rain and mud and forest. The intelligence was that the Japanese were preparing a big stand just ahead, in a few days, or less, or more, no one really knew. The going had been interrupted by ambush and counter-attack and snipers. But the night attacks had reduced in number over the past three days. That, more than anything, convinced Sam that the Jap was pulling back to regroup.

There could be no relaxation, but Sam remembered, or thought he remembered, a feeling that despite a level of savagery which had seared his mind and shattered the world he had known, despite the depression and burden and recurring sense of futility and anger, there was, in that evening, ready for instant battle though they were, a sense of rightness; even, though he could not explain this to himself, a sense of calm. The Japanese, unprovoked, had viciously trampled through Thailand, French Indo-China, Malaya, Borneo, the Philippines, Indonesia, and now Burma, and but for their defeat at the battle of Imphala they would even at this moment have been terrorising India. And there were too many reports of their thinking cruelty to prisoners and to natives to dismiss them as exceptional or as propaganda. Only very rarely did this feeling of rightness come through the weary, cynical, day-to-day slog of going on going on. But it was there, in the grain of that evening.

Ian had gathered enough slivers of bamboo and somehow dried them well enough – a much appreciated art – to start the fire under the tin of water into which, precisely at boiling point, he cast treasured tea leaves followed by two broken matchsticks to attract the stray leaves. Condensed milk and sugar were added to taste. His bush hat was set goofily square, pressing on his ears. As he went quietly about his business, he crooned the sentimental song of the moment:

'My thoughts wander homewards

'As evening draws near.

'I see your face smiling

'With maybe a tear.

'And I see a vision of all I hold dear

'In my letter from you.'

Sam knocked Ian's hat, lightly, as he walked past to have a word with the corporal in the next section. As he talked to him, he looked over his own men.

Doug was cleaning the light-coloured Lee Enfield which from day one he had resolved to steal from His Majesty when the war was over. When they had first been given their rifles, Doug had thought it was the most beautiful thing he had ever beheld and when the sergeant had said, 'She's your wife, treat her well and she won't let you down', Doug had muttered, 'I'll treat her a bloody sight better than that'. While appearing engrossed in the rifle, he was carrying on some sort of conversation with Titch, who had taken off his boots to reveal his large white spongy feet, the soles devoid of all feeling.

'These feet'll do for me in the end,' he said. 'It always starts in the feet. My Dad told me that. In the last war. Watch your feet was what he said when I left.'

'You do bugger all else,' said Doug.

'Your feet are the biggest killers of the lot.' As he talked, Titch pinched and kneaded the spongy substance with his fubsy fingers.

'Not as big as mosquitoes.' Doug squinted down the barrel.

'Feet get more in the end.'

'Not as bad as beriberi. Look at the size Jimmie ended up.'

'Feet's the slow killer.'

'Or cholera. Or dysentery. Or scabies.'

'Feet,' said Titch, heavily, bringing the debate to a close, 'is a law unto their own.'

A few yards beyond them, Alex – the Prof – was scribbling away. Sam had expected that Alex's writing would have a philosophical turn – comments on their condition, thoughts, ideas. When he read it, it turned out, in Sam's opinion, to be disappointing. 'Spotted two flying foxes. No idea they were that size. Crows extremely bold – would they attack us if they were hungry and we were weak? Must find out how they train elephants. What is this famous memory of theirs? For the first time can see why sailors were attracted to parrots.' Nothing to do with the war, nothing to do with the big subjects he would happily talk about at the drop of a hat. Yet he concentrated on that little notebook as if he were spelling out his last will and testament. The tiny neat writing used up every last piece of the paper.

Ugly Spud, who would always skive if he could get away with it, was sat leaning against a tree stump smoking a cheroot and dreaming of the beautiful Burmese girl who had sold it to him two weeks back. He needed maximum comfort and maximum peace of mind to think about her properly. She was not only the most beautiful girl Spud had ever seen but after selling him admittedly twice as many cheroots as he had first intended to buy, she had given him the 'come on'. There was no doubt about that. On Spud's bashed-in features, the battle between incredulity and desire had been epic. The definite 'come on'. And sod's law, at that very moment they'd been ordered back. Another ten minutes. Another five. The definite 'come on'. The cheroot smoke wreathed into the air, a signal to her, way behind them now, that she would never be forgotten.

Yoke and Buster, who was his second man on the Bren gun, were wringing out some of their gear and then flapping it between them, knowing it was hopeless but somehow cheered by the effort. They chuntered away, all the time, those two. But when Sam drew close and overheard them, there seemed neither beginning nor middle nor end to it. Buster would throw in some of his experiences as a bus driver; Yoke would ramble on about sheep or turnips; but mostly they would chatter through what had happened to them during that day. The talk was unbroken, with no highs or lows, just a steady, consoling thrum.

Sam took them all in. It could have been no more than a couple of minutes. It was one of those times when, despite movement, life grew still, almost stopped, became like a photograph, printed itself on memory, which grew to be the picture, the truth of all the best life in that place at that time. And later he thought he could remember the exceptional lightness. When you took off your pack for the last time of the day, the body seemed to know that, the shoulders could ache in peace, you floated, you discovered the secret of levitation, you walked in giant steps. Sometimes – as on that evening – it went to your head, this lightness, this bonus of euphoria, sheer physical relief alchemised into momentary happiness.

And the eight of them (including Sam: they were two under strength) were so odd planted there. The absurd improbability that those eight who would call themselves ordinary men from a sliver of north and west Cumberland, a remote edge of Europe, should be halfway round the world, where wild buffalo replaced Jersey cows, tigers not dogs disturbed the night, snakes not cockroaches snuggled into your bed and women wore silk.

Strangers to each other before they enlisted, now bound in a way that enthralled his imagination. Roped together by the place they came from, the villages, the words, the local entanglements, like a small raft on the ocean. Wrenched from mundane occupation, they had been translated into the ancient and legendary tradition of soldiers fighting a just war half forgotten by those who had sent them, forced to be sufficient to themselves and to their own history, with no prospect of return save through wounds or a victory which could take years. And miles from home.

Perhaps oddest of all, though the section had changed over the years, through death and injury, it was always the same. So they made their new home, their new mundane world, their new common landscape in the section, in the company, in the regiment.

In those moments of observation, packed and vivid as such insights are, Sam knew all those things and felt a flow of love for it – which could never be admitted nor could it be described, but it filled his body and his mind, almost mystical.

He wanted to write it down for Ellen and Joe. Joe was five now. He wanted to distil all this. Ellen would understand. She knew everything about him. Instead he knew he would say he was as well as could be expected and he missed them both and maybe something about seeing a monkey for Joe and God Bless. Nothing about this vision of the men, their past, their present, and Ian crooning at the heart of it, no special light on him from the sky brewing with rain, but somehow innocent and hopeful and bringing the picture together.

'Cha's up!'

Ian's voice sang out.

There was a low ironic cheer – 'About time' – and the men moved over to Ian, their piallas at the ready to scoop out the boiling tea.

Sam took Ian with him on the first night patrol.

The next two days were harder. The Japanese had not simply melted away. If they were preparing a stand down the road then they were also making it as difficult as possible to get down the road. Sam's section was one of those bang at the front and they thought themselves lucky in these last days that they had experienced nothing worse than the total fear that preceded the two minor clashes which they had survived.

The third day was a little easier, although there was one stretch where they were pinned down by two snipers. Doug eventually got one of them. The other was taken out by the next section along the line.

They moved on, bent low, rifles ready, green in green, the beloved and impractical bush hat bobbing like a large, exotic leaf.

The small Buddhist monastery was just outside the usual village wall. Alex saw it first. They stopped. The order came to attack and Titch cursed, as he always did, that they were always the blokes who got the sticky jobs and why hadn't he joined the pioneers? Sam loosened the pins in his grenades and led them forward.

The only sound – a loud and chilling sound – was of the half-wild pariah dogs barking frenziedly inside the village. The monastery had to be taken out first. Sam took Doug and Titch with him. The others crept near, more slowly.

The building was of the simplest and smallest kind, thank God, Sam thought, which also signalled a small and unimportant village. Titch and Doug got up to it, one on each side, and waited for Sam. Was it booby-trapped? The Japs could not have had time to do anything at all elaborate. Sam felt an engulfment of fear to which he should have become hardened, but he never did.

He went ahead, stood behind the wall, reached out with the bayonet of his Lee Enfield and pushed the door. Nothing. He pushed harder. Reluctantly, it creaked open. Nothing. Use the grenades? They would be too dug in if they had stayed. It was very quiet. He looked at Doug and Titch and nodded and they took short breaths and pressed down the fear and they were ready and went in fast, low, rifles scanning and searching.

No one.

Not even evidence of a struggle.

Something calm in that tiny space, as if abandoned recently but not despoiled, still fashioned for contemplation. The four simple rooms were empty. The search was done as rapidly and as silently as humanly possible.

They came out and moved towards the village wall. That was some protection. Sam looked hard through a crack in the wall. An empty settlement, dogs barking madly behind the huts and on a gentle rise of land, a small, whitewashed pagoda. It looked so innocent, the pagoda, so small and plain. They were lucky, Sam thought, white pagodas.

They went over the wall, fast, scaled out and were soon at the cluster of huts which formed the village.

'They've been in a bit of a rush.' Titch, who was on Sam's left, indicated some bullock carts, piled with equipment under a loose canvas cover.

Sam nodded along the line and they divided the huts between them. Followed the drill. Copybook. Covered for each other. Grenades ready to lob. Empty. Empty. Empty. Remains of fire. Cooking pots simmering.

Ian saw them first and the sight stopped him dead in his tracks. For a split second, despite no sound, Sam thought he had been hit. He swayed and Sam moved across to catch him before he fell, but Ian merely swayed and then Sam and the others saw what he had seen.

All the men had seen sights which had wounded and stunned the world they carried in their minds from England. Each one had a chronicle of horrors, of pulverised skulls and bodies ripped open, scattered entrails and spilled brains, a flopped heap of dead, of decaying flesh invaded by maggots, of this done to friends as well as enemies, and somehow it had to be ignored or put away, put deep away for the nightmares and shock of later when there was time.

None of them had seen anything like this.

The Japanese had taken, when they were all accounted for, eleven young children, some very young, boys and girls. They had tied them to trees with barbed wire and then bayoneted them to death.

Not long since.

There they hung.

Eleven trees. The children naked; ripped open, dead.

Perfectly still, save sometimes for blood which was driving the pariah dogs into a frenzy of leaping and scrabbling at the trunks, but they would catch their paws on the barbs and fall back.

Sam felt unlike he had ever felt before. His mind stopped being itself, not joined to the horror. He looked at the children so intently. He knew that the sight would never go. It scarred his mind. It existed in a time of its own. If he was conscious of anything outside the strangeness in his head it was of the same reaction in the others. Later he thought he understood from those seconds what it was to go mad, to lose your mind.

He saw flies settle greedily on the face of the nearest child, a small boy, and he moved forward, wanting to brush them off, and so found voice. It was hoarse and faint. He forced some spittle down his throat.

'Doug, Titch, Yoke, we'll take them down. You – ' he pointed to Ian and the others, 'dig the graves.'

They could not linger. But no one dissented. Nor would they have been stopped.

'Individual graves,' Sam ordered harshly.

He walked fast to the first tree and found where they had twisted the barbed wire and he untwisted it, pulling down his sleeves to protect his hands. Then he walked around the tree unwinding it, but took care that the child did not slither to the ground. He carried the warm little body over to the rise which bore the whitewashed pagoda, where Ian and the others were violently scooping out the graves.

He went back a second and then a final time and throughout all this not one word was uttered by any of the men until the eleven bodies were buried and stones were put on them and the barbed wire trailed around them to keep off the dogs.

When they had finished they stood in an awkward ragged line wondering how to take their leave. Sam looked up and stared unblinking at the white pagoda, seeking an explanation. He felt rooted to that spot.

Alex had made a bamboo cross which he knocked into the ground above the neat row of graves.

'I know you're not Christians,' he said, 'but rest in peace.'

Alex answered the unasked question.

'They did it to show us what they are going to do to us,' he said. 'They did it to intimidate us.'

Sam nodded. It was as if he could literally feel his brain hardening with anger. With such a force of anger that left him breathless. If he could bayonet every Japanese soldier from Burma to Tokyo, he would do it gladly.

'Let's go,' a voice said. It was his.

No one looked back.

PART FOUR

CHAPTER TWENTY-SEVEN

Sam liked a quiet time to himself before the morning shift. On this mid-autumn morning, he got up just after five and stirred the fire very gently. He had banked it up the night before but it did not do to rush at it and besides he did not want to disturb Ellen who lay, asleep he hoped, strictly on her side of the bed.

It was surprising how little noise you could make if you tried. Even in such a cramped space. There was some fat left over and he fried two slices of bread, setting the frying pan on the renewed glow of coal. He took the lid off the kettle so that it did not whistle when it boiled on the gas ring. Meanwhile he dressed, his pullover needed now, a real chill in the morning especially with the wind.

He sipped the hot tea silently and took care to eat just as silently as he sat on the chair and looked into the fire as if he were a boy again, with Ruth, seeking out pictures.

Ellen's breathing was steady but he was not sure. It was difficult to judge now. Strain as he could, there was no sound from upstairs. Blackie soft-padded out of nowhere and he poured a little milk into his saucer. The lapping was the loudest sound in the room.

Too soon it was time to go. He had hoped – as on many mornings over the past couple of weeks – that Ellen would wake up and he would hold her and feel her warmth and they would be as they had been, his guilt pardoned, their world to rights again. But she did not stir and he closed the door almost stealthily to make sure that if she was asleep she would not be disturbed by his leaving.

Ellen listened until she heard the distinctive hollow sound of his footsteps in the alley and then she spread herself diagonally across the bed and tried to claim a final relaxed stretch of sleep. Soon Joe crawled in with her and she retreated once more to her own side, holding him off when he tried to warm up against her back. She wanted to nurse herself through her misery without the scent of it reaching the boy and for that she needed to isolate herself whenever and however she could.

She had taken some days off during Joe's half term, to be with him. It was too late to go anywhere for a holiday. 'Come pickin' spuds with me,' said Sadie. 'Lots of kids go. And they get paid! You should see their faces when they get their own wages. You would like that, wouldn't you, Joe?'

Sadie was in their house as she had been increasingly over the past few weeks and although Joe did not quite understand what potato picking entailed nor even what getting his 'own wages' quite meant, he was always game to go along with Sadie.

'I'm not taking a holiday just to work.'

'It's not work. It's a holiday with pay. The kids love it. You get a ride there and back in a lorry. The farmer makes hot tea and maybe cocoa for the kids at dinner time. They play about the barns and whatnot. There's all the animals. Want to come, Joe?'

'Yes!'

'We'll see.'

Ellen was not easily persuaded. On the Monday she took up a standing invitation from Leonard to take Joe for a longer than usual ride in the car. At the last moment, at Grace's suggestion, Mr Kneale was inserted into the party, which rather dismayed Leonard, but Grace would not hear of Mr Kneale being rejected and besides, as she pointed out, he would find interesting things to say about the places they passed through. Which he did and, as it rained non-stop, they scarcely left the car, which meant that Leonard spun from one village to another without any chance of escape from Mr Kneale's informative commentary. Joe got over the thrill of being in the car quite soon and when Leonard began serious smoking – with the windows jammed shut against the rain – he began to feel very queasy and was sick, twice, once very nearly in the car itself.

On Tuesday she took him to Carlisle. The main purpose was to see *The Bells of St Mary's* at the Lonsdale, but Ellen caught an earlier bus so that she could wander around the shops, especially the big department store. Joe's boredom was broken once or twice – by putting a penny in the huge red weighing-machine and, more absorbingly, by a kindly young assistant explaining the system of rocketing capsules which whirled money and change around the vast store like an aerial railway set.

But he was soon bored again and after being half-impressed by tea at the select Lonsdale, he was less than enchanted with the film, although he tried to be for his mother's sake.

On Wednesday they turned up for potato picking. Joe loved it. This, Friday, was their last day and they were at the top of Station Road by eight o'clock, waiting again for the lorries.

Those who had gone out to the farms to help save the harvest that year had come largely from the bigger towns or the cities. The potato pickers were entirely local. There were no men. Many of the women were those who dominated the rose-hip, mushroom, berry-collecting sorority. Some of them were rough, all of them looked it. Old boots, often their husbands', or cut-down wellingtons, thick socks, the oldest, warmest skirt possible, layers of blouse and wool, a range of dark coats which vied with each other for shabbiness, and, the only vivid touch, coloured headscarves.

At first Ellen had been a bit self-conscious, both of her own bulky appearance – she had raided Grace's 'old' wardrobe – and the rough look of the women collected outside Miss Peters' sweetshop at the top of Station Road. But after a few cheers at the one or two men who waved at them as they cycled to work and jeers at the three cars which sped past, Ellen found herself smiling. It was like being back at the factory, the girls together, that feeling of liberty inside a group doing the same thing.

'We are Fred Karno's Army', they sang and they cheered anyone they recognised as the lorries rattled over the rutted roads down to the Solway Plain where they stopped at the farms and the farmers called out how many hands they wanted, how many women, how many children – much cheaper rate, teams of two, but two children could not work together. There were exceptions. Speed and his oldest brother made up a team and nobody objected, although the farmer paid the older boy less than the adult rate. Joe had been disappointed that Speed and Frank had been dropped off before him on the Wednesday and the Thursday and his hopes for better luck third time were dashed. The same farmer called them out again.

Because Joe was small and perhaps because Ellen did not look as hungry as some of the others, they were left to the last drop. Sadie had stayed with them out of loyalty. She was working with Big Marjorie, who wore very small spectacles and was rather slow and so, as Sadie explained – loudly, to everyone – she could make up for her. Their billet was a small farm near the sea.

The farmer had marked out their stints with wooden pegs. There were two wire baskets to each stint. First the tractor opened up the stitch, scooping the potatoes out of the heavy, clarty ground. They would start picking. He drove the tractor slowly back down the field and waited until the first stint had filled the baskets and then made his way up again. To set the pace he would put what he reckoned to be the fastest pickers on to the first stints. They would wait with their baskets and heave the potatoes into the cart behind the tractor. There would be a brief rest and then the tractor roared down the field to swing round and open up the next stitch.

Sadie announced to anyone who would listen that this was a walkover. She had been at places working two tractors. That killed you.

Like several of the more experienced women, Sadie had acquired a large coarse sack into which she had cut a head hole and arm holes. This was her uniform and as she bent to collect the potatoes she was, from a distance, indistinguishable from the earth.

It was another raw and dull day. The wind came from the north and bit the skin. The clouds were high, massed, it was possible only now and then to see that they were moving. There was a vastness of sky over the Plain and the sword of sea reflected it in a leaden dullness, alleviated only by the white horses which broke up the surface as the potato pickers broke up the surface of the dour flat landscape.

The farm was isolated. The gulls circled with their lonely, alluring cries. The line of bent backs slowly scythed across the field. From a distance they could have been mere creatures, bent to the task, bound to it, obeying the rule of the machine. The cheers drained away. It was hard and mean work and for many it was the best they would get all year and they knew it and had to live with that sullen thought. They picked the potatoes and were chided by the farmer if he spotted any loose work. Later in the day he gave one of his sons a swill and instructed him to go over the ground already worked and gather up the leftovers.

The farmer was not a young man and even the tinker women could not get a rise out of him. He ignored the women once he had seen them out from the lorry. He knew that he had the scrapings because his was the most remote and one of the smallest farms and paid least. He made them feel mean and low. He cut into their dinner hour, five minutes either end. His wife brought a pail of tea and slopped it, carelessly.

Dinner was the sandwiches they had brought and a time to stretch out in the barn. Some of the women nosed round. Joe tried to get a game of hide and seek going. Ellen found that she watched him all the time and worried when he was not in sight, even though she knew he was safe. She had not been so anxious about him since he was a small child.

In the afternoon a steady drizzle set in and the clouds were lower so that when Ellen straightened her back and looked over the Solway Firth to Scotland, she could see only a smudge, a blur of hills while, to the south, the matching fells of Lakeland were cloud-capped. Save for the tractor and the eternal gulls, it could seem a world cut off, women and children bent double over the opened earth, picking the crop, as muddied as the earth. The afternoon seemed endless and though Ellen was used to work she felt the tug at the base of her spine and the ache in her shoulders and the damp began to get hold. Joe was determined to stick it out and he knew the money was coming at the end of the day, but he was tired, he had put too much into the morning. Ellen had to work harder, doing almost all the stitch herself.

There were cries for the farmer to slow down. After asserting his authority for a time by ignoring the cries, he stopped his tractor at the bottom of the field and waited. 'He's given us ten minutes,' Sadie yelled out the message and the women walked away from the stitches, pressing their hands hard into the small of their backs, kneading the sore muscles. The children sat down or looked for a playmate.

The final stint was hard and fading light and low cloud darkened the field. They would finish the whole field that day which had been the farmer's best hope.

Joe's clogs were now padded with wet earth and he enjoyed the extra inch or two and the feeling of clump in his walk. He had taken off his gloves because they were too caked and his hands were red with cold. One of the veins on the back of his right hand was beginning to swell up. He sucked at it. His mother rubbed his hands but that made them hurt more.

The farmer collected the swills after the last stitch and they walked the big, denuded field to the barn, which had no light, where they waited for the lorry.

He had them in a line for payment and counted out the money carefully to each one, grudging it, crushing them. Joe got seven shillings and sixpence. He looked at it as if it were a bar of gold. Ellen kept it for him because he was wearing old clothes she ought to have thrown out long ago and there was not a sound pocket.

The lorry was late. The jolting which had been merry on the way out now bumped their aches into bruises and the drizzle penetrated their hearts as well as their bodies. The children were excited, with the money, with the adventure, now and then other cars, another lorry, always a cheer from the children, but the women knew the reckoning and although they would joke again in the morning, the darkening way back was a time when they drew apart.

Ellen felt a pressure of unhappiness new to her. It was like a stone laid on her and then another stone laid above that to press the life out of her. She had been unhappy often enough while Sam was away but this was entirely different and he was home.

She decided she would not come the next day.

Each jolt of the lorry was like a little tap of the hammer tap-tapping her unhappiness. She could not even react to the occasional salty rude remarks of the tinker women and when Joe sought to clamber on to her she told him it was too uncomfortable. The drizzle, the growing darkness and the fundamental grimness of this being her 'holiday' all added to the unhappiness, but these would have been sloughed off had she not nursed the tight clench of misery which seemed a solid object in her body. It drew everything to it, everything dark and miserable fed it and made it harder, more clenched, more hopeless.

Ellen and Joe limped off the lorry and up the street towards home. Ellen hoped that Sam would be there but when they reached the yard and she saw the yellowy glow through the curtain, her mood suddenly changed. When she opened the door and saw him by the fire, open-collared, a cigarette, pale and tired but with a clear hope of love on his face as he rose half-smiling indicating the kettle on the hob and the table laid, she wanted to move into an embrace but she could not. For a split second, her expression met his and then it snapped shut.

'I think we'll go down to Market Hill to get properly clean.'

She had thought no such thing until that perverse split second.

'This is not good enough for you?'

'We're both too dirty.'

Joe, plastered in mud beside her, was proof of that and she glanced at him as evidence, but his state was no more than a poor excuse and they both knew it.

'What d'you come back here then for in the first place?'

'I thought you might be out.'

The brutality of her answer silenced both of them.

Sam turned away. If only he would turn back, Ellen thought, then I would stay, but he had his back to her and she left, sick at the memory of her words.

When they returned, blooming from the hot water and the tea provided by Grace and the warmth of the house after the bitter damp chill on the flat fields, Sam was out, and it was Ellen who sat by the fire and waited.

Joe had been so tired that even Blackie scarcely diverted him. After putting his new money with the earnings from the two previous days and counting it all up and dropping it solemnly into the piggy bank, he was easy to persuade to bed and asleep, halfway down the page of the story.

Ellen told herself she was glad to be alone. She told herself that many times these days. She needed the silence to look at and examine this misery which dominated her. When she was alone she could breathe more easily. All she wanted was for this tightness to go away. She could think of little else while it was there. She was not herself. It soured her, against Sam, she knew, it made her say things she ought not to have said and would never have dreamt that she could say. This thing inside her, this compact of misery, was eating her, taking her over. She shied away from Sam. From talking to him. From being with him. Even from looking at him. As a wife in the house she did the least necessary. In bed she was cold.

Yet, at moments like this, sweetly weary, so warmed and fed after the day on the field, half drowsing by the fire, waiting for him, she wanted to tear out this awful thing inside her, she wanted to talk to the Sam she had married and loved and waited for and sort it out and start again and pretend this had never happened. How silly not to go away with him! Not to be part of his adventure! How timid and mousy of her!

Sam had always said, when they were courting, that in her quiet way she was the boldest of them all. So what was this fear? She tried to bounce herself out of it, to laugh at herself and scold herself and tease herself out of it and sometimes she thought she was succeeding. Australia would appear in her mind as the glowing Eden which Sam saw it to be. She could not imagine the particulars of what would happen there but there would be some people she knew and that would be good . . . but her enthusiasm died at the thought of what she would leave and never see again. At that thought, a terror set in, over which she had no control.

And there was Joe. Sam hitting Joe. That hardened her. That pulled her back. That, she thought, was the biggest cause of her immovable misery.

But still, would it not be a better opportunity for Joe – they said it was a better opportunity for the children – was she denying him a better life, as Sam said she was? Joe would like it well enough, she knew him. He liked what was new. He would soon forget Wigton. The trip on the ship would be the best holiday of the boy's life – unrepeatable. Sam had said that as well.

When he came in, Ellen was asleep. Her face was glowing, from health and from the fire. Her body had slid forward in the chair and she sprawled, in her sleep, provocatively. Her head rested on her right shoulder and the black hair fell over part of her face. Sam watched for a while, latched the door quietly, watched some more. The gas mantle puttered very gently and the sound of the fire was faint.

He had drunk two quick pints and then stopped there and only had another half. But he wiped his mouth with his sleeve as if this would wipe away the smell of beer on his breath. He sat down in the chair opposite and lit up. Perhaps it was the rasp of the match that woke her. She sat up straight, smoothing her skirt. Her eyes were soft, half full of sleep. They could have been loving. Sam, softened a little by the beer, was equally loving.

'Time for bed.' Ellen's tone was abrupt and uninviting.

'Can't we talk?'

'What more is there to say?'

'There's a lot to say, Ellen.' She knew that but the thing inside her had clenched tight again and would not let her soften.

'If you ask me we've said too much already.'

'How can we have said too much when we still don't know where we are?'

'I know where I am.'

Her expression darkened and Sam caught a glimpse of the misery eating into her.

'Maybe,' he said sorrowfully, 'I should give up going to Australia.'

'But you want to go.'

'Yes.'

'You've proved to me you want it badly. More than anything.'

'Not more than anything.' He spoke quietly.

'I couldn't be the one who stood in your way.'

'What are you saying, Ellen?'

'Go on your own.' The misery flooded into her face, drawing the warmth and the soft sleep out of it, tightening the skin, straining the eyes. 'Go on your own.'

'And send for you later?'

'So you have thought about it.' Ellen's accusation was almost triumphant. 'Going on your own.'

Sam was confused.

'Why don't you want to go with me?'

'Why did you hit him?'

It was the first time in the two weeks that she had asked him directly.

Sam tried to answer and then shook his head.

'You promised me.'

'I did.'

'I just want to know why.'

'If I could undo anything I've done, it would be that.'

'But it's done.'

'The first and last time.'

'How can I know that for certain?' Ellen was full of earnest enquiry. 'How can I?'

Sam looked at her for some help.

'You'll have to take my word.'

'You gave me your word.'

He had no answer. There was a silence. Ellen looked at him but Sam's gaze was turned away. There was an unhappiness in his attitude and half-averted face which touched her and this time, gently, she repeated.

'Why did you hit him?'

But to dig up the answer was too much for him. It was beyond him to articulate what might have been some sort of exonerating reason, at least an explanation, just something to give him a position.

'Mammy.'

Joe was at the top of the short flight of stairs, clutching the front on his pyjama bottom. Sam turned to him and smiled, a little. Joe looked at him with what Sam interpreted as insolence. Ellen had risen to her feet on the first syllable of Joe's little cry, her face, her body urgent with concern and Sam felt jealousy surge up inside him and, as

Ellen was passing him, he grabbed her wrist, firmly, not roughly.

'Why do you always have to jump and run after him? He's got you on a string.'

'Let go!'

'Mammy!' There was fear in the urgency now and Ellen tugged away her arm with unnecessary violence.

Again Sam looked at the boy and as Ellen went up the stairs he thought he saw victory in the child's gaze. He had to make himself go numb. He had to lie doggo now. Keep that sight away.

He heard Ellen chide the boy gently and then turn the mattress, put on a dry sheet, most likely a towel on top, make him change his pyjamas, stay to settle him down.

Sam waited. She sang, very softly; he strained to hear but it was for Joe's ears only. Sam had loved to hear her sing.

She came down with the wet sheet and the pyjamas.

'Did you think I was going to hit you?'

Sam's question came out of thin air. Once said, though, and with bitterness, he stuck to it.

Ellen, who had softened to Sam as she had sung their child to sleep, was pushed back into her defiance. 'You might have done.'

'Do you think I might have done?' Sam's question was terribly deliberate.

Ellen knew there was something of madness about herself and maybe Sam too, but she was powerless. 'You hit Joe.'

'Do you think I would ever hit you?'

She stood, holding the wet things, her misery now fully possessing her. He too was possessed, by a dreadful anger which took all his force to control.

'Well?' His voice was harsh. 'Would I?'

'Who knows?'

'Yes or no?'

Could he not see that she was imprisoned in this misery? That she had been taken over by it? And could she not see the hurt and anger and shame in him and the words which would not come to relieve it?

'Yes or no?'

She was unable to surmount this obstinate, all-oppressing un-happiness.

'If it comes to that,' she said, turning and dropping the wet things in the basket, 'then it's – yes.'

Sam took in his breath sharply, held it a while and then let it out slowly. He nodded and his lips tightened. He seemed to be staring beyond the room, beyond the town, far away.

'Well then,' he said, 'that's about it, then, isn't it? That's about it.'

Ellen opened up the bed and made it, all done swiftly. She changed as chastely as if they had never known each other. In no time she was in the bed, curled up at one edge of it, utterly lonely.

After a while Sam turned off the gas light and took out a cigarette and lit it from a live coal.

CHAPTER TWENTY-EIGHT

It was hard for them even to look at each other in the face after that night.

Joe had kept his distance for these two weeks, easing out of the house when Sam came in, edging into his mother's zone when they were together, and to Sam's sorrow Ellen had let it happen. He had endured it because he knew that time would heal it. But that time had not been granted. Ellen's other force, her helpless rootedness, had kept the wound open. Sam had been patient then and waited. Now there was nothing to wait for.

He would go alone. After he had established himself he would ask them to join him.

'Plenty of other married men do that,' Alex asserted. 'It seems to me rather preferable.'

'Yes?'

'More sensible altogether,' said Alex.

You are a very clever man, Sam thought, do you really mean this?

'I thought it would be easier for them,' he lied.

'If you want my opinion, you're dead right. Damn!'

The brown missed the corner pocket. Sam stepped up to the table. They had the snooker room to themselves. He concentrated on the game. It cleared his mind. Alex's opinion was important to him. They would go together. He had to find ways to continue on the path which had become inevitable. He was driven, he felt, and whatever the consequences, he had to follow this path. It was as if he were in the sea swimming all day and all night against a tide. But he could not give up.

When he walked down to the factory, when he did his work there, when he walked up the street, placed his bets, had a pint, had a word, he was self-conscious. Just as he had been the day or two after his return from Burma. Now, again, he felt as if he were being singled out. Going to Australia and without his family. His common sense told him that people were far too busy with their own lives to worry about him, but it was so.

He felt singled out and he did not like it. So he lied, transparently to Alex, about his reasons for going alone and, unused to lying, he felt uncomfortable, sullied by it and tried to talk about it as little as possible, although many of those he met were honestly interested. Ellen, too, lied when challenged as to why he was going alone: he preferred it that way, she said, and so did she, let him get sorted first, better for Joe. People said she was sensible. They had heard some bad stories about Australia as well as the cheerful messages, and they were not always to be trusted, cheerful messages.

If only he could see around it, in some way. But his mind was so set on it. Like a hard anger that had to find a release. It was a burden, this set purpose. It grew heavier the nearer the time drew for its execution. He had hoped Alex would support him – as he had – but secretly and more desperately, he hoped Alex would do something to dislodge this boulder in his mind and heart and let him start again.

'No quarter,' said Alex, after he had taken the game – Sam was badly off form. 'You're doing the right thing. My shout. One for the road.'

They would travel together. The boat was leaving Southampton at the end of November, less than a month away.

Sam did what had to be done without fuss, without lowering his guard. He gave in his notice to the factory. He put all his papers in order for the voyage. He paid the rent up to Christmas – to ensure the full month's notice – even though Ellen said she would probably be moving out before then.

'It's just as well she comes back to live with us,' said Leonard.

They were all in the sitting room for Sunday-afternoon tea. It had the atmosphere of cold meats after a funeral.

'And it won't be for all that long,' said Grace, smiling, provocative. Ellen shivered a little and not just at the chill which always lay on this room. There was very little got past Grace.

'Speaking selfishly and for myself,' said Mr Kneale, beaming in the light of his remarks on what was an unaccountably sombre occasion, 'it will be like the old times. Not that I would wish the war back,' he looked at Sam apologetically, 'but I have to confess that I've missed having Ellen and little Joe about the place.'

He nodded contentedly, his curls bobbed and his moon face dipped towards the cup and the little finger jutted out at polite attention.

'It's more sensible all round,' said Leonard, but he glanced at Grace as he said this and was relieved that she inclined her stately head in acquiescence. Grace had no fear of Leonard when Ellen was under her roof and under her thumb.

'We've never really done anything with your old room,' said Grace. 'We'll put that little camp bed in for Joe. You'll like that, won't you, Joe?'

Joe did not know how to react. Everything was as it had been often enough in this room but everything was different. He was aware of something that would break or go wrong or be amazing. He did not understand it. There were no clues in his mother's face, none on his father's. Aunty Grace and Uncle Leonard seemed the same but they were different too. Only Mr Kneale was as he had always been and Joe sensed his father pull back from Mr Kneale and he followed suit.

'Can I go out to play?'

'There's nobody out there.'

'I can go and ask them.'

'It's Sunday,' said Ellen.

'Let him go.'

Grace was in charge. Joe sped out.

'It'll be one heck of an adventure, that voyage,' said Leonard enviously.

'I should think Sam'll have had his fill of long sea voyages,' said Mr Kneale. 'I should think they can have their drawbacks.'

'But this is no troopship,' said Leonard. 'I've seen photographs of them setting off for Australia. It looks like a holiday jaunt to me. Fun and games.'

Ellen bided her time and then put the plates on a tray and left the room.

Sam lit up. Grace frowned on smoking in the front room – it got into the curtains and the cushions – but something about Sam this afternoon made her hold her tongue. Leonard also took advantage.

When Ellen returned, Mr Kneale glanced around the company in a way which clearly teed up the stroke he was to deliver.

'I have here,' he said, producing, from under his chair, a parcel neatly wrapped in brown paper and well tied with brown string, 'a small parting gift for Sam there.'

Everyone but Sam looked pleased.

'I know that it is premature, but I have my reasons, which will be explained after Sam opens this parcel.'

Smiling at the secrecy, he handed over the parcel – clearly a book.

'Thank you very much.'

He did not relish being the centre of attention. The parcel had to be opened. The string was knotted fast. Unthinkingly, he reached for his pocket knife, an act which drew a little gasp from Grace. Ellen took the parcel from him and with skilful tugging, including use of her teeth, she loosened it and passed it back. The guilty knife was put away.

As this was going on, Mr Kneale said, 'I believe very firmly in books as gifts. Joe, for example, when he was seven, I knew he would have liked a toy, but that *Junior Encyclopaedia* will continue to be a treasure long after any toy is broken and forgotten.'

Sam's book was revealed.

'Read out the title, Sam.'

'*Campaign in Burma*,' he read. '*Prepared for South East Asia Command by COI, written by Lt Col Frank Owen, OBE.* Thanks very much, Mr Kneale. It should be quite interesting.'

'Pass it round,' urged Mr Kneale and Sam did so. 'I saw a long reference to it in the *Cumberland News*,' he went on, 'and I thought – I must have that book. When I was about it I thought – and a copy for Sam. As a parting gift.' The cover of the book was sternly examined by Grace. 'And I confess to an ulterior motive.' His face took on an expression of mock self-reproof. 'As I'll never see you again after you go to Australia – they don't come back –' Here Ellen stared straight ahead, unblinking, at nothing. '– I wanted your views on the book. If you have the time. The observation of the common soldier on what we might call the High Command's version. It

325

would be helpful for me, Sam.' Mr Kneale was very earnest. 'It would mean a great deal to me. I'm taking this Burma business very seriously.'

Sam looked at him, drew heavily on his cigarette, nipped it out in the saucer, which he knew was the height of bad manners, slipped the dog-end into his pocket and said, 'I'll do my best, Mr Kneale. And thanks again. I think I'll go and look out for Joe.'

'He was rather moved,' said Mr Kneale, after Sam had left. 'The thoughts that must be going through his head! They have a lot to live with, those young men.'

—◊—

The days began to gather pace. It still seemed wholly unlikely, impossible, that he should be off to the other side of the world within such a short time and yet the date raced towards him mercilessly. The days began to be marked by last visits. The last visit to his relatives down on the coast. The last visit to Jackie, making no progress. The last visit to Ian's parents. And, in the last week, the final visit to his father and Ruth.

'What'll you do with your bicycle?' she asked.

'I'll leave it for Ellen to sort out.' He tried to smile. 'Maybe Joe can practise on it soon.'

'Father was glad you came.'

'He's losing ground.'

'Just forgetful.' Ruth shook her head. 'He is going back. He repeats things more and more. He has this terror that he'll end up in the workhouse – and whatever I say can't convince him. He keeps saying that I can't wait to get him in there. Me.'

Ruth bit her bottom lip.

Sam put an arm around her shoulders.

'I haven't been much help.'

She shook her head, excusing him.

'The trouble is,' she continued, steady now, 'the more he talks about it and worries about it, the more likely it is to happen. Though I won't let them take him until I can't cope.' Her tone was suddenly fierce. 'They'll not just cart him off.'

They walked down the lane, Sam wheeling the bicycle with one hand, linking the other arm with his sister.

'I thought of coming to see you off,' she said. 'But I think that it's best if it's just Ellen. And Joe. She'll be taking Joe.'

If he could break out of his cold fastness and talk to anyone, it was Ruth. She would not judge. Just to be listened to would be a release. To talk to no one about it was making him feel increasingly distant from everyone. No one knew what he was thinking or feeling and no one would get to know but the isolation was a curse. It was as if he were already way out to sea, out of contact with the town, the people, friends, even those he loved like Ruth. It was the strangeness and a determination beyond his comprehension which held him to the purpose. At whatever cost he would continue on the path and it was this which made him fearful.

'I'll pop through to Wigton next Thursday.'

He was leaving on the Friday.

'I'm sure you know what you're doing,' she said. 'I'll come through to see Ellen and Joe a bit more often.'

'It's that . . .' He looked at her, held her returned gaze, but then he looked away. 'I've got to get out,' he said. He swallowed and his tongue coaxed saliva into his throat.

'I'm sure Ellen understands.' Ruth's sincerity meant that she could not be challenged and besides, he thought, perhaps she was

327

right. Ellen had said so little lately, none of it critical, helping him get ready.

'I think she does. I'll send for them,' he nodded, 'when I've found my feet.'

But what, the thought came to him increasingly often, what if he did not find his feet, what if they did not come when he 'sent for them', what then? The flash of panic blinded him to such consequences.

'I just have to get away, Ruth.'

They stood apart, brother and sister, not embracing, nothing but the strain in their eyes showing the depth of the understanding and love between them and words would not have done much good.

It was still light enough when he walked into the yard – he had stowed away the bicycle at Grace's house – and he was pleased to see Bella, there was a lift in seeing her, innocent of the worries of others.

'Mr Richardson?'

'Yes, Bella.'

'You're going a long, long way away, Mr Richardson.'

'I am.'

'Is Joe and Mrs Richardson going away as well?'

'Not as far as me, Bella, but they'll be going down to Market Hill, sooner or later. You worried about seeing Blackie?'

'Yes, Mr Richardson.'

'I'll make sure Joe invites you to Market Hill, Bella.'

'Thank you, Mr Richardson.'

'Here.' He fished half a crown out of his pocket. 'I don't think I've ever given you anything, Bella. Buy something nice.'

'Oh, thank you, Mr Richardson.'

Bella looked at the large coin deposited on her palm, as if it would leap off and hop away. She closed her fist and took the money in to show her mother.

Sam had scarcely seen Bella's mother. He suspected she had kept in most of the time because she was ashamed of her daughter. Lately she had another reason: her sister had been diagnosed as tubercular and despite the warning of infection from the doctor, Bella's mother insisted on nursing her. He could sometimes hear the coughing through the party wall. Bella herself, he had noticed, was beginning to look paler.

He had hoped Joe and Ellen might be in but the house was empty yet again. He ate a couple of slices of bread but there was no real appetite. After half an hour's wait, he went into the town.

With winter closing in and the hint of real cold already in the air, the streets were almost bare. A few men scuttled from the fire of one pub to the warmer fire of another; better fires and better space, most times, than they could find at home. The older children were engaged in their perpetual game of chase up and down the rivulets of alleyways, across yards, over walls into lanes, darting across streets with no traffic, the town an adventure park. He came across one or two he knew and one of them said 'good luck'. Sam remembered that first day he had come back from the war with the town so unchanged but so different and now he was soon to leave it he felt the difference again and also the sameness. He found he was looking carefully at the shops which were usually of low interest and at other ordinary features of the place, as if he were taking photographs. There were none of the lads standing around the fountain doing nothing, which was a disappointment. He liked to think they were always there, always had been, always would be, the spirit of the town.

Two drinks in the Lion and Lamb were enough to convince him he was not in a pub mood and he went back on to the streets and tacked through the back alleys until he came on Vinegar Hill. This was where he had started from. This was where his father had brought him.

Even in the near-dark he could make out every bit of it. The precarious-looking central tower of dwellings – houses split horizontally, houses sliced vertically, rooms of many shapes and sizes, all strung together by steps and parapet ways. The ponies were tethered in the field that muddled around it and there were two donkeys apparently leaning against a wall. Dogs scavenged everywhere. Mongrels and the lurchers they always kept. Children war-whooped and next to the building was a fire, the men and the older boys sitting around it, as Sam remembered them doing since his childhood.

'Sit down, Sam. We've some spuds in that fire. They'll be out in no time.'

Diddler, the oldest of the men, extended the welcome. Kettler was also there, quite drunk, lolling like a lord on the mat of coats and old carpet and sacks they had put down for comfort. Diddler's was the full tinker look, the wide-gashed mouth, the high cheekbones, broad forehead, narrow-socketed blue eyes, long tangled hair. His family was Irish, now based in Wigton for two generations, some of them grown fond of the town and stayed. But they had never entirely lost their own ways.

Diddler was a big man, a kerchief around his throat, a once-fine tweed jacket, a brown trilby hat pushed back on his head, a short pipe, a jet of spit sizzling in the fire every so often.

'You never wear a hat yourself, Sam?'

'Not since I came back.'

'And now they say you're taking off again.'

Sam nodded and offered a cigarette. Diddler spat, pressed a thumb pad over the pipe and reached out for one. Sam handed them round to the three others. Only one lit up. The others put them behind their ears. Kettler put the cigarette in his mouth but did not light it.

330

'Try some of this,' said Diddler and he passed over a large jug. Sam had a good idea of what was in it but it would have been bad manners to refuse. He took a quick gulp which brought tears to his eyes and another quick gulp which somehow did the trick of cancelling out the awful taste of the first drink.

'Not for boys,' said Diddler and took a serious pull. He offered the jug to no one else for the moment.

'So where is it, Sam?'

'Australia.' The word sounded foolish, uttered to Diddler.

'Believe that . . . the other side of the world, eh? Where the men walk upside down. And the women, Sam?'

'That's the place.'

The drink had hit the spot. For the first time for weeks, Sam experienced something approaching happiness.

'Is there any more in that jug, Diddler?'

'For an old friend, the jug's never empty.' He passed it over and, to one of the younger men, said, 'Rake out the spuds and have a look.'

Sam took a serious slug, apprehending that it could be his last.

'So,' said Diddler, looking into the blaze, his face hot with it, 'what is it in Australia?'

Sam's instinctive reply, now that his head was being prised away from the lock in which it had been held, was to say 'I don't know.'

'It's a new start,' he said, with effort. 'Far away. Away from all this.'

'From Vinegar Hill?'

'No, no, not Vinegar Hill.'

'Wigton, then?'

'No. Yes. No. It isn't Wigton. It's just . . . Everything.'

'How's them spuds?'

'A few more minutes.'

'Surprising how you can hunger for a baked spud, Sam, with a bit of salt. Everything eh, Sam?' Diddler smiled at him. The big handsome head held few teeth. 'I understand about that. See the old caravan?' He pointed. 'Whenever I get a bit restless, off we go. We go where the road takes us. There's no fighting it when it comes on, Sam, so I'm with you. Australia, any place, when it comes on you, you have to follow it, Sam, or that day you start to die. There's something the old heart knows that we don't, Sam. You have to listen to it. You stop listening and your life's over, walk and talk all you like, your life's over. So you go to Australia, Sam. I'll drink to it.'

He handed the jug yet again to Sam.

'Drink up. You're my guest tonight. I want you to remember Vinegar Hill when you get off that old boat upside down.' He grinned, his gash of a mouth slashed wide across his face. 'The trouble is, Sam, my old Da used to say, wherever you go, you take yourself with you.'

'Spuds is ready.'

'Now you're talking.'

They sliced open the burnt, hot, black-coated potatoes with their pocket-knives and passed the salt around. The lurchers tried to gobble the food and yelped at the heat of it. Another jug was found and Diddler included all the company in drinking to his guest.

Sam scarcely remembered getting home, but after he got in the house he sobered up enough to light the candle at the bottom of the stairs to go up to look at Joe.

For some minutes, mercifully numbed by the drink and sluiced with a kind of happiness, he gazed down at his son, who looked so like his wife despite the red hair, and he had no idea at all why he was doing what he was doing but he did know, even there, that he had to go and he would go, even alone, and soon.

CHAPTER TWENTY-NINE

On the last day they went to Carlisle, all three. People noticed it and approved. Sam had not been enthusiastic about a send-off party although he had had a few drinks with his shift from the factory. Going to Australia or New Zealand or other Imperial outposts was no longer uncommon and besides, he had not been much in the town the last week or two, spending time with Alex, working as a pair: as they had done in Burma after Ian's death.

Tea, some desultory window shopping and the film and they were back in Wigton before dark and Joe – who had been uneasy throughout the day – was allowed to change and speed off. Both of them wished he had stayed.

'I said I might meet Leonard, at the Vic, if we were back, for a quick one.'

Ellen had filled the kettle from the tap in the yard before they had left. She lit the gas under it. 'Maybe we could talk?'

Her voice was quiet.

'Right.'

Sam sat down in his usual chair, fearing that he was about to be cross-questioned.

The water seemed to take an awful long time to boil.

After she had poured the tea she sat, in the other chair, opposite him. For the first time for many days, she looked directly at him and kindly. 'I've been going over what to say,' she began, examining the white tea cup and saucer in her hand, 'but now we're here . . .'

Sam waited.

'First of all. First of all it was wrong of me to say I thought you would hit me. You wouldn't. Not deliberately.'

To speak in the open in calm tones took effort. Ellen had rehearsed it several times. She had feared it would feel awkward and it did. It should not have needed saying. Essential matters at one time had not needed words. Understanding and forgiveness would have been in slight intimate signals, in small apparently inconsequential actions.

'Right.' He accepted what she said and was relieved, but he knew it was far from over.

She wanted to move on to Joe. By any comparison she could think of, Sam was not a stern or brutal father. She had been smacked as a child; Sam, she assumed from her encounters with his father, had been hit, even hammered, in his time. It was common practice. She had repeated all this to herself many times. But seeing him do it . . .

She took a quick breath.

'I wish you hadn't hit Joe, though.'

Sam had expressed regret more than once.

'It's been blown up out of proportion.'

'You mean I've blown it up.'

'These things pass,' he said doggedly.

'Maybe they don't.' Ellen was striking in the dark.

'We disagree. As on much else.' He could not conceal the bitterness. Her coldness had offended him and wounded him.

Ellen suppressed her instinct to fight back. Then, quickly,

'Leonard says they want a lot less for the house now. For moving in – twenty-five pounds, he says it could go for twenty, and the Council would consider contributing to basic improvements.'

'The same Council that wouldn't lend the Market Hall trestle tables to us for the kids' teas at the Carnival? The same Council that won't let ex-servicemen keep poultry on the allotments? That Council?'

'They'll have Councils in Australia.'

Sam smiled. The first with Ellen for a long time. After a second or two, it drew out a corresponding smile in Ellen.

'I'm sure they will,' he said.

'So?'

The sudden softness of tone, the smile, the pleading look in her eyes almost disarmed him.

'Can't you see that I have to get out of this place? I don't dislike it. I even like it. And the people here. But I'm set on it now, Ellen. And you'll follow, you'll see, when I'm set up.'

'Will I?'

Sam's face turned away as if it had been slapped.

'At some time. Maybe you can't go now. But, at some time.'

Ellen pressed her lips tightly together. Her words were measured and all the more final for being spoken slowly. 'I can't promise, Sam. Not and tell the truth.' She was not going to cry. Besides, it would be unfair. 'If I can't leave now, why should I be able to leave in six months? Or a year?' Sam was about to reply but he stopped when he saw she wanted to struggle through. 'You say you have to go, Sam. I don't fully understand why but I do understand you mean it. But I mean it as well.' She pressed her lips together even harder, taking a pause, concentrating with all her might. She swallowed and went on. 'It's so far away. I'll never be able to get back. And I like it here. I know where I am. Don't you see? It isn't much to say when you're offering to take us all to the other side of the world. I don't like saying it. Sometimes I think I should just pull myself together and I've tried, Sam. You might not believe it but I've tried time and again, in my head, I've thought about it 'til I'm dizzy with it.'

'So maybe you, and Joe, might not come at all?'

Sam looked so hurt that Ellen in her turn looked away.

'I have to tell you the truth,' she said.

Sam was winded. He had to wait a while. 'So if I go I won't see you again unless I come back? It could come to that?'

Ellen could not reply.

Sam drew a deep breath.

'I don't think it will come to that,' he said, 'once I've settled.'

'But I'm settled here.'

'You make your way faster as a single man. Alex has all the gen.'

Ellen simply shook her head.

For a few minutes they sat in silence, bound together in unhappiness.

'It's late,' Sam announced, abruptly. 'Joe should be back by now. I'll go and bring him in.'

The street lights were on, glowing weakly, each with its small private pool of light.

Water Street was, unusually, empty. Sam went towards the Waste. He felt shaky. He could not fully absorb what Ellen had said to him, even though the possibility had been haunting him. He stopped under a light and took out his cigarettes. His hands were not steady. He could scarcely credit it. Shaking over a talk. He lit up and looked up and down the cold street.

There was no real need to fuss about Joe now. He had found his feet. He was a little warrior now, smaller than the gang Speed had taken him into but, for all that, one of them. Sam was proud of him.

He walked along to the Waste and spotted Joe and two others – one of them had to be Speed – alongside the wash-houses. One of them saw him and all three dodged smartly behind the building. Sam decided to play it along.

'Joe,' he called out. 'Joe – time's up.'

He could just hear a rustling, a faint sound of giggle.

'Joe!' He put more urgency into his voice. 'Time's up, Joe!'

Clumpingly, so that they could not fail to hear him, he went down the cobbled path towards the wash-houses. When he came to the corner he stopped and for a third time called out.

'Joe!' Sharper now. 'Bed-time, Joe!'

No sound. He turned the corner. No sight of them.

He smiled to himself.

He took three heavy steps forward, stopped, turned and lightly went around the end of the wash-houses to catch them on the other side. No one.

This time he padded, just as quietly as he could, along the short length of the building and got to the other end. No. Around that. No. And no sound.

His smile broadened.

His eyes were used to the dark now. He leaned against the wall and slowly scanned the rump of Waste before him. He saw no unusual shadows, no movement. They could not have broken out into the big stretch of Waste behind without his hearing something: not three small boys.

They were good, he thought, pleased at their guile.

A brick jutting from the building pressed into the small of his back. That was where they were. He picked up a few tiny pebbles and lobbed them lightly onto the roof. The pebbles scattered like hail and he heard a little gulp of breath and ssshhh.

337

He cleared his throat, noisily. With a big sigh he began to clamber up the wall, taking every opportunity to make a sound. When he heaved himself over the edge, the boys exploded into giggles and activity and raced for the far end. Sam dropped to the ground and was round just in time to catch Joe.

'Got you!'

He swept him up. Joe struggled and kicked a little, but that was natural, Sam thought, and he set him down.

Speed had stood his ground. The other boy was haring back up into Water Street.

As they walked back, Speed said, 'So you're off to this Australia tomorrow then, Mr Richardson?'

'That's right.'

'They've told us about it at school. Father O'Brien's going out there on a mission after Christmas. So they've told us all about it.'

'And what do you make of it, Speed?'

'Dead good. I wish I could go.'

'Maybe you will, one day.'

'Why isn't Joe going?'

'I don't want to.' Joe's voice was rough, countering the amiability of the other two.

'He's clueless,' said Speed.

'I want to stay here with Mammy.'

Sam looked down and saw the determined set of his son's face.

'So there you are, Speed. A man who knows his own mind.'

'You could take me,' said Speed.

'Your mother wouldn't let me. Now.' They were beside Speed's house. 'Away you go,' he said to Joe, and when the boy had gone he squatted down to be nearer the same height as Speed. 'I've no change on me,' he said, 'but come round in the morning, after I've been up street, and I'll have something for you. But listen. Will you remember what I say?'

They were between two of the street lights and the boy's sharp thin face, squint-eyed, suspicious, was a little patch of white in the gloom. He nodded.

'Your mother, Speed, listen, is one of the best. You look after her. You'll be lucky if you find anybody as good as her. Okay?' Speed nodded. Sam was not sure that he had fully understood but at least it had been said. 'And. Your Daddy was a hero. He got shot at and he had to kill some people and he saw some terrible things. A lot of soldiers get badly after that. Your Daddy isn't the only one. He'll get better, in time. But remember, Speed, he was a hero, your Daddy, and I know, because I was there. Okay? Remember that as well.'

Once more Speed nodded, this time more gravely.

Sam stood up.

'About nine o'clock then.'

Sam went to the end of Water Street and lit up. He leaned against the wall of the pub and looked up and down the street. His last night. A subdued muttering came from the pub behind him and the windows of the Vaults and the Blue Bell glowed yellow and enticing. When someone went in or came out, there was a gust of sociability.

Sam remembered the cycling club which had met in the big yard behind the Blue Bell, the yard used by the farmers to wash down and groom the horses for the sales. The football team had used the King's Arms' field up the street and they had been allowed the back bar as a changing room. The library was down Station Road next to the fire station and Mr Carrick had suggested the books to read. Hoops in the gutter, striking sparks with the iron caulkers on clogs, running errands, playing, playing and talking, the street the best free room outside the house.

A hundred and one, a thousand and one, small particular memories, a bag of toffees split open over there outside Noel Carrick's and some of the bigger boys grabbing them. A crush of memories. Most of all of Ellen. The girl across the street, the walk she had! Looking round everywhere, everyone saying hello to Ellen, everyone always did, and her knowing the names, and the relations, and the lives, but no bad word. Here she came just before she agreed to become engaged, the blue dress, the white buttons, the laughing all of them did, and here when she knew she was pregnant but did not like that word – 'expecting' – that was Ellen.

The memories shifted and tumbled in a kaleidoscope but, as he turned for home, the final prospect was of a bleak, raw street, never changing, a hard winter setting in, more privation promised, a place to be trapped in, as he had thought at first sight, when he had seen it full that first morning of his return.

He let drop the cigarette and heeled it into the pavement.

It was time to go.

CHAPTER THIRTY

Ellen got out of bed just after dawn. Sam was still fast asleep. He had slept more soundly than she could remember. She thought to lie against him but shied away. She had been awake most of the night, as if waiting for him to make a move. But he had slept deeply, stirring only slightly, nothing of the old nightmares.

She had to do something to beat down the sadness. It was more like a sickness, threatening to choke her as she counted what were now no more than a few hours.

Upstairs, Joe dangled out of his bed but shifted not a degree out of his sleep when Ellen put him back in the centre of the narrow mattress and tucked him in.

She went into the corner where Sam's kitbag stood, packed. The suitcase was downstairs. She slid open the bottom drawer in the chest, reached down and found what she was looking for. It was the photo taken by Mr Kneale of the three of them on the steps of the house on Market Hill, where Sam had kissed her in public and thrown Joe high in the air that first morning back. Ellen had had it framed.

It would not do, though, to put it in the kitbag unprotected. Also in the drawer were the lengths of silk he had brought her. What could she use them for? Too fine for curtain material or cushion covers. Too flimsy and gaudy for a table. Certainly not for a dress – too exotic. She took one out, unfolded it. The spray of rich colour brought her a moment of wistful happiness. She opened another, then a third – they were so beautiful. These colours, they were so soft and loving on the skin, these silks. What had prompted Sam to buy them for her? Did he think she was like this – these colours, these silks? As she knelt on the floor, the silks pressed to her face, she realised that maybe this was what Sam wanted their life to be. They were a present, yes, but they were also a hope – that life need not be sullen, dull, raw, hard, but could be exotic and light, full of sun and a little magic.

For a while, Ellen rocked gently in her son's room, the silks held to her face. Thoughts of Sam drowned her sadness but then those thoughts themselves made her more sad.

She chose the brightest of the silks and wrapped the framed photograph inside it and pushed it down into the middle of the kitbag. Then she went downstairs, built up the fire and waited.

Suddenly everything accelerated. Speed came round well before nine. They went down to Grace's house for the last time and Leonard offered Sam a tot of rum and took one himself and Grace let it pass. It would not happen again. Mr Kneale appeared and before Sam could speak he excused him for not responding about the book. He understood that Sam had been busy but was certain that there would be plenty of time to read it on the boat and a letter would be much appreciated. Meanwhile he was bothered by the discovery that the Wigton Welcome Home Fund for 'Wigton Men and Women who enlisted in the town and served during hostilities' would be disbursed some weeks after Sam's departure. Rumour had it, he said, that it could come to five pounds a head and so he would see what he could do and send it on. And comments of the ordinary soldier would be much appreciated.

Sadie came in curlers and the pink pom-pom-less slippers, arms folded against the cold morning, threatening a little weep until she saw Ellen's fierce expression and checked herself. She told Sam again that the box he had given her was the most beautiful thing she had ever had and nobody would get their hands on it while she was alive. 'There's only berried holly this year,' she offered, finally, and then turned away when she caught Sam's eyes.

They went back to pick up the luggage and two or three people on the street said cheerio, good luck, drop us a postcard, send us some of that weather.

Bella's cup overflowed because she was given Blackie to look after until Joe and Ellen's return. Too soon – Ellen wanted to slow it all down, slow it down – too soon the three of them were on the bus, upstairs, looking over the bare hedges and into the wintry fields, frost on the windows. Ellen looked frightened when Sam asked for the tickets. One and a half returns, one single.

Alex was waiting for them at Carlisle Station. They were early. The platform was filling up. Joe surrendered to the steam and the whistles, the green flag, the men on the line with big hammers hitting the wheels, the sound ringing up to the high grimy glass roof of the big handsome station, a goods train with over forty wagons – Joe counted – going through on the middle track and the clouds of steam hissing, swirling way up in the air in all shades of white and grey, instant clouds, the huge engines taking his breath away.

But even that excitement cooled when his Mammy and Daddy moved away from the rest, found a place apart and stood, unhappy, waiting. Joe looked up at them and the flurry of pleasure he had experienced from the steam and the engines blew away and their coldness settled on him.

His Mammy asked his Daddy if he had everything. The flask of tea. The sandwiches. He said yes. He said he would try to drop a line from

Southampton. She said that would be nice. Joe stood close to them and for the first time felt the knowledge that his Daddy was really going away, going a long way away and for a long time. He felt cold and whimpered and snuggled against his mother, but she was not like she usually was and when he pushed against her, she resisted and took little notice.

From a respectful distance Alex watched them closely, his cigarette daintily held, the floppy hair thrown back out of his eyes now and then, the pose still rather foppish despite the ungainly greatcoat. He watched them closely without fear of being observed in return. Ellen and Sam were like sleepwalkers.

When the train was announced, Ellen felt the dark panic close in on her and she was giddy but held herself together. Sam looked around, thoughtfully, as if he had all the time in the world. Ellen willed it to be delayed outside the station, to break down, not to stop, but in it came, from Glasgow. The brute engine slowing its pistons as it curved into the station and very slowly, hissing white steam, came to a stop.

Sam and Ellen looked at each other, desperate.

'Well,' she said, brushing the lapel of his coat with her wool-gloved hand, 'you take care now.'

'And you.' The lump in his throat choked any other words.

'I'll miss you,' Ellen said, looking down and forcing herself to be steady and not let go.

'Me too.' It was too difficult to say more.

Almost without noticing, they moved towards the train. Alex walked some yards ahead of them, down the platform to the third class carriages. The train was only half full. Porters shouted 'Mind your backs!' and 'This way, clear the way!' The words turned into a blur of sound for Ellen.

Alex had found an empty carriage, almost at the back of the train, next to the guard's van where they were loading up parcels.

344

'Cheerio then, Ellen,' he said, holding out his hand. 'Don't worry. I'll look after him.'

Then he was in the train.

Sam stood looking at Ellen. How could he say all that was on his mind in such a place at such a time? How could he tell her that it was she alone who had seen him through everything, not just the war: she was the finest part of his life but there was this other, this hardening of his mind. Surely he had to tell her.

Ellen knew she had been weak. She was powerless to overcome it. But he was going. She screwed up her eyes as if that would help her understand it. In a minute or two he would be drawn away from her again. She looked at him and at last their glances met. How could this be happening?

A whistle blew. Doors began to slam. Sam looked down and picked up Joe, held him at arm's length.

'Now you look after Mammy, won't you?'

'Yes.'

'Give Daddy a kiss.' said Ellen.

Puzzled and a little frightened, Joe kissed Sam's cheek. He put the boy down and he and Ellen were in each other's arms. Locked, holding hard. Just holding.

'Sorry, lad.' The guard was genuinely apologetic. 'Sorry, missis.'

Obediently, they parted.

He got into the train.

Ellen's lips could get no tighter and the tears came to her eyes but she would not let them fall. Joe stood small beside her, bewildered, close to uncomprehending tears.

The green flag. The whistle.

A film of terror went across Ellen's face as, very very slowly, the long train began to pull out.

Sam stood at the window, his mind frozen. He tried to smile but failed.

Behind him, Alex said abruptly, 'You did me a favour once, Sam. Remember? I told you I'd never thanked you enough?'

Sam barely nodded, mesmerised by the wife and son he was leaving behind. Joe was waving.

Alex pushed Sam to one side and threw his kitbag out of the window. He leaned out, opened the door and shoved the suitcase into his hand.

'Jump!' he said. 'Go on, Sam. Jump!'

Sam lay sprawled on the platform. He looked back at the train. Alex executed a mock salute.

He got up and collected his kitbag and began to walk towards them. Sent by Ellen, Joe ran, though not flat out, towards him and Sam squatted down and took the impact of the small boy.

'Maybe I'll go another time,' he said. 'When we can all go. All three of us.'

'Yes,' Joe said.

'How's that straight left, eh?'

Sam half averted his head and offered his cheek. Joe looked at him waiting.

'Go on then,' he said, 'let's see it.'

Joe swung and his soft fist landed plum on target.

'That's good,' said Sam. 'You're coming on.'

He put the kitbag under his arm and took Joe's hand in his and together they walked towards Ellen who stood, in tears now, rooted to the spot.